DAY WATCH

THE NIGHT WATCH SERIES BY SERGEI LUKYANENKO

Night Watch

Day Watch

Twilight Watch

Last Watch

New Watch
(coming from Harper in May 2014)

DAY WATCH

Book Two

SERGEI LUKYANENKO
VLADIMIR VASILIEV

TRANSLATED BY ANDREW BROMFIELD

HARPER

NEW YORK · LONDON · TORONTO · SYDNEY

HARPER

Originally published as Дневной дозор (*Dnevnoy Dozor*) in hardcover in Russia in 2000 by AST.

First published in the United States as *Day Watch* in paperback in 2007 by Miramax Books.

Designed by Sunil Manchikanti

Library of Congress Cataloging-in-Publication Data has been applied for.

ISBN 978-0-06-231011-8

14 15 16 17 18   OV/RRD   10 9 8 7 6 5 4 3 2 1

This text has been banned for distribution as injurious to the cause of Light.

—THE NIGHT WATCH

This text has been banned for distribution as injurious to the cause of Darkness.

—THE DAY WATCH

The coincidence of any names, titles, or events in this book with human reality is entirely accidental and fortuitous.

UNAUTHORIZED PERSONNEL PERMITTED

PROLOGUE

THE ENTRANCE DID NOT INSPIRE RESPECT. THE CODED LOCK was broken, the floor was littered with the trampled butts of cheap cigarettes. Inside the elevator the walls were covered with graffiti, the word Spartak scrawled as often as the usual crude obscenities. The plastic buttons had been burned through with cigarettes and painstakingly plugged with chewing gum that was now rock-hard.

The door to the apartment on the fourth floor was a good match for the entrance: some kind of hideous old Soviet artificial leather, cheap aluminum numbers barely held on by their crooked screws.

Natasha hesitated for a moment before she pressed the doorbell. She must be insane, hoping for anything from a place like this. If you were so crazy and desperate that you'd decided to try magic, you could just open the newspaper, switch on the TV, or listen to the radio. Legitimate spiritualist salons, experienced mediums with international diplomas . . . It was all a swindle—that was clear enough. But at least you'd be in pleasant surroundings, with pleasant people—not like this last resort for hopeless losers.

She rang the bell anyway. She didn't want her journey to be a waste of time.

At first it seemed like the apartment was empty. Then she heard hasty footsteps, those typical of someone in a hurry whose worn slippers are falling off their feet as they shuffle along. For a brief instant the tiny spy-hole went dark, then the lock grated and the door opened.

"Oh, Natasha, is it? Come in, come in . . ."

She had never liked people who spoke too familiarly upon first meeting. There ought to be a little bit more formality.

But the woman who had opened the door was already pulling her into the apartment, clutching her unceremoniously by the hand, and with an expression of such sincere hospitality on her aging, brightly made-up face, that Natasha couldn't bring herself to object.

"My friend told me that you . . ." Natasha began.

"I don't know, I don't know about that, my dear," said her hostess, waving her hands in the air. "Oh, don't take your shoes off, I was just going to clean the place up . . . oh, all right then, I'll try to find you a pair of slippers."

Natasha looked around, finding it difficult to conceal her disgust.

The hallway wasn't so very small, but it was crammed full. The light bulb hanging from the ceiling was dull, maybe thirty watts at best, but even that couldn't hide the general squalor. The hallstand was piled high with clothes, including a musquash winter coat that fed the moths. The small open area of the linoleum floor was an indistinct gray color. Natasha's hostess must have been planning her cleaning session for a long time.

"Your name's Natasha, isn't it, my daughter? Mine's Dasha."

Dasha was at least fifteen or twenty years older than her. She could have been Natasha's mother, but with a mother like that you'd want to hang yourself . . . A pudgy figure, with dirty, dull hair and bright lacquer peeling off her fingernails, wearing a washed-out housecoat and crumbling slippers on her bare feet. Her toenails glittered with bright lacquer too. My God, how vulgar!

"Are you a seer?" Natasha asked. And in her own mind she screamed: "What a fool I am!"

Dasha nodded. She bent down and extracted a pair of rubber slippers from a tangled heap of footwear. The most idiotic slippers ever invented—the kind with all those rubber points sticking out on the inside. A yogi's dream. Some of the rubber prongs had fallen off long ago, but that hadn't made the slippers any more comfortable.

"Put them on!" Dasha suggested joyfully.

As if she were hypnotized, Natasha took off her sandals and put on the slippers. Goodbye, panty hose. She was bound to get a couple of runs, even in her famous Omsa tights with their famous Lycra. Everything in this world was a swindle invented by cunning fools. And for some reason intelligent people always fell for it.

"Yes, I'm a seer," Dasha declared as she attentively supervised the donning of the slippers. "I got it from my grandma. And my mom too. All of them were seers, they all helped people, it's in our family . . . Come into the kitchen, Natasha. I haven't tidied up the rooms yet . . ."

Still cursing herself for being so stupid, Natasha went into the kitchen, which met all her expectations: a heap of dirty dishes in the sink, a filthy table—when they appeared a cockroach crawled lazily off the top and underneath. The windows had obviously not been washed for the spring, and the ceiling was fly-spotted.

"Sit down." Dasha deftly pulled a stool out from under the table and moved it over to the place of honor—between the table and the refrigerator, a convulsively twitching Saratov.

"Thank you, I'll stand." Natasha had made her mind up not to sit down. The stool inspired even less confidence than the table or the floor. "Dasha . . . That's Darya?"

"Yes, Darya."

"Darya, I really only wanted to find out . . ."

The woman shrugged. She clicked the switch on the electric kettle—probably the only object in the kitchen that didn't look as if it had been retrieved from a garbage heap. She looked at Natasha. "Find out? There's nothing to find out. Everything's just as clear as day."

For a moment Natasha had an unpleasant, oppressive sensation, as if there weren't enough light in the kitchen. Everything went gray, the agonized rumbling of the refrigerator and the noise of the traffic on the avenue nearby fell silent. She wiped the icy perspiration off her forehead. It was the heat. The summer, the heat, the long jour-

ney in the metro, the crush in the trolley . . . Why hadn't she taken
a taxi? She'd sent away the driver with the car—well, she'd been
ashamed to give anyone even a hint of where she was going and why
. . . but why hadn't she taken a taxi?

"Your husband's left you, Natashenka," Darya said affectionately.
"Two weeks ago. Left all of a sudden, packed, threw his things into a
suitcase and just upped and left you. Without any quarrels, without
any arguments. He left the apartment, left the car. And he went to
your rival, a pretty young bitch with black eyebrows . . . but you're
not old yet, my daughter."

This time Natasha didn't even react to the words "my daughter."
She was trying desperately to remember what she'd told her friend
and what she hadn't. She didn't think she'd mentioned black eyebrows. Although the girl really did have a dark complexion, and black
hair . . . Natasha was overcome once again by a wild, blind fury.

"And I know why he left, Natashenka . . . Forgive me for calling
you 'my daughter'—you're a strong woman, used to making up your
own mind about things, but you're all like my own daughters to me
. . . You didn't have any children, Natasha. Did you?"

"No," Natasha whispered.

"But why not, my dear?" the seer asked, shaking her head reproachfully. "He wants a daughter, right?"

"Yes, a daughter . . ."

"Then why didn't you have one?" Darya asked with a shrug. "I've
got five children. Two of them went into the army—the eldest.
One daughter's married—she's nursing her baby now. The other's
studying. And the youngest, the wild one . . ." She waved her hand
through the air. "Sit down, why don't you . . ."

Natasha reluctantly lowered herself onto the stool, holding her
purse firmly on her knees. Trying to seize the initiative, she said, "It's
just the way life worked out. Well, I would have had a child for him,
but you can't ruin your career for that."

"That's true too." The seer didn't try to argue. She rubbed her face with her hands. "It's your choice . . . Right then, you want to bring him back? But why did he leave? Your rival's already carrying his child . . . and she made a real effort too. Listening to him, and sympathizing with him, and getting up to all sorts of tricks in bed. . . . You had a good man, the kind every woman wants to get. Do you want to bring him back? Even now?"

Natasha pursed her lips.

"Yes."

The seer sighed.

"We *can* bring him back . . . we *can*."

Her tone of voice had changed subtly, become heavy and emphatic.

". . . Only it won't be easy. Just bringing him back isn't all that hard; it's keeping him that's the problem!"

"I want to anyway."

"All of us, my daughter, have our own magic inside us." Darya leaned forward across the table. Her eyes seemed to be drilling right through Natasha. "Simple, ancient female magic. With all your ambitions, you've completely forgotten about it, and that's a mistake! But never mind. I'll help you. Only we'll have to do everything in three stages."

She knocked gently on the table.

"The first thing. I'll give you a love potion. This is not a great sin . . . The potion will bring your man back home. It will bring him back, but it won't keep him there."

Natasha nodded uncertainly. The idea of dividing the enchantment into "three stages" seemed inappropriate somehow—especially coming from this woman in this apartment . . .

"The second thing . . . Your rival's child must never be born. If it is, you won't be able to keep your man. You'll have to commit a great sin, destroy an innocent child in the womb . . ."

"What are you talking about!" Natasha said with a shudder. "I'm not going to end up in court!"

"I'm not talking about poison, Natashenka. I'll make a pass with my hands"—and the seer really did make a pass with her open palms—"and then clap them . . . And the job's done, the sin's committed. No court involved."

Natasha didn't say anything.

"Only I won't take that sin on myself," said Darya, crossing herself frenziedly. "I'll help you if you like, but then you'll have to answer to God!"

Evidently taking the silence as consent, she continued:

"The third thing . . . You'll have a child yourself. I'll help with that too. You'll have a beautiful, clever daughter who'll be a help to you and a joy to your husband. Then all your troubles will be over."

"Are you serious about all this?" Natasha asked in a quiet voice. "You can do all this . . ."

"I'll tell you how it is," said Darya, standing up. "You say 'yes,' and it will all happen. Your husband will come back tomorrow, and the day after tomorrow, your rival will miscarry. And I won't take any money from you until you get pregnant. But afterward I will— and I'll take a lot. I tell you that now, I swear by Christ the Lord."

Natasha gave a crooked smile.

"And what if I cheat you and don't bring you the money? After everything's already been done . . ."

She stopped short. The seer was looking at her sternly, without speaking. With an air of gentle sympathy, like a mother looking at a foolish daughter. "You won't cheat me, Natashenka. Just think for a moment and you'll realize it's not worth trying."

Natasha swallowed hard. She tried to make a joke of it:

"So it's payment on delivery?"

"Ah, my little businesswoman," Darya said ironically. "Who's going to love you, so practical and clever? A woman should always have some foolishness in her . . . ah . . . On delivery. Delivery of all three items."

"How much?"

"Five."

"You want five?" Natasha burst out, and broke off. "I thought it was a lot cheaper than that!"

"If you just want to get your husband back, that will be cheaper. But then after a while, he'll go away again. I'm offering you real help, a certain cure."

"I want to do it," Natasha said with a nod. She had the feeling that what was happening was slightly unreal. So that was all: Just a clap of the hands and the unborn child would be gone? Another clap and she would bear her beloved idiot a child of her own?

"Do you take the sin on yourself?" the seer asked insistently.

"What sin is there in that?" Natasha retorted, her irritation suddenly breaking through. "Every woman's committed that sin at least once! Perhaps there isn't anything there anyway!"

The seer pondered, as if she were listening to something. She nodded her head.

"There is . . . And I think it's definitely a daughter."

"I'll take it," said Natasha, still in an irritated voice. "I'll take all the sins on myself, any you like. Do we have a deal?"

The seer looked at her sternly, disapprovingly.

"That's not right, my daughter . . . About all the sins. Who knows what sins I might hang on you? My own, or somebody else's . . . then afterward you would have to answer to God."

"We'll sort it out somehow."

Darya sighed: "Oh, these young people are so foolish. Do you think He wastes his time rummaging about in people's sins? Every sin leaves its own trace, and the judgment matches the traces . . . All right, don't be afraid. I won't put anybody else's sins down to you."

"I'm not afraid."

The seer didn't seem to be listening to her anymore. She was sitting there as if she were listening alertly to something else. Then she shrugged: "All right . . . let's get the job done. Give me your hand!"

Natasha held out her right hand uncertainly, keeping a worried eye on her diamond ring. It didn't come off her finger very easily, but . . .

"Oh!"

The seer had pricked her little finger so quickly and deftly that Natasha hadn't felt a thing. She froze, dumbfounded, watching the red drop welling up. As if this were all perfectly normal, Darya tossed the medical needle into a dirty plate with the solidified remains of borscht in it. The needle was flat, with a sharp little point—the kind they use to take blood in laboratories.

"Don't be afraid, everything's sterile, the needles are disposable."

"What do you think you're doing?" Natasha tried to pull her hand away, but Darya shifted her grip with a surprisingly powerful and precise movement.

"Stop, you fool! Or I'll have to prick you again!"

She took a small pharmacy bottle of dark-brown glass out of her pocket. The label had been washed off, but poorly. The first letters were still visible: "Tinc . . ." She deftly twisted out the cork, set the bottle down and shook Natasha's little finger over it. The drop of blood fell into the bottle.

"Some people believe," the seer said in a contented voice, "that the more blood there is in a potion, the stronger it will be. It's not true. The blood in it has to be good quality, but the amount makes no difference at all . . ."

The medicine woman opened the refrigerator and took out a fifty-gram bottle of Privet vodka. Natasha remembered her driver calling that kind of vodka "the reanimator."

A few drops of the vodka went onto a wisp of cotton wool that wound round Natasha's little finger. The medicine woman held out the bottle to Natasha.

"Want some?"

For some reason Natasha had a clear vision of herself waking up the next morning, somewhere at the far end of the city, robbed, raped, and not remembering a single thing about what had happened. She shook her head.

"Well, I'll have a drop." Darya raised the "reanimator" to her lips and drained the vodka in a single gulp. "That's a bit easier . . . for working. And you, you've no need to be afraid of me. I don't make my living by robbing people."

The last few remaining drops also went into the little brown bottle of love potion. And then, quite unperturbed by Natasha's curious gaze, the seer added some salt, sugar, hot water from the kettle, and a bit of powder with a strong smell of vanilla.

"What is that?" asked Natasha.

"Have you got a cold? It's vanilla."

The medicine woman held the little bottle out to her.

"Take it."

"Is that all?"

"Yes, that's it. You get your husband to drink it. Can you manage that? You can put it in tea, or even in vodka—but that's not the best way."

"But where's the . . . spell?"

"What spell?"

Natasha felt like a fool again. Her voice almost broke into a shout as she said, "This is a drop of my blood, a drop of vodka, sugar, salt, and vanilla!"

"And water," Darya added. She put her hands on her hips and looked at Natasha ironically. "What did you expect? Dried eye of toad? Oriole's testicles? Or for me to blow my nose in it? What do you want—ingredients or effect?"

Natasha didn't answer. She was overwhelmed by this attack. And Darya continued, no longer trying to conceal her mockery: "My darling girl, if I'd wanted to impress you, then I would have done so. Have no doubt about it. What matters is not what's in the bottle, but who made it. Don't you worry, go home and give it to your husband. Will he be calling round again?"

"Yes . . . in the evening," she mumbled, "he phoned to say he'd come and collect a few things . . ."

"Let him collect them, only you give him some tea. Tomorrow he'll bring the things back again. That is, if you let him in, of course." Darya laughed. "All right then . . . And there's one more thing to do. Do you take this sin on yourself?"

"I do." Natasha suddenly realized that she no longer felt completely justified in laughing at what she had said. There was something here that wasn't funny. The seer had made her promise far too seriously. And if her husband did come back tomorrow . . .

"Your word, my deed . . ." Darya slowly parted her hands and started speaking rapidly: "Red water, others' grief and rotten seed and evil breed . . . What was is no more, what was not will not be . . . Return to the void, you are dissolved without trace, by my will, at my word . . ."

Her voice fell to an incoherent whisper. She moved her lips for a minute. Then she clapped her hands hard.

It must have been a trick of the imagination—Natasha thought she felt a gust of icy cold wind blow through the kitchen. Her heart started pounding; she felt a shiver run down her spine.

Darya gave her head a shake, looked at Natasha, and nodded: "That's all. Go now, my dear. Go home, my daughter, and wait for your husband."

Natasha got up. She asked, "But what . . . when do I . . ."

"When you get pregnant, you'll remember about me yourself. I'll wait for three months . . . and then if I'm still waiting—don't blame me . . ."

Natasha nodded. She swallowed hard to keep down the lump that had risen in her throat. Somehow she now believed completely in everything the seer had promised . . . and at the same time, it was painfully clear to her that in three months' time, if everything really did work out, she would be painfully reluctant to give the money away. She would be tempted to put it all down to coincidence . . . why should she give this filthy charlatan five thousand dollars?

And yet she realized that she would. She might drag it out until the final day, but she would bring it.

Because she would remember the gentle clap of those unmanicured hands and that wave of cold that had suddenly spread through the kitchen.

"Go now," the seer repeated with gentle insistence. "I still have to cook supper and clean up the apartment. Go on, go on . . ."

Natasha went out into the dark hallway, took off the slippers with a sigh of relief, and put on her shoes. Her panty hose seemed to have survived the ordeal . . . that was certainly more than she'd dared to hope for . . .

She looked at the seer and tried to find the right words to say. Should she thank her? Ask her about some details? Maybe even joke—if only she could manage it, of course . . .

But Darya had forgotten her completely. The seer's eyes were open wide and she was staring straight at the closed door, feebly waving her hands through the air in front of her as she whispered:

"Who . . . who . . . who?"

The next moment the door behind Natasha opened with a sudden crash and the hall was instantly full of people. Two men were holding the seer firmly by the arms and another had walked quickly into the kitchen without looking around first—he obviously knew the layout of the apartment very well. A young, black-haired girl had appeared beside Natasha. All the men were dressed in a simple and somehow deliberately inconspicuous manner: the same kind of shorts and T-shirts that ninety percent of the male population of Moscow was wearing in this incredible heat. Natasha suddenly had the frightening thought that their clothes were something like the unobtrusive gray suits that special service agents wore.

"That's terrible," the girl said, looking at Natasha and shaking her head. "How disgusting, Natalya Alexeevna."

Unlike the men, she was dressed in dark jeans and a denim jacket. She had a sparkling pendant on a silver chain around her neck and several massive silver rings on her fingers—fancy, complicated rings with dragons' heads and tigers' heads, intertwined snakes and patterns that looked like the letters of a strange, mysterious alphabet.

"What do you mean . . ." Natasha asked in a cheerless voice.

Instead of answering, the girl unzipped Natasha's purse and took out the little bottle. She held it up in front of Natasha's eyes, and then she shook her head again in reproach.

"Got it!" shouted the young man who had gone into the kitchen. "It's all here, guys."

One of the men holding the seer by the arms sighed and said in an oddly bored-sounding voice, "Darya Leonidovna Romashova! In the name of the Night Watch, you are under arrest."

"What watch?" There was a note of obvious puzzlement, mingled with panic, in the seer's voice. "Who are you?"

"You have the right to reply to our questions," the young man went on. "Any magical action from your side will be regarded as hostile and punished without any warning. You have the right to request the settlement of your human obligations. You are accused of . . . Garik?"

The young man who had gone into the kitchen came back out. As if she were dreaming, Natasha noticed that he had an intellectual, thoughtful, rather sad kind of face. She had always liked men like that . . .

"I suppose it's the usual set," said Garik. "The illegal practice of black magic. Third or fourth degree intervention in the conscious-ness of other individuals. Murder, tax evasion—but the last one's not for us. That's for the Dark Ones."

"You are accused of the illegal practice of black magic, interven-tion in the consciousness of others, and murder," the man holding Darya repeated. "You will come with us."

The seer gave a long, piercing, terrifying scream. Natasha involun-tarily glanced at the open door. Of course, it would be naïve to hope that the neighbors would come running to help, but they could call the police, couldn't they?

The strange visitors didn't react to the scream. The girl only frowned and nodded in Natasha's direction: "What shall we do with her?"

"Confiscate the potion and wipe her memory clean." Garik looked at Natasha without a trace of sympathy. "Let her believe there was no one in the apartment when she got here."

"And that's all?" The girl took a pack of cigarettes out of her pocket and lit one without hurrying.

"Katya, what other choice is there? She's a human being—how can we do anything with her?"

This wasn't even frightening anymore. It was a dream, a nightmare . . . and Natasha reacted as such. She grabbed the precious bottle out of the girl's hand with a sudden movement and dashed toward the door.

She was flung back as if she had run into an invisible wall. Natasha shrieked as she fell at the seer's feet; the bottle went flying out of her hand and shattered against the wall with surprising ease. A tiny patch of sticky, colorless liquid appeared on the linoleum.

"Tiger Cub, pick up the pieces for the report," Garik said calmly.

Natasha burst into tears.

No, she wasn't afraid, although Garik's tone of voice left no doubt that they really would wipe her memory clean. They'd clap their hands or do something else to wipe it clean. And she would find herself standing out in the street, firmly convinced that the seer's door had never opened.

She cried as she watched her love dribble across the dirty floor.

Someone stuck their head in through the open door from the landing. "We've got company, guys!" Natasha heard the alarmed voice, but she didn't even look around. There was no point. She was going to forget it all anyway. It would all be shattered into sharp little fragments and soak away into the dirt.

Forever.

CHAPTER 1

I NEVER HAVE ENOUGH TIME TO GET READY IN THE MORNING.
I can get up at seven, or even at six, but I still need another five
minutes.

Why is it always like that, I wonder?

I was standing in front of the mirror, hastily putting on my lipstick, and as always happens when you're in a hurry, the lipstick
was going on unevenly, as if I were a schoolgirl who'd secretly borrowed her mother's for the first time. It would have been better not
to bother at all and go out without any makeup on. I don't have any
complexes about that—I look good enough without it.

"Alya!"

Here we go.

That just has to happen, doesn't it?

"What is it, Mom?" I shouted, fastening my sandals in a hurry.

"Come here, my little one."

"Mom, I've already got my shoes on!" I shouted, adjusting a
twisted strap. "I'm late, Mom!"

"Alya!"

It was pointless arguing.

Deliberately clattering my heels, although I wasn't really angry
at all, I walked into the kitchen. Mom was sitting in front of the
television, the way she always does, and drinking yet another cup of
tea with yet another cake. What is it she likes so much about those

repulsive Danish cakes? They're such terrible garbage! Not to mention how bad they are for the figure.

"Little one, are you going to be late again today?" Mom asked, without even turning her head in my direction.

"I don't know."

"Alisa, I don't think you ought to let it happen. Normal working hours are one thing, but keeping you there until one in the morning . . ." Mom shook her head.

"They pay for it," I said offhandedly.

And then Mom did look at me. And her lips began to tremble. "So you hold that against me, do you?"

My mother always did have an expressive voice, like an actress's. She should have worked in the theater.

"Yes, we live on your wages," my mom said bitterly. "The state robbed us and threw us out to die at the side of the road. Thank you, dear daughter, for not forgetting about us. Your father and I are very grateful to you. But there's no need to keep reminding us . . ."

"Mom, I didn't mean anything of the sort. You know I don't have a standard working day!"

"Working day!" My mom flung her arms in the air. She had a crumb of cake on her chin. "Working night, more like! And who knows what you get up to?"

"Mom . . ."

Of course, she didn't really think anything of the kind. On the contrary, she was always proudly telling her friends what a fine, upstanding girl I was. It was just that in the morning she felt like arguing. Perhaps she'd been watching the news and she'd heard yet another disgusting story about our life here in Russia. Perhaps she and Dad had had a fight first thing in the morning—that would explain why he had left so early.

"And I've no intention of becoming a grandmother at forty!" my mom went on, without following any particular logic. What logic did she need, anyway? She'd been afraid for ages that I would get married and leave home and she'd be left living with just my father.

Or maybe she wouldn't—I'd taken a look at the reality lines, and it was very probable that my dad would leave her for another woman. He was three years younger than Mom, and unlike her, he took care of himself.

"You'll be fifty this year, Mom," I said. "Sorry, I'm really in a hurry."

When I was already in the hallway, I heard my mom's voice, full of righteous indignation: "You never did want to talk to your mother like a normal human being!"

"There was a time when I wanted to," I muttered to myself as I skipped out the door. "When I still was a human being I wanted to. But where were you then . . ."

I knew for sure that Mom was taking comfort in thinking about the argument she would have with me in the evening. And she was dreaming about involving Dad in it too. When I thought about that, it instantly put me in a foul mood.

What kind of way to behave is that—deliberately provoking a fight with someone you love? But Mom just loves to do it. And she doesn't understand it's her own character that killed my father's love for her.

I'll never do that to anyone.

And I won't let Mom do it either!

There was no one in the hallway, but even if there had been it wouldn't have stopped me. I turned back to face the door and looked at it in a special way, with my eyes slightly crossed . . . so that I could see my shadow.

My real shadow. The one that's cast by the Twilight.

It looks as if the gloom is condensing in front of you, until it becomes an absolutely black, intense darkness—so black it would make a starless night look like day.

And against the background of that darkness you see a trembling, swirling, grayish silhouette, not quite three-dimensional but not flat either . . . As if it had been cut out of dirty cotton wool. Or maybe it's the other way around—a hole has been cut through the great Darkness, leaving a doorway into the Twilight.

I took a step forward onto the shadow and it slid upward, enfolding my body, and the world changed.

The colors almost completely disappeared. Everything was frozen in a dark, gray blur, like what appears on a television screen if you turn the color and contrast all the way down. Sounds slowed down, leaving silence, with nothing but a barely audible background rumble, as faint as the murmur of a distant sea.

I was in the Twilight.

I could see Mom's resentment blazing in the apartment. A bitter, lemon-yellow color mixed with self-pity and her acid-green dislike of my dad, who had chosen the wrong time to go to the garage and tinker with his car.

And there was a black vortex slowly taking shape above Mom's head. A curse directed at someone specific, still weak, on the level of "I hope that job of yours drives you crazy, you ungrateful creature!" But it was a mother's curse, and they're especially powerful and tenacious.

Oh no, my dear mom!

Thanks to your efforts, Dad had a heart attack at thirty-seven and three years ago I barely managed to save him from another . . . at a cost that I don't even want to remember. And now you've set your sights on me?

I reached out through the Twilight as hard as I could, so hard I got a stabbing pain under my shoulder blades, and grabbed hold of Mom's mind—it twitched and then froze.

Okay . . . now this is what we'll do . . .

I broke into a sweat, although it's always cool in the Twilight. I wasted energy that would have been useful at work. But a moment later Mom no longer remembered that she'd been speaking to me. And in general, she was really pleased that I was such a hard worker, that I was appreciated and liked at work, that I went out when it was barely light and didn't come back until after midnight.

That's done.

Probably the effect would only be temporary. After all, I didn't want to delve too deeply into Mom's mind. But at least I could count on a couple of months of peace and quiet. And so could my dad—I'm my dad's daughter and I love him a lot more than my mom. It's only kids who can't tell you who they love more—their mom or their dad—grown-ups have no problem answering the question . . .

When I was finished, I removed the half-formed black vortex, and it drifted out through the walls, looking for someone to attach itself to. I took a breath and cast a critical glance around the entrance.

Yes, it hadn't been cleaned for a long time. The blue moss had crept over everything again, and it was thickest around our door. That was only natural. With Mom's hysterical fits, there was always something for it to feed on. When I was little I used to think the Light Ones planted the moss to annoy us. Then it was explained to me that the blue moss is a native inhabitant of the Twilight, a parasite that consumes human emotions.

"Ice!" I commanded, flinging out my hand. The cold obediently gathered at my fingertips and ran across the walls like a stiff brush. The frozen needles of moss dropped to the floor, instantly decaying.

Take that!

That will teach you to go feeding on people's petty little thoughts! That's real Power, the Power of an Other.

I emerged from the Twilight—in the human world less than two seconds had passed—and straightened my hair. My forehead was damp. I had to take out my handkerchief and blot off the sweat. And of course when I looked in my mirror I could see that my mascara had smudged.

I had no time to fuss over my appearance. I just threw on a light veil of attractiveness that would prevent any human being from noticing the faults in my makeup. We call it a "paranjah," and everybody likes to poke fun at Others who wear it, but we all use it anyway . . . When we're short of time or we need to be absolutely sure of making a good impression . . . or sometimes just for fun. One pretty young witch from Pskov—who doesn't really know how to do anything right except throw on a paranjah—has been working as a model for three years. She makes her living from it. The only trouble is that the spell doesn't work on photographs and videos, so she has to keep turning down all the offers she receives to work in advertising . . .

Nothing was going my way today. The elevator didn't come for ages, and the second one's been out of order for a long time now, and on my way out of the hallway I ran into Vitalik, the young guy who lives above us. When he saw me in my paranjah, he just froze with a stupid smile on his face. He has been in love with me since he was thirteen—stupidly, hopelessly, silently in love. It's the result of my sloppy work, to be quite honest. I was learning the love spell and decided to practice on our neighbor's little boy, since he took every chance he could get to ogle me while I was sitting on the balcony, sunbathing in my bikini. Well . . . I practiced. And I misjudged the limiting factors. He fell in love forever. When he doesn't see me for a long time, it all seems to pass off, but it only takes a fleeting encounter, and everything starts up again. He'll never be happy in love.

"Vitalik, I'm in a hurry," I said, smiling at him.

But the young man just stood there, blocking the doorway. Then he decided to pay me a compliment.

"Alisa, you look really beautiful today . . ."

"Thanks." I gently moved him aside and felt him tremble when my hand touched his shoulder. He'll probably remember that touch for a week . . .

"I've passed the final exam, Alisa!" he said hastily, talking to my back. "That's it, I'm a college student now!"

I turned back and took a closer look at him.

Was this boy, who still used acne lotion, getting wild ideas into his head? Was he hoping that now he'd got into college and launched into "adult life" he could have a chance with me?

"Squirming out of the army?" I asked. "Men today have no balls. They're all wimps. They don't want to serve their time and get a bit of experience, and then go and study."

His smile was slowly fading away. It was a wonderful sight!

"Ciao, Vitalik," I said, and skipped out of the entrance into the sweltering heat of summer. But my mood was a bit better now.

These little pups in love are always fun to watch. They're boring to flirt with, and having sex with them is repulsive, but just watching them is pure pleasure. I ought to give him a kiss sometime . . .

Anyway, a moment later I'd completely forgotten my lovesick neighbor. I stuck my hand out. The first car drove straight past—the driver looked at me with greedy longing in his eyes, but his wife was sitting beside him. The next car stopped.

"I need to go to the center of town," I said, leaning down toward the window. "Manege Square."

"Get in," said the driver, reaching across and opening the door. He was a cultured-looking man with dark hair, about forty years old. "How could I refuse such a good-looking girl a lift?"

I slipped into the front seat of the old Zhiguli 9 and rolled the window all the way down. The wind hit me in the face—that was some relief at least.

"You'd have got there quicker on the metro," the driver warned me honestly.

"I don't like the metro."

The driver nodded. I liked him—he wasn't staring too brazenly, even though I'd obviously overdone things with the paranjah—and the car was well cared for. He also had very beautiful hands. They were strong, and their grip on the wheel was gentle but secure.

What a pity I was in a hurry.

"Are you late for work?" the driver asked. He spoke very politely, but in a manner that was somehow personal and intimate. Maybe I ought to give him my number? I'm a free girl now, I can do what I like.

"Yes."

"I wonder, what kind of jobs do such beautiful girls do?" It wasn't even an attempt to strike up an acquaintance or a compliment—it was genuine curiosity.

"I don't know about all the rest, but I work as a witch."

He laughed.

"It's a job like any other . . ." I took out my cigarettes and my lighter. The driver gave me a fleeting glance of disapproval, so I didn't bother to ask permission. I just lit up.

"And what do a witch's duties consist of?"

We turned off onto Rusakov Street and the driver speeded up. Maybe I was going to get there in time after all.

"It varies," I replied evasively. "But basically we oppose the forces of Light."

The driver seemed to have accepted the rules of the game, though it wasn't really a game at all.

"So you're on the side of the shadow?"

"The Darkness."

"That's great. I know another witch, my mother-in-law," the driver said with a laugh. "But she's already retired, thank God. So why don't you like the forces of Light?"

I stealthily checked out his aura. No, everything was okay. He was a human being.

"They get in our way. Tell me, for instance—what's the most important thing in life for you?"

The driver thought for a second.

"Just life itself. And for nobody to stop me living it."

"That's right," I agreed. "Everyone wants to be free, don't they?"

He nodded.

"Well, we witches fight for freedom too. For everyone's right to do what they want."

"And what if someone wants to do evil?"

"That's his right."

"But what if he infringes on other people's rights in the process? Say I stab someone and infringe on his rights?"

This was funny. We were conducting the classic dispute on the subject "What is the Light and what is the Darkness?" We Dark Ones and those who call themselves the Light Ones—we all brainwash our novices on this subject.

"If someone tries to infringe on your rights, then stop them from doing it. You have that right."

"I get it. The law of the jungle. Whoever's stronger is right."

"Stronger, cleverer, more farsighted. And it's not the law of the jungle. It's just the law of life. Is it ever any different?"

The driver thought about it and shook his head.

"No, it isn't. So I have the right to turn off the road somewhere, throw myself on you, and rape you?"

"But are you sure you're stronger than me?"

We'd just stopped at an intersection and the driver looked at me closely. He shook his head.

"No . . . I'm not sure. But the reason I don't attack girls isn't because they might fight back!"

He was beginning to get a bit nervous. The conversation seemed like a joke, but he could sense that something wasn't right.

"It's also because they might put you in jail," I said. "And that's all."

"No," he said firmly.

"Yes," I said with a smile. "That's exactly the reason. You're a normal, healthy man, with all the right reactions. But there's a law, so you prefer not to attack girls, but court them first."

"Witch . . ." the driver muttered with a crooked smile. He stepped hard on the gas.

"Witch," I confirmed. "Because I tell the truth and don't play the hypocrite. After all, everyone wants to be free to live his or her life. To do what they want. Not everything works out—everyone has their own desires—but everyone has the same aspirations. And it's the clash of these that gives rise to freedom! A harmonious society in which everybody wants to have everything, although they have to come to terms with other people's desires."

"But what about morality?"

"What morality?"

"Universal human morality."

"What's that?"

There's nothing better than forcing someone into a dead end and making him formulate his question properly. People don't usually think about the meaning of the words they say. It seems to them that words convey truth. That when someone hears the word "red" he will think of a ripe raspberry and not a pool of blood. That the word "love" will evoke Shakespeare's sonnets and not the erotic films of Playboy. And they find themselves baffled when the word they've spoken doesn't evoke the right response.

"There are basic principles," said the driver. "Dogmas. Taboos. Those . . . what do they call them . . . commandments."

"Well?" I said encouragingly.

"Thou shalt not steal."

I laughed, and the driver smiled too.

"Thou shalt not covet thy neighbor's wife." His smile was really broad now.

"And do you manage it?"

"Sometimes."

"And you even manage not to 'covet'? You control your instincts that well?"

"Witch!" the driver said with relish. "All right, I repent, I repent . . ."

"Don't repent!" I interrupted. "It's quite normal. It's freedom! Stealing . . . and coveting."

"Thou shalt not kill!" the driver declared. "Eh? What do you say to that? A universal commandment!"

"You might as well say 'don't boil a young goat in its mother's milk.' Do you watch TV and read the newspapers?" I asked.

"Sometimes. But I don't enjoy it."

"Then why do you call 'Thou shalt not kill' a commandment? Thou shalt not kill . . . It was in the news this morning—down South they've taken another three people hostage and they're demanding a ransom. They've already cut a finger off each one of them to show their demands are serious. And one of the hostages, by the way, is a three-year-old girl. They cut her finger off too."

The driver's fingers tightened their grip on the wheel and turned pale.

"Bastards . . ." he hissed. "Monsters. I heard that all right. But they're scum, they're inhuman—they have to be to do something like that. I'd strangle them all with my bare hands . . ."

I kept quiet. The driver's aura was blazing bright scarlet. I didn't want him to crash; he was almost out of control. My thrust had been too accurate—he had a little daughter of his own . . .

"String them up on the telegraph poles!" he continued, still raging. "Burn them with napalm!"

I kept quiet and waited until the driver had gradually calmed down. Then I asked:

"Then what about those universal moral commandments? If they gave you a machine gun now, you'd press the trigger without even hesitating."

"There aren't any commandments that apply to monsters!" the driver snarled. His calm, cultured manner had disappeared without a trace now! There were streams of energy pouring out of him in all directions . . . and I soaked it up, quickly replenishing the Power that I'd spent earlier that morning.

"Not even terrorists are monsters," I said. "They're human beings. And so are you. And there are no commandments for human beings. That's a scientifically proven fact."

As I drew in the energy that was bursting out of him, the driver calmed down. It wouldn't last long, of course. That evening the pendulum would swing back, and he'd be overcome by rage again. It's like pumping all the water out of a well very quickly—it comes rushing back in again.

"But even so, you're not right," he replied more calmly. "Logic does exist, of course, yes . . . But if you compare things with the Middle Ages, then morality has definitely advanced."

"Don't be ridiculous!" I said, shaking my head. "How has it advanced? . . . Even in the wars back then they had a strict code of honor. A war then was a real war, and kings fought with their armies, risking their thrones and their heads. And now? A big country wants to put pressure on a little one, so it bombs it for three months and gets rid of its outdated armaments at the same time. Not even the soldiers risk their lives! It's the same as if you drove up onto the sidewalk and started knocking down pedestrians like bowling pins."

"The code of honor was for the aristocrats," the driver objected sharply. "The simple people died in droves."

"And is it any different today?" I asked. "When one oligarch settles scores with another, there's a certain code of honor that's observed! Because both of them have goons to kill for them, compromising material about each other, certain interests in common, certain family ties. They're just like the old aristocracy! Kings sitting up to their ears in cabbage. And the simple people are trash. A herd of sheep that are good for shearing, but sometimes it's more profitable to slaughter them. Nothing's changed. There never were any commandments, and there aren't any now!"

The driver fell silent.

After that he didn't say another word all the way. We turned off Kamergerskaya Street onto Tverskaya Street and I told him where to stop. I paid, deliberately giving him more than I should have. It was only then that he spoke again.

"I'll never give a witch a lift again," he told me with a crooked grin. "It's too hard on the nerves. I never thought a conversation with a beautiful girl could spoil my mood so badly."

"I'm sorry," I said, and smiled sweetly.

"Have a good day at . . . work." He slammed the door and drove off abruptly.

Well, well. I'd never been taken for a prostitute before, but he seemed to think that was what I was. That was the effect of the paranjah . . . and the district we were in, of course.

But at least I'd more than made up for the Power I'd used up earlier. He'd turned out to be a magnificent donor, this intelligent, cultured, strong man. The only time I'd ever done better was . . . it was with the Prism of Power.

I shuddered at the memory.

It had all been so stupid . . . everything about it had been so monstrously stupid.

My entire life had gone downhill as a result. I'd lost everything in a single moment.

"You fool! You greedy fool!"

It was a good thing that none of the people could see my real face. It probably looked about as pitiful as my stupid young neighbor's.

Anyway, what was done was done. I couldn't turn back the clock, put things right and win back . . . his affection. It was my own fault, of course. And I ought to be glad that Zabulon hadn't handed me over to the Light Ones.

He used to love me. And I loved him . . . it would have been ridiculous for a young, inexperienced witch not to fall in love with the head of the Day Watch when he looked favorably on her . . .

My fists were clenched so tight that the nails were biting into the skin. I'd struggled through. I'd survived last summer. The Darkness only knew how, but I'd survived.

And now there was no point in remembering the past and sniveling and trying to catch Zabulon's eye again. He hadn't spoken to me since the hurricane last year—the one that had hit on the day when I was captured so shamefully. And he wouldn't speak to me for the next hundred years. I was sure of it.

A car moving slowly along the curb stopped with a quiet rustle of tires. It was a decent car, a Volvo, and it hadn't come from the junkyard. A jerk with a shaven head stuck his smug face out of the window, looked me up and down, and broke into a satisfied smile. Then he hissed.

"How much?"

I was dumbstruck.

"For two hours—how much?" the idiot with the shaved head asked more specifically.

I looked at the number plate—it wasn't from Moscow. So that was it.

"The prostitutes are farther down, you halfwit," I said amiably. "Get lost."

"Anyone would think you didn't screw," the disappointed idiot said, trying to save face. "Think it over, I'm feeling generous today."

"You hold on to your capital," I advised him, and clicked my fingers. "You'll need it to fix your car."

I turned my back to him and walked toward the building. My palm was aching slightly from the recoil. The "gremlin" isn't a very complicated spell, but I'd cast it in too much of a hurry. I'd left the Volvo with an incorporeal creature fiddling about under its hood— not even a creature really, but a bundle of energy with an obsessive passion for destroying technology.

If he was lucky, his engine was finished. If he was unlucky, then his fancy bourgeois electronics would blow—the carburetors, the ventilators, all those gearwheels and drive-belts that the car was crammed full of. I'd never taken any interest in the insides of an automobile except in the most general terms. But I had a very clear idea of the result of using the "gremlin."

The disappointed man drove off without wasting too much time arguing. I wondered if he'd remember what I'd said when his car started going haywire. He was bound to. He'd shout, "She hexed it, the witch!" And he wouldn't even know just how right he was.

The thought amused me, but nonetheless, the day had been hopelessly spoiled.

I was five minutes late for work, and there was that quarrel with my mother, and that idiot in the Volvo . . .

With these thoughts in my head I walked past the magnificent, gleaming shop windows, raised my shadow from the ground without even thinking about it, and entered the building through a door that ordinary people can't see.

The headquarters of the Light Ones, near the Sokol metro station, is disguised as an ordinary office. We have a more respectable location and our camouflage is a lot more fun. This building, with seven floors of apartments above shops that are luxurious even by

Moscow standards, has three more floors than everyone thinks. It was specially built that way as the Day Watch residence, and the spells that disguise the building's true appearance are incorporated into the very bricks and stone of the walls. The people living in the building, who are mostly perfectly ordinary, probably feel a strange sensation whenever they ride the elevator up—as if it takes too long to get from the first floor to the second . . .

The elevator does take longer than it should because the second floor is actually the third, and the real second floor is invisible—it houses our duty offices, armaments room, and technical services. Our other two floors are on the top of the building, and not a single human being knows about them either. But any Other who is powerful enough can look through the Twilight and see the severe black granite walls and the window arches that are almost always covered with thick, heavy curtains. Ten years ago they installed air-conditioners—that's when the clumsy boxes of the split systems appeared on the walls. Before that the internal climate was regulated by magic—but why waste it like that, when electricity is far cheaper?

I once saw a photograph of our building taken through the Twilight by a skillful magician. It's an incredible sight! A crowded street with people walking all dressed up in their finest, cars driving along, shop windows and apartment windows . . . a pleasant old woman looking out of one window, and a cat sitting in another one, looking disgruntled and gloomy—animals can sense our presence very easily. And running parallel to all this: two entrances to the building from Tverskaya Street, with the doors swung open, and in one doorway there's a young vampire from security, polishing his nails with a file. Directly above the shops there's a strip of black stone with the crimson spots of windows in it . . . And the two top floors seem to weigh down on the building like a heavy stone cap.

If only I could show that photograph to the people who live there! But then, they'd all think the same thing—a clumsy piece of photomontage! Clumsy, because the building really does look awkward . . .

When everything was still all right between Zabulon and me, I asked him why our offices were located so strangely, mixed in with the humans' apartments. The boss laughed and explained that it made it more difficult for the Light Ones to try any kind of attack—innocent people might get killed in the fighting. Everybody knows that the Light Ones don't worry about people at all either, but they have to hedge around what they do with all sorts of hypocritical tricks—so the seven floors of apartments make a very reliable shield.

The tiny duty office on the first floor, with the two elevators (the people living in the building don't know about them either) and the fire stairs, seemed to be empty. There was no one behind the desk or in the armchair in front of the television. It took me a moment to spot the two security guards who should have been there according to the staff list: a vampire—I think his name is Kostya—who had only joined the Watch very recently, and the werewolf Vitaly from Kostroma, also a civilian employee, who'd been working for us as long as I could remember. Both guards were standing quite still, huddled over in the corner. Vitaly was giggling quietly. Just for an instant I had a quite crazy idea about the reason for such strange behavior.

"Boys, what's that you're doing over there?" I asked sharply. There's no point in being too polite with these vampires and shape-shifters. They're primitive beasts of labor—not to mention that the vampires are non-life—but they still claim to be no worse than magicians and witches!

"Come here, Aliska!" Vitaly said, beckoning to me without turning round. "This is a real gas."

But Kostya straightened up sharply and took a step backward, looking a bit embarrassed.

I walked over.

There was a little gray mouse dashing around Vitaly's feet. It stopped dead still, then jumped up in the air, then began squeaking and beating desperately at the air with its little paws. I didn't understand until I tried looking through the Twilight.

So that was it.

There was a huge, glossy cat jumping about beside the mouse. Sometimes it reached its paw out toward the tiny creature, sometimes it clattered its jaws together. Of course, it was only an illusion, and a primitive one at that, created exclusively for the small rodent.

"We're seeing how long it can hold out!" Vitaly said happily. "I bet it will die of fright in a minute."

"Now I understand," I said, beginning to see red. "Having fun, are we? Did your hunting instincts get the better of you?"

I reached down and picked up the mouse that had frozen still in fear. The tiny bundle of fur trembled on my hand. I blew on it gently and whispered the right word. The mouse stopped trembling, then it stretched out on my palm and went to sleep.

"What's it to you?" Vitaly asked in a slightly offended voice. "Aliska, in your line of work you're supposed to boil these creatures alive in your cauldron!"

"There are a few spells like that," I admitted. "And there are some that require the liver of a werewolf killed at midnight."

The werewolf's eyes glittered brightly with malice, but he didn't say anything. His rank wasn't high enough to try arguing with me. I might only be a simple patrol witch, but that was way above a mercenary werewolf.

"All right then, you guys, tell me the procedure to be followed after the discovery on the premises of rodents, cockroaches, flies, mosquitoes . . ." I said in a slow, lazy voice.

"Activate the pest control amulet," Vitaly said reluctantly. "If any of the creatures should be observed not to be affected by the action of the amulet, then it should be captured, exercising great vigilance, and handed over to the duty magician for checking."

"You do know it . . . So we're not dealing with a case of forgetfulness here. Have you activated the amulet?" I asked.

The werewolf gave the vampire a sideways glance and then looked away.

"No . . ."

"I see. Failure to carry out duty instructions. As the senior

member of the duty detail, you will be penalized. You will inform
the duty officer."

The werewolf said nothing.

"Repeat what I said, security guard."

He realized it was stupid to resist and repeated it.

"And now get back to serving your watch," I said, and walked to
the elevator, still carrying the sleeping mouse on my open palm.

"Bon appetit . . ." the werewolf muttered after me. Those creatures have no discipline—the animal half of them is just too strong.

"I hope that in a genuine battle you will be at least half as brave
as this little mouse," I replied as I got into the elevator. I caught
Kostya's eye—it seemed to me that the young vampire was embarrassed, and even glad that the cruel amusement was at an end.

My appearance in the department with a mouse in my hand caused
an uproar.

Anna Lemesheva, the senior witch on our shift, was about to
launch into her usual tirade about young people who haven't been
taught any discipline: "Under Stalin, for being five minutes late you'd
have been packed off to a camp in Kolyma to brew potions . . ."
When she saw the mouse she was struck dumb.

Lena Kireeva squealed and then howled: "Oh, how lovely."

Zhanna Gromova giggled and asked if I was going to make
the "thief's elixir"—which includes a boiled mouse as an essential
component—and what I was planning to steal afterward. Olya Mel-
nikova finished painting her nails and congratulated me on a successful hunt.

I put the little creature down on my desk, as if I never came
to work without a fresh mouse, and told everyone how the security
guards had been amusing themselves.

Anna shook her head. "Is that why you were late?"

"Partly," I said honestly. "Anna Tikhonovna, I was incredibly unlucky with the traffic. And then there were those nitwits playing
their games."

Anna Tikhonovna Lemesheva is an old and experienced witch—it's pointless trying to deceive her by putting on a brave front. She's about a hundred years old, and after all the things she's seen, the game with the mouse was hardly going to seem cruel. But even so she pursed her lips and declared: "These werewolves have no respect for duty. When we were stationed at Revel, fighting the Swedes, we had a saying: 'If they send the watch a werewolf, detail a witch to watch him.' What would have happened if an assault group of Light Ones had burst in while both guards were gawking at that rodent? They could have sent the mouse in deliberately. It's disgraceful. I think you should have demanded more serious punishment, Alisa."

"The lash," Lena Kireeva said in a quiet voice. She flicked her thick head of long red hair. Oh, that hair of Lena's, anyone would envy it. But the comforting thing is that nothing else is up to the same standard.

"Yes, it was a mistake to ban the practice of punishment with the lash," Anna replied coldly. "Throw that creature out of the window, Alisa."

"I feel sorry for it," I objected. "It's blockheads like those two who are responsible for the image of Dark Ones that exists in the mass consciousness, a caricature of vicious sadists and monsters . . . Why torment the poor mouse?"

"It does create a certain discharge of energy," said Olya, screwing the lid onto her nail polish. "But it's ve-ry ti-ny . . ."

She shook her hands in the air.

Zhanna snorted derisively. "A discharge! They used up so much energy creating the illusory cat, they'd have to torture an entire kilogram of mice to make up for it."

"We could work it out," Olya suggested. "We torture this mouse to death and count the total amount of Power emitted . . . only we'd need a pair of scales as well."

"You're terrible . . ." Lena said angrily. "And you're quite right, Alisa! Can I take the mouse?"

"What for?" I asked jealously.

"I'll give it to my daughter. She's six years old. It's time she was caring for someone and looking after them. That's good for a girl."

There was an awkward silence for a moment. Of course, it's nothing unusual. It's rare for an Other to have a child who is also an Other . . . Very rare. It's simpler for vampires—they can initiate their own child. And it's simpler for shape-shifters—their children almost always inherit the ability to change form. But the chances are not very good for us, or for the Light Ones either. Lena hadn't been lucky, even though her husband was a Dark magician and former staff member of the Day Watch who had retired after he was wounded and become a businessman.

"Mice don't live very long," Olya observed. "There'll be tears and tantrums . . ."

"That's all right. It'll live a long time with me," Lena laughed. "Ten years at least. Pavel and I will make sure of that."

"Then take it!" I said, pointing at the mouse with a magnanimous gesture. "I'll come round some time to visit."

"Did you put it in a deep sleep?" Lena asked, picking the mouse up by the tail.

"It will sleep until the evening for certain."

"Good."

She carried the mouse to her desk, shook the floppy disks out of a cardboard box, and put the little creature in it.

"Buy a cage," Olga advised as she admired her nails. "Or an aquarium. If it runs away it will gnaw everything and leave filthy droppings everywhere."

Anna Lemesheva thoughtfully observed everything that was going on and then clapped her hands.

"All right, girls. That's enough distraction. The unfortunate creature has been saved and it has found a new home. Things could hardly have been resolved more elegantly. Now let's begin our briefing."

She's a very strict boss, but not malicious. She doesn't make things hard for anyone without reason, and she'll let you fool about, or leave early, if necessary. But when it comes to work, it's best not to argue with her.

The girls all sat in their places. Our room is small—after all, the building wasn't intended for the present numbers of the Watch. All that could fit into the room were four small tables for us and one big desk, where Anna Lemesheva sat. The room reminded me a bit of a school classroom in some tiny village, with a class of four pupils and one teacher.

Lemesheva waited until we'd all switched on our computers and logged on to the network. Then she began in her resonant voice: "Today's assignment is the usual one: patrolling the southeast region of Moscow. You will choose your partners in the guardroom from the available operatives."

We always go on duty in pairs, usually one witch and one shape-shifter or vampire. If the level of patrols is raised, then instead of ordinary operatives they give us warlocks or some of the junior magicians for partners. But that doesn't happen very often.

"Lenochka, you're patrolling Vykhino and Liublino . . ."

Lena Kireeva, who had stealthily launched a game of solitaire on her computer, started, and prepared to argue. I could hardly blame her. Two huge districts and a long way off too. Nothing would come of it, of course. Anna Lemesheva would insist on having her own way as always, but Kireeva couldn't help feeling indignant.

But just at that moment, the phone on Lemesheva's desk rang. We exchanged glances, and even Lena's eyes became serious. That was the direct telephone link with the operations duty officer—it didn't just ring for nothing.

"Yes," said Lemesheva. "Yes. Of course. I understand. I accept the detail . . ."

For a moment her expression went vague—the duty magician was sending her telepathic guidelines to the situation.

That meant it was serious. That meant there was work to do.

"To your brooms . . ." Lena whispered quietly. The brief phrase from a children's cartoon was a traditional saying with us. "I wonder who they'll send . . ." she said.

But when Anna Lemesheva put the receiver down, her expression was strict and tough.

"Into the bus, girls. Everyone. Look lively!"

This meant something very serious. This meant a fight.

CHAPTER 2

THE MINIBUS WAS DRIVEN BY DENISKA, A YOUNG DARK MAGI-
cian so incredibly lazy that he preferred working in the garage
among the vampires and other small timers. But his laziness didn't
stop him knowing how to drive, and he knew perfectly a few spells
that were essential for his job. We literally flew along the road as
we made our way to the city center at a speed that the presidential
cortege could only dream about. I felt the surges of Power when he
examined the reality lines, made the militiamen look the other way,
or made other drivers steer their cars off to the side. Sitting beside
him was Edgar, a plump, swarthy, dark-haired magician from Estonia who looked nothing like a person from the Baltic, but possessed
magical abilities that were almost second-level.

There were nine of us in the vehicle. I could hardly remember
Anna Lemesheva ever leaving the Watch building before, but she was
sitting in the chair by the door, monotonously reciting the guidelines:

"Darya Leonidovna Romashova. Sixty-three years old, looks considerably younger, probably constantly nourished by Power. Pre-
sumably a witch, but could possibly be a Dark Sorceress. Under
observation for the last four years as an uninitiated Other."

At this point Lemesheva permitted herself to swear briefly and
obscenely, addressing her abuse to the members of the detection department. "Apparently she refuses all contact. She avoids conversations on mystical subjects, citing her religious piety! What has faith

got to do with the abilities of an Other? It's a different question who
that Christ of theirs was . . ."

"Anna Tikhonovna, don't blaspheme," Lena said quietly but insistently. "I believe in the Lord God, too."

"I'm sorry, Lena," Lemesheva said with a nod. "I didn't mean to
offend you. Let's continue . . . Romashova has probably been earn-
ing a bit from small-scale magic. Love potions, hate potions, hexes,
removing curses . . ."

"The standard charlatan's stock-in-trade," I put in. "No wonder
they didn't bother to check her seriously."

"And what about monitoring her results and finding out if she
really did help people?" Lemesheva asked. "No, I'm going to write a
report. If Zabulon thinks this is good work—then sack me! It's time
for me to retire."

Olga cleared her throat in warning.

"I'm prepared to say it to his face!" Lemesheva was obviously
worked up. "Well, I ask you, they suspect a woman is a witch for
four years, but they don't bother to check properly! It's a standard
procedure—we send an agent and monitor the discharge of Power . . .
And the Light Ones did it, by the way!"

So that was it. Now I understood and I immediately gathered
myself. What lay ahead wasn't just an incident with a crazy witch
who had done something she shouldn't have. It was a fight with the
Night Watch.

Vitaly growled indistinctly in his seat opposite me, more likely
trying to keep his courage up than expressing delight at the battle
ahead. He'd grown lazy standing watch, this brave mouse-hunter.
I smiled spitefully, and the werewolf snarled and bared his teeth
slightly. They had already started to grow, and his lower jaw was
stretching forward.

"Vitaly, spare us the spectacle of transformation in the vehicle,"
Lemesheva said sharply. "In this heat the stink of dog will be quite
unbearable!"

The trio of vampires on the backseat all began to laugh. I knew those guys quite well; they had been tested in action, and by and large, I didn't find them repulsive at all—not like most non-life. Three brothers, born a year apart, strong, well-built young men from an ordinary human family. The eldest had become a vampire first, when he was working in a regiment of paratroopers, and he'd done it deliberately, out of ideological considerations—his commanding officer, who was a vampire, had suggested the young man should become a vampire too. Their unit was in action somewhere in the South at the time. Things weren't going too well, and the young man had agreed. Of course, after that the unit became incredibly effective in battle. Killing a dozen enemies a night, penetrating the enemy's rear line, walking past sentries without being seen—for a vampire, even an inexperienced one, all this is child's play. Afterward, when he returned to civilian life, the young man had told his younger brothers everything, and they had offered up their own throats for biting.

"Anna Tikhonovna, how many of them are there?" Olga asked. "The Light Ones?"

"A few. Four . . . maybe five. But"—Lemesheva ran her stern gaze over all of us—"you mustn't relax, girls. There's at least one second-level Light magician."

The oldest vampire brother whistled. Facing a magician, especially one that powerful, was beyond a vampire's abilities. And if there were two of them . . .

"And the girl shape-shifter's there," said Lemesheva, looking at me.

I clenched my teeth. So, Tiger Cub was there. The shape-shifting battle magician, as the Light Ones preferred to call her. An old acquaintance of mine . . . and a close one. I seemed to feel an ache in my left arm, which she had once pulled out of its socket. And I remembered the wounds on my face—four bloody lines from her claws.

But Zabulon himself had helped me then. He had healed me completely so there was no damage either to my appearance or my health. And I used to go into battle boldly and cheerfully, feeling his approving glance and restrained, patient smile.

It's over. That's all behind you now, Aliska. What used to be is gone now. Forget it and don't torment yourself. If they tear your face, you'll have to wear the paranjah all the time, until your turn comes for magical healing, and the line's six months long. And you'll be lucky if they consider you worthy of complete healing, including cosmetic magic . . .

"Everybody check your equipment," Anna Lemesheva commanded.

The girls started bustling about, and I patted my pockets, checking on the tiny packets, little bottles, and amulets. A witch's Power doesn't lie only in controlling energy through the Twilight. We also employ auxiliary means, which is what really distinguishes us from sorceresses.

"Alisa?"

I looked at Lemesheva.

"Do you have any suggestions?"

That was better. I had to think about the future, not about the past.

"The operatives can neutralize Tiger Cub. All four of them."

"We don't need any help, Aliska," the oldest vampire brother said good-naturedly. "We'll manage."

Lemesheva thought for a moment and nodded

"All right, the three of you work together. Vitaly, you're with me, my reserve."

The werewolf smiled happily. What a fool. Anna Lemesheva would toss him into the fire like a splinter of wood. Right into the very hottest spot.

"And the four of us . . ."

"Five," Lemesheva corrected me.

Aha, so the old crone has decided to do some work herself?

"The five of us form a Circle of Power," I suggested. "And we feed it all to Edgar. Deniska maintains contact with headquarters."

The minibus bounced over a few potholes and bumps. We were already driving into the yard between the buildings.

"Yes, that's the only possible way to play it," Lemesheva agreed. "Take note, everybody! That's the way we'll work!"

I felt slightly excited that my plan had been accepted completely. I was still a genuine battle witch, after all. Even with all my personal problems. That was why I took the risk of speaking up and overstepping my bounds on the senior witch's final decision on how the group worked.

"But I would suggest summoning help in advance. If there are two second-level magicians there."

"All possible help has already been summoned," Lemesheva snapped. "And we still have an ace of trumps up our sleeves."

Vitaly looked at the old witch in surprise and grinned proudly with his wolf's fangs. A fool twice over. She didn't mean him. He was no ace, just a common low card . . . and certainly not a trump.

"Right, girls, let's get started!"

Our minibus stopped. Anna Lemesheva jumped out spryly and waved her left hand. A fine, dark dust swirled around her fingers for an instant and I felt a spell of inattention enfold the yard. Now, no matter what we did, ordinary people would take no notice of us.

We tumbled out of the minibus.

It was just an ordinary yard in South Butovo. Oh, what a dump . . . I'd rather live somewhere in Mytishchi or Lytkarino than be formally registered as a Muscovite and live in that terrible place. There seemed to be everything there should be: houses and stunted little trees trying to grow in the compressed clay, and wretched little cars standing at the entrances, but . . .

"Get on with it!"

Lemesheva gave me a kick that bounced me about three meters away from the minibus. I almost went flying into the sandbox, where a boy and a girl about five years old were discussing the mysterious art of building sandcastles.

But even the little children didn't notice me, although they're always more sensitive to the presence of Others.

The vampire brothers went dashing past me like three shadows. They surrounded the minibus, already in the process of transformation: Their fangs were growing out between their teeth, and their skin was taking on a pale, sickly tinge. The typical appearance of non-life . . .

"The Circle!" Lemesheva barked. I dashed across to the minibus like a bullet and grabbed Olya and Lena by the hand. Oh, the old witch was strong!

But there was someone standing in the entrance to the house, visible only to our sight as Others—a short, stocky guy . . . definitely a guy—you couldn't call him anything else—wearing worn Turkish jeans and a synthetic T-shirt, with a ridiculous cap on his head.

That was really bad.

The guy was called Semyon. And he was a magician of astounding power, even if he wasn't always quick to use it. Even more terrifying, he was a magician with immense experience of field operations . . .

I felt Semyon's gaze slip over me—firm, resilient, and flexible, like a surgical probe. Then Semyon turned and went back into the entrance hall.

This was really bad!

Then Zhanna grabbed Olga by the hand. Anna Lemesheva completed the circle—and all my emotions disappeared.

We became a living accumulator, connected to Edgar, who was already walking toward the entrance with a gentle, unhurried stride, at the human level of perception and in the Twilight at the same time.

Edgar walked up the stairs, just as his opponent had done. Of course, he didn't overtake him there. And when he reached the door of the apartment on the fourth floor, they were waiting for him. Fused into the Circle of Power, we were all perceiving the world through his sense organs now.

The door was standing open—at the human level of the world. In the Twilight, the doorway was blocked by a solid wall.

There were two magicians standing on the landing. Semyon and Garik. I couldn't feel any emotions now, but I still had my thoughts. Cold, calm, and unhurried. This was the end. Two magicians, each equal to or superior to Edgar.

"The entrance is closed," said Semyon. "There's a Night Watch operation taking place here."

Edgar nodded politely. "I understand. But there's also a Day Watch operation taking place here."

"What do you want?" Semyon moved aside slightly. Standing behind him in the narrow hallway of the apartment was a tigress. An immense beast with gleaming fur and its teeth exposed in a smug smile.

What is Lemesheva counting on? We can't handle this! There's no way!

"We'd like to take the person who belongs to us," Edgar said with a shrug. "That's all."

"The witch has been arrested and charged: magical intervention of the third degree, murder, practicing black magic without a license, concealing the abilities of an Other."

"You provoked her into taking this action," Edgar said coolly. "The Day Watch will conduct its own investigation of events."

"No." Semyon leaned against the wall and the blue moss crept convulsively along the surface, trying to get as far away as possible from the magician. "The matter is settled."

Garik didn't even say anything. He twirled a small amulet that looked like a cube of ivory in his fingers, and glimmers of energy pierced the air. Most likely it was an ordinary magical accumulator . . .

"I'm going through and I'm taking what belongs to us," said Edgar.

He's incredibly calm. Maybe he also knows something that I don't?

The Light magicians didn't say a word. But such a piece of obvious stupidity seemed to have put them on their guard. The witch's fate now depended on who would conduct the investigation. If we could get her, we'd be able to defend her and make her one of us. If the Light Ones got her, then her life was over.

But better her life than all of ours! Two second-level magicians, a shape-shifter, and another two or three Others in the apartment! They'd crush us!

"I'm going in," Edgar said calmly and took a step forward. The Twilight around him howled as it filled with Power—the magician had set up a defensive screen.

All I remember after that is the battle.

The Light Ones struck as soon as Edgar took that step. Not with deadly spells, but an ordinary "press," trying to force our magician off the staircase. Edgar bent over as if he were walking into a wind and the outline of the Power vortex protecting him became clearly visible. The battle was being waged at the level of pure energy. It was primitive and not at all spectacular. Ah, if only Zabulon had been there instead of Edgar! He'd have forced them to expend all their energy and tossed those upstarts aside in an instant, drained of all their abilities!

But Edgar was putting up a worthy fight. For about five seconds he moved forward using his own Power, even forcing the press back to the door of the apartment. Then I felt the cold in my fingertips.

The magician had started to draw on our Power.

I immediately sensed the Light Ones tense as they spotted the energy channel between us and Edgar. They didn't try to disrupt it—a hasty attempt would only have led to Edgar absorbing their energy as well. They simply increased their pressure, counting on their own superiority. And I had the impression that the magicians concealed inside the apartment started feeding them with Power as well.

For a few moments everything hung in the balance. The current of our combined Power had immediately increased Edgar's pressure, but the Light Ones had their own reserves. The little cube in Garik's hand crumbled and scattered across the floor in golden dust and their counterblow pushed Edgar back a meter. Olga began groaning beside me—her basic energy reserves were exhausted, and now she was pumping out the very substance of her Power, the deep reserves that can't be replenished so easily. She didn't seem to be in very good shape today.

What was Lemesheva hoping for?

There was a noise behind the backs of the Light Ones. Aha . . . the vampire brothers . . . they must have got in through the balcony . . .

But the magicians didn't even seem to notice what was happening. The tigress was the only one who went dashing toward the noise, brushing aside the puny furniture in her way and ripping the linoleum with her claws. And a moment later I heard a pitiful howl from one of the brothers.

Yes, three vampires weren't really enough for the shape-shifter . . .

"Vitaly!" Lemesheva commanded. The mental command slid through the Twilight and our werewolf dashed toward the entrance of the house, throwing off his clothes and changing into a wolf on the way. We continued feeding Edgar with energy and he started moving forward again, even managing to squeeze Garik back into the apartment. Then a huge wolf appeared from behind Edgar and rushed forward, paying no attention to the magicians.

It was a good idea. But inside the apartment the appearance of the werewolf was met with a bolt of fire. One of the Light Ones who had been kept in reserve had joined in the struggle, and he'd immediately shown that he was serious.

The werewolf's thick brown fur burst into flames and he leapt up into the air and fell on the floor, thrashing his paws about and rolling over and over, trying to put the flames out. If he had continued the attack, he would have had a chance to get to the magician before he could prepare a second fireball . . .

But he'd obviously been on watch duty for far too long.

Vitaly kept trying to put out the flames, and new charges kept striking him from out of the darkness. A second, a third, a fourth . . . Blood spurted out and burning lumps of flesh went flying through the air. The wolf howled and fell silent—only its back legs were twitching now, with its tail lying between them, blazing like a firework. It was actually quite beautiful.

The amulet hanging at my chest—a small crystal jug with a drop
of red liquid sealed inside—crunched and shattered into tiny fragments. That was bad. It was a signal that my Power was running out
and it simultaneously released my final reserve. A drop of the blood
of a woman who has died giving birth to an Other is a very powerful
source of energy, but even that wouldn't last for long.

"Lena!" Lemesheva ordered.

I felt the wordless command again and Lena left the Circle,
moving slowly, like a sleepwalker. My right hand was left empty and
the trance receded for a few seconds, before Anna Lemesheva reached
out to me. But it was enough time for me to see something standing
in the center of our Circle—a small folding table of black wood, with
a slim blade of burnished steel lying on it. And Lena was already
standing by the sandbox, frozen over the playing children as if she
were choosing between them . . .

"The girl!" Lemesheva shouted. "One girl is more use than a
dozen boys!"

Now I understood everything. Apart from one thing, that is. How
had Anna Lemesheva been granted the right to a human sacrifice,
and why had she decided to waste such tremendous Power on saving
some ordinary witch?

But then Lemesheva grasped my hand and at once I became a
mindless part of the Circle of Power.

Edgar was already squeezed back into the corner of the stairwell—
they weren't just pushing him back now, they were trying to crush
him against the wall. He threw up one hand: "Stop!"

A terrible pain . . .

The Circle was draining the very last drops of energy out of me,
and Olga wasn't giving any more at all. She'd been wrung completely
dry and she was standing there with us, twitching as if she were
holding a bare power cable, and Zhanna was groaning quietly too,
her head gradually sinking down onto her chest . . .

"We have the right to a sacrifice," Edgar said coolly. "If you don't
let her go . . ."

The Light Ones froze. I saw the way they looked at each other and Garik shook his head.

But Semyon seemed to believe it right away.

A sacrifice provides a massive discharge of energy, especially if it's the sacrifice of a child; more if it takes place inside a Circle of Power; and even more if it's performed by an experienced witch. Lena Kireeva was standing inside the Ring, the knife already in her hands and the girl lying on the black table.

If we transferred the liberated Power into Edgar, the Light Ones wouldn't be able to stand up against it. Of course, they had extreme methods of their own, but did they have the authority to make use of them?

The shape-shifter tigress sprang out into the corridor. She must have been battering the vampire brothers on the balcony and seen what we were preparing to do.

"You can't stand against us," Edgar said aloofly. "We'll take what is ours anyway, and a human child will die. And you'll be to blame."

The Light Ones were dumbfounded. It was hardly surprising: The situation behind this particular conflict didn't seem particularly important in any way. It wasn't a matter of states threatening nuclear strikes against each other if their agents were arrested for spying. Others don't threaten to use first-degree magic in the case of a petty conflict between operational agents.

But the Light Ones were still keeping up the pressure on our magician. They were maintaining the press, if only by inertia, and we had no more Power left to share with Edgar. Olga had gone rigid and lost consciousness, and now she was standing in the ring like a limp wooden puppet. Zhanna was already sinking to her knees, but heroically maintaining a grip with her hands and giving a few final crumbs of energy. Lena's face contorted in an agonized grimace and she raised the knife above the twitching little girl. She was conscious, otherwise the discharge of energy would have been reduced, but she was restrained by a spell of silence. My body felt as limp as cotton wool and I was beginning to sway. *I wish they'd hurry . . . I won't be able to hold out. . .*

"Stop!" shouted Semyon. "We surrender the witch!"

Hold it . . . hold the Circle. I tried to draw energy out of the surrounding space, out of the little girl who was frightened to death, out of the people walking by a little distance away and diligently paying no attention to what was going on.

It was useless. I'd been completely drained of everything. It was Lemesheva . . . that was why she was standing there stronger than everyone else, the lousy . . . We were all going to die here for an old woman no one needed, and she'd be left, that vile creature.

But the Light Ones had already shoved a scruffy, plump woman in a dirty housecoat and torn slippers into Edgar's arms. She didn't understand a thing—she was staring all around and trying to cross herself.

"You'll pay for this" were Semyon's last words.

Edgar pulled the witch's arm behind her back with a sharp jerk—he had no time for explanations and no strength left for magic. He dragged her down the staircase.

Hold the Circle . . .

A sacrifice is an act of such great Power that it is best held in reserve. The right to use it might have been won twenty or thirty years earlier by the cunning use of intrigue and provocation. That was why Kireeva was still standing stony-faced above the little girl, with the knife gleaming in her hand, ready to cut out her heart in a single swift movement, while Deniska monotonously recited the words of the appropriate spells. At any moment we could have received a powerful stream of energy . . . only it was better to do without it.

Hold the Circle . . .

My fury was the only thing that saved me. Fury with the entire unsuccessful day, with all the failures of the last year, and with Lemesheva, who clearly knew more than she was saying. I don't know where I found those final crumbs of Power, but I did! And I drove them through the limp bodies of Olga and Zhanna, so that Lemesheva could transmit the thin stream of Power to Edgar . . .

The first to jump into the minibus were the vampire brothers . . . those damn useless field agents . . . Then Lena let the little girl go and she went rushing off, howling. Deniska stopped reciting spells, picked up the little table, and tossed it into the back of the minibus. And it was only then that Lemesheva broke the Circle.

Everything was swimming in front of my eyes. For some reason I started coughing as I tried in vain to free my hand from Olga's rigid fingers.

"Into the bus!" Anna Lemesheva shouted. "Quickly!"

Edgar appeared—at least he looked fairly cheerful. He tossed the witch into the back of the bus and jumped into the seat beside Deniska. Anna Lemesheva dragged Olga into the bus and I helped Zhanna get in—she was in a very bad way, but she was still conscious.

"Who are you? Who are you?" the rescued woman wailed. Lemesheva slapped her across the face with all her might and the witch shut up.

"Deniska, step on it," I said. As if he needed to be told . . .

We tore out of the yard with a screech of tires. Edgar was holding his head in his hands and working—correcting the reality lines and clearing the way ahead of us.

"Feeling bad, Aliska?" Lena asked with avid curiosity. I gritted my teeth and shook my head. But Lena complained, "I'm completely exhausted. I'll have to take some time off."

The rescued witch whined quietly until she caught my hate-filled glance. Then she immediately fell silent and tried to move back and away from me, but the vampires were sitting there. Battered, bloody, and angry—I thought they'd been sensible enough to try to keep away from the shape-shifter, but each of them had caught one or two blows from her paws.

"And they burnt Vitalik to ashes . . ." Deniska said gloomily. "He was an idiot, of course, but he was our idiot . . . Anna Tikhonovna, are you sure this bitch was worth all this bother?"

"The order came from Zabulon," Lemesheva replied. "He probably knows best."

"He could have helped us then," I couldn't help remarking. "This was a job for his powers, not for ours."

Anna Lemesheva gave me a curious kind of glance. "I think not. You made a wonderful effort, my girl. Quite marvelous. I didn't expect you to provide so much Power."

I barely managed to stop myself from crying like a child. To hide my tears I looked at Olga—she was still unconscious. At least I could take comfort in that—she'd come off far worse than me. . . . I raised myself up with a struggle and slapped Olga on the cheek. No response. I pinched her. She didn't stir.

Everybody was looking at me curiously. Even the quietly swearing vampires stopped licking their wounds and waited.

"Anna Tikhonovna, couldn't you help her?" I asked. "She was hurt in the line of duty, and according to instructions . . ."

"Alisa, my dear, how can I help her?" Lemesheva asked in an affectionate voice. "She's dead. Since five minutes ago. She miscalculated and drained herself completely."

I pulled my hand away. Olga's limp body jerked to and fro in the chair and her chin lolled across her chest.

"What, can't you tell?" Zhanna whispered. "Aliska, what's wrong with you?"

Telling the living from the dead doesn't require any spells. It's elementary Power work. That subtle substance that some call the soul is sensed immediately . . . if it's there.

"You gave up too much Power!" said Lena. "Oh, Alisa, you're completely empty now! For five years—empty. Like Yulia Bryantseva, who drained herself during an operation two years ago, and ever since then she can't even enter the Twilight!"

"Don't get your hopes up," was all I said, trying to keep a calm expression on my face. "According to the instructions, they have to help me restore myself."

It sounded pitiful.

"Did they help Bryantseva?" Lena asked.

But Anna Lemesheva sighed and said, "Alisa, if only everything had been according to the instructions a year ago, when Zabulon was so fond of you."

Before I could even think of a reply, the rescued witch suddenly squealed hysterically: "Where are you taking me? Where are you taking me?"

That's when I lost it. I jumped up and started beating the solitary witch on the face, trying to scratch her as badly as I could. She was so frightened she didn't even try to resist. I pounded her for about three minutes to the approving cries of the vampire brothers, reproaches from Lemesheva, and encouragement from Lena and Zhanna. The only one who didn't say anything was dead Olga, whom I kept stumbling over in the crowded space of the minibus. But I think she would have supported me.

Then I sat down to catch my breath. The old witch was sobbing and feeling her bloodied face. *If only they were chasing us! I'd bite into those Light Ones' throats as hard as any vampire! I'd finish them off without any magic!*

But there wasn't anyone chasing us.

Nobody could have called our return triumphant.

The vampires took Olga's body and set off with it to our headquarters without saying a word, as if they even understood the full tragedy of the situation. But then why shouldn't they understand? They had swapped life for non-life, but they could still think and feel, and theoretically they could carry on existing like that for all eternity. But now Olga was gone forever.

Deniska drove the minibus away to the parking lot. Edgar took the rescued witch firmly by the arm and led her toward the Watch building. She didn't resist. We brought up the rear of the procession.

Carrying a body along a crowded street in the center of Moscow, close to the walls of the Kremlin, is not the most relaxing of occupations, even with the spell of inattention that Lemesheva had pronounced again. People didn't look at us, they just quickened their step and walked around the procession. But the Twilight became agitated.

The fabric of existence is woven too fine here. There's too much blood, too many emotions, the traces of the past are too clearly evident. There are places like that, where the boundary between the human world and the Twilight is almost imperceptible, and the center of Moscow is one of them.

If I'd been in a fit state, I would have seen the surges of Power emerging from the depths of a different reality. Probably even Zabulon couldn't explain exactly what stands behind them. All that we could do was pay no attention to the greedy breathing of the Twilight that had sensed the death of a witch in magical combat.

"Faster!" Lemesheva said, and the vampires quickened their stride. The Twilight must have become seriously agitated.

Only I couldn't tell any longer.

We went in the door that was invisible to human beings, and Lena had to take me and Zhanna through. Our colleagues were already running toward us. The witch, who had started yelling again, was dragged off to the interrogation room on the tenth floor. Olga was handed directly to magicians from the department of healing (without the slightest hope of being able to help, but the fact of death had to be registered). One of the healers on duty examined us carefully. He shook his head disapprovingly as he assessed Zhanna's condition and frowned when he looked at the battered vampires. But when he turned his attention to me, his face simply froze.

"Is it really that bad?" I asked.

"That's putting it mildly," he said without superfluous sentimentality. "Alisa, what were you thinking of when you gave out your Power?"

"I was acting according to instructions," I answered, feeling my tears welling up again. "Edgar would have been killed—he was up against two second-level magicians!"

The healer nodded. "Very praiseworthy zeal, Alisa. But the price is very high too."

Edgar was already hurrying toward the elevator, but he stopped and gave me a look of sympathy. Then he came over to me and kissed the palm of my hand. These Baltic types are always making themselves out to be Victorian gentlemen.

"Alisa, my most profound gratitude! I could sense that you were giving everything you had. I was afraid that you would go the same way as Olga." He turned to the healer. "Karl Lvovich, what can be done for this brave girl?"

"I'm afraid nothing can be done," the healer said with a shrug. "Alisa was drawing Power from out of her own soul. It's like acute dystrophy, if you get my meaning. When the body doesn't have enough food, it starts digesting itself. It destroys the liver, the muscles, the stomach—anything to maintain the brain until the very last. Our girls found themselves in a similar situation. Zhanna seems to have lost consciousness in time and stopped drawing on her final reserves. Alisa and Olga held out to the end, but Olga's inner resources were not so great and she died. Alisa survived, but her mental reserves have been totally exhausted."

Edgar gave a sympathetic nod and everyone else listened to the doctor with interest as he continued with his florid rhetoric. "The special abilities of an Other are similar in some ways to any other energy reaction—take a nuclear reaction, for instance. We maintain our abilities by drawing Power from the world around us, from people and other less complex objects. But in order to begin receiving Power, first you have to invest some of your own—such is the cruel law of nature. And Alisa has practically none of that initial Power left. Simply pumping in Power is no help in this case, just as a piece of heavily salted pork fat or an overcooked, crispy steak won't save someone who's starving to death. The body can't digest that kind of food—in fact, it will kill, not cure. It's the same thing with Alisa—we could pump energy into her, but she would choke on it."

"Could you please not talk about me in the third person?" I asked. "And not in that tone of voice!"

"I'm sorry, my girl." Karl Lvovich sighed. "But what I'm saying is the truth."

Edgar gently released my hand and said, "Alisa, don't take it too much to heart. Perhaps the chief will think of something. And by the way, talking about steaks . . . I'm absolutely ravenous."

Lemesheva nodded. "Let's go to some little bistro."

"Wait for me, okay?" said Zhanna. "I'll just take a shower, I'm lathered in sweat . . ."

I didn't even have enough strength left to feel horrified. I stood there like a fool, listening to their conversation, trying to sense anything at all at the level of an Other. To see my real shadow, to summon the Twilight, to feel the emotional background . . .

There was nothing.

And they seemed to have forgotten about me already.

If it had been Zhanna or Lena in my place, I would have behaved exactly the same way. After all, there's no point in hanging yourself just because someone else got careless, is there? Did anyone ask me to give everything, down to the very last drop? No, it was my fault for trying to be a hero!

It was all because of Semyon and Tiger Cub. When I realized who we'd come up against, I decided to take my revenge. To prove something . . . to someone . . . for some reason . . .

Now what was I going to do? I'd proved it, all right, and I'd been crippled. And far more badly than in the fight with Tiger Cub . . .

"Just be quick, Zhanna," said Lemesheva. "Alisa, will you come with us?"

I turned toward her, but before I could say anything, someone spoke behind my back: "Nobody's going anywhere."

Lemesheva's eyes opened wide and I shuddered as I recognized that voice.

Zabulon was standing by the elevator.

He was in his human form: skinny and sad-looking, with a rather preoccupied air. Many of our people only know him like that—calm and unhurried, even a little bit boring. But I know another Zabulon too. Not the restrained boss of the Day Watch, not the mighty warrior who takes on demonic form, not the Dark magician beyond classification . . . but a cheerful, inexhaustibly inventive Other.

Simply an Other, without any traces of the gulf between us, as if there were no difference in age, experience, or Power.

That's the way it used to be. Before . . .

"Everybody, come to my office," Zabulon ordered. "Immediately."

He disappeared—dived into the Twilight probably. But before that he rested his glance on me for a brief moment. There was no expression at all in his eyes. No mockery or sympathy or affection.

But he did look at me, and my heart stood still. For the last year Zabulon had seemed not even to notice the unfortunate witch Alisa Donnikova.

"So much for bistros and showers," Lemesheva said dourly. "Come on, girls."

It was an accident that I ended up sitting apart from the others.

My feet automatically took me to the armchair by the fireplace—the broad leather armchair in which I used to curl up, half-sitting, half-lying, watching Zabulon at work, looking at the smokeless flame in the hearth, the photographs hanging all round the walls . . .

When I realized that I'd unwittingly separated myself from the others, who had taken appropriate places on the divans by the wall, it was already too late to change anything. It would only have looked stupid.

Then I kicked off my sandals, pulled my feet up, and made myself comfortable.

Lemesheva glanced at me in astonishment before she started her report. The others didn't even dare to look—their eyes were fixed adoringly on the boss. The sycophantic toadies!

Leaning back in his chair behind his huge desk, Zabulon didn't react to me at all either. At least not on the outside.

Well, don't look then. . .

I listened to Lemesheva's smooth voice—she delivered her report well, speaking briefly and to the point, nothing superfluous was said and nothing important was omitted. And I looked at the photograph hanging above the desk. It was very, very old, taken a hundred and forty years earlier, using the colloidal method—the boss once gave me a detailed explanation of the differences between the "dry" and "wet" techniques. The photograph showed Zabulon in old-fashioned clothes as a student at Oxford, against the background of the tower of Christ Church College. It was a genuine original by Lewis Carroll. The boss once remarked that it had been very difficult to persuade the "dried-up prim and proper poet" to spend some time on one of his own students instead of a little girl. But the photograph had turned out very well—Carroll must have been a real master. Zabulon looks serious, but there's a lively glint of irony in his eyes, and he looks a lot younger too . . . but then, what does a century and a half mean to him . . .

"Donnikova?"

I looked at Lemesheva and nodded. "I entirely agree. If the absolutely essential goal of our mission was to free the prisoner, then forming the Circle of Power and threatening to perform the sacrifice was the best solution." I paused for a moment and then added skeptically, "Of course, that's if that stupid fool was worth all the effort."

"Alisa!" There was a metallic ring to Lemesheva's voice. "How dare you discuss the chief's orders? Chief, I apologize for Alisa. She's overwrought and not . . . not entirely well."

"Naturally," said Zabulon. "Alisa effectively ensured the success of the entire operation. She sacrificed all her Power. It's hardly surprising that she feels like asking questions."

I raised my head sharply at that. Zabulon was quite serious. Not a hint of mockery or irony.

"But . . ." Lemesheva began.

"Who was just talking about respect for seniority?" Zabulon interrupted her. "Be quiet."

Lemesheva broke off.

Zabulon got up from behind the desk and walked over to me without hurrying. I kept my eyes fixed on him, but I didn't get up.

"That stupid fool," said Zabulon, "was not worth all the effort. Of course not. But the actual operation against the Night Watch was extremely important. And all of the injuries you suffered in the battle are entirely justified."

I felt as if I'd been stabbed in the back. "Thank you, Zabulon," I replied. "It will be easier for me to live through all these years, knowing that my efforts were not in vain."

"All what years, Alisa?" Zabulon asked.

It was strange . . . we hadn't spoken at all for a whole year . . . I hadn't even received any orders from him in person . . . and now when he spoke to me, there was that cold, prickly lump in my chest again.

"The healer said it will be a long time before I can restore my Power."

Zabulon laughed. And then suddenly he reached out his hand! He patted me on the cheek . . . affectionately . . . in that old, familiar way . . .

"Never mind what the healer said . . ." Zabulon declared peaceably. "The healer has his opinion, and I have mine."

He took his hand away and I had to struggle to stop my cheek following it . . .

"I think no one will disagree that Alisa Donnikova was substantially responsible for the success of today's operation?"

Aha . . . I'd have liked to see anyone try to object! Lemesheva simply remarked cautiously, "We all made a significant effort . . ."

"From your condition it's not hard to see who made what kind of effort."

Zabulon went back to his desk, but he didn't sit down. He just leaned over with his hands on the desktop, looking at me. I think he was studying me closely through the Twilight.

But I couldn't sense it . . .

"Is everyone agreed that the Day Watch should help Alisa?" Zabulon inquired.

A glint of fury appeared in Lemesheva's eyes. The old witch had once been Zabulon's girlfriend herself. That was why she had hated me when I was in favor . . . and why she had become fond of me as soon as the chief turned his back on me.

"If it's a matter of help," she began, "then Karl Lvovich made a good comparison. We are prepared to share our Power with Alisa, only that would be like giving a dying person a piece of fatty bacon instead of light broth. But I am willing to try . . ."

Zabulon turned his head and Lemesheva shut up.

"If light broth is what is required, then she shall have light broth," he said in a very calm voice. "You can all go."

The vampire brothers were the first to jump to their feet, then the witches stood up. I started shuffling my feet about, looking for my sandals.

"Alisa, you stay, if it's no trouble," Zabulon said.

The glint in Lemesheva's eyes flared up—and then faded away. She had realized what I was still afraid to believe in.

A few moments later Zabulon and I were left alone, looking at each other without speaking. My throat was dry and my tongue wouldn't obey me. No, it couldn't be true . . . I shouldn't even try to deceive myself . . .

"How are you feeling, Alya?" Zabulon asked.

Only my mother ever calls me Alya. And Zabulon used to call me that . . .

"Like a squeezed lemon," I said. "Tell me, am I really such a terrible fool? Did I exhaust myself doing a job that is no use to anybody?"

"You did very well, Alya," said Zabulon.

And he smiled.

The same way he used to smile. Exactly the same way.

"But now I . . ." I stopped, because Zabulon took a step toward me—and I didn't need words anymore. I couldn't even get up out of the chair: I put my arms round his legs and hugged him, pressed myself against him—and burst into tears.

"Today you laid the foundation for one of our finest operations," said Zabulon. His hand was ruffling my hair, but at that moment he seemed to be somewhere very far away. Of course, a Great Magician like him could never afford to relax: He carried responsibility for the

entire Day Watch of Moscow and the surrounding region, for the
fates of the ordinary Dark Ones living their calm and peaceful lives.
He had to fight the intrigues of the Light Ones and pay attention to
people's needs . . . "Alisa, after your stupid trick with the Prism of
Power, I decided you weren't really worthy of my attention."

"Zabulon, I was a conceited fool . . ." I whispered, swallowing my
tears. "Forgive me. I let you down . . ."

"Today you made up for everything."

Zabulon lifted me up out of the armchair in a single swift movement. I stood on tiptoe, otherwise I would have been left dangling in
his arms, and I remembered how astonished I had been the first time
by the incredible strength of his skinny body. Even when he was in
his human form . . .

"Alisa, I'm pleased with you," he said and smiled. "And don't
worry about having drained your Power. We have certain special
reserves."

"Like the right to perform a sacrifice?" I asked, trying to smile.

"Yes," Zabulon nodded. "You're going on vacation, starting from
today. And you'll come back better than ever."

My lips started trembling treacherously. What was happening to
me? I was wailing like a hysterical child. My mascara must have run
all over my face, I didn't have a single ounce of Power left . . .

"I want you," I whispered. "Zabulon, I've been so lonely . . ."

He gently took my arms away. "Afterward, Alya. When you come
back. Otherwise it would be . . ." Zabulon smiled. ". . . an abuse of
my official position for personal ends."

"Nobody would dare say that to you!"

Zabulon looked into my eyes for a long time. "There are some
who would, Alya. Last year was a very difficult one for the Watch,
and there are many who would like to see me humiliated."

"Then don't do this," I said quickly. "Don't take the risk. I'll restore my own Power bit by bit . . ."

"No, it's the right thing to do. Don't you worry, my little girl."

My heart skipped a beat at the sound of his voice. At that calm, confident Power.

"Why would you take such a risk for me?" I whispered, not expecting any answer, but Zabulon did answer:

"Because love is also a power. A great power, and it should not be disdained."

CHAPTER 3

LIFE IS A STRANGE BUSINESS.

A day earlier I had left my apartment, a young, healthy witch full of Power—but unhappy.

Half a day earlier I had been standing in the Watch offices, crippled, with no hope or belief in the future . . . How everything had changed!

"Would you like some more wine, Alisa?" asked Pavel, my escort, looking quizzically into my eyes.

"A little bit," I said, looking out of the window.

The plane had already begun its descent for the landing at Simferopol airport. The old Tupolev jet creaked as it slowly heeled over, and the passengers' faces were anxious and tense. Pavel and I were the only ones sitting there quite calmly—Zabulon himself had checked to make sure the flight was safe.

Pavel handed me a crystal wine glass. Of course, the glass hadn't come from the stewardess's standard stock, and neither had the South African sauterne that was in it. The young shape-shifter seemed to be taking his mission very seriously indeed. He was flying south for a vacation with some friends of his, but at the last minute he'd been taken off the flight to Kherson and instructed to accompany me to Simferopol. The rumors that my relationship with Zabulon had been restored had clearly already reached him.

"Why don't we drink to the chief, Alisa?" Pavel asked. He was trying so hard to ingratiate himself that it was beginning to annoy me.

"All right," I agreed. We clinked glasses and drank. The steward-ess walked past us, checking for the last time that all the seat belts were fastened, but she didn't even look at us. The spell of inattention that Pavel had cast was doing its job. Even this wretched shape-shifter could do more than I could now . . .

"You must admit," Pavel told me after he'd taken a sip of wine, "that the way our chief treats the staff is pretty good!"

I nodded.

"And the Light Ones . . ." he said, putting all the contempt he could muster into those two words, ". . . they're much greater indi-vidualists than we are."

"Don't overdo it," I said. "That's not really true."

"Oh come on, Alisa!" The wine had made him talkative. "Do you remember how we stood in the cordon a year ago? Just before the hurricane?"

That cordon was probably the only place I remembered having seen him before. The shape-shifters do all the crude work and our paths seldom cross. Only during combat operations, and on those rare occasions when the entire Watch personnel is convened.

"I remember."

"Well then, that . . . Gorodetsky. That lousy servant of the Light!"

"He's a very powerful magician," I objected. "Very powerful."

"Oh, sure! He grabbed all that Power, squeezed the last drops out of ordinary people, and then what? What did he use it for?"

"For his own remoralization."

I closed my eyes, remembering how it had looked.

A fountain of light shooting up into the sky. The streams of energy that Anton had gathered from those people. He had risked everything on a single throw of the dice, even risked using borrowed Power, and for a brief instant he had acquired Power that matched or even surpassed the abilities of Zabulon and Gesar.

And he had expended all that tremendous Power on himself.

Remoralization. The search for the ethically optimum solution.

The Light Ones' most terrible problem was how to avoid causing harm, how to avoid taking a step that would result in inflicting evil on human beings.

"That makes him a super-egotist!" Pavel said with relish. "He could have defended his girlfriend, couldn't he? And he could have fought us, couldn't he? And how—with that Power! But what did he do? He used everything he collected on himself. He didn't even try to stop the hurricane . . . but he could have done that, he could have!"

"Who knows what any other course of action would have led to?" I asked.

"But he acted just like any of us. Like a genuine Dark One!"

"If that were true, he'd be in the Day Watch."

"And he will be," Pavel said confidently. "Where else can he go? He couldn't bear to give away all that Power, so he used it on himself. And afterward he made excuses—it was all so that he could make the correct decision . . . And what was his decision? Not to interfere! That was all—not to interfere! That's our way, the Dark way."

"I'm not going to argue with you, Pavlusha," I said.

The plane shuddered as the undercarriage was lowered.

At first glance the shape-shifter seemed to be right. But I could remember Zabulon's face during the days after the hurricane. The expression in his eyes was very gloomy—I'd learned to tell the difference. It was as if he'd realized too late that he'd been tricked.

Pavel carried on discussing the subtleties of the struggle between the two Watches, their different approaches, their long-term operational planning. What a strategist . . . he should have been sitting in headquarters, not roaming the streets . . .

I suddenly realized how tired he'd made me feel during our two-hour flight. But at first he'd made quite a pleasant impression . . .

"Pavlusha, who do you transform into?" I asked.

The shape-shifter started breathing heavily through his nose and answered reluctantly: "A lizard."

"Oho!" I looked at him again with more interest. Shape-shifters like that were a genuine rarity; he was no ordinary werewolf, like the late Vitalik. "That's serious! But why don't I see you on operations more often?"

"I . . ." Pavel stopped and frowned. He took out a handkerchief and dabbed his sweaty forehead. "You see, the thing is . . ."

His embarrassment was wonderful to watch. He was like an erring schoolgirl on a visit to the gynecologist.

"I transform into a herbivorous lizard," he finally blurted out. "Not the most useful kind in a fight, unfortunately. The jaws are strong, but the teeth are flat, for grinding. And I'm too slow. But I can break an arm or a leg . . . or chew off a finger."

I couldn't help laughing. I said sympathetically, "Well, never mind. We need personnel like that too! The important thing is for you to look impressive and instill fear and confusion."

"I look impressive all right," said Pavel, squinting sideways at me suspiciously. "Only my scales are too colorful, like a painted Khokhloma toy. It's hard to disguise myself."

I managed to keep a straight face.

"Never mind, I think that's interesting. When people have to be frightened, especially little children, colorful scales are just the thing."

"That's the kind of work I usually do . . ." Pavel admitted.

A sharp jolt cut short our conversation as the plane touched down on the runway. The passengers burst into applause somewhat prematurely. I gazed avidly out through the window for a few seconds, looking at the greenery, the airport terminal, a plane taxiing to take off . . .

I simply couldn't believe it.

I'd escaped from stuffy, oppressive Moscow. I had the vacation I'd been waiting for so long . . . and my special rights . . . and when I got back—Zabulon would be waiting for me again . . .

Pavel saw me as far as the trolley stop. It's the most amusing trolley route I know: all the way from one town to another, from Simferopol to Yalta. But strangely enough, it's quite a convenient way to travel.

Everything here was different, quite different. It seemed hot—but it wasn't the asphalt-and-concrete city heat of Moscow. And even though the sea was a long way off, I could sense it. And the luxuriant greenery, and the whole atmosphere of a huge resort at the height of the season.

It felt good . . . it really did. I just wanted to get a shower as soon as possible, get a good night's sleep, tidy myself up . . .

"You're not going to Yalta, are you?" Pavel asked understandingly.

"Not exactly to Yalta," I said. I looked gloomily at the long line. Even the children were all keyed up, ready to grab a seat in the trolley. I had nothing with me at all—just my purse and the sports bag over my shoulder, and I could have stood quite easily—but only if I managed to get on the trolley without a ticket.

And I didn't feel like standing.

If it came down to it, I had a thick wad of cash for my travel allowance, vacation allowance, and medical allowance—Zabulon had managed to issue me almost two thousand dollars. That was certainly plenty for two weeks. Especially in Ukraine.

"All right, Pavlusha," I said, and kissed him on the cheek. The shape-shifter blushed. "I'll get there, no need to see me off."

"Are you sure?" he asked. "I was instructed to give you every possible help."

Oh, my little protector . . . A herbivorous lizard, a cow with scales . . .

"I'm sure. You need to get some rest too."

"I'm going to go on a bicycle trip with friends," he informed me for some reason. "They're really nice guys—Ukrainian werewolves and even a young magician. Maybe we could call in to see you?"

"I'd like that."

The shape-shifter walked back toward the airport, clearly intending to board another flight, and I set off along the thin line of taxis and private cars offering lifts. It was already getting dark, and there were only a few of them left.

"Where to, lovely lady?" a stout man with a moustache called out.

He was standing beside his little Zhiguli and smoking. I shook my head—I'd never traveled between towns in a Zhiguli . . . I ignored the Volga as well, and the tiny Oka too—goodness only knew what that driver was hoping for.

But that brand-new Nissan Patrol would suit me very well.

I leaned in over the lowered window. There were two dark-haired young guys sitting in the car. The one in the driving seat was smoking and his companion was drinking beer from a bottle.

"Are you guys free?"

Two pairs of eyes stared at me, sizing me up. I didn't look too creditworthy—that was necessary for my cover . . .

"Possibly," the driver said. "If we can agree on a price."

"We can," I said. "To the Artek camp. Fifty."

"Are you a Young Pioneer?" the driver laughed. "For fifty we'll give you a ride round town."

The witty type. He was so young he shouldn't have been able to remember what a Young Pioneer was. And his ambitions were exorbitant . . . fifty rubles—that was almost ten dollars.

"You didn't ask the most important thing," I remarked. "Fifty what?"

"Well, fifty what?" the driver's friend repeated obligingly.

"Bucks."

The young guys' expressions changed immediately.

"Fifty bucks, we go fast, without any other passengers, and we don't turn the music up loud," I added. "Is it a deal?"

"Yes," the driver decided. He began looking around. "What about your things?"

"I've got them all here." I got into the backseat and dropped my bag down beside me. "Let's go."

My tone of voice seemed to have had the right effect. A minute later we were already swinging out onto the road. I relaxed and leaned back a bit more comfortably. This was it. Vacation. I needed to rest . . . eat the peaches . . . gather my strength . . .

And afterward Moscow and Zabulon would be waiting for me . . .

Just at that moment my cell phone rang in my bag. I got it out without opening my eyes and took the call.

"Alisa, how was the flight?"

I felt a warm glow in my chest. One surprise after another! Even during our best times Zabulon hadn't felt a need to take any interest in such petty details. Or was this just because I was unwell and feeling down?

"It was excellent, thanks. They say there were some problems with the weather, but . . ."

"I know about that. The guys in the Simferopol Day Watch gave us a hand with the weather conditions. That's not what I meant, Alisa. Are you in a car now?"

"Yes."

"Your forecast for this trip is bad."

I pricked up my ears. "The road?"

"No. Apparently your driver."

In front of me the young guys' cropped heads were like blank stone. I looked at them for a second, furious at my helplessness. I couldn't even feel their emotions, let alone read their thoughts . . .

"I'll handle it."

"Have you let your escort go?"

"Yes. Don't worry, sweetheart. I'll handle it."

"Are you sure, Alisa?" There was genuine concern in Zabulon's voice. And that had the same effect on me as dope on an athlete.

"Of course. Try looking further ahead in the forecast!"

Zabulon was silent for a moment. Then he said, "Yes, it straightens out . . . But keep in touch. I'll come if it's necessary."

"If they do anything to me, just skin them alive, sweetheart," I said.

"I'll do more than that—I'll make them eat their own skins," Zabulon agreed. It was no empty threat, of course, but a real promise. "Well, have a good vacation, darling."

I switched off the cell phone and slipped into a doze. The Nissan drove on smoothly and we were soon out on the high road. The young guys occasionally lit a cigarette and there was a smell of tobacco—fortunately not the worst kind. Then the sound of the motor became more labored—we were climbing the mountain pass. I opened my eyes and glanced through the open window at the starry sky. How big the stars were in the Crimea. How close.

Then I fell asleep for real. I even began dreaming—a sweet, languorous dream. I was swimming in the sea at night and there was someone beside me, and sometimes in the darkness I could almost make out the lines of his face, and I could feel the gentle touch of his hands . . .

When I realized that the touch was real, I instantly woke up and opened my eyes.

The engine was silent and the car was standing a little distance off the highway. I think it was in the emergency side road for poor souls whose brakes have failed.

My driver's brakes and his friend's had definitely failed. I could see it in their eyes.

When I woke up the driver's friend took his hand away from my face. He even gave a crooked smile as he said, "We're here, sister."

"It doesn't look like Artek, brother," I replied.

"It's the Angarsky Pass. The motor's overheated," said the driver, licking his lips. "We have to wait. You can get out for a breath of fresh air."

If he was still trying to make lame excuses, he was obviously far more nervous than his companion, who screwed up his courage and said, "You can take a piss . . ."

"Thanks, I don't need one." I carried on sitting there, watching the pair of them curiously, wondering what they'd try. Would they try to drag me out of the car? Or try to rape me where I was? And afterward?

It would be too dangerous to let me go. They'd probably throw me off a cliff. And probably into the sea—the murderer's best friend throughout the ages. The land preserves clues for a long time, but the sea has a short memory.

"We were starting to wonder," the driver declared, "if you really have the money . . . Young Pioneer."

"Since I hired you," I said, emphasizing the word "hired," "it means I do."

"Show us," the driver demanded.

Oh, how stupid you are . . . you little people . . .

I took the wad of money out of my purse, peeled off a fifty and held it out, as if I hadn't noticed the greedy eyes devouring the money. Well, now I was certainly done for.

But they still seemed to need some kind of justification. If only for themselves.

"It's counterfeit!" the driver squealed, carefully hiding the fifty in his pocket. "You bitch, you were trying to . . ."

I looked at them calmly as I listened to a choice serving of obscene language. I felt something inside me tense up, but even so, I didn't have the normal powers of an Other that would have allowed me to turn these two young runts into obedient puppets.

"Hoping your friend can help, are you?" the driver's friend asked. "Is that it? Going to skin us alive, is he? We'll skin him, you bitch!"

I laughed as I imagined the million and one amusing things Zabulon would have done to these young pups just for saying that.

The driver grabbed hold of my arm. His young face was basically rather handsome—I wouldn't have minded having a resort romance with an attractive young man like that—but now it was contorted by a mixture of anger, fear, and lust.

"You're going to pay in kind, you bitch."

Ugh. In kind. And with all my things, and a brief flight through the air down an almost vertical incline . . .

No, I didn't want my acquaintance with the warm water of the Black Sea to start that way. The other young guy reached out toward me, clearly intending to rip my blouse. The bastard—it cost two hundred and fifty bucks! His hands had almost reached me when I pressed the barrel of my pistol against his forehead.

There was a brief pause.

"My, what tough kids you are," I purred. "All right, get your hands off, and get out of the car."

The pistol had really stunned them. Maybe because I'd come out of the airport, so there was no way they could have expected me to be carrying a gun. Or maybe because their little pups' instincts told them it would be a pleasure for me to blow their brains out.

The young guys jumped out of the car and I followed them. They hesitated for a few seconds and then tried to make a run for it. But that didn't suit me now.

I put the first bullet into the ankle of the driver's friend. His legs were less important—he didn't have to work the pedals. It was a trivial glancing scrape—more like a skin burn than a firearms wound—but it was more than enough. The friend fell to the ground with a howl and the driver stopped dead in his tracks with his hands in the air. I wondered who they thought I was. A Federal Security Service agent on vacation?

"I understand your greed perfectly," I said. "The economy's in ruins, people aren't getting paid . . . And the lust too. After all, you still have the sexual hyperdrive of youth seething inside you. So do I, as it happens!"

Even the wounded one stopped making noise. They listened to me without saying a word—as night came on the highway had emptied and there was just one set of headlights approaching in the distance. It was an enchanting, still night, with the sky covered in stars—a warm Crimean night, and down at the bottom of the cliff, the sea was murmuring.

"You're both very good-looking boys," I said. "The only trouble is, I'm not in the mood for sex now. You haven't behaved well enough. But!" I raised one finger and they stared at it as if they were hypnotized. "We can find a way round that!"

Judging from the expressions on their faces, they were expecting the worst. But they needn't have. I'm not a murderer, after all.

"Since there are two of you, and you're clearly good friends," I explained, "it won't be any problem for you to satisfy each other. And after that we'll go on to the camp, calmly, with no more adventures."

"Why you!" The driver took a step toward me, but the pistol barrel aimed at his crotch had the desired effect.

"There is another possibility," I agreed. "I could relieve you of certain unnecessary body parts. And I bet you three to one I can do it with the first shot."

"You . . ." hissed the wounded one. "For us they'll . . ."

"They wouldn't give a bent kopeck for you," I told him. "Get your trousers down and get to work."

I didn't have the Power that allows an Other to break a human being's will. But my voice probably still carried the old conviction. They obeyed me. Or they tried to obey me.

We sometimes watch gay porno in our department—it's very amusing. And the vampires and magicians often show lesbian films in the duty room. In the films the actors always set about the job with enthusiastic skill, but these two halfwits were obviously upset by this sudden turn of events, and they lacked the necessary experience. So I just basically admired the night view of the sea and kept an eye out to make sure the boys weren't slacking.

"Never mind," I comforted them when I thought they'd been humiliated enough. "Like the man said the first time doesn't count. You can practice a bit more in your free time. Get in the car!"

"What for?" the driver asked when he'd finished spitting. He probably thought I wanted to shoot them in their fancy auto and push them over the cliff into the sea.

"Well, you agreed to take me to Artek, didn't you?" I said in an astonished voice. "And you've already got the money."

We drove the rest of the way without any more adventures. Except that halfway there the driver started howling that he couldn't live with himself, he had nothing left to live for, and he was going to turn the wheel and drive off the cliff.

"Go on, go on!" I agreed. "With a bullet in the back of your head you won't even feel the fall!"

That shut him up.

I kept the pistol in my hands all the way to the gates of the Artek camp.

After I opened the door, I leaned back and said, "Ah, there's just one more thing, guys . . ."

They looked at me with hate in their eyes. All that Power I could have drained off if only I'd been in good shape!

"Better not even try to find me again. Or this night will seem like paradise. You understand?"

There was no answer.

"Silence signifies agreement," I said decisively, putting the little Astra Cub back in my purse. The ideal weapon for a frail woman . . . although Pavel had had to carry it through customs. I walked toward the gates and the Nissan roared and set off back the way we'd come. I hoped the failed rapists and robbers would have enough sense not to attempt any kind of revenge . . . But then, a couple of days later I wouldn't be concerned about local petty bandits anymore.

And so I arrived at the Artek camp, where I was supposed to re-store my health, at two in the morning. "To sup light broth," as Karl Lvovich had said as he signed the necessary authorizations.

Every exemplary Soviet Young Pioneer was supposed to do three things: Visit Lenin in his mausoleum, take a vacation at Artek, and tie some little Child of October's necktie, then after that he could proceed to the next stage of his development—the Komsomol.

In the course of my brief childhood career as a Young Pioneer, I had only managed to fulfill the first point. This was my chance to make up for one of the things I'd missed.

I don't know how it was in Soviet times, but now the exemplary children's camp had a serious look to it. The fence around its terri-tory was in perfect order, and there were guards at the entrance. I couldn't actually see any weapons . . . not at a first glance . . . but the strong young guys in militia uniform looked serious enough without them. There was a kid of about fourteen or fifteen there too, looking completely out of place beside these guardians of order. Was he perhaps a hanger-on from the old days, when the bugles were sounded and the drums beaten as the neat ranks of Young Pioneers marched to the beach for their prescribed water therapy?

To be honest, I'd been expecting a lot of bureaucratic red tape. Or at least considerable surprise. But it seemed like it wasn't the first time that Young Pioneer leaders (although now my job had the simpler title of teacher) had arrived at Artek at two o'clock in the morning in a foreign automobile. One of the guards took a quick look at my documents—they were genuine, checked and approved in all the appropriate offices, certified with signatures and seals—and then he called over the kid.

"Makar, take Alisa to the duty camp leader."

"Uh-huh," the kid mumbled, looking me over keenly. He was a good kid, with no complexes. When he saw a beautiful young woman he wasn't afraid to show he was interested. He'd go a long way . . .

After we left the guards' hut, we walked past a long row of stands with lists of daily activities, announcements of various events, and children's wall newspapers . . . what a long time it was since I'd seen wall newspapers! Then we set off along a badly lit path, and I found myself trying to spot the traditional Soviet plaster statues of boy buglers and girls clutching oars along the sides of it, but there weren't any.

"Are you a new leader?" the boy asked.

"Yes."

"Makar." He held out his hand in a dignified manner.

"Alisa." I shook hands with him, barely managing to restrain a smile.

The difference between our ages was about ten years, or maybe twelve. But even the names showed how everything had changed in that time. Where were all the girls named after Lewis Carroll's Alice now? They'd gone the way of the plaster buglers, the Young Pioneer banners, the lost illusions, and the failed dreams. Marched off in tidy columns to the strains of a cheerful, rousing song . . . The little girl who had made every boy in the country fall in love with her when she played Alice in the old film was now quietly working as a biologist and merely smiled when she remembered her old romantic image.

There were other names now. Makar, Ivan, Egor, Masha . . . It was an immutable law of nature—the worse things get in a country, the more it's trampled into the mud, the stronger the yearning for the old roots. For the old names, the old ways, the old rituals. But these Makars and Ivans were no worse. They were probably better, in fact. More serious, more single-minded, not shackled by any ideology or fake show of unity. They were much closer to us Dark Ones than all those Alisas, Seryozhas, and Slavas . . .

But I still felt a bit slighted somehow, maybe because we hadn't been like that. Or maybe it was just because they were like that.

"Are you just going to be here temporarily?" the boy asked, as serious as ever.

"Yes. My friend's fallen ill. I'm going to take her place. But I'll try to come back again next year."

Makar nodded. "Do, this is a good place we have here. I'm going to come next year too. I'll be fifteen then."

Maybe I imagined it, but I thought I saw a brief sparkle in the little imp's eyes.

"And after you're fifteen?"

He shook his head and replied with obvious regret. "You can only come until you're sixteen. But anyway, at sixteen I'm going to go to Cambridge to study."

I almost choked in surprise.

"That's pretty expensive, Makar."

"I know. It was all planned five years ago, don't worry."

He had to be the son of one of those New Russians. They had everything planned in advance.

"Well, that's doing things thoroughly. Are you going to stay there?"

"No, what for? I'll get a decent education and come back to Russia."

A very serious child. No doubt about it, these human beings sometimes threw up amusing types. It was a pity I couldn't test him for Other abilities right now . . . we could use kids like that.

I followed my guide as he turned off the pathway and its square flagstones onto a narrow track.

"This is a shortcut," the boy explained. "Don't worry, I know everything round here . . ."

I followed him in silence—it was pretty dark, and I was relying on just my human abilities, but his white shirt was a reliable marker.

"There, you see that light?" Makar asked, turning back to look at me. "You go straight toward that. I'm off now . . ."

It seemed like the boy just wanted to play a trick on me . . . it was three hundred meters to the light through the dense growth of the park. He would have been able to boast to his friends about how he led the new teacher into the bushes and left her there . . .

But Makar had no sooner taken a step off to the side than he caught his foot on something and fell with a cry of surprise. I didn't even feel like gloating—it was so funny.

"Didn't you say you knew everything round here?" I couldn't resist asking.

He didn't even answer, just breathed heavily through his nose as he rubbed his bruised and bleeding knee. I squatted down beside him and looked into his eyes:

"You wanted to play a trick on me, didn't you?"

The kid glanced at me and quickly turned his eyes away. He muttered, "I'm sorry . . ."

"Do you play tricks like that on everyone?" I asked.

"No . . ."

"So why was I accorded such an honor?"

It was a moment before he answered. "You looked like . . . you were very sure of yourself."

"I should think so," I agreed simply. "I had some adventures on my way here. I was almost killed on the way—word of honor! But I got through it. So how am I supposed to look?"

"I'm sorry . . ."

All his seriousness and self-assurance had completely deserted him. As I squatted beside him I said, "Show me your knee."

He took his hand away.

Power. I know what it is. I could almost feel it, the Power pouring out of the boy: generated by the pain, the resentment, the shame—it was pure Power . . . I could almost take it—like any Dark Other, whose strength is people's weakness.

Almost.

But it wasn't what I actually needed. Makar sat there gritting his teeth and not making a sound. He wouldn't give way, and he held the Power inside himself. It was too much for me right now . . .

I took a flashlight as slim as a pen out of my purse and switched it on.

"It's nothing. Do you want me to put a Band-Aid on it?"

"No, don't. It will be okay like that."

"As you wish." I stood up and shone the flashlight around. Yes, it would have been difficult trying to find my way to that lighted window in the distance . . . "What now, Makar. Are you going to run away? Or are you going to show me the way after all?"

He got up without saying anything and set off, and I followed him. When we were already at the building, which turned out not to be small at all—it was a two-story mansion house with columns—Makar asked, "Are you going to tell the duty teacher?"

"About what?" I laughed. "Nothing happened, did it? We just had a quiet stroll along the path . . ."

He stood there sniffing loudly for a second, then repeated his apology, only this time far more sincerely: "I'm sorry. That was a stupid stunt I tried to pull."

"Take care of that knee," I advised him. "Don't forget to wash it and dab it with iodine."

CHAPTER 4

I COULD HEAR WATER SPLASHING ON THE OTHER SIDE OF THE wall—the duty camp leader had excused himself and gone out to get washed after I woke him up. He'd been dozing peacefully to the hissing of a trashy Chinese tape recorder. I don't understand how anyone can possibly sleep to the sound of Vysotsky's songs, but I suppose that heap of junk wasn't fit for playing anything else.

> There'll be poems and math,
> Honors and debts, unequal battle . . .
> Today all the little tin soldiers
> Are lined up here on the old map.
> He should have kept them back in the barracks,
> But this is war, like any other war,
> And warriors in both armies fall
> In equal numbers on each side.

"I'm done, sorry about that . . ." the duty leader said as he came out of the tiny shower room, still wiping his face with a standard-issue cotton waffle-cloth towel. "I was exhausted."

I nodded understandingly. The tape recorder carried on playing, obligingly making Vysotsky's voice even hoarser than ever:

Perhaps it's the gaps in their upbringing
Or the weakness of their education?
But neither one of the two sides
Can win this long campaign.
All these accursed problems of conscience:
How not to do wrong in your own eyes?
Here and there, the tin soldiers on both sides,
How do we decide who ought to win . . .

The duty leader frowned and turned the volume down so low I couldn't make out the words any longer. He held out his hand: "Pyotr."

"Alisa."

His grip was as firm as if he were shaking hands with a man. It immediately gave me a sense of distance: *a strictly professional relationship . . .*

Well, that was fine. I didn't feel particularly inspired by this short, skinny man who looked like a juvenile himself. Naturally, I was intending to take a lover for the period of my vacation, but someone a bit younger and better looking would suit me better. Pyotr must have been at least thirty-five, and even without any Other abilities I could read him like an open book. An exemplary family man—in the sense that he was almost never unfaithful to his wife, and didn't drink or smoke much and devoted the appropriate amount of time to his children—or rather, his only child. A responsible man who loved his work, he could be trusted with a crowd of snot-nosed kids or teenage hooligans without any concern: He would wipe away the kids' snot, have a heart-to-heart talk with the hooligans, take away their bottle of vodka, lecture them on the harmfulness of smoking, and pile on the work, the play, and the morality.

In other words, the perfect embodiment of the Light Ones' dream—not a living human being at all.

"I'm very pleased to meet you," I said. "I've dreamed about working at Artek for so long. It's a shame it has to be under these circumstances . . ."

Pyotr sighed. "Yes, it's a sad business. We're all very upset for poor Nastenka . . . Are you a friend of hers?"

"No," I said, and shook my head. "I was two years behind her in college. To be honest I can't really remember her face . . ."

Pyotr nodded and began looking through my documents. I wasn't worried about meeting Nastya. She would probably remember my face—Zabulon is always very thorough about details. If there wasn't a single Other anywhere in Artek, then someone would have come from Yalta or Simferopol, stood close to Nastya for a moment or two . . . and now she would remember me.

"Have you worked as a Pioneer leader before?"

"Yes, but . . . not in Artek, of course."

"That doesn't matter," Pyotr said with a shrug. "They have a staff of two thousand three hundred here, that's the only difference."

The tone in which he pronounced these words seemed almost to contradict their meaning. He was proud of Artek, as proud as if he'd founded the camp himself; as if he'd personally fought off the fascists with a machine gun in his hands, built all the buildings and planted the trees.

I smiled in a way that said: "I don't believe that, but I won't say anything out of politeness."

"Nastya works in the Azure section," Pyotr said. "I'll take you there—it's already time for Nastya to get up anyway. Our bus goes to Simferopol at five . . . how did you get here, Alisa?"

"There were no problems," I said. "I came by car."

Pyotr frowned. "They ripped you off, I suppose?"

"No, it was okay," I lied.

"In any case, it's a bit risky," Pyotr added. "A beautiful young woman alone in a car at night with a stranger."

"There were two of them," I said, "and they were absorbed in each other's company."

Pyotr didn't understand. He sighed and said, "It's not for me to tell you how to behave, Alisa. You're an adult with a mind of your own. But don't forget that anything can happen! Artek is a kingdom of childhood, a realm of love, friendship, and justice. It's the one small thing that we have managed to preserve! But outside the camp . . . there are all sorts of people."

"Yes, of course there are," I said repentantly. It was amazing how sincerely he pronounced those words full of inspired pathos! And how genuinely he believed in them.

"Well, all right." Pyotr stood up and picked up my bag with an easy movement. "Let's go, Alisa."

"I can manage on my own, just show me the way . . ."

"Alisa!" he said with a reproachful shake of his head. "You'll get lost. The grounds here cover two hundred and fifty-eight hectares! Come on, let's go."

"Yes, even Makar got a bit lost," I agreed.

Pyotr was already in the doorway, but he swung round sharply at that: "Makar? The fifteen-year-old boy? Was he at the gate again?"

I nodded, slightly confused.

"I see . . ." Pyotr said dryly.

We walked out into the warm summer night. It was already getting light. Pyotr took a flashlight out of his pocket, but he didn't switch it on. We set off along a path that led down, toward the seashore.

"That Makar's a real problem," Pyotr remarked as we walked along.

"Why's that?"

"He doesn't need much sleep . . . that's the trouble." Pyotr laughed gloomily. "He's always running off to the guards at the gate, or to the sea, or even somewhere outside the grounds."

"I thought he was on some kind of duty at the gate . . . A Young Pioneer post . . ." I surmised.

"Alisa!"

Pyotr was wonderful at making objections like that. He could express a whole gamut of emotions just by pronouncing a name.

"Children ought to be asleep at night! Not standing guard duty . . . at the camp gates, at the eternal flame, or anywhere else . . .

And all normal children do sleep at night—they wear themselves out horsing around before they go to bed. They can have fun here during the day . . ."

Gravel began crunching beneath his feet as we turned off the paved pathway. I took off my sandals and walked on barefoot. It was a good feeling—the hard, smooth little stones under my feet . . .

"If I wanted, I could give the guards a dressing-down," said Pyotr, thinking out loud. "Make them send the kid away. But what then? I can't tie him to his bed all night. It's better if he stays with adults, where he can be seen, than swimming alone in the sea at night . . ."

"But why does he do that?"

"He says he only needs three hours' sleep a day," said Pyotr, with a note of regret and pity in his voice. He was obviously one of those people who are more interesting to talk to on the phone or when it's dark—his face was boring, without much variety of expression, but the range of intonation in his voice! "And from the way he dashes around all day long, it must be true. But that's not the real problem . . ."

"Then what is?" I asked, realizing that he was expecting a question.

"He doesn't want to miss a moment of this summer, of Artek, of his childhood." Pyotr's tone was thoughtful now. "His first and last time at Artek, and what else has life ever given him?"

"The first and last time? But the boy told me . . ."

"He's from a children's home," Pyotr explained. "And he's already too old. It's not likely he'll be able to come here again. Nowadays, of course, a child can come to Artek any number of times, but only for money, and the charity sessions . . ."

I actually dropped a step behind him.

"From a children's home? But he was so convincing . . ."

"They're all very convincing," Pyotr replied calmly. "He probably said something really impressive, didn't he? His parents are in business, he comes to Artek three times a year and this fall he's going to Hawaii . . . They want to believe it all, so they fantasize. The little ones do it all the time, the older ones not so often. But I expect he took a liking to you."

"I wouldn't have said so."

"At that age they still can't express it when they like someone," Pyotr informed me very seriously. "Love and hate are easy to confuse in any case, and for a child . . . And you know Alisa . . . just one comment . . ."

"Yes?"

"You're a very beautiful girl, but this is a children's camp after all, with quite a few older boys. I'm not asking you not to wear makeup and all that, but . . . Try not to wear that miniskirt. It really is too short."

"It's not the skirt that's short," I replied innocently. "It's my legs that are long."

Pyotr squinted sideways at me and shook his head reproachfully.

"Sorry, I was joking," I said quickly. "Of course I won't wear it. I've got jeans, shorts, and even a long skirt. And my swimming costume is very modest!"

We walked on in silence.

I don't know what Pyotr was thinking about. Maybe he was wondering if I was suitable for educational work. Maybe he was feeling sorry about the boy in his care. Maybe he was pondering the imperfection of the world. That would have been like him.

But I smiled, remembering how smartly the kid had fooled me.

He ought to be our future brother-in-arms.

A future Dark One.

But even if he wasn't an Other and he was fated to live a boring human life, people like him were still our foundation and support.

It wasn't even a matter of the trick he'd played, of course. The Light Ones like to joke too. It was what drove the kid to play pranks like that—to lead a stranger into the middle of a park at night and abandon her, to thrust out his skinny chest proudly and pretend to be a kid with no problems from a great family . . . All of that was *ours*.

Loneliness, dejection, the contempt or pity of people around you—these are unpleasant feelings. But they are precisely the things that produce genuine Dark Ones. People or Others who are marked out by a sense of their own dignity, endowed with pride and a longing for freedom.

What kind of person would result from a child of well-off parents, one who really did spend every summer by the sea and studied in a good school, who made serious plans for the future and had been taught the rules of etiquette? Despite the widespread opinion to the contrary, he wasn't very likely to turn out close to us. And he wouldn't necessarily go over to the Light Ones either. He'd just bob backward and forward his whole life like a lump of shit in a drain—petty wrongdoings, minor good deeds, a wife he loves and a mistress he loves, waiting to take his boss's place and promote one of his friends . . . Grayness. Nothing. Not our enemy, but not our ally either. I have to admit that a genuine Light One inspires respect. He may oppose us, his goals may be unattainable and his methods may be absurd, but he is a worthy opponent. Like Semyon or Anton from the Night Watch . . .

So-called good people are equally distant from us and from the Light Ones.

But solitary wolf cubs like Makar are our foundation and support.

He would grow up knowing for certain that he would have to struggle. That he was on his own against everyone else, that it was pointless to expect any sympathy or help, and equally pointless to waste his own energy on pity and compassion. He wouldn't get any ideas about being a benefactor to the entire world, but he wouldn't play mean, petty tricks on other people either. He would train his own willpower and character. He wouldn't go under. If the kid possessed the natural abilities of an Other, the incredibly rare and unpredictable ability to enter the Twilight, which is all that distinguishes us from ordinary people, then he would come to us. But if he remained a human being, he would unwittingly assist the Day Watch. Like many others.

"This way, Alisa . . ."

We walked up to a small building. A veranda and open windows—with a faint light in one of them . . .

"This is a summer house," Pyotr told me. "The Azure section has four main dachas and eight summer houses. You know, I think in summer it's a lot more fun living here."

He seemed to be apologizing for the fact that I and my young charges would be living in the summer accommodation. I couldn't resist asking: "And what about in winter?"

"Nobody lives here in the winter," Pyotr said sternly. "Even though our winters are so warm, the conditions would be inadequate for children to stay here."

He made the transition to official bureaucratic language very easily too. It was as if he were giving a lecture intended to reassure someone's mom—"the temperature is pleasant, the living conditions are comfortable, the catering provides a balanced diet."

We stepped onto the terrace, and I felt a slight stirring of excitement.

I thought . . . I thought I could already feel it . . .

Nastya turned out to be small and swarthy-skinned, with features that had something of the Tatar about them. A pretty girl, except that now her face was too sad and tense.

"Hello, Alya . . ." She nodded to me as if I were an old friend. And in a certain sense, I was—they had obviously given her a false memory. "Look what's happened now . . ."

I stopped looking around at the room—there was nothing special about it anyway. A little, ordinary camp leader's room: a bed, a cupboard, a table, and a chair. The little Morozko refrigerator and the cheap black-and-white television looked like luxury items here.

But then, I'm not choosy . . .

"Nastya, everything will be all right," I promised her with false sympathy. The girl nodded wearily, the way she must have been doing all day long.

"It's good you were able to fly down so quickly." She picked up the bag that was already packed, but Pyotr immediately took hold of it. "Have you worked in Artek before?"

"No."

Nastya frowned. Maybe whoever implanted the false memory had got something confused, but she had no time to worry about that now.

"I'll be in time for the morning flight, Petya," she said. "Is the bus going to Simferopol?"

"In an hour," Pyotr said with a nod.

The former camp leader turned her attention to me again: "I've already said goodbye to the girls. So . . . no one will be surprised. Tell them I love them all very much and I'll definitely . . . I'll try to come back."

For an instant the tears glinted in her eyes—evidently at the thought of one of the possible reasons for a rapid return.

"Nastya," I said, putting my arm around her shoulders. "Everything's going to be all right, your mom will get better . . ."

Nastya's little face crumpled into a grimace of pain. "She's never been ill!" The words seemed to burst out of her. "Never."

Pyotr delicately cleared his throat. Nastya lowered her eyes and stopped talking.

Of course, there had been various different ways I could have been sent to work at the Artek camp. But Zabulon always prefers the simplest possible methods. Nastya's mother had suddenly suffered a massive heart attack, so now Nastya was flying back to Moscow, and another student had been sent from the university to replace her. It was elementary.

Most likely Nastya's mother would have suffered a heart attack anyway: maybe a year later, maybe five. Zabulon always calculates the balance of Power very thoroughly. To provoke a heart attack in someone who was perfectly healthy was a fourth-level intervention that automatically gave the Light Ones the right to reply with magic of the same Power.

Nastya's mother would almost certainly live. Zabulon is not given to senseless cruelty. Why kill the woman when the necessary effect can be produced simply by a serious illness?

And so I could have reassured my predecessor, except that I would have had to tell her too much.

"Here's a notebook I wrote a few things in . . ." Nastya held out a slim school exercise book with a gaily colored cover showing a popular singer grinning moronically on stage. "Just a few details, but it might be useful. A few of the girls need a special approach . . ."

I nodded. Then Nastya suddenly waved her hand through the air and said, "I don't need to tell you all this. You'll manage just fine."

But she still spent another fifteen minutes introducing me to the subtle details of the camp regime and asked me to pay special attention to some girls who were flirting with the boys too precociously. She advised me not to demand silence after lights out: "Fifteen minutes is long enough for them to talk themselves out, half an hour at the most . . ."

Nastya only stopped talking when Pyotr pointed to his watch. She kissed me on the cheek, then picked up a small bag and cardboard box—maybe she was taking some fruit to her sick mother?

"All the best, Alisa . . ."

And at last I was left alone.

There was a pile of clean linen lying on the bed. The electric bulb glowed feebly under its simple glass shade. Pyotr and Nastya's steps and their simple conversation quickly faded away.

I was alone.

But not absolutely alone. On the other side of two thin walls, just five steps along the corridor, eighteen little girls aged ten or eleven were sleeping.

I suddenly started trembling—a rapid, nervous trembling, as if I were an apprentice again, trying for the first time to extract someone else's Power. Nabokov's character Humbert Humbert would probably have trembled the same way in my place.

But then, compared to what I was going to do now, his passion for nymphets was nothing but childish naughtiness . . .

I switched off the light and tiptoed out into the corridor. How I missed my Other powers!

I would just have to make do with the human powers I had left . . .

The corridor was long and the floorboards squeaked. The thread-bare carpet runner was no help—my steps could easily be heard. I could only hope that at this early hour the girls were still sleeping and dreaming . . .

Simple, straightforward, uncomplicated children's dreams.

I opened the door and went into the dormitory. For some reason I'd been expecting some kind of state institution, halfway between a children's home and a hospital—iron bedsteads, the dull glow of a night lamp, depressing curtains, and children sleeping as if they were standing at attention . . .

But in fact it was all very nice. The only light came from the lantern on the pillar outside. The shadows swayed gently, a fresh sea breeze blew in at the open windows and I could smell the scent of wildflowers. The screen of the switched-off television glowed dully in the corner, and the walls were covered with drawings in colored pencil and watercolor paintings that looked bright and cheerful even in the semi-darkness.

The little girls were sleeping, sprawled out across their beds or tucked underneath the blankets, with all their things neatly ar-ranged on their bedside lockers or scattered untidily on the head-boards and the backs of the chairs—swimming costumes that were still wet, skirts, little pairs of jeans and socks. A good psychologist could have walked through that dormitory at night and composed a full character portrait of those girls . . .

But I didn't need one.

I walked slowly between the beds, adjusting blankets that had slid off, lifting up arms and legs that had slipped down to touch the floor. The girls were sleeping soundly. Soundly and with no dreams . . .

I only got lucky with the seventh girl. She was about eleven years old, plump with light hair. An ordinary little girl whimpering quietly in her sleep. Because she was having a bad dream . . .

I knelt down beside her bed, reached out my hand, and touched her forehead. Gently, with just the tips of my fingers.

I felt Power.

As I was now, without any Other powers, I couldn't have read an ordinary dream. But sensing the opportunity to nourish yourself is a different matter. It all takes place at the level of animal reactions, like an infant's sucking reflex.

And I saw it . . .

It was a bad dream. The girl was dreaming that she was going home—their session wasn't over yet, but she was being taken away because her mother had fallen ill and her gloomy, frowning father was dragging her toward the bus. She hadn't even had time to say goodbye to her friends, she hadn't had any time to take a last dip in the sea and take some little stones that were very important . . . and she was struggling and asking her father to wait, but he was just getting more and more angry . . . and saying something about disgraceful behavior, about how girls her age shouldn't have to be beaten, but since she was behaving like this, she could forget about his promise not to punish her with his belt anymore . . .

It was a really bad dream. Nastya's departure had affected the little girl very badly . . .

And anybody would have tried to help the child at that moment.

A human being would have stroked her hair and said something affectionate in a gentle voice, maybe sung a lullaby . . . anything to interrupt the dream.

A Light Other would have used his Power to turn the dream inside out, so that the father would laugh and say the little girl's mother was well again and go running to the sea with her . . . He would have replaced the cruel but realistic dream with a sweet lie.

But I'm a Dark Other.

And I did what I could. I drank her Power. Sucked it into myself— the gloomy father, and the sick mother, and the little friends lost forever, and the sea stones left behind, and the shameful beating . . .

The little girl gave a quiet squeak, like a mouse caught under something heavy. And then she began breathing calmly and regularly. There's not a lot of Power in children's dreams. It's not like the ritual killing that we had threatened the Light Ones with and which provides a truly monstrous discharge of energy. These were dreams, just dreams . . .

Light nourishing broth for an ailing witch . . .

I got up off my knees, feeling slightly dizzy. No, I hadn't recovered my lost powers yet. It would take a dozen dreams like that to fill the yawning gap.

But those dreams would happen. And I would do my best to encourage them.

None of the other little girls were dreaming. Well, one was, but her dream was no use to me, a stupid little girl's dream about the freckle-faced boy who had given her yet another of those stupid stones with a hole in them—what they called "chicken gods." I suppose chickens must have their own gods.

I stood beside this girl's bed—she was probably the most physically advanced of them all. She even had the first beginnings of breasts. I touched her forehead several times, trying to find at least something, but there was nothing. Sea, sun, and sand, water splashing, and that freckle-faced boy. Not a drop of anger, envy, or sadness. A Light magician could have drawn Power from her by drinking in her dream and then gone away satisfied. But I was wasting my time here.

Never mind. There would be another evening and another night. And my plump donor's dream would come back to her—I had drawn out all of her fear, but not its causes. Her nightmare would return, and I would help her again. The important thing was not to try too hard, not to push the girl into a genuine nervous breakdown—I had no right to do that. That would smack of serious magical intervention, and if the Light Ones had even a single observer in the camp, or even—who knows what tricks the Darkness might play—if there was an Other there from the Inquisition, then I would be in serious trouble.

And I wasn't about to let Zabulon down again.

Never!

It was amazing that he had forgiven me for what had happened the previous summer. But he wouldn't forgive me a second time.

At ten o'clock in the morning I went to breakfast with my charges.

Nastya had been right—I was managing just fine.

When the girls had woken up, they had been a bit cautious at first. How could they not have been, when the leader they had already come to love had gone away in the middle of the night to see her sick mother, and another young woman had come into the dormitory instead of her—a stranger, an unknown quantity, someone quite unlike Nastya? I had immediately felt the unfriendly, wary gaze of eighteen pairs of eyes on me—they were all together and I was isolated.

The situation was saved by the fact that the girls were still little and I am beautiful.

If boys of the same age had been in their place, my appearance wouldn't have made the slightest difference. Ten-year-old boys are far more interested in the ugliest of puppies than the most beautiful of girls. And if my charges had been two or three years older, my appearance would have only irritated them. But for ten-year-old girls, a beautiful woman is an object of admiration. They are already beginning to develop the desire to flirt and to please, but they still don't understand that not everybody can grow up beautiful. I know, I was the same myself, and I used to gape wide-eyed at my tutor, the witch Irina Alexandrovna . . .

So I soon established contact with the girls.

I sat on Olechka's bed because the notes in the exercise book suggested that she was the most quiet and timid of them. I talked to the girls about Nastya, about how bad it is when your mother is unwell, and told them they mustn't be offended with Nastya . . . she had really wanted to stay with them, but your mother is the most important person in your life!

When I finished, Olechka began sniveling and pressed herself against me. And the eyes of all the others were looking moist and weepy too.

Then I told them about my dad and his heart attack, and I said that nowadays they knew how to cure people's hearts, and Nastya's mother was going to be perfectly all right too. I helped the swarthy-skinned little cossack girl Gulnara to weave her braids—she had magnificent hair, but as Nastya had noted, she was a bit slow. I argued with Tanya from St. Petersburg about what was the most interesting way to come to Artek, by train or by plane, and, of course, I finally admitted that she was right—it was much more fun on the train. I promised Anya from Rostov that by the evening she would be swimming and not just floundering about in the shallow water. We discussed the solar eclipse that was expected in three days' time and regretted that it would be just a tiny bit less than total in the Crimea.

We arrived at breakfast as a united and cheerful group. Only Olga, who was "not Olechka, but always Olga," and her friend Ludmila were still sulky. But that was not surprising since they had obviously been Nastya's favorites.

Never mind . . . in another three days' time they would come to love me too.

Our surroundings were genuinely lovely. August in the Crimea is just fantastic. The sea was glittering at the bottom of the slope, the air was saturated with the scent of salt water and flowers. The girls squealed and ran about all over the place, bumping into each other. The marching rhymes in the old Pioneer camps were obviously invented for good reason—you can't do much squealing if your mouth's busy trying to sing.

But I don't know any marching rhymes, and I don't know how to march in line anyway.

I'm a Dark One.

In the dining hall I simply followed my little charges' lead—they knew where we were supposed to sit. We were surrounded by five hundred children creating a huge din who somehow managed to eat at the same time. I sat there quietly with my little band of girls, trying to assess the situation. After all, I had to spend an entire month here.

There were twenty-five leaders who had come to breakfast with their brigades. My facile pride in how skillfully I was managing my charges rapidly evaporated. These young men and women were more like the boys' and girls' older brothers and sisters. Sometimes they were stern, sometimes they were affectionate; their word was law and they were also loved.

Where did they find people like that?

My mood began to deteriorate. I prodded feebly at the "liver pancakes" that we had been given for breakfast, with our buckwheat and cocoa, and thought wearily about the unenviable plight of a spy in enemy territory. I was surrounded by too many expressions of delight, smiles, and innocent pranks. This was a pasture for Light Ones to tend their charges and raise human children in the spirit of love and goodness, not a feeding ground for a Dark One like me.

Sheer hypocrisy on every side. As false as gilded and varnished iron!

Of course, I consoled myself, if I could have looked around with the eyes of an Other, many things might have changed, and among all these nice people I might find villains, perverts, individuals who were malicious or indifferent . . .

But that wasn't definite. It could well be that I wouldn't find any. That they were all sincere—to the extent that that is possible. That they sincerely loved the children, the camp, and each other with a love that was pure. That this place really was a reservation for idiots, the kind of place the Light Ones dreamed of turning the whole world into.

But that would mean there was at least some basis for the way the Light Ones acted.

"Hello . . ."

I looked around at the boy walking past. Aha, my first acquaintance in Artek.

"Good morning, Makar." I squinted at his skinned knee. "So where's the iodine?"

"It's nothing. It'll heal on its own," the boy muttered. He gave me a slightly alarmed look—evidently he was trying to figure out if I'd found out anything about him already or not.

"Better run, or you won't have time to eat anything . . ." I smiled. "Maybe you only need three hours' sleep, but food's a different matter. The food here's institutional too, but it's good."

He strode off quickly along the line of tables. Now he knew that I was in the know—about his nocturnal wanderings and his genuine social status. If I'd been in better shape I could have drawn in a lot of Power . . .

"Alisa, how do you know him?" Olechka whispered loudly.

I put on a mysterious face. "I know everything about everybody . . ."

"Why?" Olechka asked curiously.

"Because I'm a witch!" I told her in a hollow, ghostly voice.

The little girl laughed happily.

Oh yes, it's very funny . . . especially because it's the absolute truth . . . I patted her on the head and called attention to her full plate with my eyes.

I still had to go through the official part of the proceedings—the introduction to the head of the Azure section. And then, the beach and the sea that my little girls were already twittering about.

And to be quite honest, I realized I was looking forward to it with just as much delight as the night ahead. I might be a Dark One but, contrary to common ignorant opinion, even vampires love the sea and the sunshine.

The year before, at the end of summer, I'd managed to get away to Jurmala. I don't know why I went there—I must have wanted to be somewhere uncomfortable. If so, I was lucky: August turned out rainy, cold, and miserable. The stiff Latvian waiters immediately started speaking Russian as soon as they'd added up the price of my order. The service in the hotel was primitive and Soviet-style, despite its pretentious four-star rating. I wandered all around Jurmala, sat for ages in a little beer hall in Majori, strolled on the wet sand of the deserted beach, and in the evenings I escaped to Riga. There were two attempts to rob me, and one to rape me. I enjoyed myself as best I could . . . I had my Other powers then, and no human being in the world could cause me any harm. My heart was weary and empty, but I had all the Power I needed and more.

And then I suddenly felt sick of it all. All at once, in a single day. Maybe it was because of the two Night Watch agents who detained me in Dzintari for ages while they tried to frame me for some unsolved crime involving third-level magic. They were irreproachably polite and absolutely adamant. That was probably what the Latvian Red Riflemen were like, and then the Forest Brothers later. The Latvians are a very thorough, consistent people—once they take a job on, they see it right through to the end . . .

I managed to refute the charges—they were genuinely groundless in any case. But the very next morning I took a plane to Moscow. Without having swum in the sea even once all summer.

But now it was payback time for me.

Everything was going along all right, everything was normal. I met the woman in charge of the Azure section—a very nice woman, brisk and pleasantly businesslike, who spoke briefly and to the point in a good way. I felt we had parted entirely satisfied with each other.

Maybe it was because today I'd put on my light summer jeans, and not the provocative miniskirt?

At last I had done a bit of sunbathing and been in the sea. The beach at Artek was wonderful, except that there was too much howling from the kids. But that was an inevitable evil, no matter which way I looked at things. My little girls turned themselves over in the sun in a highly professional manner, trying to get a nice, even tan.

Almost half of them had suntan lotion and after-tan lotion, which they shared generously with each other, so there was no prospect of problems in the evening with burnt shoulders and backs.

If only I didn't still have to keep an eye on the girls . . . I imagined myself swimming out a kilometer or two, or even three, throwing my arms out and lying on the water . . . looking up into the transparent sky, swaying on the gentle waves, not thinking about anything or hearing anything . . .

But no. I had to watch them. I had to teach Anya to swim and prevent Verochka, with her grade-one swimming diploma, from trying to swim off too far. I had to herd the girls into the shade—they might have suntan lotion, but rules were still rules . . . Basically, along with the wonderful sea, I had been given another eighteen capricious, noisy, fidgety little presents. The only thing that kept me smiling was the thought of the night ahead, when the time would come for me to get even with the most bothersome ones—I'd already decided it would be Verochka, Olga, and Ludmila! That night I wasn't going to gather chance scraps of Power. I was going to sow the seeds that would sprout in their dreams.

And then I saw Igor.

No, I didn't know what he was called then. I simply looked around as I was lying on the warm sand and noticed a well-built young man the same age as myself. He was messing about in the water with his little squirts—a gang of ten- or eleven-year-old boys—throwing them into the water, offering them his shoulders as a diving board, just having a really good time. He wasn't tanned at all, but that seemed to suit him somehow—in the middle of the crowd of swarthy children's bodies he stood out like . . . like a white elephant moving condescendingly through a crowd of dark-skinned Indians . . .

A handsome young man.

I felt a sweet ache somewhere below my stomach. We haven't really moved all that far away from people. I understood well enough that there's an immense gulf between Others and human beings, that this young guy was not my equal and we couldn't have any kind of lasting relationship, but even so . . .

I just like men like that: with strong muscles, light brown hair, and intelligent faces. There's nothing to be done about it.

And what would be the point of doing anything? I'd been intending to find myself a friend for the summer anyway . . .

"Olechka, do you know what that camp leader's called?" I asked the little girl pressing herself against me. Olechka clearly felt fond of me because I'd singled her out from the crowd just a little bit, and now she was staying close to me, trying to build on her success. People are funny, especially children. They all want care and attention.

Olechka looked and shook her head. "That's brigade number four, only they used to have a different leader before."

A look of alarm appeared in the girl's eyes—as if she were afraid that I would be disappointed with her for not knowing the answer. She probably really was afraid . . . "Do you want me to find out?" Olechka asked. "I know some boys in that brigade . . ."

"All right," I said with a nod.

The little girl jumped up, scattering sand around her, and ran toward the water. I turned away, hiding a smile.

So now I already had my first informer. A nervous, skinny little girl desperately seeking my attention.

"He's called Igor," Natasha suddenly said out of the blue. She was sitting beside me. This was the same girl who had been dreaming about a boy the night before. She didn't sunbathe like a child either—she sat up on the sand with her legs stretched out and her head thrown back, with her hands propping her up from behind. She must have seen the pose in some fashion magazine or a movie. Or perhaps she'd simply realized that in that position her new little breasts were clearly outlined under her swimming costume. She would go a long way . . .

"Thank you, Natasha," I said. "I thought I'd met him somewhere before."

The girl squinted at me and smiled. She said dreamily, "And he's handsome . . ."

Whatever are young people coming to nowadays!

"But he's too old, right?" I said, trying to tease her.

"No, he's still not too bad." And then she totally amazed me by declaring: "He's reliable, though, isn't he?"

"Why do you think so?"

Natasha pondered for a moment and replied lazily. "I don't know. I just think so. My mom says the most important thing in a man is reliability. They don't have to be handsome, let alone intelligent."

"That depends on what you have in mind . . ." I wasn't going to be bested by an eleven-year-old smarty-pants.

"Yes," Natasha agreed readily. "There have to be handsome ones too. But I wasn't talking about that sort of nonsense."

How delightful! I thought that if this girl turned out to be an Other, I would definitely take her on as an apprentice. There wasn't much of a chance, of course, but just maybe . . .

A moment later, shedding all her precocious wisdom in an instant, Natasha jumped up and went dashing off along the beach after some kid who had splashed water on her. I wondered if the concept of reliability included daily dousings on the beach.

I looked at the young guy again. He'd already stopped messing about in the water and was driving his charges out onto the beach. What a remarkable figure! And the form of his skull was very regular. Maybe it's funny, but apart from a good figure there are two things I like in men—a beautifully shaped head and well-tended toes. Maybe it's some kind of fetishism?

I couldn't see his toes, of course. But so far I liked everything else I'd seen.

My little spy came back to report. Wet, excited, and happy. She plumped down on the sand beside me and started whispering, nervously winding a lock of hair around her finger.

"His name's Igor Dmitrievich. He's good fun and he only came yesterday. He plays songs on the guitar and tells interesting stories.

The leader of the fourth brigade went away—his wife had a little boy. He thought it was going to be a month later, but it happened now."

"Well, wasn't that lucky," I said, thinking mostly of my own interests. Bearing in mind that I had no powers at all and I couldn't make the young guy fall in love with me, a coincidence like that was very useful. He'd just arrived, he hadn't had a chance to form any romantic attachments . . . He surely wasn't planning to spend his entire session just practicing his educational skills, was he? He was there for the taking . . .

Olechka giggled happily and added in a very quiet voice: "And he's not married either."

What on earth can you do with them?

"Thank you, Olechka." I smiled. "Shall we go in for a swim?"

"Uh-huh . . ."

I picked up the little girl, who squealed with delight, and ran into the water. It was clear that in the evening the favorite topic of conversation would be the new camp leader and my interest in him.

But that was okay.

In a couple of days I'd be able to make them forget anything I wanted them to.

The day rushed by like a film played at high speed.

The comparison was all the more appropriate because I'd arrived in Artek during the sixth session, when a children's film festival was traditionally held there. Two days later there was going to be a grand opening, and film directors and actors were already giving talks in some of the camps. I didn't have the slightest desire to watch any old or new children's films, but the festival promised to give me a short break from keeping an eye on the girls. And I already felt like taking a break—I was as exhausted as after a long, tense spell of duty on the streets of Moscow.

After the afternoon snack, which consisted of apple juice and rolls with the romantic name Azure, I couldn't hold out any longer and I phoned Zabulon. His satellite phone worked anywhere in the world, but there was no answer, which could only mean one thing—the chief was not in our world, but somewhere in the Twilight.

Well, he was a very busy man.

And sometimes his business wasn't very pleasant. Traveling through the lower levels of the Twilight, where all parallels with the human world completely disappeared, was quite an ordeal. I'd never been down there myself; it required absolutely immense powers. Except, that is, for that one time, after my stupid stunt, when I was caught gathering energy from people illegally . . .

I can hardly remember anything about what happened. Zabulon rendered me unconscious, punishing me for my misdemeanor and protecting me against the deep levels of the Twilight at the same time. But sometimes I do recall something. As if there was one moment of clear awareness in the blank grayness.

It's like a dream or a delirious vision. Maybe I was delirious? Zabulon, in the form of a demon, carrying me, thrown across his shoulder. His scaly hand squeezing my legs and my head dangling above the ground, above that shimmering, rainbow-colored sand. I look up and I see a glowing sky. A sky made entirely of blinding light. With big, black stars scattered across it. And between me and the sky there are two arches rising up to an immense height. Dull gray, as if they are made out of mist . . . there's nothing frightening about them, but for some reason I am struck with terror. And the rustling—a dry, menacing rustling sound on all sides, as if the grains of sand are trembling and rubbing against each other, or there is a cloud of insects hovering somewhere outside my field of vision . . .

I was probably delirious after all.

Maybe now, when everything had been put right between us, I could risk asking Zabulon what was down there in the depths of the Twilight?

But the day rolled on, and now it was rapidly approaching evening. I got Olga and Ludmila to make up after they quarrelled. We went to the beach again and Anya swam a few meters for the first time without any help. She beat the palms of her hands against the surface of the water, with her eyes staring wildly, but she still swam . . .

This was hard labor, not a vacation! This was for the Light Ones; they'd be only too happy to spend all their time on educational work. My only consolation was that night was approaching. The sun was already getting low in the sky, and even the indefatigable children had begun to get tired.

After fish, pancakes, and potatoes for supper—I wondered where they put it all—I was ready for action. Now I only had to amuse the girls for another two hours until the second supper (anyone would have had to agree that all the kids who came were severely under-nourished), and then it would be time to sleep.

It probably showed in my face.

Galina, the leader of the seventh brigade, came up to me. I'd got to know her that afternoon, more in order to keep up my cover than out of any real interest. She was an ordinary human girl, a standard product of the Light Ones' tedious moralizing—kind, calm, and reasonable. She had a tougher job than me—her brigade was made up of girls who were twelve to thirteen years old, and that meant they were constantly falling in love, getting hysterical, and crying into their pillows. But even so Galina was positively on fire with the desire to help me.

"Tired?" she asked in a low voice, smiling as she looked at my girls.

I just nodded.

"The first session's always like that," said Galina. "Last year, after I'd worked here for a month, I swore I'd never come back again. And then I realized I couldn't live without Artek."

"Like a drug," I prompted her.

"Yes." Galina didn't even notice my irony. "Everything here's in color, if you know what I mean. And the colors are all so pure and bright. Haven't you felt that yet?"

I managed a forced smile.

Galina took hold of my hand and, glancing mysteriously at the girls, she whispered, "Do you know what? The fourth brigade is going to build a bonfire now. They've invited us to the bonfire, and I'm inviting you! You'll get two hours' rest and your girls will be amused without you having to do anything."

"Is it convenient?" I asked quickly, although I didn't have the slightest desire to refuse. Not only because it was a chance to be free of work for two hours, but also because of the attractive camp leader, Igor.

"Of course it is!" said Galina, looking at me in surprise. "Igor comes to Artek every year. He's one of our best leaders. You ought to get to know him too. He's a nice guy, isn't he?"

Her voice had a warm ring to it. It wasn't surprising. I'm not the only one who likes the combination of firm muscles and an intelligent face.

"We'll definitely come," I agreed. "And right away."

CHAPTER 5

I FOUND MYSELF CHANGING MY CLOTHES WITH UNFAMILIAR haste. Where was I going in such a hurry? What for? Just to get to know a guy with a cute face and pumped-up muscles? In two or three days' time any man would be mine—I'd be spoiled for choice! I'm no succubus. I'm an ordinary witch, but I could already enchant a man if I liked him when I was a child and had barely learned to control Power. I only had to wait a little bit longer, and then . . .

But no, I couldn't wait! I put on my best underwear—far too good for a Pioneer camp leader. It should have been shown off by a model on a catwalk. And the slim silver chain with the diamond pendant, even though no one would realize they were real diamonds and not cheap artificial stones . . . A drop of Climat perfume behind my ears, a drop on my wrist, a drop on my pubis . . . was I really serious about trying to seduce him today?

Yes, I was—really serious!

And I even understood why.

I was used to relying on my abilities as an Other, whether they were appropriate or not, even when I could get by making ordinary conversation or simply asking. It would have been strange if it hadn't become a habit. But since I'd been temporarily deprived of my supernatural powers, why not see how I fared without them?

Could I do anything without magic?

Even something as elementary as seducing a man that I liked?

After all, I was young, beautiful, and skillful . . . there was the sea, a campfire on a summer evening . . . the pesky children had all gone to bed . . . surely I could manage it without any magic?

If not, then what was I worth?

I'd promised not to wear the miniskirt, but the shorts that I took out of my bag were even more provocative. I spun round in front of the mirror, examining myself. Not bad. A more revealing blouse would have been better, but there was no point in asking for trouble. This was a Young Pioneer camp, after all, not a normal resort.

I was so absorbed in all my preparations that I even missed the knock on the door. I only turned round when it creaked open and Olechka peeped into my room and started gabbling: "Alisa, we're all ready . . . oh!" She stared at me with admiration. With such genuine admiration that I didn't even rebuke her for entering the room without permission. "Alisa, how beautiful you are!"

I smiled proudly. It was nothing really—a word of praise from a dowdy little girl who painstakingly decorated her skinny little arms with silly bead trinkets and hung a stone with a hole in it on a string around her thin neck—but even so it was pleasant . . . Those stones with holes in them again—I was sick to death of them!

"What do you think?" I asked, "Could someone fall in love with me?"

Olechka beamed happily. She dashed over to me, put her arms around me, pressed her face into my stomach, and said passionately, "He's bound to fall in love with you! As soon as he sees you he will!"

"It will be our little secret!" I said in a whisper. "All right?"

Olechka began nodding rapidly.

"Run to the girls now, I'll be out in a moment," I said. Olechka gave me one last admiring glance and skipped out of the room.

Okay. Now just a little bit of makeup. When you're in a hurry, everything always goes awry, but . . .

I touched up my lips quickly with my softest, least-bright lipstick,

and my eyelashes with waterproof mascara. For some reason I was
sure it had to be waterproof. And that was it. Enough.

I wasn't going to a concert. Just a little Pioneer brigade campfire.

Every one of the summer houses had a campfire site. It was obviously
one of the Artek traditions. The impression was spoiled a bit by the
fact that the wood for the campfire looked a bit too "official"—it was
all neatly cut blocks. I could just imagine the camp leaders turning
up at the supply office and writing out a request: "Firewood for the
holding of a brigade bonfire to last two hours . . ."

But this was no joke. I would probably have to organize something of the kind too. Write out a request, bring the wood—or
would the workmen deliver it? Never mind, I'd find out later.

Everything was ready: the wood had been heaped up, the boys of
the fourth brigade and the girls of the seventh were sitting round it.
And space had considerably been left for my charges too. How very
thoughtful . . .

Igor was sitting beside the huge campfire with his boys swarming
all over him. He was quietly strumming the strings of a guitar, and
I almost groaned out loud when I realized that songs by the Russian
"bards" were an integral element of parties like this. What an unfortunate instrument the guitar is! An instrument of such great nobility,
a genuine monarch of music—reduced to a pitiful lump of wood with
six strings, constantly abused by people with no ear and no voice.

But I would have to put up with it.

It would just be a shame if such an attractive human specimen
turned out to be one more singer without any voice or any talent. Oh,
and what if he even sang his own songs? That's a real nightmare—
when someone who writes bad verse learns three chords, decides
that one negative quantity multiplied by another will give a positive result, and becomes a "singer-songwriter." I've seen so many of
them. When they start to sing, their eyes glaze over, their voices are
filled with mysterious, romantic, manly courage, and it's absolutely
impossible to stop them. Like wood grouse in the mating season!

The only alternative is popular songs in the garbled renditions that are the best they can manage. Numbers by Victor Tsoi and Kino or the group Alisa . . . or whatever it is that young people like today.

Anyway, whatever it was, I wasn't going to like it.

When he saw us there, Igor got up to greet us and all my forebodings immediately evaporated. Yes, he was a really handsome man. "Hello." He spoke as if we were already close. "We haven't started, we were waiting for all of you."

"Thank you." I felt myself losing control. My little girls were already sitting down, elbowing the boys aside—they were a little bit wary of the older girls—and I was still standing there like a fool, attracting knowing glances.

"You're a great swimmer," Igor said with a smile.

Aha!

So he had found time to look around on the beach after all.

"Thank you," I said again. What was wrong with me? I was petrified, like some naïve, inexperienced girl. I didn't even need to pretend. My anger at myself immediately gave me strength. I sat down on the grass between Olechka and Natasha. My own private little guard, the spy and the adviser . . . But they had no interest in me right now. They were too excited by the prospect of the campfire.

"Okay, Alyoshka, begin!" Igor said in a jolly voice, and threw a box of matches to a thickset boy with blond hair. The boy caught it deftly, then crawled up to the campfire on all fours and sat down with his legs crossed. It was like the preparations for some sacred ritual.

The boy took a match out of the box with meticulous precision, cupped his hands like an inveterate smoker, and struck it. He leaned over toward the fire. It didn't look as if there was any paper there to start the blaze, just pine needles and small chips of wood. Everybody held their breath.

It was a ridiculous performance. But even so, I was curious to see if the little pyromaniac would manage to light the campfire with one match or not.

He did. The first tongue of flame flickered in the gathering gloom. It was greeted with universal howling and squealing, as if the campfire were surrounded by a tribe of primordial humans who were freezing in the bitterly cold weather.

"Well done!" Igor reached out and shook the boy's hand and then immediately ruffled his hair with a smile. "You'll be our campfire monitor."

Alyoshka's face expressed immense pride.

Five minutes later the campfire was already blazing and the children had settled down a bit. All around they were chattering, laughing, and whispering, running away from the fire and then back again, throwing on little branches and pine cones, trying to roast pieces of sausage threaded onto twigs. The rejoicing was unconfined. Igor sat in state in the middle of the children, punctuating the conversation with phrases that sent everyone into peals of laughter, or tasting the half-burnt food, or calling back children who were getting too close to the fire. The life and soul . . .

Galina was besieged by her charges too. I was the only one sitting there like a total fool in the middle of the jolly crowd, giving irrelevant answers to the girls' questions, laughing belatedly when they did, and turning my eyes away the moment Igor looked in my direction.

Fool! What a fool I am! The last thing I need is to fall in love for real with a human being.

I failed to look away yet again and Igor smiled at me. He reached out and picked up a guitar off the grass. The silence spread out from him in a wave—the children nudged each other, stopped talking, and prepared to listen with a strange, affected sort of attention. I suddenly wished desperately that he would sing some kind of stupid nonsense. Maybe some old-time Young Pioneer song about potatoes roasted in the fire, the sea, the Pioneer camp, firm friendship, and the kids' readiness to enjoy themselves and to study. Anything that would dispel this idiotic enchantment, anything to stop me inventing all sorts of nonsense and seeing imaginary positive qualities in that handsome physical shell.

When Igor started to play, I realized I was done for. He could play the instrument. The melody wasn't all that complicated, but it was beautiful, and he didn't hit any wrong notes.

And then he began to sing:

Two boys saw a heavenly angel
Come flying into their attic.
Without telling anyone, the boys
Went rushing up the fire stairs . . .
Two boys climbed in through the window,
It was dusty, deserted and dark,
But just four steps away from the corner
A pair of white wings lay on the floor . . .
Yes, boys, oh yes!
Angels are not forever,
But stealing is a sin,
There aren't enough wings for everyone . . .
They want to soar up into the sky,
They only have to put on the wings . . .
But they didn't dare, they had been taught well,
They knew what was right, what was wrong.

This wasn't a song for children. Of course they listened to it quite attentively, but at that moment you could have sung them a math textbook set to guitar music—anything would have been good enough. A campfire in the evening, with your favorite camp leader and his guitar—in a situation like that children will like anything.

But I realized Igor was singing for me. Even if he was looking into the flames the entire time, even if the song wasn't about love, even if we'd barely spoken two words to each other. It was as if he had sensed my expectations—and decided to refute them. Maybe that was what it was, I thought—many people possess powerful intuition, even if they're not Others.

Two boys grew up and they followed
Different paths through the maze of life.
One was a bandit and one was a cop,
And both of them regretted it . . .
Yes boys, oh yes!
Angels are not forever.
But stealing is a sin,
There aren't enough wings for everyone . . .

He looked at me and smiled. His fingers ran quietly across the strings again and he repeated quietly:

There aren't enough wings for everyone . . .

The kids started kicking up a din.

They actually seemed to like the song, though I couldn't imagine what they could have understood in it. Maybe they were amused by the phrase about "right and wrong," or maybe in their little minds they imagined a real adventure—climbing into an attic that an angel had flown into . . . But I thought the song fitted the Others—Dark Ones and Light Ones.

It was a good song. Just not quite right about one thing. The boy who would later join our side would have put on the wings. Or at least tried them on. Because for us the idea of "right and wrong" doesn't exist.

"That's a good song. But it's very serious," said Galina. "Did you write it?"

Igor laughed and shook his head: "No, afraid not. It's by Yulii Burkin. Not a very well-known singer, unfortunately."

"Igor, could you play . . . one of our songs?" Galina was flirting with him for all she was worth. The stupid fool . . .

"Sure!" Igor agreed.

He strummed the strings, striking up a jolly rhythm, and started singing simple-mindedly all about "the very, very best camp of songs and friends in all the world."

That was what they wanted. From the second couplet everybody started joining in, because it was no problem to guess what the next word would be. When they sang about the sea, and how you had to go running into it with your camp leader, because he loved "the splashing water and the sand" too, they all howled with great inspiration. Everybody was pleased, even Galina and her girls. At one point Igor sang about "a stone with a hole inside it" that was found on the seashore . . . as if anyone could imagine a stone with a hole outside it. I noticed that lots of the kids reached for the stones dangling around their necks.

Well, well. Faithful devotees of the chicken god! Maybe someone in Artek had a special job producing stones with holes in them? Some drunk who never shaved, sitting in a workshop somewhere, drilling holes in stones all day long and scattering them on the beach in the evening to delight all the kids. If not, an opportunity had clearly been missed.

Igor appeared to be enjoying himself as much as the kids. He sang the song enthusiastically, except that . . . all the enthusiasm was for the children. Igor was amusing them, but he really felt nothing for the song one way or the other.

I relaxed.

At the very least he liked the look of me.

And I liked the look of him too.

Igor sang another couple of songs. Then Galina took over the guitar and coerced it into playing—the instrument resisted as hard as it could, flatly refusing to produce any normal sounds, but Galina still sang "Let's all hold hands, my friends" and yet another Young Pioneer song. Even the boy from the fourth brigade, who was barely strong enough to press down the metal strings, played better than she did.

Then Igor clapped his hands. "All right! Now we'll put the fire out and go for supper!"

They brought two buckets of water from somewhere and he began dousing the glowing embers.

I stood there for a while, following his sparse, precise movements. Igor looked as if he'd spent his entire life putting out campfires. Probably he did everything like that—playing the guitar, putting out fires, working on his computer, caressing a woman. Precisely. Conscientiously. Reliably. Satisfaction guaranteed.

White steam billowed up from the hot embers. The children scattered in all directions. Then suddenly, still dousing the fire, Igor asked, "Do you like swimming at night, Alisa?"

I shivered. "Yes."

"So do I. By one o'clock, the children will have settled down and I'll go to the beach for a swim, where we were this morning. Come along if you like."

For just a moment I lost my head. It was a feeling I'd completely forgotten. Instead of me hitting on a man, he was hitting on me!

Igor splashed the remains of the water onto the campfire and looked at me. He smiled. "I'd be really glad if you could come. Only . . . don't get the wrong idea."

"I think I've got the right idea," I replied.

"Will you come?"

I really wanted to say no. Just to provoke him. But it would have been stupid, after all, to give up my own pleasure for the sake of one little gibe.

"Probably," I said.

"I'll be waiting," Igor replied calmly. "Shall we go? A glass of *ryazhenka* before bed is very good for tired camp leaders. It guarantees sound, healthy sleep."

His smile was wonderful.

In Artek "lights out" comes at half past ten.

The bugles sounded solemnly in the loudspeakers and a gentle woman's voice wished everyone goodnight. I was standing in front of the mirror, looking at my reflection and trying to figure out what was happening to me.

Had I fallen in love?

No, that was impossible! I loved Zabulon. I loved the greatest Dark magician in Moscow! One of the few individuals who really controlled the fate of the world. And what was an ordinary human being, compared to him? Even if he was attractive. Even if he had a fine figure. Even with that idiotic reliability that oozed out of him with every move he made. He was an ordinary male of the human species with the ordinary little thoughts of human males. Pretty good for a resort romance, but nothing more than that. I couldn't really fall in love with him!

The cell phone in my purse rang and I started. Mom? Unlikely— she was terribly careful with money and never rang me on my cell.

I took it out and accepted the call.

"Hello, Alisa."

Zabulon's voice sounded tired. Affectionate and tired, as if he'd barely been able to find the strength to make the call, but really felt he had to . . .

"Hello," I whispered.

"You're feeling anxious, I can sense it. What's happened to you, my little girl?"

There's no way to hide anything from him. Zabulon knows everything . . . at least, everything he wants to know.

"I'm thinking about taking a friend for the month . . ." I sighed into the phone.

"Well, what of it?" Zabulon sounded puzzled. "Alisa, I'm not jealous of your dog, and I'm not going to be jealous of some little man who amuses you either."

"I haven't got a dog," I said miserably.

Zabulon laughed, and all my stupid thoughts just seemed to evaporate.

"All right then! I'm not bothered if you have a dog or you don't.

I'm not bothered if you have a human lover. Calm down, my little one. Relax. Recover your strength. Amuse yourself any way you like. Debauch the whole of Artek, including all the Young Pioneers and the old plumbers if you like. My little fool . . ."

"I'm behaving like a human being, aren't I?" I suddenly felt ashamed.

"It's nothing to worry about. It won't last long, Alisa. Build up your strength . . . only . . ." Zabulon paused for a moment. "Never mind. It's nothing."

"No, tell me!" I tensed up again.

"I have faith in your common sense," Zabulon said, and hesitated. "Alisa, just don't get carried away, all right? Your vacation is strictly governed by the terms of the old treaty between the Watches. You don't have the right to take a lot of Power. Only crumbs. Don't turn into some crude energy-vampire. You're on vacation, not out hunting. If you overstep the mark, we'll lose this resort forever."

"I understand," I said.

How long was that blunder with the Prism of Power going to keep coming back to haunt me?

I didn't start pouring out promises or swearing by the Darkness and my own Power. Promises mean nothing. The Darkness doesn't bother itself with petty details, and I had no Power right then. I simply promised myself that I wouldn't overstep the defined boundaries for anything. I wouldn't let down Zabulon and the entire Day Watch.

"Then have a good vacation, my little girl." I thought I caught a hint of sadness in Zabulon's voice. "Have a good vacation."

"Couldn't you come? Just for a short while?" I asked hopelessly.

"No. I'm very busy, Alisa. I'm afraid we won't be able to talk for the next three or four days. But don't you worry. What good is a tedious old miscreant obsessed with global problems as a partner for a young witch on vacation?"

He laughed.

We generally tried not to say things like that on the phone, especially the cell phone, because they listen to all of them and record everything. It all sounded like a flippant conversation . . . But what if some ordinary little human being picked up the thread and started following it? Then we would have to waste time and energy on him.

"I love you," I whispered. "Thank you."

"Good luck, my little one," Zabulon said affectionately. "I kiss you."

I switched off the phone and smiled to myself.

Well then, everything was all right. So where had that stupid feeling of alarm come from? And where had I gotten the crazy idea that I was in love with Igor? Love was something different. Love was pure delight, a fountain of emotions, sensual delights, and enjoying spending time together. But what I was feeling—this strange, timid alarm—was only the consequence of my illness. It just felt strange to associate with a man without having any idea of how to control him . . . I couldn't threaten him with a pistol, like those half-witted bandits . . .

"Alisa?" Olechka's curious little face had appeared in the doorway. "Are you coming in to see us for a minute?"

The girl was barefoot, in just her panties and top. She'd already gone to bed, but she got impatient.

"I'll be right there," I said. "Shall I tell you all a story?"

Olechka lit up: "Uh-huh!"

"A happy one or a scary one?"

The girl wrinkled up her little forehead. But, of course, curiosity won out. "A scary one."

All children like scary stories.

"Run back to bed now," I said. "I'll be right there."

Ten minutes later I was sitting on Olechka's bed in the dormitory, telling the girls a story in a low voice:

"And in the morning the little girl woke up and went over to the mirror and looked—and all her teeth were red! She tried cleaning them with toothpaste, and washing them with soap, but they were still as red as ever. She couldn't say a single word to her parents, in case they noticed. It was a good thing her younger brother had fallen ill and her parents took no notice of her at all. That's the way it always is—the little ones get all the attention and nobody even looks at you, not even if all your teeth are red . . ."

Scary children's stories are so wonderful! Especially if you tell them at night, to a pack of silly little girls, with a mysterious half-light coming in through the window.

"I've guessed it already," Natasha said in a bored voice. Such a serious girl, you couldn't impress her with scary stories. The others started hissing at her indignantly and she shut up. I carried on, feeling Olechka's little heart pounding as she pressed herself against me. There would be a good harvest for me there . . .

"On the third night the little girl tied her right braid to her bed with a piece of string," I went on in a mysterious whisper. "And at midnight she woke up because the string was stretched tight and it was pulling on her hair and hurting. And the girl saw that she was standing over her little brother's bed and her teeth were chattering! Chattering!"

Larisa gave a quiet squeal. Not because she was frightened, but because it was the right thing to do. And of course one of the girls began happily chattering her teeth together.

"Then the little girl went into the kitchen and took out the hammer and the pincers that her father kept in the cupboard, and before morning came she secretly pulled out all her own teeth. It hurt very badly, but she managed it, because she was a brave girl and she had strong hands. And the next morning her little brother got better. And the little girl's teeth grew back better than ever, because the first ones were her milk teeth!"

I lowered my voice to a whisper and said solemnly, "Only they were still pink anyway!"

One of the girls who had been waiting for a happy ending gasped in fright. I concluded solemnly: "And the parents still loved her little brother more than her. Because he was very ill that time and they were really worried about him."

And that was all. I wondered how many of the girls had younger brothers. The birth rate in Russia is low, but if the first child is a girl, people usually try for a second.

My mother had wanted to do that when she was already too old, past thirty—what a fool . . . But by then I was an Other, even at the young age of twelve, and I dealt with the unexpected problem. Though probably I shouldn't have bothered. If I did have a brother, what would have been so bad about that? Even if he was only a half brother . . . and only I would have known that for sure (even my mom had her doubts) . . . He could have turned out to be an Other—not just a brother but an ally . . . But what's done can't be undone.

"And now—to sleep!" I ordered the girls in a cheerful voice.

Of course, they started asking me to tell them another story. But I refused. It was half-past eleven already, and I still had to get to the beach . . . the girls' voices were already ragged and sleepy. When I left, Gulnara tried to tell a scary story of her own, but all the pauses and hesitations suggested that she would fall asleep halfway through it.

I went back to my room, stretched out on the bed, and started waiting.

I wondered what Igor was doing right then.

Was he entertaining his kids too?

Or was he drinking vodka with some other camp leaders?

Or was he screwing one of them?

Or had he forgotten he was intending to go swimming that night and sleeping peacefully in his bed?

I shook my head. No. Anything but the last option.

He was reliable. Almost . . . almost like Zabulon. What an absurd comparison: There weren't many, even among the Dark Others, who could call Zabulon reliable. But I could. I had a perfect right to do it. Love is a great power, and such a strange power . . .

What if Igor turned out to be a potential Other?

I squeezed my eyes shut tightly in simultaneous sweet anticipation and panic. What would I do then? Then it wouldn't be the tryst with an ordinary man that Zabulon had approved, but a genuine love triangle . . .

What was wrong with me! There couldn't be any triangle. Not even if Igor did turn out to be an uninitiated Other. He'd go running off with his tail between his legs and forget he ever had a romance with Zabulon's girl.

And I would forget it too.

The time dragged by unbearably slowly. The hands on my watch crept along hesitantly, as if they weren't even sure that time was passing. I had planned to wait for half an hour, but I gave in after twenty minutes. I didn't have the strength to hold out any longer . . .

I got up and walked quietly through the girl's dormitory . . .

There was silence in there. The calm, pleasant silence of a large children's dormitory with just a few sounds—breathing, snuffling, lips smacking sleepily.

"Girls," I called quietly.

No answer.

I set off along the row of beds, gently touching shoulders, arms, hair . . . Nothing . . . nothing . . . nothing . . .

Here was something.

It was Olechka. I knelt down beside her bed and lowered my hand onto her sweaty forehead. I heard her dream and felt the flow of Power. The dream was confused and incoherent; it had nothing to do with my bedtime story. Olechka was dreaming that she was climbing to the top of a tower—an old tower that was leaning slightly, with half-ruined stone banisters that had huge gaping holes in them. Down below at the foot of the tower there was either a medieval town or an ancient monastery. And the strange thing was that although the tower was in semi-darkness, down below the sun was shining. And there were people wandering about between the decrepit buildings—happy and cheerful, dressed in light summer clothes, holding cameras and colorful magazines. They were enjoying themselves so much, it couldn't possibly occur to them to look up at the sky and see the little girl walking toward a gap in the banisters as if she were under a spell . . .

I needed to hang on just a little bit longer. Wait until Olechka started falling—that was where the dream was leading her. I don't know what happened, but I suddenly gathered my strength and sucked in her dream. Every last scrap of it.

The dark tower above the cheerful crowd, and the gaping holes in the banisters, and the cold indifference, and the fearsome, alluring height. Everything that could give me Power.

Olechka held her breath for a moment. I even felt afraid that she might fall into a coma—it's rare, but it sometimes happens to people when you draw Power from them too suddenly.

But she started breathing again.

I got up off my knees. I'd even broken into a sweat myself. I could feel that a bundle of energy had fallen into the empty gap left by my usual Power. No, it still hadn't filled it, not by a long way . . . and I'd acted hastily for some reason . . .

But I was recovering.

Again—the gentle touches, the soft hair, the lips parted in sleep, the relaxed fingers . . .

Nothing here . . . nothing here . . . but there was something here.

It was Natasha.

And her dream had been prompted by me.

Natasha was standing in a bathroom, naked and covered in soapy lather. She was holding a boy, about five or six years old, and hammering his head against the tiled wall, saying over and over again: "Are you going to peep again? Are you going to peep?"

The boy was dangling in her hands like a rag doll. His eyes were wide open in terror, but he didn't say anything. He seemed to be far more afraid of being punished by his parents than hurt by his sister.

But Natasha wasn't feeling too good either. Her soul was filled with a mixture of furious anger at her insufferable brother, and fear that she would hit his head against the wall too hard, and shame, even though only very recently she and her brother had been given their baths together, and guilt . . . because she'd deliberately left the door unlocked in the expectation that her brother would try to peep in, driven by the natural urge of children to violate all prohibitions.

This was really something! Passions like that in someone who wasn't even twelve yet!

Natasha gave a deep sigh, and in her dream she hit her brother's head so hard against the wall that it started to bleed. I couldn't see where the blood came from, but it suddenly covered the entire head.

I sucked in her dream.

Completely. The fury, the fear, the shame, the guilt, and the budding sensuality, still vague and ill-defined.

But the dream didn't end!

Natasha had just released her grip when she grabbed her brother again by the shoulders and, with the cold calculating movement of an executioner, forced his head into the bath water, which instantly turned pink. Even the clumps of foam on the surface of the water turned pink. The boy began twitching helplessly, struggling to pull his head out of the water.

I froze in surprise. A murder committed in a dream gives almost the same discharge of Power as a real one. Now I'd be able to fill the gap in my soul in a single moment!

All I had to do was draw Natasha's newly awakened fear out of her, and . . .

But I didn't do anything. I stood there, leaning down over the bed, watching another person's dream as if it were a horror movie that was showing on TV instead of the children's cartoons.

Natasha suddenly jerked her brother's head out of the water and he gulped in air greedily. There was no blood on him any longer—he just had a small bruise under one eye. Dreams have their own laws.

"You'll tell them you fell in the bath yourself and banged your head, all right?" Natasha hissed. The boy nodded in fright. Natasha quickly pushed him out of the bathroom and closed the door, then slowly got into the foamy water. The nice, bright-pink water . . .

I waited for another second or two and then drank in the remains of the dream. Triumph, excitement, tranquillity.

And the gaping wound in my soul was immediately half-filled.

I should have let Natasha kill her brother. I only needed to take away her fear, and she would have drowned her little brother like a kitten.

I was covered in perspiration. My hands were shaking. Who could ever have expected nightmares like that from such a rational little Miss Know-it-all?

All right. Slow and steady does it.

I moved on.

By half past midnight I had absorbed another three dreams. They weren't such sumptuous feasts, but they provided fine surges of Power. This was a good place for a vacation, if the girls accumulated that much energy.

I had almost completely restored the strength that I'd lost. The lion's share, of course, had come from Natasha. I had the feeling that if I could just suck in one more dream, then I would be completely restored and become a normal Other. But nobody had any more dreams that were of use to me. There was one that simply repelled me: Gulnara was dreaming that she was taking care of her old grandfather. Dashing around the kitchen, pouring his tea, constantly asking him solicitous questions. Oh, how I hate that awful Eastern culture . . . Turkish delight laced with arsenic.

If it wasn't for Igor . . .

I would only have had to wait half an hour, or an hour, and one of my eighteen donors would have had a frightening dream.

But . . .

I didn't hesitate for long.

I would collect all the Power I needed, absolutely everything, the next night. But today I could relax and try out the role of an ordinary woman.

I closed the door firmly and slipped out into the summer night.

The camp was sleeping. There were lamps lit here and there on the pathways and an almost full moon hung in the sky. Nights like this are great for the werewolves: They're at the peak of their powers, they can transform easily and at will, they're full of high spirits, the thirst for life, and the urge to hunt, to tear living flesh to pieces, to stalk and pounce on their prey. Of course, the vampires and the shape-shifters are the very lowest caste of the Dark Ones. And most of them are simply stupid and primitive. But . . . on nights like this I envied them just a little bit. I envied them the primitive power that comes from the deepest animal depths of their nature. The ability to transform into a beast—and get rid of all those stupid human feelings.

I started laughing and set off along the path at a run, flinging my arms out and throwing my head back to look up at the sky. I might not have the powers of an Other yet, but my blood was seething with fresh Power, and I didn't stumble even once or hesitate for a moment in my choice of direction. It was like just before my initiation, when "mother's old friend" Irina Alexandrovna had arrived at our apartment unexpectedly. I could sense that my parents were behaving oddly, awkwardly, and every now and then Irina Alexandrovna would look at me in a strange way, as if she were evaluating me, with a gentle, condescending smile. And then my parents suddenly decided to go out somewhere in a great hurry, leaving me alone for the entire evening with "the old friend." And my future mentor told me everything. She said this was the first time she had ever seen my parents, that she had simply put a spell on them. She told me about the Others, and about the Twilight that gives them miraculous powers and said that the first time I entered the Twilight would determine who I would be, a Light One or a Dark One . . . She said I was a future Other. That I had been noticed by a certain "very, very powerful magician." Later I wondered if it could have been Zabulon himself, but I couldn't bring myself to ask . . .

Back then I hesitated for a long time . . . I was a little fool. I didn't like the words "Dark Ones." In the fairy tales and films the Dark Ones were always bad. They had power over the entire world, ruled countries and commanded armies, but at the same time they ate all sorts of disgusting things, spoke in horrible, repulsive voices, and betrayed everyone whenever they got the chance. And, in the end, they always lost.

Irina Alexandrovna laughed for a long time when I told her all that. She admitted that all the fairy tales were invented by the Light Ones. The Dark Ones didn't usually bother with that kind of nonsense. She said what the Dark Ones really wanted was freedom and independence. They didn't strive for power, they didn't impose their own foolish desires on others. She demonstrated some of her abilities to me—and I learned that my mom had been unfaithful to my dad for a long time already, and my dad wasn't nearly as courageous as I thought, and that my best friend Vika told people all sorts of horrible things about me . . .

I knew about my mom already, even at the age of ten. I tried not to think about her and Uncle Vitya. I felt so hurt for my dad. But when I heard about Vika, I got really furious and I realized that I wanted to get even with her. It seems funny to me now, but when I was ten, to learn that my friend had told our classmate Romka my most terrible secret—that I used to wet the bed until I was in second grade—was really horrible! I'd been wondering why he smirked in that disgusting way when I gave him a card and some colored pens for Army Day on the twenty-third of February . . .

Irina helped me to enter the Twilight for the first time. She said while I was there I would decide for myself who I would be. The Twilight would see straight through my soul and make the most appropriate choice.

After that my friend Vika started getting bad marks all the time and swearing at all the teachers, even the head teacher. Then they took her out of our school; I heard she spent a long time in a children's psychiatric hospital being treated for a rare condition, Tourette's syndrome. The handsome Romka pissed his pants in the middle of Russian dictation and had to live with the nickname "Pisser" for two years afterward, until he and his parents moved to a different district.

Uncle Vitya drowned while he was swimming in the shallow pond at the dacha, but that wasn't until three years later. That's quite a difficult task for a child, after all. And it still makes me feel sick to remember the way I managed to get hold of a lock of his hair . . .

I didn't regret my choice the tiniest bit.

There are some who think that we Dark Ones are evil. But that's not true at all. We're simply just. Proud, independent, and just.

And we decide things for ourselves.

The beach at night is filled with a wistful enchantment. Like a park in autumn, or a concert hall after a premiere. The tired crowd goes away for a while to gather its strength for new insanities; the sea licks its wounds and throws the melon rinds, sodden chocolate wrappers, corn cobs, and other human rubbish up onto the beach; the cool, wet sand covers over the tracks of the seagulls and the crows.

I heard Igor when I was still approaching the beach. First his guitar and then his voice.

As he sang, I suddenly realized with piercing clarity that nothing was going to happen. There was a group of people sitting over there on the sand, enjoying themselves with a bottle or two and some bread rolls stolen from the supper table to go with them. And the most that I could count on, stupid fool that I was, was an invitation to spend the rest of the night in his room . . .

But even so I walked toward the sound. Just to make certain . . .

You say there's no such thing as love,
There's nothing but the carrot and the stick,
But I say flowers bloom
Because they don't believe in death.
You tell me that you never want
To be a slave to anyone at all.
I say that means the slave will be
Whoever you have by your side.

I never liked that song. I don't like the group Nautilus Pompilius in general—their songs sound almost as if they were ours, but there's something subtly different about them. No wonder the Light Ones are so fond of them.

But I particularly disliked that song.

I was only two or three steps away from Igor when I realized that he was there on the beach alone. Igor noticed me too—he raised his head and smiled, still singing:

Maybe I am wrong,
Maybe you are right.
But I have seen with my own eyes
The grass reaching for the sky.
Why should we argue all night long
And lie sleepless till the dawn?
Maybe I am wrong,
Maybe you are right.
What good is arguing to us,
The day will come and then
You'll see for yourself
If there's a bottom to the sky
And why
The grass reaches up to it . . .

I sat down beside him on a large fluffy towel spread out on the sand and waited patiently for the song to end. When Igor finally put down his guitar, I asked him: "Playing for the waves and the sand?"

"For the stars and the wind," he corrected me. "I thought it would be hard for you to find me in the dark. And I didn't like the idea of bringing a tape deck."

"Why not?"

He shrugged. "Surely you can feel it? This is a time for living sound."

Igor was right. Maybe I didn't agree with his choice of song, but I was all for the idea of living sound . . .

I looked him over without saying anything—or rather, I tried to look him over in the darkness. He was barefoot, dressed in nothing but his shorts. His hair had a wet gleam to it—he must have been in the sea already. He reminded me of someone at that moment . . . someone from one of the old fairy tales, either a jolly troubadour or a prince dressed up as a troubadour . . .

"The water's warm," Igor said. "Shall we go in?"

That was when I realized I'd been in too much of a hurry to get to the beach.

"Igor . . . you'll laugh at me . . . I can't go swimming. I forgot my bathing costume."

He thought for a moment and then asked very calmly, "Are you shy? Or are you afraid I'll think you did it deliberately?"

"I'm not afraid, but I don't want you to think that."

"I don't think that at all," Igor said, and stood up. "I'll go into the water and you come and join me."

He took off his shorts right at the water's edge, started to run, and dived almost immediately. I didn't hesitate for long. I hadn't even thought about seducing Igor in such a primitive way—I really had forgotten my bathing costume in my room. But there was no way I was going to feel shy, especially in front of an ordinary human being.

The water was warm and the waves caressed me like a lover's hands. I swam after Igor, and the shoreline receded and blurred until only the lighted lamps marked Artek out in the night. We swam far beyond the buoy, probably a kilometer from the shore. I caught up with Igor, and then we were swimming beside each other in silence, not saying a single word. Not competing with each other, moving in the same rhythm.

Finally he stopped, looked at me, and said, "That's enough."

"Are you tired?" I asked, a little surprised. It had seemed to me that he could go on swimming forever . . . and I—well, I could have swum across the Black Sea and got out in Turkey.

"No, I'm not tired. But the night is deceptive, Alisa. This is the maximum distance I could pull you to the shore if anything happened."

I remembered what Natasha had said about him being "reliable." Looking into his face, I realized it wasn't bravado and he wasn't joking. He really was in control of the situation at every moment. And he was ready to save me.

You funny little human being. In the morning or tomorrow night I'll gather a little more Power—and then I'll be able to do whatever I like with you. And it won't be you who'll save me if anything happens. I'll save you—you big, strong, confident, reliable man . . . But right now you're sure of yourself, sure of your ability to protect and save, like a little child walking along a dark street with his mother and telling her, "Don't be afraid, Mom, I'm here . . ."

Maybe it is in the style of the Light Ones, but even so, I like it somehow. . .

I swam slowly up to Igor. Right up to him. I put my arms around him and whispered, "Save me."

The water was warm, but his body was hotter than the water. He was as naked as I was. We kissed, sometimes going under the water, then surfacing with a rush and gulping in the air and searching for each other's lips again.

"I want to go back to the beach," I whispered. We started swimming, sometimes touching each other, sometimes stopping to exchange another long kiss. I had the taste of salt and his lips on my lips, my body seemed to be on fire, the blood was pounding in my temples. You could drown like that . . . from the excitement, from the impatience, from the longing to be closer.

About five meters from the beach, where the water was already shallow, Igor picked me up in his arms as easily as if I weighed nothing at all, carried me to our clothes and put me down. I felt the towel under my back and the stars swayed over my head.

"Come on . . ." I whispered, spreading my legs. Like a depraved little girl, like a seasoned slut . . . and this was me, a witch of the Moscow Day Watch who was loved by Zabulon himself!

But right now that didn't bother me at all. There was only the night, the stars, Igor . . .

He lowered himself toward me, his right hand slid under my back and caught me between the shoulder blades, his left hand slid across my breasts and for just a moment he looked into my eyes—as if he were doubtful, hesitating, as if he weren't feeling the same burning desire for intimacy that I was. I arched up involuntarily to meet his body, felt for his aroused member with my hips, swayed—and it was only then that he entered me.

How I wanted him . . .

It was like nothing else in the world. Not like sex with Zabulon, who always took on the form of a demon for this. With Zabulon I had always experienced a wild, painful pleasure, but it had always had a feeling of humiliation in it, sweet and arousing, but still humiliation. Not like sex with ordinary men, whether they were inexperienced youths full of strength, hefty hunks, or experienced, aging womanizers. I'd tried everything. I knew it all and I could make an evening with any man interesting in its own way.

But this was different.

It was as if we really did become one, as if my desires were immediately transmitted to him and his to me. I could feel the trembling of his member that had entered my body, and I knew that he could come at any moment, but he was putting that moment off and I was balanced there on the same agonizingly sweet, timeless boundary of pleasure.

It was as if he had known me for years and could read me like an open book. His hands responded to the desires of my body before I could even feel them myself, his fingers knew where to be gentle and where to be rough, his lips slid over my face without stopping for an instant, his thrusts became more and more powerful, carrying me up into the dark sky on a swingboat of delight, and I whispered something without knowing what I was saying . . .

And then the world stopped and I groaned, clutching at his shoulders and scratching, moving after him, not wanting to let him go.

The pleasure was as brief as a flash of lightning, and as blindingly bright. But he didn't stop, and I was buoyed up again, balancing on that wave of sweetness—and at the precise moment when his eyes opened wide and his body went totally rigid, I came again. But this time in a different way—the pleasure wasn't as piercing, it was long and pulsating—as if it were following the rhythm of his sperm, spurting into my body.

I couldn't even groan anymore. We lay beside each other—I was on the towel and Igor was on the sand—touching each other, caressing each other, as if our hands had a life of their own. I pressed my cheek against his chest, catching the salty smell of the sea and the sour smell of sweat, his body shuddering under my hand. And I didn't even realize when I started kissing him, moving lower and lower and burying my face in the rough hair, caressing him with my lips and my tongue, feeling the excitement mounting in him again. Igor lay there without moving, just touching my shoulders with his hands. And that was right, that was what he should do, because now I wanted to give him pleasure. And when he came again with a quiet groan, unable to restrain himself, I felt as happy as if he had been caressing me.

Everything was just the way it should be.

Everything was like nothing that had ever happened before.

No orgy, not even the very liveliest, had ever given me so much pleasure. I had never felt such happiness, not with one man or two or three, never felt this feeling before . . . this feeling of . . . completeness? Yes, that was it, completeness! I simply didn't need anyone else.

"I love you," I whispered. "Igor . . . I love you."

He could have answered that he loved me too—and he would have spoiled everything, or almost everything. But he only said, "I know."

When Igor got up and took something out from under the heap of clothes on the sand, I could hardly even believe my eyes at first.

A bottle and a glass. A crystal glass. Just one.

Igor smiled, the cork went flying into the air and the foaming champagne poured into the glass. I took a mouthful. Brut, and cold too.

"Now am I good or bad?" he asked.

"Bad," I said, holding out the glass to him. "For hiding a precious treasure like that!"

Igor smiled and drank the wine. Then he said thoughtfully, "You know, I think I'm getting that feeling again . . ."

He started, and stopped speaking, straightening up abruptly. I jumped up—just in time to see an indistinct shadow slip away into the night from behind a beach parasol not far away.

"That's not good," Igor whispered.

"Who was it?" I asked. The realization that someone had been watching us didn't increase my excitement as it usually did. Completeness. Total completeness. Even the sip of champagne was just a pleasant extra after sex now, but not really necessary. And I certainly didn't need any outsiders.

"I don't know . . . it looked like one of the children." Igor was clearly upset. "That's really bad . . . how stupid."

"It's no disaster," I said, putting my arms around his shoulders. "The little ones are already asleep, and it's good for the older ones . . . it's part of their education too."

He smiled, but he was obviously concerned. That's people for you . . . always making a big deal out of nothing . . .

"Let's go to your room," I suggested.

"Okay," said Igor with a sharp nod. He looked at me. "But remember, in that case you won't get any sleep today."

"I was just going to warn you about that," I said. And it was true.

CHAPTER 6

WHEN I WAS A FULLY FUNCTIONAL OTHER, I COULD EASILY GO without sleep for five or six days. But even now I wasn't feeling sleepy at all. Quite the opposite. I could feel my blood simply seething with energy.

I got back to our summer house half an hour before reveille and looked in on the girls—some of them were tossing and turning as they woke up, but everything was all right. No one had run off to go swimming and drowned, no one had been kidnapped by evil terrorists, no one had got it into her head to go looking for their brigade leader in the middle of the night.

I went into my room with a smile of stupid satisfaction. I got undressed slowly and lazily, standing in front of the mirror, then ran my hands sensuously over my thighs and stretched like a satisfied cat.

An insane night. A magical night. I must have done just about all the wild things that a woman can do when she's in love with a man. Even things I hadn't liked before had suddenly become tantalizing pleasures that night. Surely I couldn't really have fallen in love with a human being? It wasn't possible . . . Not with an ordinary man, even if he did understand me better than anyone else in the world.

It just wasn't possible.

"Darkness, let him be an Other," I whispered. "Great Darkness, I implore you . . ."

It's a dangerous game to bother the primordial Power with such petty requests. Although . . . I don't believe the Darkness is able to hear a simple witch. But I expect Zabulon can shout loud enough for it to hear him . . .

Zabulon . . .

I sat on the bed and covered my face with my hands.

Only two days ago nothing would have brought me more joy than his love. But now?

Of course, he himself had suggested that I should amuse myself. And of course, he couldn't give a damn for banal human dogmas, especially those that made up the repertoire of the Light Ones. Infidelity meant nothing to him. And as for jealousy . . . he wouldn't even say a word against it if Igor and I . . .

Stop! Where is this taking me?

"Alisa, you've lost your wits . . ." I whispered.

Was I really still so much like ordinary people? Could I really think—what a terrible thing to say—of getting married? To a human being? Of cooking him borscht, washing his socks, bearing his children and raising them?

It was just like the old saying: The Watch by day, disgrace by night . . .

But yes, I could . . .

I shook my head, imagining how the other girls would react. No, there was nothing unusual about the actual fact. Most witches are married and, as a rule, to human beings. But . . .

It was one thing to cast a spell on some wealthy and influential man, an oligarch, or even a deputy of the State Duma or some major Moscow gangster. But a simple young guy, a student, without any money or contacts? I imagined the kind of jokes that would be hurled at me . . . and with good reason—that was the most terrible thing!

But it wasn't the sex that was driving me insane.

What was it that was happening to me?

It was as if I'd been enchanted by an incubus . . .

I shuddered at the monstrous thought. What if Igor was an ordinary incubus? A colleague . . . from one of the primitive types of Dark Ones?

No. It was impossible. An incubus would have sensed that I was an Other. A Dark Other, even if I had been temporarily deprived of Power. And he would have never turned his Power on a witch, knowing the price he would have to pay for that. I'd grind him into dust if my Power returned and I discovered love had been imposed on me . . .

Love? So it was love then? "Oh, Alisa . . ." I whispered. "What a fool you are . . ."

Well all right, so I am a fool!

I took a clean pair of panties out of my bag and went into the shower.

I dashed about like someone possessed all day long until the evening. Everything went quickly, but that didn't bother me in the slightest. I even had a bit of a quarrel with the camp commandant when I was trying to get good places for my girls at the movie festival. But I got them, and I think I left her with an improved opinion of me. Then they gave out the pieces of dark glass that had been brought from somewhere in the town of Nikolaev for watching the next day's eclipse of the sun. Five pieces of glass were given out to every brigade, but I managed to get hold of six. I hadn't even expected anyone in Ukraine to think of making them, but since they had . . .

After that came the beach, but of course didn't it just happen that today the boys' brigades had gone off on some stupid trip or other! Even the sea brought me no joy. But at a certain moment I looked at Natasha, understood her sad glance, and realized the comedy of the situation. I wasn't the only fool. There were two of us: the girl, pining for her boy and barely even daring to fantasize about kisses, and me, who had done things the night before that you wouldn't even find in the porn videos in the alley at the Gorbushka Market . . . Opposite extremes meeting.

"Are you missing him?" I asked in a quiet voice. Just for a moment it seemed Natasha was going to get furious and she looked at me indignantly . . . then suddenly she sighed: "Uh-huh . . . you too?"

I nodded without speaking. The girl hesitated for a second and asked, "Were you with him until morning?"

I didn't lie to her, especially since there was no one else there. I just asked, "Did you follow me?"

"I felt afraid in the night," the girl said quietly. "I woke up. I was having such horrible dreams . . . I came to you, but you weren't in your room."

"Until the morning," I confessed. "I like him very much, Natasha."

"Were you making love?" she asked in a businesslike tone of voice.

I wagged my finger at her: "Natasha!"

She wasn't embarrassed at all. On the contrary, she lowered her voice and told me, as if I were her bosom friend, "I can't get anywhere with mine. I told him that if he tried to kiss me, I'd punch him in the eye, and he said, 'As if I wanted to!' Why are boys so stupid?"

"He'll kiss you," I promised her. And I thought to myself: I'll do my best to make sure he does.

After all, what could possibly be simpler? The next day I would have my powers back, and the boy with ginger hair and freckles would follow Natasha around, gazing at her with eyes filled with genuine love. Why shouldn't I give my best donor a little happiness?

"What were you dreaming about?" I asked.

"Something horrible," the girl answered briefly. "I can't honestly remember. But it was something really, really horrible!"

"About your younger brother?" I asked.

Natasha wrinkled up her forehead. Then she replied: "I don't remember . . . But how did you know I have a younger brother?"

I smiled mysteriously and stretched out on the sand. Everything was all right. The dream had been extracted completely.

* * *

That evening I realized I just couldn't stand it any longer. I found Galina and asked her to keep an eye on my girls for a couple of hours. There was a strange look in her eyes. No, it wasn't hurt, although she'd obviously understood everything, and she'd had designs on Igor herself. And it wasn't anger. It was more like the sad look of a dog who has been punished unjustly.

"Of course, Alisa," she said.

That's the trouble with these so-called good people. Spit in their faces, thwart their desires, trample on them—and they put up with it.

But then, of course, it is very convenient.

I set off toward the fourth brigade's small house. Along the way I frightened two little boys in the bushes—they were smoking shards of glass on a little fire of disposable plastic cups. Actually, to say I frightened them is putting it rather strongly. The kids frowned and tensed up, but they didn't stop what they were doing.

"Tomorrow they'll give everyone special pieces of glass," I said amicably. "But you'll cut yourselves with those."

"There aren't enough of the special ones," one of the kids objected reasonably. "We'll smoke some for ourselves—the cups make great smoke."

"And we'll stick Band-Aids round the edges," the second one added. "And they'll be just fine."

I smiled, nodded to them, and went on. I liked the kids' attitude. Proud and independent. The right attitude.

I was already getting close to the summer house and I could hear the sounds of a guitar when I saw Makar. The kid was standing by a tree, as if he weren't really hiding, but so that he couldn't be seen from the direction of the house. Just standing there looking at Igor, who was sitting in the middle of his boys. When Makar heard my steps, he turned around sharply, started . . . and lowered his eyes.

"It's not good to spy on people, Makar."

He stood there, chewing on his lip. I wondered what he'd been planning to do. Play some nasty trick on Igor? Challenge him to a duel? Or had he just clenched his fists in helpless fury as he looked at the grown man who'd been making love to the woman he liked the evening before? You stupid, stupid boy. You ought to be looking at girls your own age, not at enchanting grown-up witches with long legs.

"You'll have it all, Makar," I said softly. "Girls, and a night beside the sea, and . . ."

He raised his head and looked at me derisively, even rather condescendingly. *No I won't,* his eyes seemed to say. *There won't be any sea, there won't be any beautiful naked woman by the edge of the foaming sea. It will all be quite different—cheap wine in a tiny room in some dirty hostel; a girl who could be anybody's after her second glass; a sweaty body turned flabby before its time and a whisper hoarse from smoking: "Where do you think you're sticking that thing, you greenhorn!"*

I knew that, as an experienced and cynical witch. And he knew it, this chance visitor to Artek, this short-term guest in "the realm of friendship and love." And there was no point in us pretending with each other.

"I'm sorry, Makar," I said, and patted him affectionately on the cheek. "But I really like him very much. You grow up strong and clever, and you'll have every . . ."

He turned and ran away, an almost grown-up boy who didn't want to waste even a minute of his brief happy summer, who didn't sleep at night and invented a different, happy life for himself.

But what could I do? The Day Watch has no need for human servants. There are enough werewolves, vampires, and other small-timers. I would check Makar, of course. He would make a magnificent Dark One. But the chances were very, very slim that the boy had the natural gifts of an Other . . .

My girls were probably just perfectly ordinary people too.

And the chances were just as slim that Igor had the gifts of an Other.

Maybe that was for the best? If he were human, then we could be together. Zabulon couldn't give a damn about a petty detail like his girl having a human husband. But he would never tolerate a husband who was an Other . . .

I looked down thoughtfully at my feet as I walked out of the trees toward the little house. Igor was sitting on the terrace, tuning his guitar. There were only two of his boys there with him—the "campfire monitor" Alyoshka and a plump, sickly looking child I didn't think had been at the campfire.

Igor looked at me and smiled. The boys spoke, greeting me, but we didn't say anything to each other—we read everything in each other's eyes. The memory of that night, and the promise of the next one . . . and the ones after that . . .

But there was a hint of confusion and anguish in Igor's eyes too. As if there were something making him feel very sad. *My darling . . . if only you knew how great my sadness is . . . and how difficult it is for me to smile. . .*

I don't care if you don't have the gifts of an Other, Igor. I don't care if my colleagues laugh at me. I'll put up with it. And you'll never know anything about Zabulon. Or about the Watch either. And you'll be amazed at your own success, at the way your career develops, your magnificent health—I'll give you all that!

Igor strummed his guitar strings, gave his boys an affectionate look, and started to sing:

I'm afraid of babies, I'm afraid of the dead,
I feel my own face with my fingers.
And I turn cold with horror inside—
Am I really the same as all these people?
These people who live above me,
These people who live below me,
Who snore on the other side of the wall,
Who live underneath the ground . . .
What wouldn't I give for a pair of wings,
What wouldn't I give for a third eye,
For a hand with fourteen fingers on it!
I need a different gas to breathe!
Their tears are salty, their laughter is harsh,

They never have enough for everyone.
They love seeing their faces in fresh newspapers,
But next day the papers are flushed away.
These people who give birth to children,
These people who suffer from pain,
These people who shoot at people,
But can't eat their food without salt.
What wouldn't they give for a pair of wings,
What wouldn't they give for a third eye,
For a hand with fourteen fingers on it—
They need a different gas to breathe.

Something cold and sticky stirred inside me. A terrible, dreary, hopeless feeling . . .

That was our song. This was like our song . . . far too much like a song for the Others.

I could feel the emotions of the boys sitting beside him. I was almost a normal Other now and felt as if I'd be able to summon the Twilight any moment. It was like when we were having sex the night before—that gathering momentum on a swing, that balancing on a razor's edge, that waiting for the explosion, the chasm beneath my feet . . . There were streams of Power flowing all around—still too coarse for me, not the light broth from children's nightmares, just the fat-cheeked boy's depression because he was missing his parents: He had some problem with his heart, he didn't play much with the other boys, he followed Igor around more or less the same way as Olechka stuck to me.

It wasn't light broth.

But it was still almost exactly what I needed . . .

I can't wait any longer!

I swayed forward, reached out, and took hold of the boy's shoulder, drawing in his blank sadness, and the sudden surge of energy almost made me throw up. But then the world turned cool and gray, my shadow fell across the worn floorboards of the veranda like a black chasm, and I fell into it, into the Twilight, just in time to see . . .

. . . to see Igor drawing in Power from the boy Alyoshka who was pressing against him—a thin lilac stream of Power: the expectation of pranks and adventures, delights and discoveries, joys and frights—the entire bouquet of feelings and emotions of a healthy, happy child, content with the world and with himself . . .

A Light bouquet.

Light Power.

The dark unto the Dark Ones.

The light unto the Light Ones.

I stood up, still half in the real world, half in the Twilight, to face Igor, who was also standing up, to face the lover that I loved, a Light magician of the Moscow Night Watch.

To face my enemy.

I heard him shout: "No!"

And I heard my own voice shout: "Don't!"

The very first thought that had come into my head proved to be wrong. No, Igor hadn't been working against me, playing out some insidious plans of the Night Watch. He had lost his Power—exactly as I had. He hadn't seen my aura, he couldn't have had any idea that he was looking at a witch.

He had fallen in love with me. With his eyes closed. Exactly as I had with him.

The world was gray and dreary. It was the cold world of the Twilight that makes us what we are—Power-hungry—but also helps us to find that Power. No sounds, no colors. The leaves frozen still on the trees, the frozen figures of the two boys, the guitar suspended in midair—Igor had let go of it as he entered the Twilight. Thousands of icy little needles pricked my skin, drawing out of me the energy I had only just acquired, drawing me down into the Twilight forever . . . but I was an Other again and I could draw Power from the world around me. I reached forward and scraped out every last little drop of everything dark that there was in the fat boy. I no longer had any problems absorbing Power. I no longer had to focus on what I was doing and how. It was all easy and familiar.

And Igor did the same thing with Alyoshka. Maybe a bit less skillfully—the Light Ones only rarely harvest Power from people directly. They're shackled by their own stupid restrictions, but he drank in all of the boy's joy, and I felt an unnatural joy for my beloved, for my enemy, for a Light Other who had just acquired Power . . .

"Alisa . . ."

"Igor . . ."

He was suffering. It was far harder for him than for me. The Light Ones spend all their lives chasing illusions. They're filled with false hopes and don't know how to survive a heavy blow, but he was handling it and I was handling it too . . . I was . . . I was . . .

"How absurd," he whispered, and shook his head sharply—a strange gesture in this gloomy haze, in the Twilight. "You . . . you're a witch . . ."

I felt him reach out to my mind—not deep into it, just to the very surface, simply trying to make sure . . . or hoping to be proved wrong . . . and I didn't try to resist. I just reached out in reply.

And I laughed—at the unbearable pain.

South Butovo.

Edgar standing against the Light magicians.

We were feeding Edgar with Power, and the Light Ones were being fed by the magicians in their second line.

Including Igor.

I recognized his aura, remembered his Power profile. Things like that are never forgotten.

And he recognized me . . .

Of course, I didn't know him by sight and I'd never heard his name. But why should an ordinary patrol witch know all one thousand agents of the Moscow Night Watch? All those magicians, wizards, enchanters, shape-shifters . . . When we needed to know, they gave us a specific briefing. The way they had for Anton Gorodetsky, when we'd followed him on Zabulon's secret instructions a year and a half earlier and managed to catch him committing an illegal intervention . . . And there were some you just couldn't help remembering . . . like Tiger Cub, for instance.

But I'd never known about Igor. A third-level Light magician. Probably a bit more powerful than me, although it was hard to compare the powers of a natural magician and a witch. My beloved, my lover, my enemy . . .

My fate . . .

"What made you do it?" Igor asked. "Alisa . . . why did you do it?"

"What do you mean why?" I almost shouted out, but I stopped myself because I realized he wouldn't believe me. He would never believe that what had happened was mere coincidence—just a stupid and tragic accident—that there hadn't been any evil intent, that a cruel twist of fate had brought us together in the moment of our weakness, when we could not recognize each other, could not sense our enemy . . . at the very moment when all we could do and all we wanted to do was to love.

How can we say why anything in this world happens? Why am I a Dark One? Why is he a Light One? After all, both of these are mixed together in all of us—at the beginning . . .

Igor could have been my friend and colleague, a Dark One . . .

And I . . . probably . . . could have become a Light One. And then I wouldn't have been taught by a wise witch, but a wise enchantress . . . and I wouldn't have paid my enemies back in kind, but sentimentally set them on "the true road" . . . by turning the other cheek . . . and I would have delighted in every pompous piece of their stupid nonsense.

I only realized that I was crying when the world started spinning around me. You must never cry in the Twilight—everybody knows that. The more emotion we allow ourselves to show, the more eagerly the Twilight drains our Power. And to lose your powers in the Twilight means to stay in it forever.

I tried to draw Power from my donor, the fat boy, but he was already drained; I reached toward Alyoshka, but he was absolutely neutral, squeezed dry by Igor. I couldn't draw energy from Igor and I didn't want to anyway, and everyone else was too far away, and the world was spinning . . . how stupid . . .

My knees struck against the ground and I even had the stupid thought that I would stain my skirt, although no dirt from the Twilight ever stays with us in the real world.

An instant later Igor hurled a charge of energy at me.

No, not to finish me off. To save me.

It was alien, Light Power. But it passed through him and then was given to me.

And Power is always Power.

I stood up, breathing heavily, as exhausted as during that night of our senseless, impossible love. Igor had helped me to hold out in the Twilight, but he didn't reach out his hand.

He was crying now. He was in a bad way too. "How could you do it?" he whispered.

"It was an accident, Igor!" I took a step toward him and held out my arms, as if I could hope for something. "Igor, it was an accident!"

He jumped away from me as if I were a leper, with the light, elegant movement of a magician who is used to working in the Twilight.

Fighting in the Twilight. Killing in the Twilight.

"Accidents like that don't happen," he said, spitting the words out. "You're . . . you're filthy scum . . . you witch . . . You . . ."

He froze as he absorbed the remaining traces of my magic. "You take Power from children!"

I couldn't stop myself from answering. "And you, what are you doing here, Light One?" My tongue almost refused to obey me. It was impossible, unthinkable to call him that, but he really was a Light One, and the abuse had become a simple statement of fact.

"What are you doing here if not grazing on little human children?"

"Light cannot be removed." He shook his head. "What is taken returns a hundredfold. You take Darkness, and the Darkness grows. I take Light and it comes again."

"Tell that to the boy Alyoshka, who'll be miserable the whole evening!" I shouted. "Make him feel better by saying his joy will return!"

"I shall have other things to do, witch! Saving the children you have driven into the Darkness!"

"Console them," I said indifferently. Everything in the world seemed to be covered with a crust of ice. "That's your job . . . my darling."

What am I doing?

He'll only be convinced that I knew everything in advance, that the Day Watch planned a cunning operation, that he has been cruelly mocked and deceived, that everything that has happened between us was only a cunning pretense . . .

"Witch . . ." Igor said contemptuously. "You will leave this place. Do you understand?"

I very nearly answered him: "Gladly!" After all, what joy was there left for me in this summer, this sea, this abundance of Power? I could restore myself little by little; the important part of the work was already done.

"You can leave," I said. "I have permission for a vacation and the use of human energy. You can ask your own organization . . . But do you have permission . . . darling?"

What are you doing, you fool? What are you doing, my love? What am I doing?

What am I doing? I am a Dark One. I am a witch. I am beyond human morality, and I have no intention of playing petty childish games with those primitive organisms known as people. I came here to rest, and that's what I'm doing! And you, what are you doing? If you really do love me? And you do, I know! I can see it right now, and you can see it too . . . if you want to. . .

Because love stands above Darkness and Light.

Because love is not sex or a shared faith, or "the joint maintenance of a household and the upbringing of children."

Because love is also Power.

And Light and Darkness, people and Others, morality and law, the Ten Commandments and the Great Treaty have damn all to do with it.

And I love you anyway, you bastard, you skunk, you Light son of a bitch, you good-hearted blockhead, you reliable cretin! I love you anyway! Even though only three days ago we stood against each other and dreamed of only one thing: destroying the enemy. Even though we are separated by an abyss that nobody can ever bridge!

Don't you understand, I love you!

And everything I say is only to protect myself, my words are my tears, but you don't see them, you don't want to see them . . .

Oh, come to me, it doesn't matter where—in the Twilight, where no one can see us, or in front of the astonished boys. Take me in your arms and we will cry together, and there'll be no need for words, and I'll clear out and go back to Zabulon in Moscow, back to Lemesheva's smug tutelage . . . or do you want me to leave the Day Watch? Do you? I wouldn't stop being a Dark One. That's not in my power, and I don't want to do it, but I will withdraw from the endless war between Darkness and Light. I will simply live and not even take anything from the ordinary, little people, even if you don't want to be with me. I don't even ask that, only leave me the memory of our love for each other!

Simply come to me.

No, do not reply to my words!

I am a Dark One!

I cannot be any different!

I love only myself in this world!

But now you are a part of me. The greatest part. The most important part. And if I have to—I will kill part of myself, and that means I will kill all of myself.

But don't do this!

You are a Light One!

You sacrifice your entire lives, you protect people and stand up for each other . . . oh, try to look at me in the same way, even if I am a witch, even if I am your enemy! You know that sometimes you can . . . understand. The way Anton Gorodetsky understood . . . when he gathered such immense Power for one purpose—and never made use of it. I can only admire Anton as a worthy enemy, but I love you, I love you, I love you! Oh, why won't you understand what I'm saying and take a step toward me, you scum that I love, my darling rat, my only enemy, my beloved idiot!

"Idiot," I shouted.

And Igor's face contorted in such monstrous torment that I understood everything.

Light and Darkness.

Good and Evil.

They're nothing but words.

Only we speak different languages and we just can't understand each other—even if we're trying to say the same thing.

"Leave, or I'll destroy you."

And with those words he left the Twilight. His body became blurred and indistinct and immediately reappeared in the human world, beside the two boys on vacation at Artek. And I rushed after him, tearing myself out of my shadow—if only it were as simple as that to escape from myself, from my nature, from my fate!

I was even in time to see what Igor did as he emerged from the Twilight: He caught the guitar that had almost touched the floor, threw a paranjah—I don't know what the Light Ones call it—over his face that was contorted in pain, and brought the boys out of their trance. He must have put them into a stupor when he entered the Twilight so that they wouldn't be frightened by the camp leaders' sudden disappearance . . .

What was that you said, little Natasha?

Reliable?

Yes, he's reliable.

"It's time for you to go, Alisa," Igor said. "What do we say, boys?"

Only I could see his real face now. Full of grief, nothing but grief . . .

"Goodbye," said the fat boy.

"Ciao," said Alyoshka.

My legs felt like cotton wool. I tore myself away from the railings of the veranda that I was leaning on . . . and took a step.

"Goodbye now," said Igor.

It was dark.

It was good that it was dark.

I didn't have to waste any energy on a paranjah. I didn't have to pretend to be happy. I just had to be careful with my voice. The weak light coming from the window didn't matter.

"And then they divided into Light Ones and Dark Ones," I said. "And the Light Ones believed that they should teach others to tear their lives to pieces. That the most important thing was to give, even if those who took were not worthy of it. But the Dark Ones believed that they should simply live. That everyone deserves what he has taken from life, and nothing more."

They didn't say anything, my stupid little girls . . . these human children—I hadn't found a single Other among them, Dark or Light. Not a single enchantress, or witch, or even vampire . . .

"Good night, girls," I said. "Sweet dreams, or even better—no dreams at all . . ."

"Good night, Alisa . . ."

So many voices. I was rather surprised. It wasn't even a fairy story, it was a fable that every Other knew, Dark Ones and Light Ones. But they hadn't gone to sleep . . . they had listened.

I was already halfway out of the door when Natasha's voice asked, "When the eclipse happens—will it be frightening?"

"No," I said. "It's not frightening at all. Just a little bit sad."

In my room I picked up my cell phone yet again and dialed Zabulon's number.

"The number you have dialed is temporarily unavailable . . ."

Where can you be, Zabulon, if your famous Iridium isn't receiving my call? Where are you, where?

I don't love you, Zabulon. And I probably never did love you. I think I've only just realized what love is. But you do love me! We were together and we were happy. You gave me this whole world and . . . please answer! You're my chief, you're my teacher, you're my lover, so tell me—what should I do now? When I'm left face-to-face with my enemy . . . and my beloved? Run? Fight? Die? What should I do, Zabulon?

I entered the Twilight.

The shadows of the children's dreams flickered all around me. A banquet . . . those streams of energy. Light and dark. Fears and sorrows, misery and resentment. I could see right through the whole Azure section. There was the boy, Dimka, feeling offended in his sleep because his friends hadn't called him to drink some of their lemonade. There was the tireless little girl, Irochka, who was nicknamed the Energizer, whining quietly into her pillow because someone had stolen her inflatable ring for swimming . . . And there was my faithful energy donor Natasha—she'd lost her little brother in the strange, dark back alleys of a dream and now she was running, crying as she tried to find him . . .

I don't want to gather Power. I don't want to prepare for battle. I don't want anything.

"Zabulon!" I shouted into the shimmering gray gloom. "I call to you! Zabulon . . ."

No answer.

It was easier for Aunt Polly to get an answer from Tom Sawyer with his hand stuck in the jar of jam than for me to get through to Zabulon . . .

"Zabulon . . ." I repeated.

This isn't the way I imagined this night . . . nothing like it.

Igor . . . Igor. . .

What are you doing now? Gathering Power? Consulting with the all-wise Gesar? Or are you sitting staring dully into the mirror . . . like me. . .

Mirror, mirror . . . can you tell my fortune?

I'm not very good at fortune-telling, but sometimes I have managed to see the future . . .

No.

I don't want to.

I know there's nothing good there.

They reached the beach when the eclipse had already begun. My girls were squealing and grabbing the pieces of dark glass from each other. They couldn't understand why I didn't ask for a piece. Oh girls, girls . . . what difference does the blinding light of the sun make to me? I can look the sun full in the face and not blink.

The boys of the fourth brigade were jumping around Igor, hurrying him on. They couldn't understand why their beloved camp leader wasn't going faster. They couldn't understand why he'd led them to the beach by such a long, roundabout route.

But I understood.

Through the Twilight I could see the faint flashes of Power being gathered.

What are you doing, Igor . . . my beloved enemy . . .

At each step the smile faded on one more face. Now a ten-year-old fidgety nuisance was no longer feeling happy about making up with his friend. Now an eleven-year-old fidget had forgotten about the black shell he found on the seashore. Now the serious man of fifteen years had stopped thinking about the date he was promised this evening.

Igor was walking through Artek in the same way that Anton Gorodetsky had once walked through the streets of Moscow.

And I, who was his primordial enemy, wanted to shout out, "What are you doing?"

Anton didn't outwit Zabulon because he gathered more Power than everybody else. Zabulon was still more powerful.

Anton knew how to use it properly . . .

Will you?

I don't want you to win. I love only myself. But what am I to do if you have become the greater part of me? Transfixed my life like a bolt of lightning?

Igor was collecting everything. Every last drop of Light energy around him. He was breaking all the laws and agreements and staking everything on a single throw of the dice—including his own life. And not just because he was burning with desire to protect the little human children from the evil witch.

He didn't want to live either. But, unlike me, he was prepared to live for others. If that was the way it had to be.

The last one he drew Power from was Makar.

I'd been feeling the boy looking at me for a long time. With the miserable, longing gaze of a boy in love with a grown-up woman. Miserable, and filled with the sadness of farewell.

It wasn't the kind of sadness that we Dark Ones can use. It was a bright sadness.

Igor drank it all up.

He had transgressed all the boundaries. And I couldn't even respond in the same way—I was bound by the promise I had given to Zabulon, bound by my old misdemeanor.

And also by the insane hope that he would do the right thing. That my enemy would win his victory, but I wouldn't lose either.

Up in the sky the bright disk of the sun was slowly dying. The children were already tired of staring at it through their pieces of glass. They were wallowing in the sea under the strange spectral light that reminded the two Others on the beach of the Twilight.

I turned to Igor and caught his eye.

"Leave," his lips whispered silently. "Leave, or I will kill you."

"Kill me," I answered silently.

I am a Dark One.

I will not leave.

What is he going to do, this enemy of mine? Attack me? Despite my legal right to be here? Call in the Yalta division of the Night Watch? He must already have consulted with them . . . and he knows there are no charges that can be brought against me.

Igor took a step closer.

"By the Light and the Darkness, I challenge you . . ." his lips whispered.

I shuddered.

I hadn't been expecting this. Not this.

"Beyond Light and Darkness, you and I, one against one, to the end."

He had challenged me to a duel.

It's an old custom that came into being with the Great Treaty between the Light Ones and the Dark Ones. A custom that is hardly ever used. Because the victor has to answer to the Inquisition. Because a duel only takes place when there is no legitimate basis for conflict, when the Watches have no legal competence to intervene, when emotions speak louder than reason.

"And may the Light be my witness."

Nobody else could have seen the tiny petal of white fire that flared up for an instant on Igor's open palm. He himself started when he saw it. The higher powers rarely respond to appeals from simple Watch agents . . .

"Igor, I love you . . ."

His face quivered as if I had struck it. He didn't believe me. He couldn't believe me.

"Do you accept my challenge, witch?"

Yes, I can refuse. Go back to Moscow, humiliated but secure, with the stigma of having refused a challenge . . . every lousy werewolf would spit as I walked past . . .

Or I could try to kill Igor. Gather so much Power that I could stand up to him . . .

"May the Darkness be my witness . . ." I said, opening my hand. And a tiny scrap of Darkness quivered on my palm.

"Choose," said Igor.

I shook my head. I wasn't going to choose the place, the time, or the type of duel.

Why can't you understand me? Why?

"Then the choice is mine. Now. In the sea. The press."

His eyes are dark. An eclipse isn't frightening—it's only something cutting off the light.

The sea was unnaturally warm. Maybe because the air had turned cold, as if it were already evening? All that was left of the sun was a narrow crescent at the top of the disk—now even a human being could look at it without blinking.

I swam through the warm water without looking back at the shore, where no one had noticed the two camp leaders slip into the sea without paying any attention to the jellyfish that hurried out of their way.

I remembered the first time I ever went to the sea. I was still very little. I still didn't know that I didn't belong to the human race, that fate had decided I would be an Other. I was staying at Alushta with my dad, and he was teaching me to swim . . . I remembered the feeling of delight when the water first submitted to my will . . .

And I remember how strong the waves were in the sea. Very strong. Or was it just that all waves looked huge to me then? My dad was holding me in his arms, he was jumping up and down in the waves, making me laugh. It was such fun . . . and I shouted that I could swim across the sea, and my dad said of course I could . . .

You'll be really hurt, Dad.

And it won't be easy for Mom, either.

The shore, full of delighted children and contented adults, had been left far behind. I didn't even feel the start of the press. It just got harder to swim. The water just stopped supporting me. There was suddenly a weight on my shoulders.

A very simple spell. Nothing fancy. Power against Power.

Dad, I really did believe I could swim across the sea . . .

I extended a defensive canopy above myself and it took the invisible weight off my shoulders. And once again I whispered, "Zabulon, I appeal to you . . ."

The strength that I had managed to gather was rapidly melting away. Igor struck again and again, battering my defenses mercilessly.

"Yes, Alisa."

He has responded after all! He has answered me! Just in time, as always!

"Zabulon, I'm in trouble!"

"I knew already. I'm very sorry."

I didn't realize immediately what those words "I knew" meant. And that impersonal tone, and the feeling that there was no Power on its way . . . He always used to share his Power with me, even when I didn't really need it that badly . . .

"Zabulon, am I going to die?"

"I'm afraid so."

My defensive canopy was dissolving, and I still couldn't make sense of what was happening. He could intervene! Even from a distance! A small part of his strength would be enough for me to resist the pressure and fight out a draw.

"Zabulon, you said that love is a great power!"

"Have you not been convinced of that? Goodbye, my little girl."

It was only then that I understood everything.

Just as my strength melted away and I felt the invisible pressure on my shoulders again, forcing me down into the warm, twilit depths.

"Igor!" I shouted, but the splashing of the water drowned out my voice.

He was swimming about fifty meters away, not even looking in my direction. He was crying, but the sea has no place for tears.

And I was being dragged down, down into the dark abyss.

How could it have happened . . . how?

I tried to gather Power from the beach. But there was almost no Darkness there for me to take. That sweet delight and those cries of joy were of no use to me.

Only a hundred meters behind Igor and myself, the young teenager who had fallen so hopelessly in love with me was vainly trying to lie on the waves and relax the leg that was contorted by cramps. Somehow he must have noticed us going into the water and swum after us, this proud boy called Makar, who had already realized that he couldn't swim back to the shore now.

Love is a great power . . . how stupid you all are, you boys, when you fall in love. . .

There's Makar, floundering about as his panic grows . . . I can take his fear and prolong my own agony for a minute or two. . .

And there's Igor, swimming in the sea: not seeing anything, not hearing anything, not sensing anything around him, not thinking about anything except that I have killed his love. The stupid Light magician doesn't know that there are no winners in duels, especially when the duel has been carefully prepared by Zabulon . . .

"Igor . . ." I whispered as I sank, feeling the pressure force me down, down to the dark, dark seabed.

Forgive me, Dad . . . I can't swim across this sea. . .

A STRANGER AMONG OTHERS

PROLOGUE

HE COULD ALREADY MAKE OUT THE LIGHTS OF THE STATION glimmering up ahead, but inside the gloomy, neglected park beside the Zarya factory the darkness remained as dense and chill as ever. The thin crust of ice over the snow crunched under his feet—it would probably thaw out again before noon. Locomotive whistles in the distance, incomprehensible announcements over the radio relay system, and the crunching under his own feet—these were the only sounds anyone who happened to be out strolling could have heard if he wandered into the park at that time of night.

But no one had set foot in here at night for a long time now. Not even people out walking massive canines with huge teeth—dogs could not save them from what they might meet in the darkness of night among the oaks that had grown tall here over the last forty years.

The solitary traveler with a bulky bag over his shoulder was clearly late for a train. He decided to take a shortcut and go through the park, along the path, with his feet sometimes crunching the thin ice, sometimes the gravel. The stars gazed down in amazement at this bold spirit. The round disk of the moon, as yellow as a pool of Advocaat liqueur, shone its light through the jagged, naked branches. The fantastic forms of the lunar seas were like the shadows of human fears.

The traveler noticed the twin gleam of a pair of eyes when he was still thirty meters from the final trees. He was being watched from the gaunt, skeletal bushes that stretched along both sides of the path. There was the vague, dark form of something over there, in the low thickets; perhaps not even something, but someone, because this dense patch of darkness was alive. Or at least it could move.

A dull growl—nothing like a roar, more like a low, hollow squawk—was the only sound that accompanied the lightning-swift attack. A wide mouthful of sharp teeth glinted in the moonlight.

The moon had readied itself for fresh blood. For a fresh victim.

But the attacker suddenly stopped dead in his tracks, as if he had run into an invisible barrier, stood there for a moment, and then collapsed onto the path with a ludicrous squeal.

The traveler paused for a second.

"What are you doing, you blockhead?" he hissed at his attacker. "Do you want me to shout for the Night Watch?"

The patch of darkness at the traveler's feet growled resentfully.

"It's lucky for you that I'm late . . ." said the traveler, adjusting the bag across his shoulder. "What damn nonsense is this, Others attacking Others . . ." He strode on rapidly across the last few meters of the park and hurried toward the station without looking back.

His attacker crawled off the path, under the trees, and there he transformed into a young man of about twenty, completely naked. The young man was tall with broad shoulders. The crust of ice crunched under his bare feet, but he didn't seem to feel the cold.

"Damn!" he whispered fiercely, and then shivered for the first time. "Who the hell was that?"

He was still hungry, still feeling savage, but this strange victim who had escaped had robbed him completely of any desire to carry on hunting. He was frightened now, although only a few minutes earlier he had been certain that everyone should be afraid of him—a werewolf out on the hunt. The heady, intoxicating hunt for human flesh. And the hunt was unlicensed—which made the sensation of risk and his own daring even keener.

Two things in particular had completely blunted the hunter's ardor. First, the words "Night Watch"—after all, he didn't have a license. And second, the fact that he had failed to recognize his intended victim as an Other. An Other like him.

Not long ago the werewolf and any of the Others that he knew would have said that was simply impossible.

Still in the form of a naked human being, the werewolf hurried through the low thickets to the spot where he had left his clothes. Now he would have to hide for many, many days, instead of prowling through the park at night hoping to chance upon a victim. He would have to stay hidden away, waiting for sanctions from the Night Watch, or maybe even from his own side.

His only hope was that this solitary traveler, who had not been afraid to cut across the park in the dark, this strange Other—or someone pretending to be an Other—really had been hurrying to catch a train. That he would catch it and leave the city. And then he wouldn't be able to contact the Night Watch.

Others also know how to hope.

CHAPTER 1

I ONLY CALMED DOWN COMPLETELY WHEN I COULD RELAX AND listen to the regular, hammering rhythm of the wheels. Although even then, not completely. How could I possibly feel calm? But at least I had recovered the ability to think coherently.

When that creature in the park broke through the bushes and threw itself at me, I hadn't been afraid. Not at all. But now I had no idea how I had found the right words to say. Afterward I must have surprised plenty of people with the way I staggered across the square in front of the station, past the tight ranks of route taxis parked for the night. It's not easy to walk with a steady stride when your knees are buckling under you.

What the hell was all this? The Night Watch . . . What on earth had I meant by saying that? And that beast with the teeth had immediately started whining and crept back into the bushes . . .

I took another mouthful of beer and tried once again to make sense of what had happened.

So, first I left the house . . .

Stop.

I put the bottle down on the little table, feeling confused. I must have looked very stupid at that moment, but there was no one to look at me—I was the only person in the compartment.

Stop.

I suddenly realized I couldn't remember my own house at all.

I couldn't remember a single thing about my past life. My memories began there, in that chilly winter park, just a few seconds before the attack. Everything before that was hidden in a mysterious darkness. Or rather, not even darkness, but a strange, gray shroud—sticky and viscous, almost completely impenetrable. A dense, gray, swirling twilight.

I didn't understand a thing.

I cast a confused and frightened glance around the compartment. It was a perfectly ordinary compartment. A little table, four bunks, brown plastic and maroon imitation leather, with lights occasionally sliding by in the night outside the window. My bag lying on the other bunk . . .

My bag!

I realized I didn't have the slightest idea what was in my bag. It had to be my things, and things can tell you a lot. Or remind you. For instance, they might remind me why I was going to Moscow. For some reason I felt certain the things could help reawaken my failed memory. I must have read about that somewhere or heard about it from someone.

I suddenly had a better idea and reached under my sweater because I realized my passport was in the left pocket of my shirt. If I started with my name, then maybe I would remember everything else.

As I looked at the yellowish page, with its dark pattern of fanciful curlicues, my feelings were mixed. I looked at the photograph, at the face that I had probably been used to identifying with my own unique personality for about thirty years—or was this the very first day?

The face was familiar in all its minutest features, from the scar on the cheekbone to the premature hint of gray in the hair. But never mind the face. That wasn't what interested me just at the moment.

The name.

Vitaly Sergeevich Rogoza. Date of birth—September 28, 1965.

Place of birth—the city of Nikolaev.

Turning over the page, I read the same information in Ukrainian and also ascertained that my sex was male and that the passport had been issued by an organization with an exceptionally clumsy acronym DO PMC ADIA—the District Office of the People's Municipal Council of the Administration of the Department of Internal Affairs of Ukraine. The "Family Status" page was an unsullied, virginal blank. I heaved a sigh of relief, or perhaps disappointment.

Then came the eternal burden and curse borne by every ex-Soviet citizen: my residence permit and address. Apartment 28, 28 Tchaikovsky Street, Nikolaev.

Well, well, there was the number 28 again, twice in a row.

Then the associations really began to click—I remembered that my house stood on the corner of Tchaikovksy Street and Young Guard Street, next to School No. 28 (that number yet again!). I remembered everything quite clearly and distinctly, right down to the charred poplar standing under my window—the victim of chemical experiments conducted by the young kid who lived on the floor above me (he had poured all sorts of garbage out the window onto the long-suffering tree). I remembered a drunken party five years ago in the next house, when someone had casually told the neighbor from downstairs what she could do with herself when she complained about the noise. She'd turned out to be Armenian, the wife of some local bigwig, and later an entire mob of those swarthy Armenians had come bursting in and started battering our faces to a pulp. I'd had to clamber out through the little window in the end room, because the main window wouldn't open, and climb down the drainpipe. When they noticed that one of the woeful drunks had disappeared from the blockaded apartment, the Armenians stopped waving their fists about and some kind of agreement was eventually reached with them. I also remembered my bitter disappointment when I asked for assistance from some close local acquaintances of mine whom I'd often drunk beer with at the kiosks in the district, and not a single one of them came.

I tore myself away from my surprisingly vivid memories.

So I did have a past after all? Or were these merely the forms of memories with nothing real behind them?

I had to try to figure it out.

From the passport I also gleaned the entirely useless piece of information that I had "exercised the right to privatize without payment the following volume of living space"—the volume was not indicated—"subject to the standard maximum of 24.3 square meters."

And that was all.

I thoughtfully put the document away in my pocket—the same one, on the left side of my chest, and looked hard at the bag. *What will you help me remember, my black-and-green traveling companion with the foreign inscription FUJI on your bulging side?*

Well, let's hope you'll help me remember at least something. . .

The zipper opened with a quiet whoosh. I threw back the flap of cloth covering the contents and looked inside. The polythene bag on the top contained a toothbrush, a tube of Blend-a-Med toothpaste, a pair of cheap disposable razors, and a small, fragrant black bottle that obviously contained eau de cologne.

I put them on the bunk.

In the next plastic bag I discovered a warm wool sweater that was obviously knitted by hand, not on a machine. I set that aside too.

I spent two or three minutes rummaging through the other bags—clean underwear, T-shirts, socks, a warm checkered shirt . . . Aha, here was something that wasn't clothing.

A small cell phone in a leather case, with an extendable aerial. My memory instantly reacted: *When I get to Moscow, I'll have to buy a card . . .*

The charger was there too.

And finally, at the very bottom, one more plastic bag. Filled with some kind of blocks. When I looked inside, I was astounded. This ordinary plastic bag, with its logo half worn away so that it was completely unrecognizable, contained wads of money, stacked in two layers. American dollars. Ten wads of hundred-dollar notes. That was a hundred thousand.

My hand automatically reached out for the door and clicked the latch shut.

Jesus, where had I got this from? And how was I going to get such a huge amount of money across the border? But then, I could probably stick a hundred dollar bill under every customs officer's nose and they'd leave me alone.

The discovery aroused almost no associations, apart from the memory of how expensive hotels are in Moscow.

Still in a mild state of shock, I put all the things back in the bag, zipped it shut, and pushed it under the bunk. I felt glad there was a second, unopened, bottle of beer standing beside the one I'd already started. I don't know why, but the sedative substance had a distinctly soporific effect on me. I was expecting to spend a long time lying there, listening to the hammering of the wheels, screwing up my eyes when the bright light suddenly broke in for a few moments, and racking my brains painfully.

Nothing of the sort happened. Before I'd even finished the second bottle of beer, I slumped onto the bunk, still fully dressed, and crashed out on top of the blanket.

Maybe I'd got too close to something taboo in my memories?

But how would I know?

I woke up with cold winter sunshine flooding in through the window. The train wasn't moving. I could hear indifferent official voices in the corridor: "Good morning, Russian customs. Are you carrying any arms, narcotics, or hard currency?" The replies sounded less indifferent, but most of them were unintelligible.

Then there was a knock at the door. I reached out and opened it.

The customs officer turned out to be a burly, red-faced guy with eyes that were already turning puffy. For some reason, when he spoke to me, he abandoned the standard routine and simply asked me, without any officialese: "What have you got? Get the bag out . . ."

He looked around the compartment carefully, got up onto the steps, and glanced into the luggage rack just under the ceiling. Then he finally focused his attention on the bag lying all alone in the middle of the bottom bunk.

I lowered the other bunk and sat down without saying anything.

"Open the bag, please," the customs officer demanded.

Can they smell money, or something? I thought sullenly, and obediently opened the zipper.

One by one the plastic bags migrated to the bunk. When he reached the bag with the money, the customs officer brightened up noticeably and reached out in a reflex response to slam the door of the compartment.

"Well, well, well . . ."

I had already prepared myself to listen to a hypocritical tirade about permits and even to read a paragraph from a book—like every written law, this one consisted of perfectly understandable words strung together so that they made absolutely no sense at all. To listen, read, and then ask hopelessly: "How much?"

But instead of that, I mentally reached out my hand toward the customs officer's head, touched his mind, and whispered, "Go now . . . Go on. Everything's fine here."

The officer's eyes instantly turned as stupid and senseless as the customs regulations. "Yes . . . have a good journey . . ."

He swung around stiffly, clicked the lock open, and staggered out into the corridor without saying another word. An obedient wooden puppet with a skillful puppet master pulling his strings.

But since when had I been a skillful puppet master?

The train moved off about ten minutes later, and all that time I was trying to figure out what was happening. I didn't know what I was doing, but I was doing exactly what was needed. First that creature in the park beside the factory, and now this customs officer whose mind had instantly gone blank . . .

And why, in hell's name, was I on my way to Moscow? What was I going to do when I got off the train? Where was I going to go? Somehow I was already beginning to feel certain that everything would be made clear at the right moment—but only at the right moment, not before. Unfortunately, I wasn't quite a hundred percent certain yet.

I slept for most of the day. Maybe it was my body's reaction to all the unexpected answers and new skills. How *had* I managed to set off the customs officer? I'd reached out to him, felt the dull crimson aura with the shimmering greenish overlay made up of dollar signs . . . And I'd been able to adjust his desires.

I didn't think people could do that. But what was I, if I wasn't an ordinary human being?

Oh, yes. I was an Other. I'd told that to the werewolf in the park. And only just that moment did I realize it was a werewolf that had tried to attack me. I remembered his aura, that bright yellow and crimson flame of Desire and Hunger.

I seemed to be gradually clambering up a stairway out of the blackness, out of a blank chasm. The werewolf had been the first step. The customs officer had been the second. I wondered just how long the stairway was, and what would I find up there, at the top? So far there were more questions than answers.

When I finally woke up we had already passed Tula. The compartment was still empty, but now I realized that was because it was the way I wanted it. And I realized that I usually got what I wanted in this world.

The platform at Kursk Station in Moscow drifted slowly past the window. I was standing in the compartment, already dressed and packed, waiting for the train to stop. The female announcer's muffled voice informed everyone that train number sixty-two had arrived at some platform or other. I was in Moscow, but I still didn't understand what I was doing.

As usual, the most impatient passengers had already managed to block the way through. But I could wait, I was in no hurry. After all, I'd be waiting anyway, until my slowly reviving memory prompted me or prodded me, like a muleteer with a stubborn, lazy mule.

The train gave a final jerk and came to a halt. There was a metallic clang in the lobby of the carriage; the line of people instantly started and came to life and spilled out of the carriage little by little. There were the usual exclamations of concern, greetings, attempts to squeeze back into a compartment to get things that couldn't be taken out the first time . . .

But the confused bustling around the carriage was soon over. The passengers had already got out and received their due allocations of kisses and hugs from the people meeting them. Or not, if there was no one there to meet them. There were a few still left, craning their necks as they gazed around the platform, already shivering in the piercing Moscow wind. But the only people left in the carriage were waiting to pick up the usual parcels of food and other things that relatives had sent with the conductor.

I picked up my bag and walked toward the door, still not under-standing what I was going to do in the immediate future.

Probably I ought to change some money, I thought. I didn't have a single kopeck of Russian money, only our "independent" Ukrai-nian currency, which unfortunately wasn't valid here. Just before we reached Moscow I'd prudently slit open one of the wads in the plastic bag and distributed some of the bills around my various pockets. I always did hate billfolds . . .

What was that thought I'd had? Always . . . My "always" had only begun last night.

I shuddered reflexively at the cold embrace of winter and strode off along the platform toward the tunnel. Surely there had to be some-one changing money at the station?

Rummaging about in my unreliable memory, I managed to es-tablish two things: First, I didn't remember the last time I'd been in Moscow but, second, I had a general idea of how the station looked from the inside, where to look for the bureau de change, and how to get into the metro.

The tunnel, the large waiting hall in the basement, the short es-calator, the ticket hall—my immediate goal was on the second floor, beside another escalator.

But this currency exchange point looked to have been closed very securely for a very long time. No light showing in any chink, no essential board with the current exchange rates. All right. Then I had to go to the exit and turn left, toward the ramp sloping down to the Chkalovskaya metro station . . . and the place I needed would be near there.

A white trading pavilion, a staircase up to the second floor, empty little shop spaces flooded with light, a turn . . . The security guard glanced up at me quickly and then relaxed when he recognized someone newly arrived in town.

"Go in, there's no one inside," he told me magnanimously.

I carried my bag into a tiny little room, in which the entire furnishings consisted of a rubbish bin in the corner and, of course, a tiny window with one of those little retractable drawers that had always reminded me of an eternally hungry mouth.

Hey, I reminded myself, *don't forget just how young your "always" is. . .*

But even so—if I thought like a man who really had lived thirty-five years, surely there must be some reason for it?

All right, we could get to that later.

The hungry mouth instantly devoured five one-hundred-dollar bills and my passport. I couldn't see who was concealed there behind the blank partition, and I wasn't really concerned to get a look at them. All I noticed were the fingers with pearly polish on the nails, which meant it was a woman. The mouth reluctantly slid open and belched out a sizeable heap of one-hundred-ruble bills and several bills of smaller denominations. Even a couple of coins. Without counting the money, I put it into my breast pocket, under my sweater, keeping just the smaller bills and the coins for my trouser pocket. I put my passport in my other breast pocket and threw the receipt—a small rectangle of green paper—into the rubbish bin.

Right, now I was someone. Even in this insane city, which was just about the most expensive on the planet. But no . . . that wasn't right. It had to be almost a year since Moscow had relinquished that dubious title.

Outside, winter greeted me again with its ice-laden breath. The wind carried fine, hard crumbs, like grains of semolina, a kind of immature hail. I strolled back along the front of the railroad station and then down to where I wanted to be—on the metro circle line.

It felt like I was beginning to remember where I needed to get to. Well, I could enjoy making some progress, even if I didn't enjoy the state of uncertainty. And I could hope that whatever business had brought me to Moscow was entirely good, because somehow I didn't feel I had the Power to serve Evil.

Only native Muscovites go home from the railroad stations in taxis. If their financial status permits it, of course. Any provincial, even if he has the kind of money I had, will take the metro. There's something hypnotic about this system of tunnels, with its labyrinth of connections, about the rumbling of the trains as they go hurtling past and the rush of air that fades away and then starts up again. About the constant movement. Down here there is unspent energy seething and swirling around under the vaults of the station halls: free for the taking, more than I could possibly use.

And there is protection. I think it's connected somehow with the thick layer of earth above your head . . . and all the past years that are buried in that earth . . . Not even years—centuries.

The doors of the train parted and I stepped in. There was a repulsive, insistent buzzing from the loudspeakers, and then a finely modulated man's voice announced: "Please mind the closing doors. The next station is Komsomolskaya."

I was riding the circle line. Counter-clockwise. And I was definitely not getting out at Komsomolskaya. But after that . . . after Komsomolskaya I apparently would get out. That would be Peace Prospect. And, by the way, it would be worth walking up the platform at Komsomolskaya to get closer to the front of the train. Then I'd be nearer the exit for my connection.

That meant I was changing onto the brown line, and probably going north, because otherwise I'd have gone around the circle line in the opposite direction and changed at Oktyabrskaya.

The carriage shook as it moved, and since I had nothing better to do, I studied the numerous advertisements. There was a long-haired man standing on tiptoe, but squatting down at the same time, who was advertising panty hose for women, and someone with a felt-tip pen had taken the opportunity to endow the hairy poser with a phallus of impressive proportions. The next stick-on poster suggested that I should go chasing around the city after a jeep painted in bright colors, but I failed to grasp the point of this pursuit. A prize, probably. Miracle tablets for almost every ailment—all in a single bottle—real estate agencies, the most yogurty yogurt of all yogurts, genuine Borzhomi mineral water with a picture of a ram on the bottle . . . And here was Komsomolskaya.

I was fed up with the advertisements, so I dropped my bag by the door and went to look at the plan of the metro system. I don't know why, but at the first glance my attention was immediately caught by the little red circle with the letters AEEA above it—the All-Union Exhibition of Economic Achievements.

That was where I was going. No doubt about it. To a massive horseshoe-shaped building. The Cosmos Hotel.

No one can deny that life feels easier when you know what your goal is. I heaved a sigh of relief, went back to my bag, and even smiled at my dull reflection in the glass of the door. The door also bore traces of the mindless hyperactivity of the city's own pithecanthropoids—the inscription "Do not lean against the doors" had been reduced to "Do lean again do."

The unknown author of this pointless statement wasn't even a pithecanthropus; he was more likely a monkey, a dirty, smug little monkey. Dirty and stupid, precisely because he was too much like a human being . . .

I was glad that I was an Other, and not a human being.

Here was Peace Prospect; stairs, a turn to the right, an escalator, and there was the train just arriving. Rizhskaya, Alexeevskaya, AEEA. Out of the carriage and turn right—I'd always known that.

A long, long escalator, on which for some reason I have no

thoughts about anything at all. Those annoying advertisements again. A pedestrian underpass. And there's the hotel. A horseshoe-shaped monstrosity of French architecture. The hotel has changed, though, and quite noticeably. They've added illuminated billboards and bright lights; and then there's the casino, with the prize foreign automobile displayed on a pedestal. Some street girls standing around outside smoking, despite the hard frost. And the doorman inside, whose hands instantly swallow up a hundred-ruble bill.

It wasn't really late yet, so it was still busy in the foyer. Someone was talking on a cell phone, rapping out phrases in Arabic loud enough for everyone to hear, and there was music coming from several directions at once.

"A deluxe suite for one," I said casually. "And please, no phone calls offering me girls. I've come to work."

Money is a great thing. A suite was found instantly and I was immediately offered dinner to be delivered to my room and promised that no one would call me, although I didn't really believe it. And they suggested I should register straightaway, because I had a Ukrainian passport. I registered. But then, instead of quietly making for the elevator to which I was solicitously directed, I set out toward an unremarkable little door in the darkest and emptiest corner of the foyer.

There were no plaques at all on this door.

The receptionist watched me go with genuine admiration. I think everyone else had stopped noticing me at all.

Behind the door I discovered a grubby little office—probably the only space in the hotel that hadn't been given a European makeover. It looked as if it had come straight out of the uncivilized Soviet '70s.

A standard-type desk—not really shabby, but it had seen plenty of service, a standard-type chair, and an ancient Polish "Aster" telephone in the center of the desk. Perched on the chair was a puny little guy wearing a militia sergeant's uniform. He looked up at me inquiringly.

The sergeant was an Other. And he was a Light One—I realized that straightaway.

A Light One . . . Hmm. Then who was I? I didn't think I was a Light One. No, definitely not a Light One.

Well then, that decided the matter.

"Hello," I said to him. "I'd like to register in Moscow."

The militiaman addressed me through clenched teeth, with a mixture of surprise and irritation in his voice: "The receptionist handles registration . . . When you check in. You have to check in to register." He rustled the newspaper that he had been studying with a pencil in his hand before I arrived—I think he was marking interest ing announcements from the incredibly long list.

"I've been through the ordinary registration already," I explained. "I need the *Other* registration. By the way, I haven't introduced myself: Vitaly Rogoza, Other."

The militiaman immediately straightened up and looked at me differently, with a perplexed expression now. He didn't seem able to recognize me as an Other. So I helped him.

"Dark," he muttered after a while, with a feeling of relief, or so it seemed to me. He also introduced himself: "Zakhar Zelinsky, Other. Night Watch employee. Let's go through . . ."

I could clearly hear in his tone of voice the old complaint about *all these foreigners flooding into our Moscow.* Others could never help dragging human models and stereotypes into their own relation-ships. This Light One definitely seemed annoyed by the arrival of yet another provincial and the need to get up off his backside, tear his eyes away from the newspaper, drag himself to his computer, and go through the hassle of a registration . . .

There was another door in the middle of the wall, one that an ordinary person never could have seen. But there was no need to open it—we walked through the wall, surrounded by the gray twi-light that had instantly filled the space around us. Our movements became soft and slow, and even the flickering of the light bulb on the ceiling became visible.

The second room looked far more presentable than the first. The sergeant immediately sat down at a comfortable little desk with a computer and offered me a seat on a plump divan.

"Are you staying in Moscow for long?"

"I don't know yet. I think for at least a month."

"Show me your permanent residence registration, please."

He could have seen it for himself, using his sight as an Other, but apparently the rules obliged him to use the simplest method.

My jacket was already open, so I just pulled up my sweater, shirt, and T-shirt. There on my chest was the bluish mark of a permanent registration in the Ukraine. The sergeant read it with a pass of his open hand and began slowly fingering the keyboard of his PC. He took a while to check the data, then rustled away on the keyboard again. He opened a massive safe that was locked with more than just keys, took something out, ran through the necessary procedures, and concluded by flinging a small bundle of bluish light at me. For an instant my entire upper body was flooded with fire, and a second later I had two seals decorating my chest. The second was my temporary Moscow registration.

"Your registration is temporary, but it has no fixed period," the sergeant explained without any particular enthusiasm. "Since our database indicates that you are an entirely law-abiding Dark Other, we can go easy on you and issue an unlimited registration. I hope the Night Watch won't have any reason to change its opinion about you. The seal will self-destruct as soon as you spend twenty-four hours outside the Moscow city limits. If you have to leave for more than twenty-four hours, I'm afraid you'll have to register again."

"I understand," I said. "Thank you. Can I go?"

"Yes, you can go . . . Dark One."

The sergeant said nothing for a few moments, then he locked the safe (with more than just keys), left the computer as it was, and gestured with his hand toward the door.

Back in the grubby little room, he asked me uncertainly: "Pardon me, but who are you? Not a vampire, not a shape-shifter, not an incubus, not a warlock—I can tell all that. And not a magician either, I think. I don't quite understand . . ."

The sergeant himself was a Light magician, about fourth level. That wasn't very high, but it wasn't exactly nothing either . . .

Yes, indeed—who was I?

"That's a difficult question," I replied evasively. "More a magician than anything else, I think. Goodbye."

I picked up my bag and went back out into the foyer.

Five minutes later I was already making myself at home in my suite.

I'd been right not to believe the receptionist—the first call with an offer to provide me with entertainment caught me while I was shaving. I morosely but politely asked them not to call again. The second time there was less politeness in my tone of voice, and the third time I simply poured so much sticky, viscous Power into the innocent phone that the person at the other end choked and stopped in mid-word. But at least they didn't call me anymore.

I'm learning, I thought. *But am I really a magician or not?*

To be honest, I hadn't really been surprised by what the Light sergeant had said. Vampires, shape-shifters, incubuses . . . They all exist. They certainly do. But only for their own kind, for the Others. For ordinary people, they don't exist. But for the Others, ordinary people are the very source of existence. Their roots and their nourishment. For both the Light Ones and the Dark Ones, no matter what nonsense the Light Ones might trumpet on every street corner. They also draw their energy from the lives of human beings. And as for their goals . . . We both have the same goals. It's just that we and the Light Ones both try to overtake our competitors and reach our goals first.

I was distracted from this torrent of revelations by a knock at the door—they had brought my dinner. After I'd fed the waiter a hundred-ruble bill (where did I get this lordly habit of handing out such incredibly generous tips?), I tried to concentrate again, but I'd obviously lost the wavelength. A pity.

But in any case, I had climbed up one more step. At least now I knew there were two different kinds of Others: Light Ones and Dark Ones. I was a Dark One. I wasn't very fond of Light Ones, but I couldn't say that I hated them. After all, they were Others too, even if they did follow rather different principles from us.

And I'd begun to understand a bit more about what lay behind my threat to the werewolf in the park, behind the vague but imposing title "Night Watch." What it signified was the observation of Dark Ones at night—precisely at night, because the Dark Ones' time was the night. Naturally, there was a Day Watch as well. They were my kind, but I had to be careful with them too, because if I did something wrong it wouldn't earn me a pat on the back. And this whole system was in a rather shaky state of equilibrium, since both sides were constantly seeking means and methods to finally rout their opponents and acquire undivided control over the world of human beings . . .

That was all I had so far. And from the height of this step I couldn't make out anything more in the encircling Twilight . . .

I heard the Call just as I was finishing my dinner.

Neither too quiet, nor too loud, neither pleading nor imperious. The person it was intended for heard it too. And couldn't resist.

It wasn't intended for me. So it was strange that I could hear it . . .

That meant I had to do something.

Something implacable inside me was already giving orders. Put your jacket on! Put the bag in the cupboard! Lock the windows and the doors! And not just with the locks and latches, you blockhead!

Drawing in Power from everywhere I could reach, I made sure that ordinary people wouldn't take any interest in my room. Others had no business being here anyway.

The dead-drunk Syrian in the next room suddenly sobered up. On the next floor down the Czech who had been suffering torment with his stomach finally puked and collapsed in relief with his arms round the toilet bowl. In the room across the corridor an elderly business-man from the Urals slapped his wife on the cheek for the first time in his life, putting an end to an old, lingering quarrel—an hour later the couple would celebrate their reconciliation in the restaurant on the second floor. If there was a Light One around then, I'd already set the table for him . . .

But all this didn't really interest me. I was following the Call. The Call that wasn't intended for me.

Evening was smoothly merging into night. The avenue was full of noise, the wind howled in the trolley wires. For some reason the sounds of nature drowned out the voices of civilization—maybe because I was listening so intently?

To the right, along the avenue. Definitely.

I pulled my cap down tighter on my head and set off along the sidewalk.

When I had almost reached a long building with shop windows along its first floor displaying absurd phoney samovars, the Call stopped. But I already knew where to go.

Beside the next building there was the dark tunnel of a narrow alley. And right now it was filled with genuinely intense darkness.

As if to spite me, the wind grew stronger, lashing at my face and shoving me back like a rugby player, and I had to lean forward in order to move at all.

There was the alley. It looked like I was too late. An indistinct silhouette froze for a moment against the vague patch of light that was the other end of the alley; all I could make out was a pale face that was obviously not human and the dull gleam of two eyes. And I think I saw teeth.

That was all. Someone had been here and disappeared, but there was someone else still here, and they wouldn't be going anywhere.

I leaned down over the motionless body and took a close look. A girl, still very young, about sixteen, with a strange mixture of bliss and torment in her glazed eyes. There was a fluffy knitted scarf and a matching hat lying beside her. Her jacket was unbuttoned, exposing her neck. And there were four puncture marks clearly visible on her neck.

Somehow I wasn't surprised that I was able to see in almost total darkness.

I squatted down beside the girl. Whoever had drunk her blood—not a lot of it, no more than a quarter of a liter—had also drunk her life. Sucked out all of her energy right down to the last drop. A lousy way to go.

And then people burst into the alley from both ends simultaneously, or rather, not people—Others.

"Stop there! Night Watch! Leave the Twilight!"

I straightened up, not realizing immediately what they wanted from me, and received a hard blow—but not from a fist or a foot. It was something white, as white as a surgeon's coat. It didn't really hurt, but it was annoying. One of the watchmen was pointing a short rod at me. There was a red stone on the end of it, and he looked as if he were getting ready to hit me again.

And then I was immediately thrown one more step up the stairway. Not even just one, but two at least.

I left the Twilight. Now I understood what was happening when everything around me slowed down and I could suddenly see in pitch darkness. It was the world of the Others. And I'd been ordered—not asked, but ordered—to return to the world of human beings.

So I did, obeying without any objections. Because it was the right thing to do.

"Name yourself!" they demanded. I couldn't see who they were, because they were shining a flashlight in my face. I could have made out their faces, but just at that moment that wasn't the right thing to do.

"Vitaly Rogoza, Other."

"Andrei Tiunnikov, Other, Night Watch agent," said the one who had struck me with his battle wand, clearly taking pleasure in introducing himself.

Now I could tell that I hadn't been hit with full Power; it had just been a warning shot. But if they wanted, they could strike a lot harder—the charge in the wand was strong enough.

"Well now, Dark One. What do we have here? A fresh corpse, and you standing beside it. Are you going to explain? Or maybe you have a license? Well?"

"Andriukha, hold your horses," someone called sharply to him from out of the darkness.

But Andriukha took no notice and just gestured in annoyance.

"Wait!"

He spoke to me again: "Well, then? Why don't you talk, Dark One? Nothing to say?"

I wasn't saying anything.

Andriukha Tiunnikov was a magician. A Light magician, naturally, and just barely up to the fifth level.

I'd been that strong yesterday.

He obviously hadn't charged the amulet himself—I could sense the work of a much more experienced magician than him. And I thought the two young guys behind his back looked a bit more powerful too.

On the other side the alley was blocked off by a girl, standing on her own. She was young and not very tall, but she was the most experienced and dangerous member of the group. She was a shapeshifting battle magician. Something like a Light werewolf.

"Well, come on, Dark One!" Andriukha insisted. "Still got nothing to say? I see. Show me your registration! And someone let the Day Watch know we have a Dark poacher here . . ."

"You're a fool, Andriukha," I said derisively. "So delighted because you've caught a Dark poacher! Why don't you try taking a look at the victim? Who do you think finished her off?"

Andriukha broke off and squinted sideways at the dead girl. He seemed to be getting the picture.

"A va . . . vampire . . ." he muttered.

"And who am I?"

"You're a ma . . . magician . . ." Andriukha was so confused, he'd begun to stammer.

I turned to the girl, because I'd decided she was the one I ought to talk to. "When I got here it was all over. I saw the vampire, but he was already outside the alley. He took off into the yard. The girl was already dead, she's been completely drained, but only a mouthful of her blood has been taken. I'm new in town, just off the train two hours ago. I'm staying at the Cosmos Hotel."

And I couldn't resist adding, "Not the first time vampires have used this alley for poaching, is it?"

Now I could see the traces of the past there, on the ground and on the walls. I'd jumped several steps at once.

"Only last time you were luckier, Light Ones . . . But I must say you did a lousy job cleaning up—the signs are still visible now."

"Don't get any idea we're grateful to you," the girl answered darkly through her clenched teeth. "And let me take a look at your registration anyway."

"By all means." I meekly showed them the seal. "I hope I'm not required any longer? I wouldn't like to hinder your superlative detectives in their search for the poacher."

"We'll find you tomorrow," the girl told me dryly. "If we need you."

"Please do!" I said with a grin. Then I moved one of the watchmen aside and walked out onto the avenue.

I cast off the guise of an ordinary Dark One about a hundred steps farther on.

CHAPTER 2

FOR THE NEXT TWO DAYS AND NIGHTS ABSOLUTELY NOTHING interesting happened. I wandered around Moscow, making unexpected purchases and practicing my new abilities, trying not to make it too obvious. I switched on my cell phone, without having the slightest idea why—I had nowhere to ring and there was no one to ring me. I bought a mini-disk player and spent a couple of hours putting together a disk for it from the catalog, looking for old and new songs that triggered some response in my recalcitrant memory. I gradually got used to the changes in Moscow, which behind the tinsel glitter of its bright, festive neon had remained just as dirty and scruffy as ever. The hotel staff all said hello to me, and they seemed to have organized a line for the right to serve me—I was still living like a man who didn't acknowledge any bills worth less than a hundred rubles. But strangely enough, I was still careful to collect my correct change in the shops, even the little nickel-plated coins that are no good for anything except maybe souvenirs for foreigners.

During those two days I only met Others three times: Once in the metro, entirely by chance; once at night, when I ran into a drunk witch trying unsuccessfully to fly up to a third-floor balcony because she'd lost her keys and didn't have enough Power left to go through the Twilight. I gave the witch a hand. And once during the day I was taken for an uninitiated Other by a rather powerful Light magician—I even remembered his name: Gorodetsky. He'd just happened to go into the shop for the same thing as me—to put together a new mini-disk for his player. The magician was surprised when he saw my official seals and backed off immediately. He was even going to leave, out of disgust, I think, but they'd just finished cutting my disk, so I was the one who left.

I was left wondering for a while why he hated the Dark Ones so much.

But then, everybody hates us. Well, almost everybody. And they just don't want to believe that what we feel about them is mostly indifference—just as long as the Light Ones don't get in our way. And they do, all the time. But I suppose we get in their way too.

No one from the Night Watch bothered me. I don't think they even made any attempt to find me and question me. They must have realized that a Dark magician has no need to drink human blood. Of course, I could have done it, and given myself a chronic digestive disorder—if I hadn't been sick in disgust . . . I was totally absorbed in waiting for the next step up along the stairway, for when something inside me would force me to make use of magic, but apparently for that to happen required an extreme, unambiguous situation. Not just minor actions, like getting rid of the fat-faced ticket inspectors in the bus with their shaved heads, or a mantle of calm for the agitated people standing in line for metro cards when I couldn't be bothered to wait—no, all that was quite literally yesterday's level as far as I was concerned. In order to learn something new and reveal another layer of my sealed memory, in order to take possession of the knowledge that was still slumbering, I needed more serious shocks.

I had to wait for them, but not very long.

Like many other Dark Ones, I turned out to be an inveterate night owl. Since I was living among ordinary people, I couldn't completely ignore the day, but I didn't feel like resisting the alluring call of the night either. I rose late, about midday or even later, and I only returned to the hotel at dawn.

My fourth night in Moscow was already streaked with the first hints of dawn, the blackness had already admitted the first shades of dark gray into itself, when I ran smack into the next step upward. I was strolling along deserted Izmailovsky Boulevard when I suddenly sensed the flash of a powerful magical discharge somewhere in among the buildings in the distance.

When I say "discharge," I don't mean that uncontrolled energy had simply escaped. No. The energy was discharged and then immediately absorbed, otherwise the final result would have been a banal explosion. Others transform themselves, and the world, and energy. But in the final analysis the balance of energy emitted and absorbed always amounts to zero, otherwise . . .

Otherwise the world simply couldn't exist. And we couldn't exist in it.

I felt something urging me to go there. Go!

So I had to go.

I walked for about twenty minutes, confidently turning corners at intersections and sometimes taking shortcuts through courtyards. When I was almost there I sensed Others—they were approaching rapidly from two different directions, and at the same time I heard the sound of several automobiles. Almost immediately I picked out the house and the apartment I needed from the faceless palisade of high-rises. That was where the event had occurred that had caught the attention of the other me, still concealed somewhere in the depths of my ordinary being.

A standard five-story Khrushchev-period building on Thirteenth Park Street. Rubbish containers standing along the end wall, and not a sign of the trading kiosks I was so used to seeing in the South.

Three vehicles at the entrance: a Zhiguli, a humble and very unkempt-looking station wagon, and a pampered BMW. There were actually plenty of other cars standing all around, but they were obviously parked for the night, while these had just arrived in a hurry and been dumped.

The fifth floor. At the entrance to the stairwell (the metal door, by the way, was standing wide open) I sensed powerful magical blocks, and they made me pull my shadow up from the ground and enter the Twilight.

I think the Twilight draws Power out of Others—if they don't know how to resist it, of course. Nobody told me what to do. I just started doing it instinctively, as if I'd always known how. Maybe I always had, and I just remembered when I needed to.

The blue moss that inhabits the first level of the Twilight had spread in luxurious abundance over the walls and the stairs, even the banisters. The people living in this entrance must be highly emotional if it was flourishing so well.

Here was the apartment I wanted. More powerful blocks, and the door locked even in the Twilight.

And at that point I was flung up another two steps. Overcoming a momentary weakness, I raised my own shadow from the floor again and went deeper.

I could immediately tell this was a place where not many came. There was no building. There was almost nothing at all except a dense, dark gray mist and the moons that I could vaguely make out through it. All three of them. There ought to have been a raging wind—the wind doesn't recognize any difference between the ordinary world and the Twilight—but at this level, time flowed so slowly that I could hardly feel it at all.

I began slowly falling, sinking into this mist, but I held myself up. Apparently I knew how to do that. A certain effort—as always, hard to describe and more instinctive than conscious—and I moved forward. Another effort, and I glanced out into the preceding level of the Twilight.

Everything was happening in syrupy slow motion, as if the world had sunk into a layer of transparent gray tar, and at first, sounds seemed like deep, distant peals of thunder, but I managed to adjust to their slowness. I must have set my rate of perception to the same pace, attuned myself to this new reality, and from that moment on, everything that was happening began to remind me again of the ordinary world—the world of human beings.

A narrow hallway, as they all are in those buildings. Two doors on the left—to the bathroom and the kitchen. One room farther along on the left and one on the right. The room on the right was empty. In the room on the left there were five Others and a body lying on a disheveled bed. The body of a guy about thirty: He had several ragged wounds in the area of his crotch and stomach, which immediately put to rest any idea that he could be saved. The wounds were covered with a crumpled, bloody bedsheet.

There were three Light Ones and two Dark Ones. The Light Ones were a lean young guy with a rather asymmetrical face and two acquaintances of mine—the music lover Gorodetsky and the girl shape-shifter. The Dark Ones were a plump magician with a keen, intense expression, and a gloomy individual who looked to me like an unsuccessful parody of a lizard—he was wearing clothes, but his hands and face were green and scaly.

The Others were arguing.

The Light One I didn't know was talking.

"It's the second incident this week, Shagron. And another murder. I'm sorry, but it's beginning to look like you've thrown the treaty out the window."

The Dark One glanced involuntarily at the corpse.

"We can't keep track of everybody, you know that perfectly well," he blurted out, but I didn't hear any trace of guilt or regret in his voice.

"But you undertook to warn all the Dark Ones about Clean Week! Your chief promised officially."

"We did warn them."

"Well, thank you!" The Light One clapped his hands in theatrical applause. "The result is impressive. I repeat: We, the agents of the Night Watch, officially request your cooperation. Call your chief out!"

"The chief isn't in Moscow right now," the magician replied morosely. "And, by the way, your chief knows that perfectly well, so he needn't have bothered to authorize you to request cooperation."

"Does that mean," Gorodetsky asked with the hint of a threat in his voice, "that you are refusing to provide cooperation?"

The Dark magician shook his head rather more quickly than he need have. "What do you mean, refusing? No. We're not refusing. I just don't understand what we can do to help."

The Light Ones seemed to be filled with righteous wrath at that. The magician I didn't know spoke again. "What can you do? Some shape-shifting hooker rips the balls off a client—an uninitiated Other, by the way—and gets clean away! Who knows all your countless low-life best—you or us?"

"Sometimes I think you do," the Dark magician retorted, and glanced at the girl. "If you remember the conversation in the Seventh Heaven when they caught the Inquisitor and him . . ."—he nodded at Gorodetsky and paused, as if he were thinking about something.

"Most likely the shape-shifter's not registered. And most likely the client got a bit too boisterous and er . . . er . . . Well, let's put it this way: He wanted something that was unacceptable even to a hooker. And this is the result."

"Shagron, you can't unload this on the human cops, because she killed him when she was in her Twilight form. Like it or not, the Watches are involved. So tell me straight: Are you going to carry out an investigation or will you force us to deal with it? And don't even hope that you can just drag things out. We want Saturday's vampire and this cat up in front of a tribunal, and before next weekend. Do you understand our demands?" The skinny young guy was leaning on Shagron, insisting on his rights, and he obviously enjoyed doing it, as an Other who didn't often get involved in showdowns. And he seemed to have justification for putting on the pressure . . .

"These lousy, lecherous cats," the scaly one suddenly muttered. "Brainless bitches . . ."

"Shut up," the Light girl told him coldly. "You overgrown gecko."

Ah, yes, she was a cat too, even though she was Light . . .

"Cool it, Tiger Cub," Gorodetsky said to her. Then he turned to the Dark magician again. "Do you understand our demands?"

At this point I returned to the first level of the Twilight. To describe the seconds that followed as a dumb show would be a gross understatement.

"You!" the girl gasped. "You again!"

"Buenos noches, lady and gentlemen. Pardon me, I saw the light, so I just dropped in."

"Anton, Tolik," Tiger Cub said in a ringing voice that trembled slightly, pointing one finger at me in a childish manner. "Andriukha found him standing over the vampire's victim on Saturday! This Dark One from Ukraine!"

All five of them carried on staring straight at me.

"I hope," I said ironically, "that I don't resemble a shape-shifting hooker any more than I do a crazy vampire?"

"Who are you?" the Dark magician, the one they called Shagron, asked in a hostile voice.

"A magician, dear colleague. A Dark magician. From out of town."

When he tried to probe me, I could tell that if I hadn't yet climbed up the next step, then I was right there in front of it. He didn't get anywhere. And meanwhile I noticed that Shagron's defenses were not entirely his own—I could sense a framework that had been put together by a top-class magician. Probably the famous chief who wasn't in Moscow at the moment.

"A second murder, and here you are again," Tolik drawled suspiciously, also making an attempt to probe me—quite unsuccessfully, as I noted with some satisfaction. "I don't like it. Perhaps you would care to explain?"

Tolik certainly looked annoyed, but now he was behaving correctly, and that suited me just fine. He was obviously the leader of the three Light Ones and now he was busily thinking over the possible courses of action. There seemed to be plenty of choice.

"Yes, I would," I agreed readily. "I was out strolling not far from here. I sensed something bad going on. And I came to see if I could do anything to help."

"Do you work in the Watch back home in Ukraine?" the scaly one asked unexpectedly.

"No."

"Then how can you help?"

"Who knows?" I said with a shrug.

Of course, the scaly one's tongue was long and forked. Our people's imagination is certainly pretty limited. You'd think the Twilight image of a Dark One offered plenty of scope for fantasy—unlike what the Light Ones have, which is just a standard outfit: a luminescent glow and white clothes. The more sentimental ones, mostly the women, have a white garland as well. But even so . . . almost all the Dark Ones go for the old, worn-out cliché of a scaly demon with horns and a forked tongue.

"Of course, you have nothing at all to do with these murders?" the girl said with poorly concealed sarcasm.

"Naturally."

"I don't trust him," said the girl, and turned away. "Anton, you have to probe him."

"We will," Anton replied without thinking. "When we get back I'll personally request all the data on him . . ."

I laughed ironically.

"All right. If you don't want any help, I don't mind. I'm not going to impose myself on you. I'll be going then . . ."

I started toward the door.

"Hey, Dark One," Tolik said to my back. "I'd advise you not to leave Moscow. That's an official ban from the Night Watch."

"I'll bear it in mind," I promised. "In any case, I wasn't planning to leave . . ."

"I'll go with you," Tolik said to Anton and Tiger Cub. "I have something to say to you."

Anton thought gloomily that he must have done a bad job cleaning up again—for some reason this strange Dark One's words had really stung him. Tiger Cub had imitated the stranger's way of

speaking very precisely, right down to the intonation pattern, and
when Anton saw the Dark One, he was convinced yet again that
Tiger Cub had the makings of a skillful actress. Who could tell what
she might have been if she hadn't been an Other . . .

Shagron and his partner had driven off in their fancy BMW a
long time ago. Tolik reached out his hand demandingly and Anton
obediently gave him the keys to the office Zhiguli. Tiger Cub got
into the back without speaking. Anton sat beside Tolik, who drove
rapidly out onto Sirenevy Boulevard and headed east.

"Who is he, this Dark One?" Anton asked to break the silence.
He was in a foul mood. Another body—and this time an uninitiated
Other!

"He's a very powerful magician," Tolik said abruptly. "More powerful than me. I tried to probe him and I failed—he closed up instantly."

"Closed up?" Tiger Cub said in an excited voice from the back.
"You mean he came without a shield?"

"That's just the point," Tolik exclaimed gloomily. "When he
came in, he looked exactly like an ordinary magician, maybe third
or fourth level. Like me and Anton."

Anton didn't say anything—strictly speaking, Tolik was incor-
rect, but in essence he was right. Gesar had called Anton a second-
level magician, but Anton's powers had only risen to that level on a
few occasions. It would be more honest to admit that for the time
being he was still third level.

"But as soon as I tried to probe him," Tolik went on, "that was
it. A blank wall. He's definitely more powerful than me. Anton. Did
you try to probe him?"

"No."

"Looks like he's first level . . ." Tolik, said with a sigh. "If it comes
to it, we'll have to call in Ilya . . ."

"I'm afraid we might even have to call in Olga and Sveta and the
boss," Anton remarked. Nobody answered him. Nobody liked the
idea of asking the Higher Magicians for help.

Tiger Cub started squirming about, making herself more comfortable on the seat. "There's no way he's not connected with these murders. I can understand the first time—he arrived in Moscow, went out for a walk, and accidentally stumbled across a poacher. But this time? What was he doing on Pervomaiskaya Street?"

"But did he definitely arrive on Saturday?" Tolik asked.

"Definitely," Tiger Cub assured him. "I didn't like the look of him, you know? I even found the train he was on and scanned the conductress for memories. He almost never came out of his compartment, but he was on the train all right."

"And do we have anything on him?"

Anton thought he caught a hint of concealed hope in Tolik's question: "Compromising material, you mean? Not a thing. Not a single violation. He doesn't need any licenses, he's not a vampire or a shapeshifter. And he was only initiated fairly recently, just seven years ago . . . Like me."

Tolik nodded thoughtfully. "There aren't many Others in Nikolaev. So the Watches are small as well, only twenty or thirty agents . . ."

"Okay, when we get back, I'll dig a bit deeper," Anton promised. "Did you lock up your station wagon, eh?"

"What's going to happen to it?" Tolik asked with a shrug. "Yes, we'll have to phone the boss after all. Or will we be able to handle this on our own?"

He was obviously feeling uncomfortable. Tolik had been in charge of the IT department for more than a year now, since Anton made the move to operational work. But no member of the Night Watch has the right to let his qualifications slip—and the time had come around for Tolik's month of field duty. And on the very first day there was an unpleasant incident like this . . .

"We'll probably have to tell him," Anton decided.

"Then there's no point in putting it off . . ." Tolik sighed.

Tiger Cub eagerly held out her cell phone, but before Tolik could even touch it the phone started chirping the tune of "Midnight in Moscow."

Anton was about to take the phone, but he restrained himself. You never know . . . It was obviously one of their own calling, but he couldn't sense the tense, nervous energy of a work call. Maybe it was simply some member of the Watch calling Tiger Cub? Everybody had a personal life, even the members of the Watch.

Tiger Cub took the call. Most of the time she just listened, and once she said, "I don't know."

"It's Garik," she explained in a voice filled with quiet alarm. "Andriukha's disappeared."

"Tiunnikov?"

"Yes. Garik thought he was with us."

"The last time I saw him was this afternoon," Tolik told her. "He was planning to go and catch up on his sleep."

"His phone's not answering. Garik can't sense him either—and he's Andriukha's mentor . . ."

Anton turned toward Tiger Cub: "After Saturday he was like a man possessed. What did that Dark One say to him in the alley?"

Tiger Cub shrugged. "Nothing special—I've told you a hundred times already. He called him a detective. But Andriukha really had screwed up—it was obvious straightaway that the Dark One was no vampire. I explained that to him myself."

"He doesn't have to be a vampire," Tolik declared in a bored, didactic voice. "This Dark One could quite easily be the organizer of the whole grisly mess. And it goes without saying that his organizational talents are clearly above average!"

"One of Zabulon's pawns," Anton mused. "Yes, it's possible. Perfectly possible."

"Aim a bit higher. Not a pawn, not even a knight or a rook. A bishop. A serious piece. Maybe even a queen . . ."

"Tolik, don't exaggerate. Without Zabulon there's no way the Dark Ones can match us. And Zabulon's not in Moscow."

"That's what the Dark Ones say. But who knows what the truth is . . ."

"Zabulon hasn't shown his face much at all recently," Anton put in.

"That's just it. He's been keeping quiet, planning an operation . . . The lousy thing is that I can't imagine what its objectives are. What do we have so far? Two suspicious killings, with absolutely no idea of how they're connected."

"If they are connected at all," said Anton, but even he didn't seem to believe his own words.

"No, say what you like, but they're connected," Tolik insisted stubbornly. "I can sense it. And the link is that magician from out of town."

"Why bother thinking about it?" Tiger Cub asked. "Since Svetlana appeared we've had a substantial advantage. The Dark Ones have yielded one position after another—remember how the boss put the pressure on Zabulon at the last round of negotiations? And Zabulon gave way—what other choice did he really have? It looks as if the Dark Ones have launched an operation to restore the balance. But the timing's terrible—just before Clean Week . . ."

"For the Dark Ones that's the best possible time," Anton growled. "They know we won't start anything serious without a good reason. But so far there doesn't seem to be any reason."

"Be careful what you say . . ." Tolik told him in a pained voice.

The Zhiguli flew on along Leningradsky Prospect, overtaking the advancing dawn.

They drove the rest of the way to the office without saying another word. Either no one wanted to predict the worst, or they all felt they were in for something serious.

Garik was standing outside the entrance, shifting nervously from one foot to the other. And Ilya was there beside him, short of sleep and squinting out from behind his spectacles.

"Right," Tolik said cheerlessly. "Brace yourselves."

Ilya and Garik quickly got into the car, squeezing Tiger Cub from both sides, and Anton immediately realized why they'd got in like that, and what the pale, furious, and therefore very restrained Garik would say next . . .

"The Cosmos Hotel. Andriukha's dead, guys . . ."

Tolik slammed the accelerator to the floor, but even the most powerful car isn't fast enough to overtake death. Tiger Cub jerked feebly, squeezed tight between her friends, and then froze.

"How did it happen?" Anton asked in a dull voice.

"That Dark One—Vitaly Rogoza—just phoned. He said he'd found the body of an Other in his room."

"I'll personally bite his throat out," Tiger Cub promised in a hoarse voice. "And don't you try to stop me!"

"I phoned Bear just in case," Ilya said in a very neutral tone. "I think he's already in the Cosmos."

Anton got the idea that his colleagues had understood everything in advance and come to terms with the fact that a fight was inevitable. He secretly stroked the pistol in the holster under his armpit— the weapon that had never been any real use to him even once.

I had a nagging feeling that the events of the night were still far from over. I felt I was just beginning to be able to foresee the immediate future. Not in detail—far from it, in fact—more as a tangled ball of probability threads. But I had begun to sense where the thickest strands were leading.

Alarm, trouble, disaster, danger—that was what the night had in store for me. At first I thought I would wait for the Dark Ones downstairs, beside their BMW outside the entrance, but then I realized I shouldn't do that. I shouldn't enlighten them as to . . . well, as to my total ignorance. Let them think that I really was playing a game. The chief of the Day Watch was out of town, and the others didn't seem to be any competition for me . . .

But just who was I? Wasn't I aiming too high? Was Moscow so short of powerful magicians? Even if they didn't work in the Watches? I couldn't keep being led on up the steps forever, could I?—there are no infinite stairways. Some way would be found to keep me in check—the Moscow magicians had plenty of experience, many of them had an entire century of it. And I didn't really know what I could do and what I couldn't. I was still an unknown quantity. And how did I know my Power wouldn't evaporate just as miraculously as it had appeared?

So you take your time, Vitalik, don't try to force things along. Better think about what bad things this fading night could bring you. But better not drag things out, lengthen that stride . . .

I walked quickly, as far as Sholkovskoe Shosse, darted into an underpass, and then started hitching a lift on the opposite side of the road.

What I like about Moscow is that even in the dead of night or early in the morning, all you have to do is raise your hand and an automobile will immediately pull in at the curb. In Nikolaev you can stand there for half an hour and no one will even think of stopping. But here everything is decided by money. Everyone needs it.

The Exhibition of Economic Achievements, fifty rubles. The standard rate.

I got into the sporty Volkswagen and set off toward problems that I could almost feel already.

When I reached the hotel, I immediately sensed that my room's defenses had been compromised. The defenses had worked just as they were intended to do, and that was my main problem. Without looking at anyone, I went up to the sixth floor, walked to my suite, put the key in the lock, and froze for a moment, looking at the door.

Okay, whatever was about to happen, I had to go through it.

He was lying in the middle of the lounge with his arms flung out to the sides. There was an expression of childish surprise and resentment on his face, as if he'd opened a wrapper and instead of the candy he'd been hoping for he'd found an angry hornet that had instantly sunk its stinger into his carelessly exposed finger.

He had stumbled into my Shahab's Ring. Not complex magic, but very powerful. And, naturally, he hadn't known the word that was needed. He was the unfortunate young detective, Andriukha Tiunnikov, a Light One from the Night Watch, who had been trying to prove that I'd murdered the girl on Saturday.

If he'd been more experienced, he would never have stuck his nose into the area enclosed by the Ring. I hadn't even set it around the whole room—only the safe with the bag in it.

This was the very last thing I needed—the Light Ones regarded the deaths of ordinary people as poaching, but the killing of an Other was a different matter altogether. It already smacked of a tribunal.

But I had simply closed off my own territory, closed it off in a way that Others understood! This is mine! Keep out! No entry!

Only he hadn't kept out. And he'd met his end in the Twilight . . . The infantile booby! Had he been trying to impress his bosses?

I had to own up. Otherwise they'd ask in a way I couldn't refuse to answer.

I reached for the phone—not my cell, but the ordinary phone that was standing on the table. The number obligingly surfaced from my memory.

"Night Watch? Vitaly Rogoza, Other, Dark. If I'm not mistaken, I have your employee Andrei Tiunnikov here. He's dead. You'd better come . . . Cosmos Hotel, suite six hundred twelve."

Strangely enough, the Light Ones weren't the first to arrive. The moment the first Others reached my floor—there were two of them—I felt as if I were suddenly flooded with energy from someone. The pair were Dark magicians and they were both brimful of a Dark Power that reminded me in some ways of the Twilight, except that it was even denser and darker. A long tongue of Twilight ran straight down through the floors of the hotel, gradually growing thinner as it approached the ground and seeming to run on beyond it, to somewhere lower, somewhere underground.

There was a knock at the door, emphatically correct.

"Yes, yes," I replied, without getting up out of my armchair. "It's open, come in!"

They came in. My acquaintance from the apartment on Pervomaiskaya Street, Shagron. And another one, also a magician, as far as I could tell. A bit overweight, like Shagron, with dark hair. And powerful. More powerful than his partner. But even so, despite my expectations, it was Shagron who started talking. It seemed that the accepted thing among members of the Watches was for the most important member of a team to keep quiet—Anton had preferred to listen too.

"Good morning, colleague."

"What's good about it? You must be joking, colleague."

I deliberately pronounced the word "colleague" in the same tone as Shagron. But he wasn't so easily provoked, and that was where he had the advantage over me. In experience. All I had to rely on were cheap wisecracks like that, plus moments of sudden illumination and the mystical stairway that obligingly offered me one step after another, and then arranged a kick up the backside at the appropriate moment.

"I'm not joking, colleague, simply greeting you. It's a pity you didn't wait for us back there . . . you know where I mean. I'd been counting on having a word with you."

"I didn't want to get in your way," I confessed, and it was more than half-true. A normal response from an Other—Dark or Light.

"I was counting on help. Help from a brother-in-arms. But you chose to disappear."

That "I" was strictly a Dark way of speaking. In Shagron's place, any Light One would definitely have said "We," and been perfectly sincere. And he'd have meant exactly what Shagron had meant, no less sincerely, of course.

"Okay. Let me introduce you. This is Edgar, our colleague from Estonia, recently a member of the Moscow Watch. What have you got here?"

"What I've got here is yet another body," I confessed. "A Light Other. A Watch member. But then you already know all about it, don't you, colleague Edgar?"

"There's not much time? The Light Ones will be here any minute? Is that what you wanted to say?" Edgar asked, casting aside diplomacy and addressing me in a familiar fashion. I realized there was no point in arguing with this dark-haired Estonian.

"Last Saturday evening, when I'd just arrived, this Light One was in charge of the operation dealing with a poaching vampire . . ."

"A vampiress," Edgar corrected me with a frown. "And then?"

"By sheer chance I just happened to be there beside the victim. They found me beside the corpse and recognized me as a Dark One. Clearly out of inexperience—I can't see any other reason—Tiunnikov accused me of what the vampire . . . that is, the vampiress . . . had done. I put him in his place, and I admit I did it quite sharply, but he'd asked for it. And that's really the whole story . . . When I left my room today, I left some protective spells. And when I came in, there he was. He was already beyond my help."

The last phrase simply burst out on its own—I hadn't been planning to say it. It felt like I was beginning to talk nonsense again.

"This snot-nosed kid was in charge of the operation?" Shagron asked incredulously. "When there were Light Ones with far more experience—the tigress, the magicians . . ."

"Tiunnikov was in training, that's perfectly normal," Edgar barked at his partner, and then suddenly glanced at me. "But you set up a Shahab's Ring so strong that it killed the Light Ones' trainee on the spot?"

The question was almost rhetorical. Apparently I'd cast a simple spell, but put too much Power into it. Maybe . . .

I sensed the approach of the Light Ones at the same time as Edgar, just as they were nearing the hotel. A few seconds later Shagron picked them up too.

"What did you tell them?" Edgar asked, obviously in a hurry. "But keep it short."

I sensed that he had covered us with a cowl of invisibility, and quite a powerful one too. Before I said a single word, I added some Power of my own to the cowl, drawn partly from somewhere inside myself, from my own mind, and partly from outside. It happened quite spontaneously, but I read the dumb astonishment in Edgar's eyes.

"I phoned and said there was a dead Light One in my room. And told them his name. That's all."

Edgar gave a barely perceptible nod and glanced significantly at Shagron, who gave the slightest of shrugs.

We stood there in silence until the knock at the door—a far less polite one this time.

The Light Ones didn't wait to be invited. They just walked straight in.

There were five of them—Tolik, Anton, and the girl shape-shifter could barely have had enough time to get from Pervomaiskaya Street to their office. Two others had come with them—a cultured-looking young guy wearing spectacles with eighty-dollar frames and another with a suntanned face, as if it weren't winter in Moscow.

These last two and Tolik carefully examined, probed, and scanned every centimeter of my suite. The walls here had probably never seen such intense magical activity.

Anton and the girl didn't interfere, but I could clearly sense the aversion emanating from them. Not even hatred—the Light Ones don't really even know how to hate properly. More like a desire to pin me into the corner, have me condemned and punished. Or simply to hit me with so much Power that I'd be driven into the Twilight forever.

And I also sensed there was at least one more Light One somewhere outside the room. Probably somewhere else on the same floor, or by the lifts. He was obviously covering the others' backs, and he had shielded himself really well for the job. I only spotted him, you might say, by accident. But I don't think that Shagron and Edgar had any idea he was there.

I frowned. The Light Ones had the numerical advantage—there were twice as many of them. And the two of them that I was seeing for the first time were very powerful magicians, almost certainly first level. In any case, the two of them together would be stronger than Shagron and Edgar. And Anton was no pushover either—he could give Shagron a good fight, or even Edgar. Plus the girl—she was a warrior. And that unknown one somewhere nearby. The balance of forces was not good at all. They'd grind us to dust, grind us as fine as powdered vanilla . . .

Meanwhile the Light Ones had finished their scanning. The one in spectacles came up to me and inquired with emphatic indifference: "Tell me, did you really need to use a protective spell of such great Power?"

"Well, why do you think I would have used so much Power?"

The one in spectacles and the other one I didn't know exchanged a quick glance.

"We demand to see your things."

"Stop, stop," Edgar put in hastily. "On what grounds, exactly?"

The one in spectacles smiled bleakly—with just his lips. "The Night Watch has reason to suspect that a forbidden artifact of immense Power has been smuggled into Moscow. You must know that such actions contravene the terms of the Treaty."

My Dark colleagues looked at me doubtfully. They were apparently expecting some unambiguous response. But what was it? On this occasion my magical internal help-all chose not to prompt me. But on the other hand, I knew perfectly well that there weren't any forbidden artifacts in my bag. And so I gestured magnanimously and said, "Let them look! All night long if they want."

"I protest," Edgar said quietly, and apparently without any great hope. "You don't have the sanction of your chief."

"The protest is rejected," the one in spectacles parried in an inflexible voice. "I'm the chief here. Show us your things, Dark One."

I didn't have to be asked twice. I neutralized the remains of the defenses with a single gesture and opened the door of the safe, where my bag was lying in total isolation, apart from a pair of clothes brushes. Part of its logo seemed to gaze out at us reproachfully: Fuj . . . I imagined a bored, squeaky voice pronouncing it as "phooey . . ."

I took the bag and tipped its contents out onto the bed. The Light Ones didn't take much interest in my things, but the sight of the final plastic bag put them on their guard—the second unknown magician even grasped the amulet in the pocket of his jacket.

When I shook the money out onto the bedcover, everybody looked at me. My own side and the Light Ones. As if I were some kind of psycho. An absolutely hopeless case.

"There," I said. "That's all I have. A hundred thousand. Actually a bit less now."

The magician in spectacles stepped toward the bed and rummaged disdainfully through my things, glancing into the plastic bags. But I realized that what he really wanted was tactile contact.

He wasn't even satisfied with remote scanning!

Good grief, what did they suspect me of? Probably some cretin really had tried to bring something forbidden into Moscow, and since I'd overdone it a bit protecting my miserable heap of bucks, now they suspected me of everything. That was really funny, and it was getting funnier all the time.

The one in spectacles spent about a minute sniffing at my baggage. Then he gave up.

"All right. There's nothing here. We're declaring this suite off-limits. You'll have to change rooms."

The girl shape-shifter started and gave him a puzzled look. He spread his hands and I understood the meaning of his gesture. There was nothing to charge me with. No grounds. The shape-shifter tensed up, but the other magician put his hand on her shoulder, as if he were warning her not to do anything rash.

"Ye-es?" Edgar drawled insinuatingly, and something Estonian finally came through in that "Ye-es" of his. "Change rooms? In that case we request official permission for a seventh-level intervention. In order to avoid unnecessary questions from the hotel management."

The Light Ones were annoyed by that—but then, they were all annoyed already in any case.

"Why? We can influence the staff without any psychic correction."

"But you have a habit of declaring any influence a violation," Edgar explained in a very innocent voice.

"I will per . . ." Ilya drawled slowly, and then broke off. "No. I won't permit it. Anton, you go with them and do it all yourself. Try to make sure they move him as far away from here as possible, so that . . . Anyway, just do it."

Edgar sighed in disappointment. "Okay . . . if you say no, then it's no. But tell me, dear fellow, do you have any more questions for our colleague?"

Edgar's tone of voice was so prim and polite that I was afraid the Light Ones might decide he was mocking them. But they clearly knew Edgar pretty well. And maybe this caustic, biting politeness was the norm of behavior between the two Watches.

"No, we don't dare detain him any longer. But permit us to remind you that until our investigations are concluded, he is forbidden to leave Moscow, in connection with three cases."

"I remember," I put in as innocently as I could.

"In that case, permit us to take our leave. Colleague Vitaly, pack your things . . ."

I shoved all my bits and pieces into the first plastic bags that came to hand, put the plastic bags into the large bag, picked up my jacket from where I had dropped it on the armchair, and stood up. Edgar pointed to the door in invitation.

We went out into the corridor and took the elevator down to the vestibule, where Edgar suddenly turned to the Light One with us.

"Anton! Our colleague is not going to stay in this hotel any longer. We're taking him with us. If you need him, you can inquire at the Day Watch office."

The Light One seemed to have been taken by surprise; he glanced uncertainly at the hotel administrator sleeping behind his counter, then nodded indecisively. And we set off toward the exit.

I didn't put my jacket on because I'd already spotted the familiar BMW standing outside the door of the hotel—I'd only been able to see it because I was an Other.

It was warm and cozy inside the car. And spacious too—my knees didn't press against the back of the front seat. I made myself comfortable and asked, "And where am I going to stay now?"

"At the Day Watch office, colleague. Or, rather, in the office hotel. You should have gone there straightaway."

"If only I'd known where to go . . ." I muttered.

The BMW went darting off, turned smartly out of the parking

lot toward the entrance, dived under the boom almost before it had time to rise high enough, and eased into the sparse flow of traffic on Peace Prospect.

Shagron might not be the strongest of magicians, but he could drive a car superbly. Peace Prospect flashed by and disappeared, followed by the arc of the Garden Ring Road. And all I saw of Tverskaya Street was an endless row of shop windows with tinted glass . . . but then, it wasn't really endless after all.

We got out of the car very close to the Kremlin. The magicians left their BMW at the curb, without even bothering to lock it. I decided to take a look at it through the Twilight, simply out of curiosity and a desire to assess the quality of the protective spells so that I wouldn't overdo things again.

I was astounded. Not by the sight of the car, but by the sight of the building, which had looked so ordinary in the ordinary world.

In the Twilight the building had grown by three whole floors. One of them was inserted between the ordinary first and second floors, while the other two were on top, making the already big building even taller. The Twilight floors were made of polished black granite. Almost all the windows were curtained and dark, but the first weak rays of sunlight were already glinting on the white boxes of modern air conditioners.

I forgot about the protective spells in an instant.

There was a small portal leading straight out onto Tverskaya Street; behind the glass door I could sense, rather than see, the silhouette of an Other.

"Well, well, well!" I said. My voice sounded hollow, like all sound in the Twilight. My colleagues all turned their heads as if by command.

"What? Haven't you seen it before?"

"No."

"It impresses everybody the first time. Come on, you'll have plenty of time to admire it."

We went up a few steps and found ourselves in a tiny duty office. The vague figure behind the door had materialized into a skinny, dismal-looking young guy—I think he was a shape-shifter. But he was laughing in joyful delight as he read Victor Pelevin's story, "A Werewolf Problem in Central Russia."

But the moment Edgar entered the duty office, the young guy was transformed. His eyes flashed and the book dropped onto the desk.

"Hi, Oleg." Edgar greeted him in a Baltic accent that had suddenly appeared out of nowhere.

Shagron simply nodded.

I decided to say hello too: "Good morning."

"This is a colleague of ours from Ukraine," Edgar said, introducing me. "When he wants, let him through into the guest sector without any checks."

"Understood," Oleg agreed immediately. "Shall I enter him in the database?"

"Yes."

Oleg glanced into my eyes and bared his teeth in a friendly grin, read my registration mark with some effort, sat down at the desk, and took a notebook PC out of one of the drawers.

"And where's your partner?" Edgar asked.

Oleg's face took on a guilty expression.

"He went out for cigarettes . . . Just for a moment."

"Let's go," Edgar said with a sigh, taking me by the sleeve and drawing me toward the elevators. Shagron had already pressed the call button.

We seemed to be in the elevator for a long time. At least longer that I'd been expecting. But then I remembered the additional floors and everything fell into place.

"The guest sector is on the ninth floor," Edgar explained. "Basically it's just like a hotel, only it's free. I don't think there's anyone staying there at the moment."

The elevator doors parted soundlessly and we found ourselves in a square foyer, decorated with a rational combination of luxury and economical functionality. Leather divans and armchairs, a live palm tree in a tub, engravings on the walls, a carpet on the parquet floor.

A counter like the ones in hotels, but there was no sign at all of any table and chair for a bellhop. Just a locked secretaire, with an elegant metal key protruding from the lock.

Edgar opened the secretaire to reveal neat rows of horizontal wooden pegs, with a key hanging on each one. And beside the pegs there were numbers.

But I was being too hasty—there were no keys on two of the pegs: numbers two and four.

"Take your pick. If the key's here, it means the apartment's free."

He said "apartment," and not "suite," as if the fact that this accommodation for Others was free distinguished it from faceless hotel suites and put it in the category of places that could be called home.

I took key number eight. From the right end of the second row.

"You can look the place over later," Edgar told me. "Leave your things and come straight back."

I nodded, wondering what my Dark colleagues were planning. No doubt a polite but thorough interrogation.

That was okay. I'd survive. They were my kind, after all.

The apartment really was an apartment. With a kitchen, a separate toilet, and three spacious rooms—and a huge hallway. It was a typical Stalin-period apartment refurbished to "European" standards. The ceilings were three and a half meters high, if not four.

I hung my jacket on the coatrack and dropped my bag in the middle of the hallway. Then I went out into the corridor and pulled the door shut.

I could hear faint music coming from apartment number four: A minute earlier, as I was walking past, it had been something light and foreign. But now the song had changed. The words were almost drowned out by the harsh rhythm and the background of hard rock—I guessed at them rather than heard them:

Cast down by the power of fate,
You are humiliated and crushed.
It's time to forget who you were,

And remember who you've become!
Cast into the depths, where it doesn't matter
Why fame used to court you before—
Villains set a brand of fire on you,
And your soul is empty.
People in the depths prowl through the darkness,
Ready to eat each other up.
Anything to prolong this wild life,
And snatch something for themselves . . .
Angry like them, all angry and pitiful,
You rush round and round in the same herd,
With them you crawl for food at knifepoint,
Like a slave or a prophet.

I don't know why, but I froze outside that other person's door. These were more than just simple words. I absorbed them through my skin, with my entire body. I had forgotten who I used to be, but how could I remember who I'd become? And hadn't I entered a new circle now, running with a herd that I still didn't know?

Oh, if I could listen just to silence.
Not lies, or flattery, not the midday or the darkness.
Be like snow melting in the sun,
And love, knowing no betrayal,
Then you would die of anguish and anger!

No, I clearly wouldn't get any chance to listen to silence in the immediate future. Too many others had taken an interest in my modest person. Light Ones and Dark Ones . . .

Meanwhile the singer's voice had grown stronger and taken on a triumphant, challenging note:

Hey, you inhabitants of the skies!
Which of you has not plumbed the depths?

Without passing through hell,
You can never build heaven!
Hey, you inhabitants of the depths!
The thunder is laughing at you.
To be on equal terms with them—
There is only one way upward!
There is only one way upward . . .

So that was it . . . The way upward. And you couldn't get to heaven unless you'd already done your time rattling around in hell. Except that heaven and hell were different for everyone—but then that was what Kipelov was really singing about anyway.

Strange. I'd heard the song before, and the singer's name had stuck in my memory. I'd even included it in the mini-disk I put together for my player. But now it sounded completely new; it had suddenly slashed across my mind like an invisible shard of broken glass.

"Colleague! Please hurry!" Edgar called to me.

I stepped regretfully away from the door.

I'll have to listen to it later . . . Buy the whole album and listen to it . . .

The singer's voice faded away behind me:

But if the light flares up in your brain
And dislodges all the submission,
The old days will come alive in your soul,
And a new sin will be committed.
Blood on your hands, blood on the stones,
And over the bodies and the pitiful backs
Of those willing to die as slaves,
You strive upward once again.

It somehow seemed to me that Kipelov knew only too well what he was singing about. About blood. About the lower depths. About the sky. This long-haired idol of the Russian heavy metal set could easily turn out to be an Other. At least, I wouldn't be surprised if he did.

I went up to the next floor with Edgar and Shagron, and we found ourselves in a genuine office space, with a large hall divided into little booths separated off by screens, individual offices at one side and an open area overlooking Tverskaya Street through a huge window of lightly tinted glass. I noticed that the Dark Ones used hardly any desktop PCs: at least the three Watch staff members who were there—they must have been either very late owls or very early larks—were all sitting with their noses stuck in the screens of their notebooks.

"Hellemar!" Edgar called, and one of the three—a werewolf, like the guard on duty downstairs—reluctantly tore himself away from some game on the screen.

"Yes, Chief?"

"I want an urgent news update! All movements of reagents or artifacts of great Power. Lost, disappeared, smuggled. All the latest events!"

"What's happened?" the werewolf Hellemar asked. "Is there something dangerous going on?"

"The Light Ones have information that someone's trying to smuggle an artifact into Moscow. Move it, Hellemar!"

Hellemar turned to the other players:

"Hey, you blockheads! Get to work!"

The blockheads instantly dropped what they'd been doing and seconds later I could hear the quiet rustling of keyboards, and on the screens the endless corridors filled with monsters had been replaced by the bright windows of Netscape.

Edgar took me into an office separated off from the large hall by a glass wall and blinds. Shagron went off somewhere for a moment, but he soon came back with a jar of Tchibo and a carton of Finnish glacier water. He poured the water into an electric kettle and pressed the appropriate switch. The kettle started murmuring industriously almost immediately.

"I hope you have sugar here?" Shagron muttered.

"I'll find some." Edgar lowered himself into one armchair and offered me the other: "Have a seat, colleague. You don't mind if I call you simply Vitaly, do you?"

"Of course not. Feel free."

"Excellent. Well, then, Vitaly, I'll do the talking, and you correct me if I get something wrong. Agreed?"

"Certainly," I said readily. Because I had almost no idea what weird stories would surface out of my subconscious for me to tell to these intent agents of the Day Watch.

"Have I understood correctly that you possess no information about the aforementioned artifact?"

"You have," I confirmed.

"A pity," Edgar said with genuine disappointment. "It would have greatly simplified matters . . ."

As a matter of fact, not only didn't I possess any information about the aforementioned artifact, I didn't possess any information at all about any artifacts that Edgar might be interested in. This was no doubt an area where experienced Others felt like connoisseurs, but I still understood less about it than a pig does about oranges.

"Then let's move on to the next point. You arrived in Moscow from Ukraine, if I understand correctly?"

"Yes. From Nikolaev."

"For what purpose?"

I pondered for about half a minute. Nobody tried to hurry me.

"It's hard to say," I confessed honestly. "Clearly without any particular purpose. I just got fed up sitting at home doing nothing."

"You were only initiated very recently, am I right?"

"Yes."

"Did you just get the urge to see a bit of the world?"

"Probably."

"Then why Moscow, and not the Bahamas, for instance?"

I shrugged. But really—why? Surely not just because I didn't have a passport for foreign travel yet?

"I don't know. The Bahamas are a place to go in summer."

"It's summer now in the Southern Hemisphere. And there are plenty of places to go."

Yes, that was true. I hadn't thought about that.

"All the same, I don't know," I answered. "Later, maybe . . ."

I had the feeling that Edgar wanted to ask about something else, but at this point Hellemar entered the office without knocking. His eyes were as wide as the cartoon mouse Jerry's when he suddenly spots his eternal pursuer, Tom, just behind him.

"Chief! Berne, Fafnir's Talon! It's been taken from the Inquisition's vault! The whole of Europe's been in an uproar for over two hours now!"

Shagron couldn't restrain himself—he leapt to his feet. Edgar held back, but his eyes glinted and even without entering the Twilight I could see the orange streaks that sprang up in his aura. But he quickly took himself in hand.

"Is this open information?"

"No. It's restricted. The Inquisition hasn't made any official statements yet."

"Your source?"

The werewolf hesitated. "The source is unofficial. But reliable."

"Hellemar," Edgar said with a hint of emphasis, "your source?"

"One of our men in the Prague information agency," Hellemar confessed. "An Other. Dark. I caught him in a private chat room."

"I see, I see . . ."

I wanted very much to ask a few questions, but naturally all I could do for the time being was stare stupidly and keep quiet as I absorbed the important but, alas, incomprehensible things they were saying.

"And how do the Light Ones know about this?" Shagron asked in puzzlement.

"Who can tell?" said Edgar, twitching his eyebrows in a funny manner. "They have a wide network of informers . . ."

"Status 'Aleph,'" Edgar said abruptly to Hellemar. "Call in the staff . . ."

About half an hour later the office hall was crowded. Of course, all the individuals there were Others. And all Dark.

But I still didn't understand a thing.

When Anton got back to suite six hundred twelve, Ilya was sitting in an armchair and massaging his temples, and Garik was striding nervously to and fro across the carpet between the window and the divan. Tolik and Tiger Cub were sitting on the divan, and Bear was hovering in the doorway of the bedroom.

". . . he spotted me, by the way," Bear was saying gloomily. "Your 'cloud' didn't help."

"The Estonian?"

"No, the Estonian didn't spot me. And neither did Shagron, of course. But the other one did, almost straightaway."

"But that's nonsense, guys. He can't be more powerful than the Estonian, can he?" said Garik.

"But why can't he, really?" Ilya asked without raising his head. "A couple of hours ago I thought I knew all four of the Dark Ones in Moscow I wouldn't be able to handle one-on-one. But now I'm not sure of anything."

Anton slumped back against the refrigerator. The question his tongue was poised to ask had remained unspoken so far—the conversation was more interesting than Anton had thought it would be at the beginning.

And then Tiger Cub got in before him: "Ilya! Why don't you fill us in? About the artifact."

Ilya abruptly stood up and began: "To keep it short, Fafnir's Talon has been removed from the Inquisition's vault in Berne. Two . . ."—he glanced at his watch—"no, already three hours ago now. The Swiss department is in a panic. The Inquisition is fuming and thundering, but so far it hasn't issued an official communiqué. The details are unknown; all we do know is that the Talon is at the seasonal peak of its Power. In the Dark phase, of course. Simple calculations indicate that liberating even part of the Power accu-

mulated by the Talon in the territory of Central Russia is likely to
result in powerful discharges, up to and including a localized Inferno
breakthrough. And that's the way things stand . . ."

"And Zabulon's not in Moscow . . ." Tolik drawled with slow emphasis.

"You mean the Dark Ones are behind this?" asked Tiger Cub.

"Well, we aren't, are we?" Ilya asked, and his shoulders twitched
as if he were suddenly feeling chilly.

"Does Gesar know about this?" she asked.

"Of course," Ilya said. "He was the one who told me. He ordered
me not to worry, but just keep on working away . . ."

Ilya sat down again.

"I don't even know what to think," he said in a voice that somehow sounded tough and helpless at the same time. "To be quite
honest, when I heard about a Shahab's Ring killing a Light One, I
suspected the Talon was already here. There's no point in setting up
a Ring with such monstrous Power—it's just a waste, a sheer, unnecessary waste. I'd understand if it was to protect the Talon, but for
a lousy heap of bucks . . . it's simply idiotic . . ."

"A Dark One wouldn't have left the Talon in his suite without
someone to watch it," Garik put in.

"Of course not. It would be stupid," said Tiger Cub.

"Yes, it would," Ilya agreed. "But we had to check."

"And what can we do now?" Tiger Cub asked gloomily. "Now
Andriukha's dead, and we can't even punish his killer?"

"Katya," Ilya said, looking at her sympathetically, "it's sad, but
that's the way it is. And now we've been hit with a problem that
makes Andrei's death seem almost unimportant. Our analysts have
been following the approximate balance between global nexuses of
Power since four o'clock this morning. If the Talon is moved, the balance is bound to be disrupted."

"And have they come up with anything?"

"Yes. About an hour ago it became clear that the Talon is either
already in Moscow or due to appear here at any moment."

"Hang on," Tolik put in again, "so the recurrences of poaching and unmotivated aggression by Dark Ones are due to the influence of the Talon?"

"Probably."

"But the first incident took place on Saturday!" Tiger Cub protested in surprise.

Ilya massaged his temples again; it was obvious now that he was very tired. "The Talon is a very powerful thing, Tiger Cub. The lines of probability extend far into the future. And the Dark Ones are more powerfully influenced by Dark artifacts than we are. So the small fry have already started running wild . . ."

"If it's such a powerful thing, how come the Inquisition has mislaid it?"

"I don't know," Ilya retorted, "I wasn't there. But I'm quite sure of one thing: If it's possible to do something, sooner or later someone's going to do it."

"Our people are coming," Garik remarked, off the point.

He was right—someone from the service section had arrived. Obviously Andrei Tiunnikov's body had to be taken away after the poor unfortunate had stumbled into a matrix of Power that was still way beyond his level.

"And what about this Dark One?" Anton finally asked. "Do you think he's connected with the thieves?"

"Not necessarily." Ilya watched morosely as Tiunnikov's body was zipped into a black polythene bag. "He could be distracting us. Or he might not even be aware of what he's doing. That's what it actually looks like most of all. The Talon is controlling him, or the person who now possesses it. And the Dark One has definitely become more powerful since our clash with him last Saturday in the alley near the All-Union Exhibition."

"Then shouldn't we be following him?" Tolik suggested. "If he's connected with the Talon, isn't he bound to lead us to the thieves?"

"If he is connected, he'll lead us to them."

"And if he doesn't?"

Ilya sighed. "Then we'll have more surprises and emergencies. And that Dark One will be there all the time, just on the edge of our field of vision. He's bound to be."

"Wait," Garik said tensely. "What if he's predestined for the Talon?"

"That's what I'm afraid of . . ."

Anton shook his head sharply. After the events of a year and a half earlier, for a while he'd thought he could regard himself as an experienced and hardened watchman. But now he felt like an apprentice among virtuosos again. And he didn't like having to admit it.

The phone rang—the local hotel phone. It felt strange to hear the ring of an ordinary phone after the trilling of all the cells.

"Hello?" Tolik picked up the receiver, listened for a moment, and turned to Ilya. "For you. It's Semyon."

Ilya took the receiver and held it to his ear, then immediately ran a piercing glance over all of them.

"Mount up, guys. The boss is already in the office."

Anton thought with a vague feeling of weariness that now he would see Svetlana again. And again he would feel the gulf between them widening with every second.

I didn't stay in the Day Watch office for long after it livened up. I was dozing off where I sat, so I was simply sent off to catch up on my sleep. I didn't object, because I'd been on my feet for more than twenty-four hours and I couldn't keep my eyes open.

As I slipped into sleep I could hear the faint strains of Kipelov's singing coming from somewhere:

Hey, you inhabitants of the skies!
Which of you hasn't plumbed the depths?

CHAPTER 3

I WOKE UP WHEN I REALIZED I WAS BEING CALLED. CALLED THE same way that vampires call their prey. Still not fully awake, I got up and fumbled for my clothes on the chair.

The Call was sweet and alluring, it enveloped me—caressing and urging me, it was impossible, absolutely impossible to resist it. Sometimes it sounded like music, sometimes like singing, sometimes like whispering, and in every form it was perfection, the reflection of my own soul.

And then, like a sudden blow just below the knees, came the jerk up onto the next step.

The Call instantly lost its power over me, although it hadn't stopped. I dropped the trousers I was holding and gave my head a quick shake . . .

Oh, that hurt . . .

The sweet hypnotic syrup slowly drained out of me. Drained out and disappeared somewhere under the floor. Spent Light energy, faded Power.

I suddenly understood very clearly why vampires' victims smile as they present their necks to be bitten. When the call sounds, they're happy. This is the sweet moment they have been waiting for all their lives, and compared with this, life is as empty and gray as the world of the Twilight.

The Call is a kind of gift. A liberation. Only it was still too soon for me to be set free.

I had no idea why, but this time the new ability I acquired was immunity to the magical Call. I could hear it and understand it, but I remained completely in control of myself. And naturally, I screened my mind off from the caller, so that he wouldn't suspect his victim had been transformed from a sleepwalker into a hunter . . .

"A hunter?" I asked myself curiously. "Hmm . . ."

So I was going hunting. Well now, that was interesting.

The Call continued.

"Well, well," I thought. "This is the residence of the Day Watch. Everything here is saturated with magic. The defenses here are quite incredible. But the Call is still effective . . . was effective?"

The Light Ones had invested a lot of effort in this trick. And in concealing it from prying eyes. It was their good luck that the chief of the Day Watch was out of Moscow—the Light Ones would never have been able to trick him, no matter how hard they tried.

Meanwhile I calmly got dressed, thinking sadly that my dream of visiting a restaurant and grabbing a bowl of hot, spicy soup and a plate of something like duck in cherry sauce would be postponed again for an indefinite period. I set two or three weak protective spells and left my suite . . . I mean, my apartment. If they called them apartments here, I might as well maintain the tradition. I had the flat bread-cake of my mini disk-player attached to my belt, of course; I stuck the little beads of the earphones into my ears and pulled my cap down tight onto my head.

"Why not set it on random selection?" I thought, manipulating the controls. "Play a little game with fate."

And once again fate chose me a song from the album by Kipelov and Mavrin. A different one this time.

There is silence above me,
A sky full of rain,

The rain goes straight through me,
But there's no more pain.
While stars whispered coldly,
We burned our final bridge.
And everything has tumbled into the abyss
I shall be free
From evil and good,
My soul's been walking the razor's edge.

Mm . . . well. A rather gloomy prophecy. Just when was it that I burned my final bridge? Or maybe that was what I'd just left my apartment to do, instead of going up to the next floor and inquiring after the fate of some extremely powerful Talon or other? But I was being urged to follow the Call by that certain something that had already been lying concealed somewhere deep inside me for a while.

I'm free! Like a bird in the heavens.
I'm free! I've forgotten the meaning of fear.
I'm free! I am the wild wind's equal.
I'm free! In the real world, not in a dream.

Kipelov's voice was no less enchanting than the Call. It had a hypnotic resonance; it was as convincing as truth itself. And I suddenly realized I was listening to a hymn of the Dark Ones. An embodiment of their ideal of rebellious souls who acknowledge no boundaries or rules:

There is silence above me,
The sky full of fire,
The light goes straight through me,
But I'm free once again,
Free from love,
Free from hate and from rumors,
From a fate foretold in advance

And from earthly shackles,
From evil and from good.
My soul no longer holds a place for you.

Freedom. The only thing that genuinely interests us. Freedom from everything. Even from domination of the world, and it's incredibly sad that the Light Ones just can't understand that and believe it; they just carry on spinning their interminable intrigues, and just to maintain the status quo we have no choice but to obstruct them.

The elevator slid smoothly downward, past the Twilight floors and the ordinary ones. I'm free . . .

If Kipelov was an Other, he had to be Dark. No one else could sing about freedom like that. And no one but the Dark Ones would hear the song's most profound, true meaning!

The two taciturn warlocks on watch below let me out without any trouble—Edgar had done well to have the image of my registration seal entered in the operational database. I walked out onto Tverskaya Street, into the thickening dusk of another Moscow evening, and set out toward the Call, but free from it. And from everything in the world.

Who wanted me so badly? There are no vampires among the Light Ones—no ordinary vampires, that is. All Others are energy vampires—they can all draw Power from people. From their fears, from their joys, from their sufferings. The only fundamental difference between us and the Twilight moss is that we're able to think and move about. And we don't use accumulated Power simply for nourishment.

The Call led me along Tverskaya Street, away from the Kremlin, toward the Belorussian railroad station. I walked along, all alone in the evening crowd, as if I'd been singled out, chosen. And I had been chosen—by the Call. Nobody saw me, nobody noticed me. Nobody was interested in me—not the girls warming themselves up in the automobiles, not their pimps, not the tough-looking young guys in the foreign cars pulled up at the curb. Nobody.

A right turn. Onto Strastnoi Boulevard.

The Call was getting stronger. I could feel it—that meant the encounter would be soon.

The herds of automobiles tore through the driving, sticky snow, the fine snowflakes dancing whimsical roundelays in the beams of their headlights.

Cold and dusk. Moscow in winter.

The snow settled in an even layer on the paths of the boulevard and on the benches that were empty at this time of year, and on the bushes, and on the railings that separated the roadway from the pedestrian park area.

They tried to grab me halfway toward Karetny Ryad.

The spell of isolation seemed to fall from the sky—ordinary people just lost interest in what fate had in store for the boulevard, the cars carried on rushing past, minding their own business, the small number of pedestrians who were nearby faltered for a moment and then wandered away, even if they had been moving toward me.

The Light Ones slid out of the Twilight one after another. Four of them. Two magicians and two shape-shifters, already in battle form. A massive polar bear as white as snow and a tigress with bright ginger stripes.

I was almost flattened when the magicians struck together from both sides. But they had underestimated their quarry—the blow had been calculated for the old me, the one that would have submitted to the Call.

I had already become someone else.

Mentally parting my hands, I halted the walls that were about to come together and envelop me. I halted them, drew in Power, and pushed them away from myself. Not very hard.

I don't know what a tsunami looks like—I've never seen one—but it was the first thing that came to mind when I examined the result.

The Light magicians' walls, which had appeared so monolithic and impregnable only a second earlier, crumpled like rice-paper partitions. Both magicians were swept away, tossed onto the snow, and dragged about ten meters across the ground, and only the railings fencing the park off from the road prevented them from falling under the wheels of the cars. A cloud of powdery snow flew up into the air.

The Light Ones probably realized that they couldn't take me with just magic, so then the shape-shifters came rushing at me in their animal forms.

I hurriedly drew more Power from wherever I could, and immediately there was a dull thud on the road, followed by the tinkle of broken glass, then another thud, followed by the carsplitting screech of car horns.

I took the bear's impact on a Concave Shield and sent him tumbling away along the boulevard. At first I simply dodged the tigress.

I'd taken a dislike to her from the very beginning.

I don't know where shape-shifting magicians get the mass for transformation. In her human form this girl couldn't have weighed more than forty-five or fifty kilos. But now she was at least a hundred and fifty kilos of muscles, sinews, claws, and teeth. A genuine combat-killing machine.

The Light Ones like that.

"Hey!" I shouted. "Wait. Maybe we can talk?"

The magicians were back on their feet, and they made another attempt to snare me, but it didn't cost me much of an effort to tie the greedy, trembling threads of energy into knots and fling them back at their owners. Both shots hit their targets again, but this time no one was sent skidding onto his back—I had simply returned their own energy. The bear stood on one side, shifting his weight menacingly from one foot to the other. He was hunching up, as if he were about to stand on his hind legs.

"I wouldn't advise it," I told him, and struck at the attacking tigress.

Not too hard. I didn't want to kill her.

"Just what is the damn problem?" I shouted angrily. "Or is this just the way things are done in Moscow?"

Calling the Night Watch would have been stupid—my attackers served in the Watch themselves. Maybe I should get help from the Day Watch? Especially since it was no real distance—their office was very near and I could be there in a flash. But would it do me any good?

The magicians weren't about to give up; one was holding a flaming wand charged up to the hilt, and the other had some kind of restraining amulet that looked pretty powerful too.

It took an entire two seconds to deal with the amulet—I had to tear apart the net that was cast over me with an ordinary Triple Dagger—but the amount of Power that went into that extremely simple spell was enough to reduce the entire center of Moscow to ashes. Then the second Light magician hit me with the Fire of Bethlehem, but his blow only made me angry and, I think, even stronger.

I froze his wand. Simply turned it into a long icicle and put a spell of rejection on it. Fragments of ice spurted out of the Light One's hands like some weird, cold firework display, and at the same time the liberated energy went soaring up into the heavens.

I couldn't really dump on the people around us, could I? I'd already done enough damage with those collisions on the nearby intersections . . .

The bear stayed put. Apparently he'd realized that, despite their numerical superiority, the balance of Power was far from equal. But the tigress just wouldn't stop. She came for me with all the aggression of a crazed female animal when an enemy gets too close to her young. Her eyes blazed with unconcealed hatred, as yellow as the flames on church candles.

The tigress was taking revenge. Taking revenge on me, a Dark One, for all her old grudges and losses. For Andrei, who had been killed by me. And who knows for what else . . . And she didn't intend to stop for anything.

I don't want to say she had nothing to avenge—the Watches have always fought, and I'm not in the habit of mincing words. But I didn't intend to die.

I'm free. Free to punish anyone who gets in my way and refuses to resolve things peacefully. Wasn't that what the song had been trying to tell me?

I struck out at her with the Transylvanian Mist.

The tigress's body was twisted and stretched, and even above the roar of engines and the piercing beeping of horns I heard the crunching of bones quite clearly. The spell crumpled the shape-shifter the same way a child crumples a plasticine figure. The broken ribs tore through the skin and their bloody ends thrust into the snow. The head was squashed into a flat, striped pancake. In an instant the beautiful beast was transformed into a tangled mess of bloody flesh.

With a final, calculated blow, I consigned the tigress's soul to the Twilight.

Once I'd begun, I had no right to stop.

The Light Ones froze. Even the bear stopped stamping his feet.

And what now? I thought wearily.

Maybe I would have had to kill them all, but thank heaven—or hell—it didn't come to that.

"Day Watch!" I heard a familiar voice say. "An attack on a Dark One has been registered. Leave the Twilight!"

Edgar spoke sternly and without any Baltic accent.

But he needn't have said that about the Twilight. Those who were alive hadn't been fighting in the Twilight, and the tigress had no-where to come back to.

"The Day Watch demands that a tribunal be convened immedi-ately," Edgar said ominously. "And in the meantime be so good as to summon the chief of the Night Watch."

"Why, he'll scatter all of you like kittens," one of the Light magi-cians said angrily.

"No, he won't," Edgar snapped, and pointed at me. "Not with him here. Or haven't you got the point yet?"

I just barely caught the movement as someone shuffled Power in space. Then a swarthy man with pointed features appeared nearby.

He was wearing a colorful Eastern robe and looked totally absurd in the middle of the snowy boulevard.

"I'm already here," he barked, mournfully surveying the scene of the recent battle.

"Gesar!" Edgar said in a more lively voice. "Hello. In the chief's absence you will have to explain yourself to me."

"To you?" said Gesar, glancing sideways at the Estonian. "You're not worthy."

"Then to him," said Edgar, shrugging his shoulders and shuddering as if he felt cold. "Or is he not worthy either?"

"No, I'll explain myself to him," Gesar said coolly and turned toward me. His gaze was as bottomless as eternity. "Get out of Moscow," he said with almost no emotion at all. "Right now. Catch a train or ride a broomstick, but just clear out. You've already killed twice."

"As I see it," I remarked as amicably as I could, "certain other individuals have attempted to kill me. And all I did was defend myself."

Gesar turned his back to me—he didn't want to listen. He didn't want to speak to a Dark One who had dispatched one of his best warriors into the Twilight forever.

"Let's get out of here," he said to his people.

"Hey, hey!" Edgar protested angrily. "They're criminals, they're not going anywhere, in the name of the Treaty I forbid it!"

Gesar turned back toward the Estonian. "Yes they are. And you can't do anything about it. They're under my protection."

I was seriously expecting a hike up onto the next step because the powers that I already had were enough for me to realize I couldn't go head to head with Gesar yet. He'd crush me. Not without an effort—after all, I'd already come a long way up the invisible stairway. My powers were pretty strong. But he'd still crush me.

But nothing happened. Probably the time hadn't come yet for me to fight Gesar.

Edgar gave me a plaintive glance—apparently he'd been hoping for great things from me.

The Light Ones slipped away into the Twilight, taking with them the remains of their dead sister-in-arms, and then they dived deeper, to the second level. It was over.

"I really can't stop him," I admitted guiltily. "Sorry, Edgar."

"A pity," the Estonian said, with just his lips.

They took me to the Day Watch office in the trusty BMW—for the first time in Moscow I was feeling tired.

But still as free as before.

I paid the price for using so much Power—I can barely remember how they drove me back, urged me toward the elevator, led me to the office, sat me in an armchair, and stuck a cup of coffee in my hand. I had a painful ache in my overworked muscles, an ache in my entire being, which just a short while ago had been commanding the powers of the Twilight. I'd beaten them off with convincing skill—it would be a long time before the Light Ones forgot this battle. And my attackers hadn't been young novices either—I reckoned that both Light Ones had been first-level magicians at least.

"Give the analysts a kick up the backside," Edgar ordered one of his subordinates. "I want to find out at last what's going on."

I glanced at him, and Edgar realized I was coming around.

"Talk to me!" he said.

"A Call!" I said in a hoarse voice, and started to cough. I tried to take a sip of coffee, burned myself, and hissed in pain. "A Call," I said when I could talk again. "They caught me while I was sleeping."

"A Call?" Shagron echoed in surprise. He was sitting in an armchair like mine at the next desk. "The Light Ones haven't used that for about thirty years . . ."

"They caught you with a Call in the Day Watch building?" Edgar asked suspiciously. "That's really something! And you mean no one else noticed anything?"

"No. It was a very subtle call, aimed with masterly precision and camouflaged as natural background noise from the residential floors."

"And you submitted to it?"

"Of course not." I made another attempt to take a sip of coffee, this time successfully. "But I decided to investigate what the Light Ones were up to."

"And you didn't tell anyone?" Edgar was balancing halfway between disbelief and annoyance. "That was a crazy risk . . ."

"If I'd gone trailing after the Call with backup, they'd have spotted it in a moment," I explained. "No, I had to go alone and without cover. So I did. They tried to grab me on Strastnoi Boulevard and I had to fight them off. I knocked the tigress down two or three times and tried to persuade her to stop, and it was only after that I hit her really hard."

Edgar stared at me without blinking.

"You're a dark horse, Vitaly," he said.

"Yes, Dark," I confirmed happily. "They don't come any Darker."

"Are you a magician beyond classification?" he asked.

"Alas, no," I said, spreading my hands—but slowly, so as not to spill the coffee. "Otherwise I wouldn't have let Gesar go."

Edgar drummed his fingers on the desk, squinting sideways impatiently at the door.

"What are those analysts doing . . ." he muttered.

The door opened and a brisk middle-aged woman, a witch, appeared in the doorway, with two men, both magicians.

"Hello, Anna Tikhonovna," Shagron greeted her hastily. He ought to have been more powerful than the witch, but he seemed to be afraid of her. And he was right, of course. A witch's Power is slightly different in nature from a magician's. And a witch can easily screw things up even for a very powerful magician.

Edgar just nodded.

"Is this him?" one of the magicians asked, looking at me.

"Yes, Yura."

Yura was an old and powerful magician—I realized that straightaway. I also realized that Yura wasn't his real name. Magicians like that keep their real names hidden so incredibly deep, there's no way you can ever get to them.

And that's the right way. If you're really following the path of freedom.

"Have a seat, Anna Tikhonovna," said Shagron, giving up his armchair and going across to join the magicians, who had occupied the broad windowsill.

"Edgar," said the witch. "The Light Ones went for broke. They haven't pulled anything as wild as this since '49. They must have really serious reasons to violate the Treaty!"

Edgar shrugged and explained curtly: "Fafnir's Talon."

"But we haven't got it," the witch declared emphatically, looking around significantly at everyone there. "Or have we? Shagron?"

Shagron began hastily shaking his head. It looked to me as if he'd had a few run-ins with the witch and not come out on top in them. She was a pretty strong witch.

"Kolya?"

The second magician who had come in replied in a calm voice: "No, and it's by no means clear that we want it . . ."

"I'm not asking you," the witch barked at Edgar and Yura. And then for the first time she glanced at me.

"Anna Tikhonovna," I said with feeling. "I only learned that the Talon exists yesterday, and I've been asleep for most of the time since then."

"Why are you in Moscow?" she asked sternly.

"I don't know that myself. Something gave me the urge, told me to come, and so I did. And I was barely off the train before I got caught up in that business with the vampire. Off the boat and into the party, as they say . . ."

"If I understand anything about anything here," the magician Yura put in, "then this is predestination. That explains everything— the increased powers, and the missing Talon, and the way the Light Ones acted. They're simply trying to eliminate him, or at least isolate him, before he can get his hands on the Talon. Because afterward it will be too late."

"But why didn't they bring in their enchantress?" Edgar asked, beginning to draw out his vowels slightly again. Apparently his accent only appeared at moments of agitation, when he was concentrating on something apart from what he was saying.

"And even Gesar only intervened at the critical moment," Shagron remarked. "And then all he did was cover their retreat."

"Who knows?" The witch pierced me with her sharp glance again. "Maybe they simply can't keep up with him?"

"My name's Vitaly," I told her. "Pleased to meet you." After all, who likes to hear himself referred to as "this" and "him" all the time?

The others just seemed to ignore what I'd said. Yura looked into my eyes and instantly probed me. I didn't bother to screen myself—but why not?

"Good first-level," he declared. "With some gaps, though. Just yesterday I would only have been delighted by the appearance of a magician like this among us."

"But today it upsets you, does it?" the witch snorted.

"Today I refrain from drawing any conclusions. The Light Ones have cut loose, and we've been left on our own, without Zabulon. Gesar, plus that enchantress, plus Olga—even if she doesn't have her full powers—and then Igor, Ilya, Garik, Semyon . . . We can't stand against them."

"But we have the Talon and this . . . Vitaly," the witch countered. "And then Zabulon has a habit of appearing just at the crucial moment."

"We don't have the Talon," Yura remarked. "And what guarantee is there that we will have it? In any case, Kolya's absolutely right: What would we do with the Talon? Of course, I understand, it possesses ancient, mighty Power. But if we don't think carefully before we let it loose . . . We can't afford to mess things up."

"Well, we'll try hard not to," the witch said ingratiatingly. "Edgar, what have the analysts got?"

As if in response, there was a knock at the door and Hellemar, the lord of the notebooks, appeared in the doorway.

"Got it!" he said triumphantly. "Vnukovo airport! Flight fifteen zero zero from Odessa. It was delayed twice by bad weather conditions, and has only just left. It will land in an hour and twenty minutes. The Talon's on board."

"Right," said Edgar, leaping to his feet. "Set up field HQ at the airport. Keep track of the weather. Cut off the Light Ones. And they can go whistle for an observer."

"Chief," Hellemar said with a sour expression, "the Light Ones already set up their field HQ at Vnukovo fifteen minutes ago. Better bear that in mind."

"We will," the witch promised. "Now let's get moving . . ."

Everyone got up; someone grabbed the phone, someone raked the charged amulets out of the safe, someone else started issuing loud orders to the staff . . .

And I just wearily set down my empty coffee cup on the desk.

"Do they at least feed people in your headquarters?" I said to nobody in particular. "I've been running on empty for twenty-four hours now . . ."

"You'll survive," I was told sharply by Edgar. "Get downstairs and don't even think of trying any more solo heroics at all."

But strangely enough, just at that moment I didn't feel the slightest desire to try any heroics.

We reached Vnukovo with incredible speed. The driver of our comfortable minibus was a lippy young guy the others called Deniska. He was a magician, but he handled a steering wheel even better than Shagron. First we drove around the embankments, then along Ordynka Street and Lenin Prospect, into the South-West district, around the Ring Road . . . Everything flashed by so fast I barely had time to see anything. Shagron and Edgar had gone off somewhere, Yura and Kolya had disappeared too. I was left with Anna Tikhonovna and a trio of girl witches; every now and then I caught them looking at me curiously. Anna Tikhonovna must have told them to leave me alone, because none of them made any attempt to talk to me. A fat werewolf floundered about heavily in the baggage compartment behind us and growled huskily whenever Deniska threw the minibus into a tight curve as he overtook someone. The tires squealed, the driveshaft groaned, and the engine hummed like an industrious bumblebee in May.

We were the first to reach the airport. Deniska drove up to the service entrance and two other vehicles came rushing up almost immediately—Shagron's BMW and another minibus carrying the technicians. The Watch members set to work with fantastic coordination; they immediately cast information spells that made us empty space as far as ordinary people were concerned, and a line of technicians carrying notebook computers set off for the entrance. Someone had already chosen a place for the HQ—a spacious office with a plaque on the door that said "Accounts." The human employees had been herded into the next room—either an office or a boardroom—and put into a blissful trance. I would have chosen the boardroom for the HQ, but Hellemar said there were more telephone lines in the accounts office.

Yura appeared, and I wondered irrelevantly why Edgar was carrying out the duties of senior deputy while the chief was away, even though he was only just on the border of the second level. Yura seemed more powerful to me. But the affairs of the Day Watch were none of my business, so I just hunkered down in a corner and tried to figure out if I could make a dash to the restaurant for ten minutes. The young technicians were already scraping away at the touch pads of their notebooks.

"The flight's making its approach, ETA is twenty minutes plus or minus five."

"Have you located the Light Ones?" Anna Tikhonovna asked.

"Yes. In the overnight transit rooms, beside the lounge. That's in the next building."

"What are they doing?"

"Looks like they're tinkering with the weather," someone said.

"What's the point? To stop the plane landing?"

"They won't do anything that might kill the passengers," Anna Tikhonovna snorted.

It seemed to me the simplest thing would have been to bring the plane down, and that would have put an end to the whole business. But Light Ones are Light Ones. Even in a situation like this they worry about ordinary human beings. And then, who knew if a plane crash would even damage the artifact from Berne? Maybe it wouldn't touch it. Power is Power, after all.

"Who's a weather specialist here?" Anna Tikhonovna inquired.

"Me!" two witches answered in chorus.

"Right then, feel out what's going on here . . ."

The witches began feeling things out—that is, scanning the immediate area for weather-changing spells. I could sense dense arrays of sensitive energy impulses that were intangible and invisible, even to many Others. It wasn't that the Others couldn't have traced them—most of them simply didn't know how. Weather magic has always been a specialty of witches and a small number of magicians, and like any other specialized field, it involves plenty of subtle points.

"They're intensifying the cloud cover," one of the witches announced. "We need Power . . ."

One of the reserve magicians immediately picked up an amulet and groped for one of the witches' hands. They concentrated for a while, and finally all three of them held hands, closed their eyes, and sank into something like a light trance.

"Everybody, help them if you can," Anna Tikhonovna ordered.

I was in no state to help them yet. At least the energy I could have put into the effort was insignificant compared to the Power of the amulet. I'd pretty well drained myself back there on Strastnoi Boulevard . . .

The Watch continued with its work. The headquarters was really buzzing—nobody seemed to be running, nobody seemed to be agitated, but the air was alive with tension. I even began feeling a bit uncomfortable—I was the only one in the whole headquarters sitting there and doing nothing. And something told me I still wouldn't be able to do anything for quite a few minutes.

So I sneaked out. I stood up and slid into the Twilight. And then I moved deeper, to the second level.

Falling to the ground from the second floor took me about three minutes, even though I hurried it along as much as I could. It was strange—I'd expected the Twilight to drain me completely but, on the contrary, I felt invigorated, as if I'd just taken a shower and downed a shot of vodka. Amazing.

And by the way, that shot sounded like a good idea.

When I surfaced from the Twilight, I set out for the next building, a long glass-and-concrete slab quite unlike the administrative building, which was crowned by a tall spire—a souvenir of the architectural pomposity of the Soviet '50s.

I'd left my jacket in the field headquarters, so I had to sprint for the door. The wind was carrying fine pellets of snow, and I wondered how the plane from Odessa was going to land. Darkness and driving snow—it was a night you wouldn't put a dog out in. And then the Light Ones would be doing their best to spoil things. But if the plane didn't land, where would it go to? Would they redirect it to another Moscow airport? Maybe Bykovo or Domodedovo?

That was an idea. I ought to tell Edgar or Anna Tikhonovna they should send Watch members, just in case . . .

And then again, they could divert the plane to Kaluga or Tula. If the weather was better there. Which it very well could be—after all, here in Butovo the Light weather magicians were obviously giving it their best shot.

After being outside, the terminal building felt warm and cozy. I went straight up to the second floor, to the bar where Boryansky and I once drank beer while we were waiting for a plane and ate nuts while we listened to a song that had literally dogged our footsteps during that trip: ". . . the summer has flown by, it's all behind us now . . ."

It took me a moment to realize that this was a memory—and I hardly had any of them left. What murky depths of my mind had it surfaced from? I couldn't tell.

I tried to think exactly who Boryansky was, but I couldn't even remember his face. And as to where we'd been flying to, and what for . . . For some reason the only memory that kept on coming back was that then, in those ancient Soviet times, he had a huge bidet in his apartment. Of course, it didn't work . . . and anyway, what would a Soviet citizen want with a bidet?

But the bar was still exactly the same as I remembered it. A counter, high stools, gleaming beer taps. And a TV in the corner. But the video clip they were showing on it was quite different. A young guy with suspiciously red eyes and a girl in a scarlet dress. He was kissing her hand. And the action after that was like a good thriller—complete with slashing wolf's jaws and all the rest. The moment I really enjoyed was when the young guy, who for some reason was now dressed in the girl's scarlet dress, came into the ballroom and then split apart into several wolves. And I liked the final shot, when the girl's red eyes glinted as she surveyed her guests . . .

Hmm. Well, the guys who made that didn't know too much about shape-shifting Others. Just as the unfailingly fashionable writer Pelevin didn't know much about real, gluttonous, dirty werewolves. But the clip was well produced, you couldn't deny that. The werewolves must have all chipped in to pay the producer and influenced the musicians—and what they'd ended up with was a beautiful, romantic video about themselves. The Russian vampires had done the same thing only just recently.

I remembered the name of the group—Rammstein—for future reference, so that I'd be able to find the song and listen to it a bit more carefully.

I ordered beer and a couple of hamburgers and then sat at one side near the television, with my back to the room. My stomach already thought my throat had been cut, and I was determined to do something about the situation.

I sensed the Light Ones when I'd just started my second hamburger—literally felt them with my back. And I immediately clammed up—I knew how to do that already, and I knew for certain that they hadn't spotted me.

I was a powerful Other, after all, even if I was inexperienced, and these two were still apprentices at best: a weak magician, about twenty or twenty-two years old, and a novice soothsayer. I figured I could see the future a lot more clearly than the soothsayer—the whole vast gamut of possible variants—and I could predict more precisely which of them was more probable.

The two Light Ones were talking in low voices; both of them were covered by a skillful spell of inattention—a fairly exotic variety, in fact. It had been cast by someone who was very powerful indeed.

I listened.

". . . already here. The boss says things could get rough," the magician said quietly.

"They'll stick us in the security cordon anyway," the soothsayer objected wearily. "Especially after Tiger Cub and Andrei."

"Oleg, we'll need all our Power, you understand. All of it. Every last drop. The Dark Ones mustn't get their hands on the Talon—that would be the end of everything. The end of the Light . . ."

"Ah, come on," the soothsayer objected skeptically. "How can it be the end . . ."

The magician corrected himself: "Well, the end of our superiority. We won't be able to put the Dark Ones under pressure for the foreseeable future."

"But is it really possible to do that anyway?" There was a note of very healthy, frank skepticism in the soothsayer's words. "The Light Ones and the Dark Ones have existed side by side for thousands of years. They've been fighting for thousands of years. Look at how long the Watches have been competing with each other. And then there's the Inquisition—it doesn't allow any violations of the balance of Power . . ."

The Light Ones broke off their conversation for a moment, walked to the front of the line of three people at the bar, and gently clouded everyone else's minds, including the barman's.

"Twenty hamburgers and a carton of juice," the magician said, and then turned back to his companion.

I pretended my mind was clouded too. Others are basically pretty happy-go-lucky. Especially young ones. The feeling of their own superiority over ordinary people is pretty intoxicating, and it takes years before they can understand that sometimes being human is much simpler and better than being an Other.

"Anyway, there's going to be a fight. Anton told me the Dark Ones have got some sorcerer from out of town, and he laid out Farid and Danila with an easy sucker punch. And he killed Tiger Cub. The bastard . . ."

"She had no business attacking a peaceful Dark One," I thought, feeling annoyed. "I wasn't chasing her, she was the one who was after me . . ."

But the Light Ones were wrong about the sucker punch. I'd paid a heavy price for that fight.

A moment later I realized that something was happening. As if on command, the Light Ones turned their faces toward the airfield and immediately withdrew into the Twilight. A second later, so did I.

Outside the building, one of the Dark Ones was standing on a snow-covered runway with his wand held out in front of him. A long tongue of flame licked at the frozen concrete. Once, twice. The magician was drying out the runway before the plane from Odessa landed. But there were Light Ones hurrying toward him from the terminal building, sinking into the snowdrifts as they ran.

The magician launched a few more tongues of flame and then shifted deeper into the Twilight.

It looked to me like it was Kolya.

My two Light chatterboxes hastily tipped their food supplies into white-and-green plastic bags and set off at a fast trot, trampling the ever-hungry covering of blue moss. It had an easy life here. All those people, all those emotions . . . A single passenger who was late for a plane was enough to feed this entire ravenous carpet for a day.

I hopped off my stool too, leaving my unfinished beer on the counter. I could barely make out what was happening through the wall of the terminal building—all I could see were the vague shadows of Others with the colored patches of auras above their heads and viscid bursts of Power being discharged. At the same time, I could still see the inside of the terminal hall and the people sitting in plastic chairs, patiently waiting for their flights.

Low, rumbling sounds threaded themselves through the Twilight—it was a woman's voice announcing that "flight fifteen zero zero from Odessa has landed." I went hurtling down the stairs, maneuvering between the people who were hardly even moving.

Down. Forward. And now to the right.

I leapt over the turnstile and found myself facing the exit to the airfield.

There was a full-scale battle going on out there—I could literally sense the discharges of energy on my skin. All that Power from the amulets, all that skill from the magicians—and it could all have been used for other purposes, instead of fighting each other. The Light Ones were so rigidly dedicated to their righteous struggle! It hadn't even entered their heads simply to reach an agreement with us—they'd gone rushing straight into the attack.

I could sense that the Dark Ones were having a tough time of it. It looked like the chief of Night Watch, Gesar, had got involved. And there were at least another two very powerful magicians out there now, beside the plane that was taxiing to its stand.

And then four figures burst in through the wall of the terminal. They were all Others, of course. All tall, with broad shoulders, blond hair, and blue eyes. As if they'd been specially picked to match—a standard matching set of twentieth- or twenty-first-century Vikings. All wearing identical warm winter parkas and carrying identical bags. They weren't wearing hats and their hair looked disheveled, but something told me it wasn't the wind that was responsible for that.

At first I couldn't understand why they had remained in human form. But then I looked at them in the human world and laughed in surprise when I got the idea: An Other's image in the Twilight—his subconscious dream—can take all sorts of forms . . .

They walked quickly across the hall, almost running, moving

past me and toward the exit and the bright patch of light in front of the terminal that was the airport parking lot.

Walking past me.

But just as they drew level with me, a dark-blue flower the size of a heavy Ural construction truck sprang up to the right of them. Everyone in the Twilight was thrown to the ground.

As I lay there on my back, I raised my head and saw a blue veil shimmering in midair, looking like a gigantic *Aurelia* jellyfish. But I could sense that something was about to happen behind that transparent curtain.

And I was right—a portal opened up in the blue haze, right there in the baggage hall, behind that hazy blue curtain. My eyes were stung by a blinding white glow and it was suddenly abnormally light in the Twilight, even though there were still no shadows. That was a really weird sight: unbearably bright light and not a hint of a shadow.

There were two Light Ones. The Night Watch chief and an attractive young woman. An enchantress of very impressive Power.

"You are in my power," Gesar declared loudly, making a short, economical pass with his hands. "Stand up!"

He was talking to the Vikings. The Light Ones hadn't noticed me lying there closer to the portal than anyone else.

One of the Vikings said something angry and abrupt in English. Gesar replied. I regretted gloomily that I didn't understand a single word. Then the Vikings stood up and began obediently walking toward the portal. I was preparing to stand up and had even got on all fours already, but when the third Viking drew level with me, the fourth abruptly withdrew deeper into the Twilight.

Gesar reacted instantly—he cast a Net over the others and disappeared. The enchantress stayed where she was.

The remaining Vikings were pinned to the ground and so was I—from being on all fours I was flattened back against the floor, this time facedown, like a squashed frog on a major highway. It felt as if a slab of concrete had dropped on top of me from a passing dump truck—I couldn't catch my breath or move a muscle. And damned

if there wasn't some object jabbing unbearably into my chest, some
long, slightly curved object.

Lying with my nose pressed to the floor was not at all pleasant; I
made an effort and turned my head.

My eyes met the eyes of the Viking lying beside me.

I felt a frost more chilly than any Moscow winter.

"You!"

"I . . ."

"You're an Other!"

"Yes . . ."

"You serve the Darkness . . ."

"Probably . . ."

"Take care of it!"

"What?"

But the Viking had already closed his eyes. The silent dialogue
had only lasted a few brief moments.

Take care of what? This damn thing that was poking me in the
ribs?

Just to be sure of things, the enchantress dropped another concrete slab on us—the Vikings began wheezing painfully and something like a groan was torn from my chest.

And then I thought: Ah, what the hell!

I closed my eyes and focused on searching for Power . . . and I
sensed an almost inexhaustible source right there—the portal that
was still open.

Well, well, how simple everything was, really! It would take no
more than a few seconds to restore the Power I'd expended on Strastnoi Boulevard. And the fact that it was a Light portal didn't bother
me in the least—the nature of Power is similar in any case.

I began drawing in the Power of the portal. Taking it slow, so that
the Light Enchantress wouldn't immediately realize what was going on.

The first thing I tried was to shift the weight off myself slightly—
I managed that okay, and I can't say it was really too difficult. Then
I enveloped the thing underneath me in a cocoon and stuck it inside

my sweater, still fumbling about on the floor. I thought the enchantress was beginning to feel uneasy.

I was all set to stand up, but then Gesar came back; he was radiating white light, just like a peasant's idea of an angel. With one hand he was clutching the shoulder of the Viking who had fled. One step, then another, and he dropped the limp, submissive fugitive beside his comrades, like a rag doll. But what I saw on Gesar's face was not joy, but something else.

"Where's the Talon?"

He glanced briefly at the enchantress, who pulled her head back into her shoulders in alarm—I sensed her scanning all of us at once.

Oh no, my girl! You won't break into my cocoon.

And Gesar won't break into it either. I can tell you that for sure, from the height of the next step up the stairway.

But Gesar wasn't wasting any time. He came straight up to me.

"You again . . ."

I didn't catch any hint of hate in his voice. Only infinite weariness.

I stood up and dusted my clothes off for some reason.

"Me."

"You amaze me," Gesar confessed, drilling right through me with his glance. "Amaze me one more time. Give back the Talon."

"The Talon?" I asked, raising my eyebrows expressively. "What are you talking about, colleague?"

Gesar gritted his teeth—I distinctly saw the muscles at his temples twitch.

"Cut the comedy, Dark One. You've got the Talon, there's nowhere else it can be. I've stopped sensing it, but that doesn't change matters. Now you're going to give me the Talon and clear out of Moscow forever. That's the second time I've told you—and let me tell you it's the first time I've ever given anybody a second chance to leave in peace. The first time in very, very many years. Am I making myself clear?"

"Nothing could be clearer," I growled, weighing up my own strength and deciding that it was worth going for it.

I mentally reached out toward the enchantress, who wasn't prepared for anything bad to happen, and drew as much Power as I could from her before she realized what was happening. Then I added some from the portal, and all as quickly as possible.

I opened my own portal directly under my own feet, and at the same time I emerged from the Twilight.

The effect would basically have been the same if I'd been standing on the manhole of a sewer and the cover had suddenly disappeared. I just fell through the floor, as far as Gesar and all the others could see. Fell straight through the floor and disappeared.

I hadn't dared try drawing Power from Gesar—something had told me it wasn't worth tangling with him yet.

You can create a cocoon that Gesar couldn't see into without special preparation, you can steal energy from an enchantress who's very probably going to be a great enchantress—that's all pure childish mischief and it will only work once. But it's a bit too soon for you, Vitaly Rogoza, Dark Other, to get involved in an open fight with the chief of the Night Watch.

Just say "thank you" that got you away in one piece.

I said "thank you" and fell straight into a snowdrift from a height of several meters. It was dark all around. Or almost dark. Just the moon overhead. With a forest stretching out on both sides.

I was in a clearing in the forest, a clearing as straight as Lenin Prospect in Nikolaev and very wide, about fifteen meters across. There was a blank wall of forest on my right and a blank wall of forest on my left, and straight ahead, hanging above the silvery strip of untouched snow, there was the moon. Almost full.

It was beautiful, incredibly beautiful—the moonlit clearing, the night, the snow . . . I could have just lay there and admired it.

But I started feeling cold.

I scrambled out of the snowdrift with a struggle and looked around. The snow still looked untouched. But somewhere in the distance I could hear the distinctive hammering rhythm of the wheels of a commuter train.

Hmm. Some great magician I was. Lord of the Dark portals. I'd opened a portal all right, but I hadn't bothered about where it would end. And this was the result: Here I was all alone in the winter forest in nothing but my sweater—no jacket or hat.

Furious with myself, I felt the long, hard object under my sweater, decided not to remove the cocoon yet, and set off toward the moon, across the miraculous virgin snow of the moonlit forest clearing.

I soon realized that walking through snowdrifts was a very dubious pleasure, so I veered toward the forest, having sensibly decided that there ought to be less snow near the trees.

To my own amazement, I was proved right twice over. First, there were indeed no snow drifts at the edge of the forest, and second, I found a narrow path, pretty well trodden. I simply hadn't noticed it before in the shadow.

One of the ancients once said that roads always lead to the people who built them. And anyway, I had no other option. I set off along the path. First I walked, and then I started running to warm myself up.

"I'll run until I get tired," I decided. "And then I'll enter the Twilight . . . to warm up."

I just hoped I'd have enough strength for running and the Twilight.

I ran for about fifteen minutes: There was absolutely no wind, so I actually did manage to warm myself up a bit. The clearing went on and on, an unbroken stretch of silvery, glittering snow. I wasn't the one who should have been running here; it should have been some knight of old in a doublet with fur on the outside and his enchanted sword on his belt, his faithful tame wolf running a few steps ahead . . .

Almost as soon as I thought about the wolf, I heard barking from somewhere on my left. Dogs. A wolf's bark is different. And they don't bark in winter.

I stopped and looked. There was a warm orange glow flickering through the trees. In addition to the barking I could hear voices—people's voices.

I didn't waste much time thinking. I walked forward a bit until I reached the path branching off toward the campfire and turned onto it.

Soon two dogs came bounding toward me—a white Karelian Laika with a tight coil of a tail, almost invisible against the background of the snow, and a shaggy Newfoundland terrier, as black as pitch. The Laika was yelping in a voice that rang like a sleigh-bell and the Newfoundland was barking gruffly: "Booff! Booff!"

"Petro! Is that you?" someone asked from the campfire.

"No," I replied regretfully. "It's not Petro. But can I warm myself up a bit?"

To be quite honest, the first thing I wanted to do wasn't warm myself up, but find out where I was, so I wouldn't have to go wandering through the forest at random, but could go straight to the suburban railroad.

"Come on over here! Don't worry about the dogs, they won't touch you."

And the dogs didn't touch me. The little Laika ran around me cautiously at a constant distance of about four meters, and the Newfoundland simply came skipping up to my feet, sniffed my shoes, snorted, and ran back to the campfire.

There were more than ten people sitting by the campfire. Hanging on a long chain, thrown over a thick horizontal branch of the nearest pine tree, there was a big pot, with something bubbling promisingly inside it. The people were sitting on two logs. I could see metal mugs in most of their hands and somebody was just opening a new bottle of vodka.

"Oh, look at that!" a young, bearded guy who looked like a geologist said when I emerged from the darkness into the light. "Just a light sweater!"

"I'm sorry," I sighed. "I've got a few little problems."

"Sit down!" said someone who had come over to me. They sat me down almost by force and immediately thrust a mug of vodka into my hand.

"Drink that!"

I didn't dare disobey. It burned my throat, but a few seconds later I'd already forgotten it was the middle of winter.

"Styopa! Didn't you have a spare jacket somewhere?" the bearded guy asked, still giving the orders.

"Yes," someone answered from the opposite log, and then ran off briskly to one side, where there were dark tents pitched in the gaps between the trees.

"And I've got a hat," said a plump girl with braids like a schoolgirl's. "Just a moment . . ."

"Been out in the cold long?" the bearded guy asked me.

"Not very. Only about twenty minutes. Just don't ask how I got here."

"We won't," he replied. "We'll find a place for you to sleep, and a spare sleeping bag too. And tomorrow we're going to Moscow. You can come with us, if you like."

"Thanks," I said. "I'd be glad to."

"We've got a birthday here," Styopa explained as he came up to me, holding a bluish-green ski jacket. "Here, take this."

"Thanks a lot, guys," I said sincerely, thanking them mostly not for the hospitality, but for not asking any unnecessary questions.

The jacket was warm. Warmer than it looked.

"And whose birthday is it?" I asked.

One of the girls stopped kissing her latest bearded admirer.

"Mine," she told me. "My name's Tamara."

"Happy birthday," I said. It sounded a bit flat. I felt genuinely sorry that I had nothing to give her as a present, and I felt ashamed to hand her a hundred-dollar bill. It would have been too much like my generous tipping in the hotel.

"What's your name?" the first bearded guy asked me. "I'm Matvei."

"Vitaly." I shook the hand that he held out. "A birthday party in the forest in the middle of winter—I've never been at one of those before."

"There's a first time for everything," Matvei remarked philosophically.

The dogs started barking again and dashed off into the dark night.

"Well, is it Petro this time at last?" the birthday girl asked hopefully.

"Is that you, Petro?" Styopa roared in a surprisingly resonant baritone quite unlike his normal speaking voice.

"Yes," said a voice in the forest.

"And have you brought the champagne?"

"Yes," Petro confirmed happily.

"Hoo-ray," all the girls shouted together. "Hooray for Petro, our savior!"

I felt stealthily under my jacket for the case that must conceal the mysterious Fafnir's Talon. I thought that I could relax until morning and soak in the relaxed atmosphere of somebody else's celebration. The people around the campfire made a point of not singling me out—they filled my mug with vodka as if I were one of them, then handed me a plate of steaming pilaf, as if the light of their fire attracted underdressed travelers out of the forest every day of the week.

It was a great pity there wasn't a single Other among them. Not even an uninitiated one.

CHAPTER 4

SEMYON WALKED INTO GESAR'S OFFICE, FROZE FOR A MOMENT just inside the door, and shook his head very slightly.

"He's not in Moscow. Definitely not."

"That's kind of stupid," Ignat snorted from his armchair. "If he's supposed to do something with the Talon in Moscow, then what's the point of opening a portal to somewhere outside the city?"

Gesar glanced sideways at Ignat. There was something mysterious in his glance: The first name that came to mind for it was "higher knowledge."

"Maybe not so stupid," he objected quietly. "The Dark One had no choice. Either stay in Moscow and lose the Talon, or clear out and take the Talon with him, and then try to break back in again. What's bad about all this is that the Brothers managed to get the Talon to this Dark One from Ukraine, and he managed to trick us."

Gesar sighed, closed his eyes for a moment, and corrected himself: "No, not us, of course . . . It was me he tricked. Me."

Svetlana was huddling miserably in the corner of the divan by the window. She started sobbing again. "I'm sorry, Boris Ignatievich . . ."

So far Anton had been sitting as straight as a ramrod, but now he moved close to her and put his arm around her shoulders without speaking.

"Don't cry, Svetlana. It's not your fault. If I couldn't guess what the Dark One was going to do, then you can't possibly be blamed for anything." Gesar's voice was cool, but basically neutral. The chief of the Night Watch really didn't have anything to reproach Svetlana with—what had happened was simply beyond the range of her present knowledge and skills.

"There's just one thing I don't understand," Olga said abruptly. She was sitting on the pouffe between Gesar's desk and the window, smoking nervously. "If the Dark One's actions couldn't be read in advance at all, doesn't that mean he was acting on intuition? Without planning or thinking anything through in advance?"

"Yes, it does," Gesar agreed. "He prefers to create probabilities, rather than choose from the ones that already exist. It's a pretty bold way of doing things, but it has its dangers. Intuition can be deceptive. And that's how we'll get him."

There was a brief silence; Semyon walked silently across the office and sat on the divan, a little distance away from Anton and Svetlana.

"Actually, there's something else bothering me," Gesar said darkly, reaching into his pocket and taking out a pack of Pall Malls. He looked at it in surprise, put it back in his pocket, and took out a Cuban cigar in a metal tube, a clipper to cut off its tip, and a huge tabletop ashtray. But he didn't open the cigar. "Something quite different."

"The fact that the Dark One had no trouble using the energy of the portal and some of Svetlana's too?" Semyon asked, guessing immediately. "But that was to be expected."

"Why was it?" Gesar asked cautiously.

Semyon shrugged.

"It seems to me that he's more powerful than we think. He simply disguises the fact. In principle Ilya and I, and even Garik, can make use of the Dark Ones' Power. Under certain circumstances. And with certain consequences for ourselves."

"But not so brazenly and not so quickly," Gesar said with a shake of his head. "Remember Spain. When Avvakum tried to draw Power from the Dark portal. Remember how that ended?"

"I remember," said Semyon, not fazed in the least. "All that means is that our Dark One is significantly more powerful than Avvakum. And nothing else."

Gesar looked at Semyon for a few seconds, then shook his head and turned his gaze to Svetlana.

"Sveta," he said in a voice that was noticeably gentler. "Try once again to remember everything that you felt at the time. But don't hurry. And please, don't get upset. You did everything right, the trouble is it just turned out not to be enough."

Semyon glanced in surprise at Svetlana, with the expression of someone who has missed the most interesting thing. "What do you mean, try to remember? Create the image and the job's done," he advised them.

"The image won't materialize," Gesar growled. "That's the whole problem. What does materialize is some kind of gibberish, not an image."

"And have you tried creating a different one?" Semyon asked eagerly. "An abstract image, not connected with the Dark One?"

"She has," Gesar answered for Svetlana. "Any other image is okay, but this one just doesn't work."

"Hmm," Semyon muttered. "Maybe the impressions are too vivid, too oppressive. Remember how I tried for twenty years to re-create the image of the Inferno vortex over the Reichstag when Hitler was speaking. But I just couldn't get it to look real . . ."

"We're not talking here about trying to get it to look real," said Gesar. "There isn't any picture at all. Just a gray blur, as if Svetlana's trying to remember the Twilight world."

Anton, who still hadn't uttered a single word, glanced hopefully at Sveta.

"Well, then," she began. "At first I didn't notice anything at all. When you left to follow the Brother who made a run for it, Boris Ignatievich, I stayed with the portal. Then I noticed that the Dark Ones on the floor had started moving and I fed some Power into your Net. The Dark Ones were pressed flat against the floor again; then you came back. And almost immediately—it was like a fainting fit, everything went black, I felt weak . . . And then there's a blank. I came around on the floor when Anton splashed water in my face. The memories are all I have left . . . And I can't even remember anything properly." The enchantress bit her lip, as if she were about to burst into tears. Anton looked at her as if he hoped just his look would be enough to calm her down.

"I have no rational explanation," Ilya put in. "There's simply nothing to go on—too little data."

"There's more than enough data," Gesar snorted. "But I don't have any explanation either . . . Not in the sense of a hundred percent correct explanation. I have a few suspicions of my own, but they need to be checked out. Olga?"

Olga shrugged. "If you have nothing to say, I won't even try. Either he's a top-flight magician who's never been registered anywhere by anyone, or someone's messing with our heads. For instance, I still can't understand why Zabulon hasn't got involved. You'd think smuggling in the Talon was an operation of supreme importance. But he hasn't raised a finger to help his rabble."

"That's right," Gesar drawled thoughtfully and finally took the cigar out of its tube, looked at it carefully, breathed in the aroma of its tobacco with obvious delight, and put it away again. "The Moscow Day Watch might have nothing at all to do with the operation to smuggle in Fafnir's Talon. The Regin Brothers could easily have been acting on their own initiative. In that case we have absolutely no claims against Zabulon. His rabble appears to have been acting independently. And not all that effectively, either, otherwise they'd never have allowed us to intercept the Brothers."

"What good are the Brothers to us, boss?" Ignat said in annoyance, getting up. "If the Dark One from Ukraine really is predestined for the Talon, then the Dark Ones won the fight at the airport."

"If the Dark One from Ukraine was predestined for the Talon," Gesar said in a quiet voice, "we'd all be settling into spending the rest of eternity in the Twilight. Even I wouldn't have been able to save any of you. Not any of you. Is that clear, Ignat?"

"Is that right?" Semyon asked calmly. "It's that serious?"

"It's exactly right, Semyon. I have only one hope: The Dark One doesn't even understand his own role in all this yet. That's why he's thrashing about like this. Our only chance is to outguess him and take the Talon. And in principle that would balance out the odds."

"But how can we outguess him?" Ignat persisted. "Maybe I should try talking to him, convincing him. I'm good at convincing people. If only we can find him . . ."

"The Dark One won't be able to just sit around doing nothing with the Talon burning his fingers. He's bound to turn up in Moscow." Gesar stood up and surveyed his subordinates, then rubbed his cheek in a tired gesture. "That's it. Get some rest. Everybody get some rest."

He turned to Anton.

"Anton . . . Stay close to Sveta. Stick like glue. And you shouldn't go home—not to your place or hers. Stay here."

"All right, Boris Ignatievich," said Anton. He still had his arm around Sveta's shoulders.

Ten minutes later Anton and Sveta were alone in the comfortable duty staff lounge. Anton held out his mini-disk player and the earphones to the exhausted enchantress.

"You know," he said, "there's this sort of game I play. There's a lot of music on that disk. All sorts. I put it on random selection, but somehow it always comes up with the songs I need. Why don't you give it a try?"

Svetlana smiled faintly and took the earphones.

"Press here."

She pressed the button. The player blinked its green eye as it spun the disk; the laser slid across the tracks and stopped on one.

I dream of dogs and of wild beasts,
I dream that animals with eyes like lamps
Bit into my wings high in the heavens,
And I fell clumsily, like a fallen angel . . .

"It's Nautilus Pompilius," said Svetlana, adjusting the earphones slightly. "'Fallen Angel.' It certainly suits the mood . . ."

"You know," Anton told her with emphatic seriousness, "call me superstitious, but I was sure Nautilus would come up. I really love that song."

"Let's listen to it together," Svetlana suggested, sitting down on the divan.

"Okay," Anton agreed, and mentally thanked the person who invented mini-earphones with no hard frame.

I don't remember the fall, I only remember
The impact as I struck the cold stones.
How could I have flown so high and then
Tumbled down so cruelly, like a fallen angel?
Straight back down into the place that we
Had left behind, hoping for a new life.
Straight back down into the place from where
We stared avidly up into the blue heavens.
Straight down . . .

They sat there for a long time with their arms round each other, each with a tiny Nautilus Pompilius singing in one ear. The three of them shared the feeling of bitterness and happiness—the magician, the enchantress, and the fallen angel.

"But when I went into the terminal building," Shagron said, "there was nobody there. They'd just closed the portal, over near the entrance, just a bit to the right, where the baggage hall is. The Light Ones had already removed their HQ and I could just barely sense them, somewhere near the edge of the airport. Either they were getting into their vehicles or they'd already driven off."

"What about the Brothers?" Edgar asked.

"Damned if I know what's happened to them. I think one of them got killed. The Light Ones immobilized the others and took them away with them."

"What for?" Deniska asked in surprise, even putting down his coffee. "Why didn't they finish them off on the spot?"

"Come on, they're Light Ones!" said Yura, amazed by the question. "The Brothers surrendered, so they just arrested them. They'll probably hand them over to the Inquisition . . . The sadists. It would have been better just to kill them."

"I think he got away after all," said Nikolai, toying idly with his discharged wand. The Power it had contained only recently had melted the snow on the airport runway in a few brief moments and then dried out the ground. "Well, Yura, what do you think?"

"I can't sense the Talon. It's not in Moscow."

"But how could he have got away?" said Anna Tikhonovna. She kept pursing her lips, and it made her look like a strict school-teacher. "How could he slip through Gesar's fingers? Somehow I can't believe it."

"I don't know," Yura snapped, "but something happened back there."

"Maybe he could have used a portal?" Edgar asked cautiously.

"A portal?!" Yura snorted. "Can you use a portal?"

"Not easily," Edgar admitted. "I don't have the Power."

"Oh!" Yura said emphatically, jabbing his finger toward the ceiling in a vague gesture. "And apart from that, after the fight on the boulevard our friend looked like a squeezed lemon."

"But after the fight in the airport it was the Light Ones' enchantress who looked like a squeezed lemon," Nikolai remarked innocently. "And don't anyone try to convince me she gave the Power away voluntarily."

"Yes, that's right," said Shagron, brightening up. "When you think about it, the energy picture of events at Vnukovo looks pretty much like straightforward vampirism. Everything was kind of purple . . ."

Yura shook his head skeptically.

"I must admit the Ukrainian didn't strike me as capable of that. In order to snatch Power from the Light enchantress right under Gesar's nose, you have to be Zabulon at least. And have the right to a first-level intervention . . ."

"What have rights got to do with it?" Anna Tikhonovna exploded. "During the last twenty-four hours we've registered three gross violations of the Treaty by the Light Ones, including one violent attack using Power! The Light Ones have forgotten what rights mean!"

"Anna Tikhonovna," Edgar said with feeling. "The Inquisition has given the Light Ones another indulgence. As long as their actions are directed to returning the stolen artifact, the Treaty is suspended. Until Fafnir's Talon is handed over to the Inquisition, the Night Watch has the right to do whatever it likes. In effect, we're at war. Like in '49—you should remember that."

The silence in the room was like outer space.

"And you didn't say anything?" Anna Tikhonovna asked reproachfully.

"What's the point of making our young people nervous? I'm sorry, Deniska. We're already at a disadvantage as it is. First—the chief isn't here, and second—we've just had two pretty unsuccessful years . . . How many times have we been forced to give way to the Light Ones during those two years? Five, ten?"

"So we're trying to avoid defeatist attitudes, are we?" Yura inquired acidly. "Keeping quiet about things? Protecting the young people from pernicious influences? Well, well . . ."

"What's the point of just saying 'well, well'?" Edgar snarled. "Why don't you try suggesting where we go from here?"

"The chief left you in charge," Yura said indifferently. "So you do the thinking."

"You and Kolya refused, that's why he appointed me," said Edgar, turning gloomy and sulky. "Some fighters you are . . ."

"Hey, boys, just shut it, will you!" said Anna Tikhonovna, turning scarlet with indignation. "This isn't the right time. Even my witches work together better than this."

"Okay, let's forget it," said Yura with a wave of his hand. "You're asking me what we do now? Nothing. The Ukrainian can't go too far out of Moscow. I think he has the Talon with him. If he hasn't done anything yet, it means the time still hasn't come. We wait until he comes back. He has to come back—the Talon has to be in Moscow within the next two days. Otherwise the probability peak will have passed, and it will just be a powerful artifact, nothing more."

Nikolai nodded approvingly.

Edgar looked closely, first at one magician, then the other.

"Then we wait," he sighed. And he added: "Yes. Our Ukrainian friend has turned out to be cunning, all right. More cunning than Gesar."

"*Ne kazhi gop,*" Kolya advised him. "That's Ukrainian for 'don't count your chickens' . . ."

"Anna Tikhonovna," Shagron asked in a rather ingratiating tone, "tell the girls to make some coffee. After all this, I feel like I can hardly move . . ."

"You're an idle lazybones, Shagron," said Anna Tikhonovna with a shake of her head. "But all right, I'll be nice to you, since you distinguished yourself. You'll be an example for the others."

Shagron grinned happily.

To my great amazement, it was warm in the tent all night long. Of course, we slept without getting undressed—I just took off my jacket and my shoes and climbed into the sleeping bag I was offered. The tent belonged to the bearded Matvei, and it could have held three or even four people if necessary, but there were just the two of us. The next tent was about twenty meters away. Immediately after everyone wandered away from the campfire, I could hear the birthday girl moaning sweetly in it, wrapped in someone's tight embrace—so we weren't the only ones who were warm. It was strange. As a southerner, I'd always thought it was cold and miserable in the forest in winter.

I'd been wrong. Maybe it was cold and miserable in the forest, but man can bring his own warmth and comfort with him anywhere he goes. Of course, nature has to suffer a bit as a result, but that's a different matter. A different matter altogether . . .

Matvei woke up first. He crawled out of his sleeping bag, stopped at the entrance for a minute as he fiddled with his stylish mountain boots (far superior to my clumsy, thick-soled shoes), unlaced the flap, and went outside. A breath of frost immediately licked at my face. At the same time I felt against my chest the elongated object that the Vikings had passed on to me at the airport. I hadn't taken a proper look at it since then—there hadn't been any opportunity.

And I also realized that overnight the cocoon, which hadn't been fed any further energy, had melted away. I could feel a breath of Power from the object. Or rather, not Power, but POWER. If there had been even one Other there, he couldn't have helped sensing the Talon.

I pulled the long, curved object—a case?—out from under my sweater. It looked like a scabbard for a dagger, but it opened like a bivalve seashell. That is, of course, if there are any shells like that in the sea—thirty or thirty-five centimeters long, and narrow.

The case was locked in the Twilight, so no ordinary person could possibly have opened it. Crossing my eyes, I moved closer to the entrance of the tent and threw the flap back a bit so that there was more light.

Inside, lying on dark red velvet, there really was a blackish-blue claw from some huge beast. It looked as sharp as a Circassian dagger—stretching along the entire length of its curved inner surface, there was a groove that looked like it was for drawing blood. The wide end looked as if it had been roughly broken off, like the talon had been hacked out of someone's foot very crudely, with no ceremony. And I supposed it probably had been.

But then, what kind of beast could have had talons like this? It would have to be some kind of legendary dragon. What else could it be? But did dragons ever really exist? I rummaged through my memory, trying to find an answer to this question, and shook my head doubtfully. Witches and vampires were one thing—they were just Others—but dragons . . .

The snow squeaked under Matvei's feet as he walked back from the stream. With a regretful sigh, I slipped into the Twilight for a moment, closed the case, and stuck it back under my sweater.

"Awake already?" Matvei asked as he came closer.

"Uh-huh."

"You weren't cold, then?"

"No. It's incredible. I thought in the middle of winter, in the forest, I was bound to feel cold. But it was warm . . ."

"You southerners are strange people!" Matvei laughed. "You think what we have here is a real frost? In Siberia they have real frosts. You know what they say? A Siberian isn't someone who doesn't feel the cold, he's someone who's warmly dressed!"

I laughed. It was well put. I ought to remember that.

Matvei smiled into his beard too.

"There's a stream over there. You can get a wash."

"Aha." I clambered out of the tent and took a short walk to the frozen stream. At the point where the path reached the low bank, someone had broken a neat hole in the ice: Overnight the hole had frozen over with a thin, almost transparent layer of ice, but Matvei had broken it open again. The water was cold, but not cold enough to make even my warmth-loving soul afraid of splashing a few hand-fuls onto my face. The wash invigorated me, and I immediately felt I wanted to do something, run somewhere . . .

Or perhaps it wasn't the wash at all. The day before I'd almost completely drained myself before the airport. And I'd felt exactly the way you'd expect. I'd grabbed some Power from the portal and a little bit from the enchantress, and then expended almost all of it again. But overnight I'd apparently been drawing Power from the Talon.

Its Power was the right kind—Dark Power. I hadn't really enjoyed using the Light Ones' Power—it was alien, hard to control. But the Talon's Power was like mother's milk to a little infant. It even seemed to breathe in a mysterious way that was almost painfully familiar.

I felt as if I could overturn mountains.

"When are you planning to break camp?" I asked when I got back to the tent. Or rather, not to the tent, but the campfire. Matvei was chopping firewood. The two dogs were circling around him, gazing hungrily up at the pot hanging over the fire.

"When everyone wakes up, we'll warm up the pilaf, take another shot of vodka to warm ourselves up, and then we'll move on. Why? Are you in a hurry?"

"I probably ought to get going soon," I said vaguely.

"Well, if you're in a hurry, go. Keep the jacket . . . I'll give you Styopa's address, you can take it around sometime."

If only you knew who you're helping, human . . .

"Matvei," I said in a low voice, "I seriously doubt that I'll have a chance to go looking for Styopa. Thanks, but I won't freeze."

"Don't be silly," said Matvei, straightening up and holding the ax out in his hand. "If you don't give it back, you don't. Your health's more important."

I tried to make my smile look wise and sad.

"Matvei . . . it's a good thing there's nobody else here. You know, I'm not actually human."

Matvei's eyes immediately glazed over in boredom. He'd probably decided I was some kind of crazy psychic charlatan. Well . . . I'd just have to prove it to him.

Both dogs instantly lost their joyful bounce, started whining, and huddled down at Matvei's feet. I raised my barely visible morning shadow from the snow and slipped into the Twilight.

Matvei's reaction was funny to watch—he was so startled he dropped his ax. It landed on the Newfoundland terrier's paw and the poor dog yelped deafeningly.

Matvei couldn't see me. But he wasn't supposed to see me.

I pulled off the jacket; Matvei wouldn't be able to see it either, until I threw it out of the Twilight. I felt for some money in my shirt pocket and stuck two hundred-dollar bills in the pocket of the jacket. Then I tossed it at Matvei.

Matvei shuddered and caught the jacket awkwardly when, as far as he could tell, it suddenly appeared out of thin air. He looked around and, to be quite honest, he looked rather pitiful, but I could tell that without this kind of demonstration there was no way I could ever convince him.

I didn't want to take anything belonging to anyone else away with me, not even a lousy jacket. If people ask no questions and help a stranger who comes wandering up to their campfire out of the forest, you shouldn't take anything from them if you can avoid it. The jacket was comfortable and obviously not cheap. I didn't want it. I'm a Dark One. I don't need other people's things.

I emerged from the Twilight behind Matvei's back. He carried on staring wildly into empty space.

"Here I am," I said, and Matvei swung around abruptly. His eyes were completely crazy now.

"A-a-a-a . . ." he murmured and fell silent.

"Thanks, I really will get by without the jacket."

Matvei nodded. He obviously didn't feel like objecting anymore. I think he was seriously concerned that he'd spent the night in a tent with some kind of monster who could disappear in front of his eyes. And who knew what he might be capable of apart from that?

"Just tell me one thing: How do I get away from here?"

"That way," said Matvei, waving his hand in the direction of the path I'd followed to get there. "The trains are already running."

"And is there a highway over there? I'd rather hitch a ride."

"There's a highway. Right behind the railroad."

"Excellent," I said in delight. "Okay, be seeing you! Thanks again. Give the birthday girl my congratulations . . . and I tell you what . . . give her this . . ."

It was remarkable how easily I managed the simple, but unfamiliar spell. I put my hand behind my back, touched a frozen twig, broke it off . . . and held out a living rose, only just cut from the bush. There were drops of dew glistening on the small green leaves and the petals were flame-red. A fresh rose looks very beautiful in a snowy forest.

"A-a-a . . ." Matvei mumbled as he automatically took the rose. I wondered if he'd give it to the birthday girl or just bury it in a snowdrift to avoid the hassle of having to give long, awkward explanations.

But I didn't ask. I withdrew into the Twilight again. I certainly didn't want to drag myself over the frozen snow again. And what had been good for the previous day, when I thought I was running away from Gesar, was no good today, when I was rested and full of fresh Power.

There was something else I'd forgotten . . . Ah, yes! The hat. That wasn't mine either, and I was still wearing it. I tossed it onto the jacket . . . and set off.

I moved in leaps of a hundred or two hundred meters, opening weak little portals at the limit of my visibility and stepping through them, eating up the distance like a giant.

By day the clearing looked perfectly ordinary. All of its magical charm had completely disappeared. It was obviously no accident that the genuine romantics and lovers of freedom—the Dark Ones—had chosen the night as their time, and not the day, when all the dirt and garbage of the world assaults your eyes, when you can see how unattractive and cluttered our cities are, when the streets are full of stupid people and the roads are full of stinking automobiles. Day is the time of bonds and chains, of duty and rules, but Night is the time of Freedom.

And for a genuine Other, nothing can take the place of that Freedom. Neither ephemeral Duty, nor service to cheap, fuzzy ideals invented by someone long before you were even born. That's all a myth, a fiction, *ucho od Śledzia*—ear of the fish—as our Slav brothers, the Poles, say. There is only Freedom, for everybody alike, and there is only one limitation: No one has the right to limit the Freedom of others. And let the cunning and hypocritical Light Ones seek apparent paradoxes and contradictions in this—everyone who is Free gets along just fine with others who are just as Free, and they don't get in each other's way at all.

I had to use my Other powers to stop a car—for some reason no one wanted to pick up a man without any jacket or coat. I had to touch the mind of one of the drivers in his dolled-up Zhiguli 9, the color of wet asphalt.

Naturally, he stopped.

The driver was a young guy of about twenty-five with short-cropped hair and absolutely no neck. His head was just attached in a very natural way directly to his body and his eyes were blank. But his reflexes turned out to be quite fantastic. I seriously suspected that he could have driven the car even if he was unconscious.

"Eh?" he said to me when I'd made myself comfortable in the back, beside his huge leather jacket.

"Drive on, drive on. To Moscow. You'll let me out on Tverskaya Street."

And I touched him gently again through the Twilight.

"Ah . . ." the young guy said, and set his Zhiguli moving. Despite the slippery road and the trance he'd been put in, he drove at over a hundred kilometers an hour. The car held the road so magnificently, I wondered if he had special tires on it.

We drove into Moscow from the northwest side after turning onto the Volokolamsk Highway, which meant we sliced through half of the megalopolis very quickly, driving in a straight line almost the whole time, straight to the Day Watch office on Tverskaya Street.

I was lucky to have found such a remarkable driver, and the highway encouraged him to put his foot down to the floor. Plus, we rode a wave of green lights.

As we were driving past the Sokol metro station, I realized they'd spotted me.

Me and the Talon.

But in the middle of Moscow it's almost impossible to catch a Zhiguli 9 hurtling along in a straight line without changing lanes.

I got out on Tverskaya Street and handed the neckless driver a hundred. Rubles, not dollars.

"Eh?" he gasped out, and started gazing around. Of course, he didn't remember a thing, and now he was straining his meager intellect to solve the almost insoluble puzzle of how he'd got from a suburban Moscow highway to the very center of the city.

I didn't interfere and left him alone with his unsolved puzzle.

He had really tremendous reflexes: the Zhiguli set off almost immediately. But the young guy's face was turned toward the side window, with his jaw hanging open. It was still like that when he drove out of sight. I crossed the street and headed for the entrance to the office.

The lobby was full of cigarette smoke, and a tape deck—a Phillips boom box—was quietly playing some song with a laid-back, powerful melody. The voice was so hoarse and low I didn't realize straight away that it was Butusov:

The wind is cold through the open window,
And long shadows lie on the table,
I am a mysterious guest in a silver cloak,
And you know why I have come to you.
To give you strength,
To give you power,
To kiss your neck,
Kiss to my heart's content!

At the sight of me, the young vampire who had his eyes half-closed and was blissfully lip-synching along was struck dumb. But the other guard on duty, an equally young alchemist-magician, was already gabbling his report into the phone.

"They're waiting for you," he told me. "Ninth floor."

Even though he'd been struck dumb, the vampire had managed to call the elevator.

But I suddenly got the feeling I shouldn't get into the elevator, and I certainly shouldn't go up in it. I just shouldn't, and that was all.

"Tell them I'm alive and everything's okay," said that someone there inside me.

I went back out onto the street.

I was being guided again. Without the slightest hesitation I turned left—toward Red Square.

I still didn't know what was driving me and what for. But I could only obey the Power inside me. And I could also feel that Fafnir's Talon had come to life—it was breathing.

Every meter of ground here, every square centimeter of asphalt, was saturated with magic. Old magic that had eaten its way into the stone of the buildings and the dust on the street.

The massive form of the State Historical Museum towered up on my right. I didn't even know if it was still open or whether it had been transformed into a casino by the latest fundamental shift in the history of long-suffering Russia. But anyway, I had no time to find out. I walked on past.

The cobblestones of Red Square, which remembered the leisurely steps of the czars, and the tramping boots of revolutionary soldiers, and the caterpillar treads of Soviet armored monsters, and the columns of May Day demonstrations, seemed like the embodiment of Moscow's unshakable permanence. The city had stood here through the ages. It would always stand here, and nothing—not the squabbles of ordinary human beings, or even the eternal altercations between the Watches—could shake its calm grandeur.

I walked out into the square and looked around. Nearby on my left GUM—the old state department store—was teeming with life. On my right were the battlements of the Kremlin wall, with the pyramid of Lenin's Mausoleum rising up in front of it. Could that be where I was being led?

No, not there. And that was good. No matter what people in Russia felt about their former leader, it was a sin to disturb the peace of the dead. Especially of those who had died irrevocably, forever—he wasn't an Other . . . and it was a good thing he wasn't.

I walked across the square without hurrying. A line of official government cars snaked out of the Kremlin and tore off into the side streets. The Execution Site greeted me in silence. The statue of

Citizen Minin and Prince Pozharsky watched as I walked by. The bright-painted domes of St. Basil's Cathedral breathed a sigh.

Power. Power. Power . . .

There was so much of it here that an Other who had exhausted himself could restore his strength in moments.

But nobody would ever do anything of the kind, because it was strange, alien Power. It belonged to no one. It was unruly and uncontrollable, the Power of the past centuries. The Power of dethroned czars and general secretaries of the Communist Party. Touch it and it would blow you to pieces.

I looked around yet again.

And I spotted him.

The Inquisitor.

It's impossible to confuse an Inquisitor with anyone else, either Light Ones or Dark Ones, let alone an ordinary human being.

The Inquisitor was looking straight at me, and I couldn't understand why I'd only just noticed him now.

He was alone, completely alone, outside and above any worldly balances of power, alliances, and treaties. He embodied Justice and the Inquisition. He maintained Equilibrium. I didn't need to ask what he was there for.

I walked right up to him.

"You did right not to disobey," said the Inquisitor.

Somehow I knew his name was Maxim.

He reached out his hand and said, "The Talon."

There was no imperious tone to his voice, not even a hint of pressure. But I had no doubt that anyone would obey that voice, up to and including the chief of either of the Watches.

I reached gloomily inside my sweater, with obvious regret.

The Talon was seething, processing the surrounding Power. The moment I held it in my hand I was swamped by a dense wave of it. The Power given to me by the Talon rushed into every cell of my body; it felt as if the whole world were ready to go down on its knees and submit to me. To me. The owner of Fafnir's Talon.

"The Talon," the Inquisitor repeated.

He didn't add anything else or tell me not to do anything stupid. The Inquisition is above giving meaningless advice.

But I was still hesitating. How was it possible to give up voluntarily a source of such inexhaustible Power? An artifact like that was every Other's dream!

I automatically noted the redistribution of energy as a Light portal opened up nearby. Of course, it was Gesar, the chief of the Moscow Night Watch.

The Inquisitor didn't react to the appearance of the unexpected witness. Not at all. As if no portal had even opened up and no one had surfaced out of the Twilight.

"The Talon," the Inquisitor repeated for the third time. The third and last. He wouldn't say another word. I knew that.

And I also knew that even if all the Dark Ones of Moscow appeared beside me, it wasn't worth trying anything. They wouldn't help me. On the contrary, they'd take the Inquisitor's side. The intrigues played out around the Talon could only continue until the guardians of the Treaty put in a personal appearance.

I squeezed my eyes shut and drew in as much Power as I could hold within myself, almost choking on the pressure. With a trembling hand, I held out the case with the artifact in it to the Inquisitor. As I did so, I could just sense the vague desire that Gesar was struggling to control—to dash forward and take possession of the Talon. But naturally, the chief of the Night Watch didn't move a muscle. Experience is primarily the ability to restrain our fleeting impulses.

The Inquisitor glanced at me. I probably ought to have read satisfaction and approval in his glance: Well done, Dark One, you didn't flinch; you did as you were told, clever boy.

But I couldn't see anything of the kind in the Inquisitor's eyes.

Not a thing.

Gesar was gazing at us with open curiosity.

Without hurrying, the Inquisitor put the case with the Talon into the inside pocket of his jacket and then disappeared into the Twilight without even saying goodbye. I stopped sensing him instantly. Instantly. The Inquisition has its own paths.

"Ha," said Gesar, looking away to one side. "You're a fool, Dark One." Then he looked straight at me, sighed, and added: "A fool, but clever. And that's remarkable."

Then he left too, quietly this time, without any portal. I could still sense him for some time in the deeper layers of the Twilight.

I was left on Red Square, out in the piercing wind, alone, without the Talon after I'd already got used to its Power, with no warm clothes, still wearing the same sweater, trousers, and shoes, and my hair was as tousled as a film actor's in some dramatic solo scene. Only there weren't any viewers to appreciate this fine shot, now that Gesar had gone on his way too.

"You really are a fool, Vitaly Rogoza," I whispered. "A clever and obedient fool. But then, maybe that's the only reason you're still alive?"

But the person inside me suddenly came to life and reassured me: *Everything's happening as it should. You did the right thing by getting rid of Fafnir's Talon.* I was overwhelmed by such a blissful, unshakeable certainty that I was right, that I even stopped feeling the cold, piercing wind.

Everything was just fine. Everything was right. Children shouldn't play with atom bombs.

I twitched my shoulders, turned around, and strode off in the direction of Tverskaya Street. I'd only gone a few steps when I came across the entire top level of the Day Watch (the only ones missing were the magician Kolya and—naturally—the chief), plus about fifteen mid-level agents, including Anna Tikhonovna's young witches, three vampire brothers, and a rather stout werewolf. The entire company was staring at me like idle bystanders gaping at a penguin that has escaped from the zoo.

"Hi," I said in a surprisingly cheerful voice. "What are you all doing here, eh?"

I'm getting carried away again, I thought miserably. Oh-oh . . .

"Tell me, Vitaly," Edgar asked in an odd, unnatural voice, "why did you do that?"

His attention was distracted for a second as he diverted an over-vigilant militiaman who was all set to approach a gathering that he thought looked suspicious. Then his gaze returned to me: "Why?"

"Do the Dark Ones really need a pointless fight? Do they need pointless casualties?" I said, answering a question with a question, like some joker from Odessa.

"I think he's lying," Anna Tikhonovna said aggressively. "Maybe we should probe him?"

Edgar frowned gloomily, as if to say: How can we probe him? So they were already afraid of me in the Day Watch! Would you believe it!

"Anna Tikhonovna," I said, addressing the old witch in a sincere voice, "Fafnir's Talon is an incredibly powerful destabilizing element, capable of disrupting the balance of Power like nothing else. If it had stayed in Moscow, a bloody battle would have been inevitable. As a law-abiding Other, I accepted the Inquisition's verdict and gave back the Talon. That's all I have to say." I was keeping quiet about the Power that had settled in me after my contact with the Talon—until the right time came. "Surely you wouldn't have done anything else?" I added, realizing that no one would dare object to that. All of them had wanted to touch the artifact . . . to draw Power from it . . . And all of them had been afraid of the consequences of doing it.

"Why don't we go back to the office?" the magician Yura growled. "Instead of standing around in the wind like the three poplars on Plushchikha Street in the old film."

His words made a lot of sense—I was beginning to shiver again, and it would have been unforgivably stupid to waste the Power that I'd stored up.

With Edgar's support, Yura called up an economical portal, and two minutes later the entire Watch had already ridden the elevator up to the office in groups. I couldn't help remarking that my portal would have been more stable and would have worked for longer. Apparently I'd moved up another step on the stairway to nowhere when I parted with Fafnir's Talon. And apparently I was now more powerful than everyone else there, taken together. But I was still as inexperienced and naïve as ever, and I still had to learn the most important thing of all: how to use my Power properly.

The technicians, led by the unsleeping Hellemar, were working away hard on their headquarters notebooks. When the hell did these young guys ever rest? Or was it just that they all looked alike?

"What's going on, Hellemar?" Edgar asked.

"The Light Ones are withdrawing their outposts," the werewolf reported cheerfully. "One after another. Not just changing them, but removing them completely. And they've lifted the cordons at the entrances to the city and the railroad stations."

"They've calmed down," sighed Anna Tikhonovna.

"Of course they've calmed down," Yura snapped. "The Talon's gone now. They've probably already transferred it to Berne. In fact, I'd bet on it."

He was right. A few seconds earlier I'd sensed the source of my Power suddenly disappear into the Twilight and move somewhere far, far away. I wondered if I was fated ever to hold it in my hands again just one more time . . . I didn't know . . .

"For the life of me, I don't understand why all this fuss over the Talon was started in the first place. What were the Regin Brothers trying to achieve? Why didn't they let us know what they were doing? It's all some kind of crazy nonsense, absolute nonsense."

"And what makes you so sure the Regin Brothers didn't achieve their goal?" I asked innocently. They looked at me as if I were a child who'd asked an awkward question in adult company.

"You have a different opinion?" Yura inquired cautiously, exchanging a quick glance with Edgar.

"Yes," I said honestly. "Only don't ask me about the details—I don't know them anyway. There was a serious imbalance of Power developing in Moscow in favor of the Light Ones. So serious that Europe was beginning to feel worried. Measures were taken. The Regin Brothers' escapade is one piece of a jigsaw that will eventually add up to a new equilibrium."

"And your appearance is another piece of the jigsaw?" Edgar surmised.

"Obviously."

"And the absence from Moscow of Zabulon, our chief?"

"Probably."

The Dark Ones looked at each other, wondering.

"I don't know about that," Anna Tikhonovna drawled in a displeased tone of voice. "It all looks pretty strange. If we had the Talon, we'd soon have the Light Ones in a corner."

"But would we be able to keep it under control?" Yura remarked. "I don't know . . ."

"In any case," said Edgar, after thinking for a while, "we still have the right to demand satisfaction from the Light Ones. There were several serious interventions committed. What they've done over the last two days goes way beyond the recent killings. Tiunnikov's death should really be classed as an accident, and if Gesar tries to dispute that, the tribunal will soon demolish all his arguments. And the vampire poacher and the shape-shifting hooker aren't such very serious violations, only sixth level, or fifth at most. They were acting independently, the Day Watch had nothing to do with it . . . Now we have the right to demand several second-level interventions at least. That's what I think . . . So in the final analysis the Day Watch has still come out best from everything that's happened. Even without the chief and his powerful support."

"Better hold the fanfares for a while," Yura remarked skeptically. "Wait and see."

Edgar shrugged and spread his arms in the gesture of a man sticking to his own opinion. He really believed what he'd just said. And I could understand him.

There's no way of knowing how the argument would have ended.

The cell phone on Edgar's belt trilled and everyone automatically turned toward him.

It could have been a private call, or a call from the technical section. But the Others gathered together in the office were pretty powerful. Almost all of them were capable of calculating probabilities and the consequences of very simple events.

This call had a dense central thread that was clearly visible. A thread connecting it to events of supreme importance.

Edgar raised the phone to his ear and listened for a while. "Show him through," he said, then canceled the call and put the cell back on his belt. "An Inquisitor," he said with a stony expression, "with an official announcement."

Less than thirty seconds later the warlock from the duty watch opened the door into the Day Watch main office. And a second after that the impassive Inquisitor called Maxim strode in through the doorway.

There was absolutely no emotion or other coloration in his voice; his tone was strictly informative. And it would have been stupid to suspect an Inquisitor of sympathizing with one side or the other. "In the name of the Treaty," he declared, "tomorrow at dawn there will be an extended session of the local board of the Tribunal, under the patronage of the Inquisition. The subject is a number of actions taken by Light Others and a number of actions taken by Dark Others which are incompatible with the stipulations of the Treaty. Attendance is compulsory for all who have been informed. If anyone who has been informed fails to attend or arrives late, it will be regarded as an act incompatible with the stipulations of the Treaty. Until the session starts all magical interventions at the fifth level of Power and above are prohibited. May Equilibrium triumph."

When he finished his speech, the Inquisitor turned around unhurriedly and walked out into the lobby, to the elevators. The warlock cast a fleeting glance at his superiors and closed the door behind him. He regarded it as his duty to show the Inquisitor out. The office was quiet for a while; even the technicians and their notebooks had fallen silent.

"Just like in '49," Anna Tikhonovna remarked quietly. "Exactly the same."

"Let's hope so," the magician Yura said in a low voice. "Let's hope so, Anna Tikhonovna. Let's hope real hard."

CHAPTER 5

EVERYBODY GETS THE FEELING SOMETIMES THAT WHAT IS HAP-
pening just at the moment has already happened before. There's even
a special term for it, déjà vu, a kind of false memory.

The Others have it too.

Night Watch agent Anton Gorodetsky was standing in front of
the door of his apartment and struggling with his memories. He had
hovered in front of this open door in exactly the same way before,
wondering who could have got inside. And when he went inside that
time, he'd discovered that his uninvited guest was his sworn enemy,
the chief of the Day Watch, known to the Light Ones by the name
of Zabulon.

"Déjà vu," Anton whispered, and stepped inside the door. The defense system remained silent again, but there was definitely a visitor
in the room. Who was it this time?

Anton squeezed his talismanic medallion tightly in his hand as
he entered the room.

Zabulon was sitting in an armchair and reading the newspaper
Arguments and Facts, wearing a severe black suit, a light-gray shirt,
and black shoes with blunt, square toes, polished so that they shone
like mirrors. He took off his spectacles. "Hello, Anton."

"Déjà vu . . ." Anton muttered. "Well, hello."

Strangely enough, this time he wasn't scared of Zabulon at all.

Maybe that was because the last time Zabulon had conducted his surprise visit in an entirely correct manner?

"You can take my amulet. It's in the desk—I can sense it."

Anton let go of the talisman hanging round his neck, took off his jacket, and went across to the desk. Zabulon's amulet was hidden in among some papers and all the other office clutter that inevitably seems to appear out of nowhere.

"Zabulon, you have no Power over me," Anton declared in a voice that didn't sound like his own.

The Dark magician nodded in satisfaction. "Excellent. Allow me to compliment you. That other time you were trembling like a withered leaf. But today you're calm. You're growing, Anton."

"I suppose I ought to thank you for the compliment?" Anton asked coolly.

Zabulon threw his head back and laughed soundlessly.

"All right," he said a few seconds later, "I see you're in no mood to waste time. Well, neither am I. I came to offer you the chance to commit an act of betrayal. A small, calculated act of betrayal from which everyone will benefit, including you. Sounds paradoxical, doesn't it?"

"It does."

Anton looked into Zabulon's gray eyes, trying to understand what trap he'd fallen into this time. Trust a human being half way and a Light One a quarter of the way, but don't trust a Dark One at all.

Zabulon was the most powerful—and therefore the most dangerous—Dark One in Moscow. And probably in the whole of Russia.

"Let me explain," said Zabulon, without hurrying, but not hesitating either. "You already know about tomorrow's session of the Tribunal, do you not?"

"I do."

"Don't go to it."

Anton finally decided to sit down, on the divan by the wall. Now Zabulon was on his right.

"And for what particular reason?" Anton inquired.

"If you don't go, you and Svetlana will stay together. If you go, you'll lose her."

Anton felt a sudden burning sensation in his chest. It wasn't a question of whether he believed Zabulon or not. He wanted to believe him. He wanted to very much.

But he couldn't forget that Dark Ones can't be trusted.

"The leadership of the Night Watch is planning yet another global social experiment. You must know that. And Svetlana has been given a rather important role in this project. I shan't try to change your convictions or win you over to the Darkness—that's an entirely hopeless proposition. I shall simply tell you what the danger of realizing such an experiment is: the disruption of the balance of forces. Obviously a rather desirable thing for the side that grows stronger. In recent times the Light has been growing stronger and, naturally, I don't like it. It is in the Day Watch's interest to restore the equilibrium. And you are the one who can help us."

"Strange," Anton said thoughtfully. "The head of the Day Watch asking for help from a Night Watch agent. Very strange."

"Well, your help isn't absolutely necessary to us. We could manage on our own. But if you help yourself in the first instance, then you will also help us. And Svetlana, and everyone else who will inevitably suffer from the next global experiment."

"I don't understand—how can I help myself and Svetlana?"

"What don't you understand? Svetlana is potentially a very powerful enchantress. As she grows stronger, so the gulf that separates you grows wider. Her Power is the factor that is shifting the balance in the favor of the Light. If Svetlana is deprived of her Power for some time, equilibrium will be restored. And there will be nothing to keep you apart, Anton. She loves you—anyone can see that. And you love her. Surely you wouldn't sacrifice your happiness and that of the woman you love to the Light? Especially since the sacrifice is meaningless in any case. That's why I'm proposing you commit this little, perfectly painless act of betrayal."

"Betrayal is never little."

"Sometimes it is, Anton. It most certainly is. Loyalty itself is built up from a series of little, calculated betrayals. You can trust me on that—I've lived in this world long enough to be quite sure of it."

Anton paused for a while before he spoke. "I'm a Light One. I can't betray the Light. By my very essence I can't do it—and you should understand that."

"No one's trying to make you go against the Light. And what's more, if you do this, you'll be helping many people. Very many people, Anton. Isn't that the goal of a Light magician—to help people?"

"And how will I be able to look my colleagues in the eye?" Anton asked with a bitter laugh. "After that?"

"They'll understand," Zabulon said with an assurance that seemed strange to Anton. "They'll understand and they'll forgive. And if they don't—what kind of Light Ones are they?"

"You're good with the sophistry, Zabulon. Far better than I am, no doubt. But just because you call things by different names, it doesn't change their essential nature. Betrayal is always betrayal."

"All right," Zabulon agreed with surprising readiness, "then betray love. Basically, you have a choice between two betrayals— surely you can understand that? To betray yourself or to prevent yet another cycle of bloodshed from happening. To forestall the inevitable battles between the Watches or to allow them to happen. Or haven't there been enough deaths for you yet? You went out on patrol with Andrei Tiunnikov more than once. You were friends with the girl shape-shifter, Tiger Cub. Where are they now? Who else are you willing to sacrifice in the name of the Light? Don't go to the Tribunal session tomorrow, and your friends will stay alive. We don't need any more deaths, Anton. We're willing to avoid conflict. To settle things peacefully. That's why I'm suggesting you should help everybody. Everybody. Dark Ones and Light Ones. And even simple, ordinary people. Do you understand?"

"I don't understand how my absence from the Tribunal session will help restore equilibrium."

"You've already run into the Dark One from Ukraine, haven't you? Vitaly Rogoza?"

"Yes, I have," Anton replied reluctantly.

"He's not an Other."

Anton was startled.

"How do you mean, not an Other?"

"He's not entirely an Other. He's only a Mirror. And he doesn't have long left to live."

"What, or who, is a Mirror?"

"Definitely 'what,'" Zabulon said with a sigh. "Alas, only a 'what' . . . That's not important, Anton. It's more useful for you to know something else. If you stay away from the session of the Inquisition, no more blood will be spilled. If you go, a bloodbath is inevitable."

"Failure to appear at a Tribunal is punished by the Inquisition."

"The Inquisition will regard your reluctance to engage in combat with Rogoza as legitimate. There have been precedents; if you wish, I can even obtain the relevant documents. But you can take my word for it. I've never deceived you yet."

"I don't like the sound of that 'yet.'"

Zabulon smiled with just the corner of his mouth. "It can't be helped. I am a Dark One, after all. I just don't think it's useful to lie without any reason."

Zabulon stood up, and Anton also got to his feet.

"Think, Anton. Think, Light One. And remember: Your love and the lives of your friends depend on your decision. That's the way things turn out sometimes: In order to help your friends, first you have to help your enemy. Better get used to it."

Zabulon walked rapidly out of the room, and then out of the apartment. That very instant the sentry sign started howling in the Twilight, and the mask of Chkhoen on the wall pulled a terrifying face. As Anton listlessly put everything in order, he tried to gather his thoughts.

Should he believe Zabulon or not?

Should he be with Svetlana or not?

Should he call Gesar and tell him everything or keep quiet?

Every conflict, from a simple, crude brawl to intrigues between different states and the Watches, is a battle of information. Whoever has the most precise idea of the strength and aims of his enemy will win.

Zabulon's aims and Anton's could not be the same. That was absolutely impossible. But what if the head of the Day Watch had told Anton what he had, precisely in order to make him reject the very idea of missing the Tribunal?

Where was the truth, and where was the lie? Zabulon's words were a cage, but inside the cage there was a mantrap, and inside the mantrap there was a mousetrap, and inside the mousetrap there was poisoned bait . . . How many layers of falsehood had to be peeled away in order to expose the truth?

Anton took a coin out of his pocket. He tossed it in the air and caught it, then laughed and put it back in his pocket, without even looking to see if it had come up heads or tails.

That wasn't the right way.

If one of the two choices was a trap, then he had to look for a third.

In order to get to the Tribunal at dawn, I either had to get up very early, or not go to bed at all. I chose the second option. I could catch up on my sleep later.

My Dark colleagues had grilled me stubbornly for a while, trying to extract the motives for my actions, but since I myself didn't understand very much about why I behaved the way I did and not some other way, they didn't get much out of me.

Nothing really interesting happened until the evening; I went to the shop where they burned mini-disks for my stylish little player and asked if they kept the lists of the collections ordered by their clients. It turned out they did. And for some reason I chose to order a copy of the disk that Anton Gorodetsky, the Light magician, had

put together. Maybe I was trying to get an idea of his view of the
world from his musical preferences? I don't know . . . Just recently I'd
got out of the habit of asking questions, because most of the time I
didn't get any answers. And correct answers were even rarer.

There was one other thing that stuck in my memory that evening:
someone I met in the metro. I was on my way back from the music
shop. On the metro. Sitting there with my hands in the pockets of
my jacket (my Dark colleagues had kindly brought my things back
from the field HQ at the airport) and listening to the disk I'd just
bought. I was in a good mood, feeling calm.

The essence of things and the sequence of years,
The faces of friends and the masks of enemies
Are clearly visible, they cannot be concealed
From the sight of the poet—he owns the centuries.
The light of distant stars and the beginning of dawn,
The secrets of life and the mysteries of love
At the moment of inspiration, warmed by the sun,
All is reflected in the poet's soul,
In the mirror of the world . . .

Suddenly there was a subtle change of some kind in my surroundings. The announcer was just warning the unfortunate passengers
to be careful because the doors were closing. I pressed "pause" and
raised my head, glancing around.

Then I saw him. A teenage kid, fourteen or fifteen years old.
There was no doubt that he was an Other. He must have been initiated, because he was staring at me in fascination through the Twilight and shielding himself against the Twilight pretty skillfully
at the same time. But his aura was absolutely pristine. As pure as
the newly fallen snow, an identical distance from the Light and the
Darkness. He was an Other, but at the same time he wasn't either
Light or Dark.

We looked at each other for a long time, all the way to the next stop. Probably we would have carried on looking at each other for even longer, but a rather attractively built woman, obviously his mother, roused the kid from his trance.

"Egor! Are you asleep? We're getting off."

The teenager started, looked at me one last time with obvious anguish in his eyes, and stepped out onto the platform. I was left behind in the carriage.

It took me about a minute to gather my thoughts. I was still wondering what had struck me so much about this Other. He had reminded me of something. Something very important, but elusive. I just couldn't think what it was.

Then I went back to Nikolsky and his "Mirror of the World," and that made me feel a bit calmer.

The mirror shows me how a man has lived,
Who has composed his song out of lies,
Who wants it to be night everywhere,
Shows me that I must help people.
I have the mirror of the world,
If you want to look—don't fear the fire,
The fire that I will glorify in song,
Let people know there is a good power
In the mirror of the world . . .

Strange. This song would suit the Light Ones better. So why did I, a Dark One, feel that strange aching in my heart?

I carried this vague, uncertain feeling back to the Day Watch office with me. The elderly, worldly-wise vampire at the entrance started away from me like a sanctimonious hypocrite from sudden temptation. Shocked, I suddenly realized that there were a few bluish-white streaks glowing in my own aura.

"I'm sorry," I said, putting my aura in order. "It's a disguise."

The vampire gave me a suspicious look. A female vampire stuck her head out of the duty office—it was a sure bet she was his wife.

They checked my seals very thoroughly and it looked as if they were going to stall me as long as they could, but at this point Edgar came into the office with a pretty young witch. He understood what was happening from the first glance, and a single movement of his eyebrow was enough for the over-vigilant couple on watch. Edgar nodded to me and walked toward the elevators. The witch was devouring me with her eyes.

In the elevator she plucked up her courage and asked, "Are you new here?"

Her voice expressed an entire spectrum of emotions and aspirations that I felt no desire to analyze. Somehow I didn't feel like demonstrating my own Power in front of Edgar and the other powerful Dark Ones.

But Edgar's attention had been caught, and I could see he was genuinely interested in how I would answer.

"Well, in a certain sense, I'm new."

The young witch smiled. "Is it true that you defeated four Light warriors single-handed and killed the tiger-woman?"

Edgar curved his lips very slightly in a sarcastic smile, but he still said nothing, listening with interest.

"Yes."

The witch had no time to ask any more questions. We'd arrived.

"Alita," Edgar said in a deep, hollow voice, "you can pester our guest later. First go and report to Anna Tikhonovna . . ."

Alita nodded enthusiastically and then turned to me: "Can I come around and see you for coffee? In about an hour?"

"Yes, okay," I agreed. "Only I haven't got any coffee."

"I'll bring some," the pretty witch promised, and she set off for the office.

She didn't ask where I was staying, which meant she already knew.

For a few seconds I watched the witch from behind. Her stylish silver jacket, the kind that mountain skiers and tourists wear (I was immediately reminded of my acquaintances from the forest), was decorated with a brightly colored image: a cartoon of a girl with big eyes and her foot thrust out in a kick, with the caption "Battle Angel Alita." The drawing and the caption were partly covered by the witch's long hair, which was hanging down across the jacket.

Edgar also looked as Alita walked away. There was plenty to look at, despite the winter outfit.

"She'll come," Edgar said thoughtfully. "She's already asked about you."

I shrugged. "The Tribunal's tomorrow," I said, changing the subject. "What should I do? Skip it? Go with everyone else?"

"Go with everyone else, of course. You're a witness." Edgar looked around. "Would you come into the office for a moment?"

"All right."

Somehow I was quite sure this office had never been used by the genuine head of the Day Watch, who wasn't in Moscow right then. It was more likely Edgar's office or the office of one of the senior Dark Ones. I slumped gratefully into an armchair, noting to myself that it was far more comfortable than the sagging seats in the metro carriages. Edgar took an already opened bottle of cognac out from somewhere under the desk.

"Shall we take a shot?" he suggested.

"Sure."

Who would want to refuse old Koktebel?

"I'm glad you've come back," said Edgar, pouring the cognac. "Otherwise we would have had to go looking for you."

"In order to clarify our tactics and strategy at tomorrow's session of the Tribunal?" I asked, guessing.

"Exactly."

It was good cognac. Smooth and aromatic. Maybe it wasn't the most famous and prestigious brand (which one is, anyway?), but I really enjoyed it.

"I won't even ask any more why you behave so strangely. To be quite honest, I've been instructed not to. From up there." Edgar raised his eyes expressively to the ceiling. "And I'm not going to try to figure out who you really are, either. For the same reason. All I want to ask is: Are you on our side? Are you with the Day Watch? With the Dark Ones? Can we count on you as one of ours tomorrow?"

"Definitely," I said, without even pausing for thought. Then I made it even clearer: "That's the answer to all your questions."

"That's good," Edgar said with a rather weary sigh and drained his spherical glass in a single gulp.

I didn't think he believed me.

We finished the cognac in total silence. Edgar didn't find it necessary to hold a consultation on how to behave at the next day's session of the Tribunal. He had clearly decided that I'd behave however I wanted to anyway. And he was absolutely right.

I spent the night with Alita, over coffee and conversation. The young witch had even managed to get hold of that long-forgotten brand Casa Grande. We settled down in the armchairs and chatted—about everything and nothing. It was a long time since I'd had such a good time, just sitting and chatting. About music, which I turned out to know quite a lot about. And literature, which I knew rather less about. And movies, which I knew absolutely nothing about. Every now and then, Alita tried to get me to talk about myself and my abilities, but she did this so artlessly that I never even suspected she could have been sent by the vigilant Anna Tikhonovna.

An hour before dawn there was a knock at the door.

"It's open," I shouted.

Edgar and Anna Tikhonovna came in.

"Are you ready?" Edgar asked.

"Always prepared, like a Young Pioneer," I assured him. "Are we moving out in close formation? In armored vehicles or in marching order?"

"Don't play the clown," said Anna Tikhonovna, pursing her lips and giving Alita a severe look. Alita gazed back innocently.

"All right, I won't," I promised. "Where are we going? I don't even know."

In fact, I had no doubt that the reliable internal guide, buried somewhere in the depths of my mind, would tell me where we were going and which direction to follow. But I asked anyway.

"The main building of Moscow University," Edgar told me. "Up in the tower. Shagron's waiting downstairs with his car—you can go with him."

"Okay. I'll go with him."

"Good luck," said Alita, heading for the door. "I'll call around tomorrow, okay, Vitaly?"

"No," I said gloomily. "You won't."

I knew for certain that I was right. But as yet I didn't understand why.

Alita shrugged and walked away. Anna Tikhonovna slipped out after her. Hmm . . . maybe the old hag had sent the girl after all? But then she'd decided to do her own thing and not tried to get anything out of me. If I was right, I had to feel sorry for Alita. Anna Tikhonovna would extract her very soul, squeeze it out and hang it up to dry. She'd regret she'd ever been born.

I reached for my cell phone and dialed Shagron's number, too fast even to be surprised that I knew it.

"Shagron? This is your guest from the South. Can you give me a lift? Uh-huh, I'm on my way."

"Okay, I'll get going too," said Edgar. "Don't drag it out. The Inquisition gets very touchy when someone's late."

I put my coat on, locked my door, and went down in the elevator. The vampires on watch looked at me a lot more calmly this time—either their immediate superiors had had a heart-to-heart talk with them, or they'd realized the truth for themselves. But then, what was the truth? It refused to reveal itself even to me. There were only sudden, brief glimpses of one piece of the mosaic when the curtain was raised for an instant and then descended again, and that impenetrable, misty shroud obscured my sight.

Shagron's BMW was snorting out exhaust fumes about twenty meters away, right under the No Stopping sign. I got in on Shagron's right.

"Good morning."

"I hope it's a good one," Shagron barked. "Shall we go?"

"Yes, if we're not waiting for anyone else, let's go."

Shagron slid into the dense stream of traffic without saying another word.

Driving around snow-covered Moscow in rush hour is a really special experience. Occasionally Shagron pacified the over-keen nearby drivers through the Twilight. Otherwise they would have been cutting in front of us, forcing us over into the next lane, and then squeezing us out of the gaps that suddenly opened up. I put my safety belt on just in case. Shagron muttered something with his teeth clenched. He was probably swearing.

After my sleepless night I had an almost irresistible yearning for a blissful doze, especially since the seats in this quality German automobile encouraged just that. If I'd tried listening to music, I'd have been sure to be lulled into sleep. But I didn't feel like listening to music just then, so I stayed in this world filled with the roar of dozens of engines, the quiet hum of the air-conditioner, the shrill honking of car horns, and the swish of dirty gray slush under our mudguards.

If we'd gone by metro, we would have got there a lot sooner. But as it was, half an hour later we were still crawling along jam-packed Ostozhenka Street toward Vernadsky Prospect. The traffic jam was getting bigger, sprouting a tail that reached back toward the center of Moscow.

"Hell's bells," Shagron hissed angrily. "We could get stuck in this."

"Let's open a portal," I said with a shrug.

Shagron gave me a strange look. "Vitaly! We're on our way to a session of the Tribunal under the patronage of the Inquisition! Your portal would collapse two kilometers away from where we're going!"

"Ah, yes," I said light-heartedly. "That's right. I forgot."

Actually, I could easily have guessed that for myself. Magical interventions and any use of magic were forbidden while the Tribunal was at work. The Other-I inside me helpfully informed me that there had been violations in the past, but only during times of violent upheaval that was the direct cause of the violations themselves.

But then, this was a time of change too. The end of the millennium. A turning point. I remembered how terrified people had been in the summer, when they were waiting for the eclipse, how badly the earthquake in Turkey had frightened them . . . But it was all right, we'd survived.

Only, of course, in surviving we'd become slightly different. All of us, Others and people, especially people.

"Shi-it!" Shagron yelled, jolting me out of my reverie.

I didn't even have time to glance out through the windshield. There was a deafening crash, and in the same instant I was thrown forward and my ribs were squeezed together painfully as the safety belt bit into my chest; with a repulsive, shrill squeak, a fat, round cushion sprouted from the driving wheel, and Shagron's face and chest slid up around it until he crashed into the spot where the windscreen met the roof. There was an unpleasant sort of jangling sound outside the car, and a fine shower of crumbs of glass shot up in the air, falling silently on the snow, but drumming an irregular tattoo against the bodywork of the cars around us. Then, to add insult to injury, we were rammed from behind. Someone had run straight into our trunk.

There were two or three seconds that felt like the launch of a space shuttle, and then I stopped being twisted and tossed about. The blissful moment of dynamic equilibrium had arrived.

Shagron slid back down off the steering wheel into his seat, leaving a trail of blood on the balloon. I thought his arm was broken too. The fool hadn't fastened his belt . . . How long would he be regenerating now?

All around us there were car horns blaring.

With mixed feelings, I unclasped my belt, pushed the door open, and got out onto the road covered in compressed snow and sprinkled with broken glass.

The hood of our car had been rammed at a slight angle by a red Niva. The trunk had been crumpled so it looked as if someone had taken a bite out of it; there was the front end of a well-cared-for Japanese jeep sticking into it. Well, it had been well cared for. In fact, the jeep hadn't suffered all that badly: One headlight on the impact bar had been broken, and the bar itself was bent a bit. He'd obviously had enough time to brake.

"You stupid or something, jerk?" someone from the jeep yelled as he dashed at me. He seemed to consist of dark glasses, a shaved head, a barrel-like torso squeezed into something crimson and black, and stylish shoes that were size forty-something plus. This individual's eyes were as pale as the aura of a young infant . . . or the aura of that kid Egor in the metro.

Couldn't he see that the Niva had rammed us?

And then the crimson outfit of this barrel-shaped individual suddenly flared up in a dull bluish flame, and the individual squealed like a hog under the knife.

I recognized a transatlantic spell popularly known as Spider Flame. And then, before I could recover my wits from the attack by the scarlet-clad individual, someone took me by the collar and swung me around.

If there was one person I hadn't expected to see, it was him. The Light magician and music lover Anton Gorodetsky.

"Who are you?" he whispered furiously. "Who are you, may the Darkness take you? Only don't lie!"

His eyes were even paler than the eyes of the individual from the jeep, who was now furiously dancing something like a jig.

Something seemed to click inside my head. And my lips whispered the words of their own accord: "The mirror of the world . . ."

"The mirror . . ." the Light One echoed. "Damn you! Damn everything!"

I felt like replying that curses were the province of the Dark Ones, but I restrained myself. And I was right. Anton's aura was a blaze of crimson and purple. I was certainly more powerful than Gorodetsky . . . but just then he seemed to be supported by some incomprehensible force that was neither Light nor Darkness, but no less powerful. And if there had been a duel, I couldn't have told you which way it would go.

Anton let go of the collar of my jacket, swung around, and wandered off blindly, squeezing his way between the cars, ignoring the horns and the curses hurled at him through the wound-down windows. Traffic police sirens began howling somewhere quite close. The traffic jam had completely blocked Ostozhenka Street, except for a narrow channel in the oncoming stream of traffic, through which a few lucky drivers were squeezing their cars one by one, swearing and beeping their horns.

I looked at my watch. I had fifteen—no, now it was fourteen minutes left to get to the university. And I knew for sure that I couldn't use any transport magic.

But first things first—how was Shagron?

I walked round the Niva with its door hanging open and approached the BMW from the driver's side. Shagron was unconscious, but in the first instant of danger his immediate reflex response had been to set up a protective membrane and slip into the Twilight. And now he was regenerating, like a pupa, and the greedy Twilight could do nothing to him.

He would survive. He'd recover, and fairly quickly too. Most likely in the ambulance, if it could get here through the traffic jam. Shagron was too powerful a magician to be seriously hurt by something as minor as a traffic accident.

All right then, till we meet again, Shagron. I don't think the Inquisition will charge you with anything. It was force majeure, after all.

And just then I saw my salvation. A young guy deftly maneuvering his way along the very edge of the road on a feeble little orange motorbike. There was someone who didn't have to worry about traffic jams . . .

Of course, it was the wrong season for that kind of transport. But even so . . .

I slid into the Twilight.

In the Twilight the mini-motorbike looked a bit like the little hump-backed horse in the fairy tale. A small animal with handlebars for horns and one big headlight-eye.

"Get off," I told the young guy.

He obediently got off the saddle and stood there.

Leaping over the hood of a beige-colored Opel, I took hold of the handlebars. The mini-motorbike's engine was idling and snorting devotedly.

Okay then, forward. The young guy was standing there frozen like a dummy on the sidewalk, clutching the dollars I'd stuffed in his hand. I twisted the grip that controlled the gas toward me and just avoided scraping the polished side of the nearest car as I set off, squeezing my way through the traffic toward the edge of the jam and the Garden Ring Road. It was fairly simple to get the hang of the tiny Honda, even though it was meant for the warm asphalt of Japan, and not the icy roads of Moscow. And I managed to maneuver between all the cars pretty smartly too. But the bike couldn't give me any real speed—thirty kilometers an hour at most. I realized I still wouldn't get there in time, even if I abandoned the laboring Honda and dived into the nearest metro station—it was still a long way from the University metro station to the spire-topped central building of the university itself. Of course, I could take over any driver's mind on the way, but what guarantee was there that we'd escape the morning traffic jams? I remembered vaguely that in the area of the university the main roads were immensely wide, but I still wasn't certain. If I rode the Honda farther, I would retain my mobility almost all the way to my destination. But on the other hand, I only had a very general idea of the route. I was no Muscovite, unfortunately. Maybe I should just rely on the inner helper who had never let me down so far? I could, of course. But what if this was the very moment he chose to let me down? The most critical moment of all? That was the way things usually happened.

I listened for an inner voice. The cold wind lashing my face was full of exhaust fumes. Moscow was breathing carbon monoxide . . .

My faithful assistant was obviously asleep.

I skipped past the Garden Ring Road and the Park of Culture metro station. But when I saw the Frunzenskaya station up ahead, I decided to go underground. Time was pressing.

Before I even reached the steps at the entrance to the metro, the bike had already been stolen. The motor gave a brief grunt as it was started up, and some quick-thinking individual drove the reliable little Japanese machine away, disappearing into the side streets as quickly as possible. Ah, people, people . . . The Light Ones take care of you, protect you, cherish you, but you're still the same old trash you always were. Animals with no conscience or compassion. Elbow everyone aside, steal, sell, stuff your belly, and the world can go to hell. It's so repulsive . . .

I simply jumped over the turnstiles—in the Twilight, an invisible shadow. I had no time to buy a ticket and stick it in the slot of the magnetic reader. That was okay: The country wouldn't go bankrupt because of me.

I slid down the escalator too, without leaving the Twilight. Jumped up onto the slow-moving handrail and went hurtling downward, barely managing to set one foot after the other in the sticky gray jelly. A train was just about to leave the platform; while I was still figuring out if it was going in the right direction, the doors closed. Never mind, that was no hindrance to me. But traveling back into the center certainly wasn't what I wanted.

I jumped into the carriage straight through the closed door—in the Twilight. Then gently moved aside the astonished passengers as I seemed to appear out of nowhere.

"Oh!" someone exclaimed.

"Tell me, is this Moscow?" I blurted out for some reason. Probably out of a boisterous sense of sheer stupid mischief.

No one answered. Well, all right. At least now there was noticeably more free space around me. I took hold of the handrail and closed my eyes.

Sportivnaya station, Sparrow Hills station, still closed—the train was barely crawling along; every now and then, in the cracks between the metal doors that didn't quite meet, I caught glimpses of electric lights and the gray half-light of early morning. Dawn already . . .

Finally, here was the University station. The escalator, very long and very crowded. I had to wait again. That was it. I was definitely late.

Up at the top it was almost light. Finally realizing that I wouldn't get there for the beginning of the session, I suddenly felt completely calm and stopped hurrying. Completely. I took the button headphones out of my pocket, switched on the player with Anton Gorodetsky's disk in it, and walked off to stop a car.

"It's time," the Inquisitor announced quietly. "All those who have not arrived on time will answer for it later in strict accordance with the terms of the Treaty."

Everyone present got to their feet. Dark Ones and Light Ones alike. The members of the Watches and the judges. Gesar and Zabulon, whom everyone had thought was away from Moscow. The Inquisitor Maxim and the Inquisitors who were there as observers, shrouded in their long, loose gray robes. Everyone who had gathered in the turret of the main building of Moscow University. The small, five-sided chamber of the invisible Twilight story stood on top of the agricultural museum and was used exclusively for holding the infrequent sessions of the Inquisition's Tribunal. In the postwar years it had been quite common to include Twilight structures in buildings—it had been cheaper than putting up with the constant opposition from the state security forces and militia, who were always sticking their noses into other people's business. There was an excellent view from there of the scarlet glow of dawn creeping out from behind the horizon and the incredible shimmering streaks of light that had been dancing above the university building, slowly fading, ever since Jean Michel Jarre's concert for Moscow's anniversary celebrations. The Others would be able to see the traces of that laser show for a long time yet, even without entering the Twilight, where colors fade and disappear. Huge numbers of people had gazed rapturously at the colorful show, pouring their emotions out into the Twilight.

Maxim, wearing an ordinary business suit—not loose robes like the other Inquisitors—waved his hand, unfurling in the Twilight a gray canvas covered with letters of red flame. Thirty voices began chanting together: "We are the Others. We serve different powers. But in the Twilight there is no difference between the absence of Darkness and the absence of Light . . ."

The immense city and the entire vast country were unaware that almost everyone who decided the fate of Russia was gathered here now, and not in the Kremlin. In a neglected, crowded chamber under the spire of the Moscow University building, with wooden chairs, light armchairs, and even sun loungers set in the old, thick dust—everyone had brought what they could manage. No one had bothered to bring a table, so there wasn't one.

The Others are not very fond of cheap rituals: A court is action, not spectacle. And so there were no gowns, wigs, and tablecloths. Only the gray robes of the observers, but no one really remembered why the Inquisitors sometimes wore those.

"We limit our rights and our laws. We are the Others . . ."

The scarlet letters of the Treaty blazed in the semi-darkness, the embodiment of Truth and Justice. And the voices rang out:

"We are the Others."

Thirty voices:

"Time will decide for us."

After the Treaty had been read, the Tribunal proper began, by tradition, with the least important cases.

Without getting up off his rotating piano stool, a judge, one of the Inquisitors clad in the loose robes, announced in a perfectly ordinary voice, with no special solemnity: "Case number one. Poaching by the Dark Side. Bring in the guilty party."

Not even the accused, but the guilty party. Guilt had already been proven. The witnesses would only help to determine the circumstances and the degree of guilt. And the court would give its verdict. Pitiless and just.

"Unfortunately, not all the witnesses are present. We are missing Vitaly Rogoza, an Other registered in Nikolaev in Ukraine and temporarily registered here in Moscow, who is absent for reasons unknown; and also Andrei Tiunnikov and Ekaterina Sorokina, who were killed in cases that will be considered a little later . . ."

The trial was brief and strict: "Victoria Manguzova, Dark Other, registered in Moscow, is guilty of the offense of unlicensed hunting. The verdict is dematerialization. Are there any objections or proposed amendments to the verdict from the Watches?"

There were no objections from the Dark Ones and, of course, not from the Light Ones either.

"The sentence will be carried out immediately," said the Inquisitor. He looked at the Light Ones—verdicts were traditionally carried out by members of the Watches.

Ilya stood up and adjusted his spectacles. He looked intently at the female vampire, who howled, because she knew there was no escape. There was neither hate nor joy in the magician's glance. Nothing but concentration. He reached out his hand and touched the registration seal on the vampire's chest through the Twilight. A moment later Victoria slumped onto the floor. She didn't crumble to dust as an older vampire would have done; her body still hadn't lived out its time yet. But the force that replaces life in vampires, drawn over the years from human beings, had dissolved irretrievably into the Twilight. The room had turned a little bit colder. Ilya frowned and dispatched the body into the Twilight with another restrained gesture.

Forever.

Thus is the verdict of the Others applied.

"Case number two. The killing of an uninitiated Other by a Dark Other, a shape-shifter. Bring in the guilty party . . ."

Questions. Answers. A brief consultation by the Inquisitors.

"Oksana Dashchiuk, Dark Other, registered in Moscow, is adjudged not guilty of premeditated murder; her actions are categorized as self-defense. But she is found guilty of using excessive force to defend herself and therefore deprived of her license to hunt for a period of ten years. In the event of a repeat offense or any violation of the fifth level or above, she shall be subject to immediate dematerialization. Are there any objections or proposed amendments to the verdict from the Watches?"

Ilya looked at Gesar and rose to his feet again. "We have objections. There was no actual threat to the life of this Other. There was no need to kill the man. We demand that she be deprived of her license for a period of fifty years."

"Thirty," replied Maxim, as if he'd been expecting this demand. And in fact he had been . . .

"Forty," Gesar said in a cold voice, without getting up. "Shall I present all the necessary grounds?"

"Forty," Maxim agreed. He looked at the Dark Ones, but they didn't intervene, believing quite correctly that the shape-shifter's fate wasn't worth arguing about.

"Release the prisoner from custody . . ."

The door opened in front of the pale, frightened girl and she dashed out happily, still not realizing that she might as well have been sentenced to execution. Forty years is a very long time for a shape-shifter who can only draw Power from human lives. Long enough for her to grow decrepit and maybe even die, without any way of opposing the implacable advance of age.

"Case number three. An attack on a Dark Other by members of the Night Watch. Since the victim is not present, the court judges it appropriate to cross-examine the surviving guilty parties and the head of the Night Watch, who permitted the unsanctioned use of force against a Dark Other. All protests from the side of the Light Ones are rejected in advance."

Gesar frowned. Zabulon permitted himself a restrained smile.

Svetlana Nazarova, the Light enchantress, glanced at her watch in concern. She was feeling nervous because the Light magician Anton Gorodetsky was late.

"Might it not be more expedient to establish the reason for the absence of three individuals who were invited to attend?" Gesar asked cautiously, involuntarily adopting the judges' official style of speech. "I assure you that I am not trying to play for time at all. I am alarmed by the absence of a member of the Night Watch and one of the greatest troublemakers in these recent weeks."

The Inquisitors exchanged glances as if they were silently taking an official decision.

"The Inquisition has no objection," Maxim said in a dispassionate voice. "Permission is granted for the necessary magical intervention."

The Inquisition observers' robes swayed as they moved their protective amulets. Maybe that was why they wore the robes, so that no one could see how they used the amulets and exactly what kind of amulets they had? The Inquisition has its own methods, its own laws, and its own weapons . . .

An observation sphere sprang into sight in midair. Gray haze, streaked with wavy lines. Most of them disappeared, leaving only three.

Three threads of fate that had recently crossed at a single point. One thread was faded and barely glowing at all. An Other was hurt . . .

"That's Shagron," said Edgar, who had now relinquished the responsibilities of deputy chief of the Dark Ones. "That's Shagron!"

The two other threads parted, but they were about to cross again at any moment—right outside the University building.

A clash. Another clash between Dark Ones and Light Ones. But so far with no fatalities.

"The Night Watch requests the Inquisition to intervene!" Gesar barked. "Maxim, Oscar, Raoul—they'll kill each other!"

A woman stood up beside the head of the Night Watch—it was the Light Other Olga, who had only recently reacquired her abilities as an enchantress, and a very powerful one, which meant that she had lost her right to a surname, but not yet acquired the right to a Twilight name. She touched Gesar's elbow and looked at the judges inquiringly.

Svetlana had turned pale and her face looked as if it were made out of wax.

The Dark Ones didn't say anything. Zabulon scratched the tip of his nose thoughtfully.

"The Tribunal forbids any intervention," one of the judges announced dryly

"Why?" Svetlana asked helplessly. She tried to get up out of her light wicker armchair, but she didn't have the strength. The physical strength. But Svetlana's real strength, the magical Power of an Other, began circling around her in a dense spiral.

Just like people, when Others are angry, or in extreme situations, they are often stronger than when they're calm.

"Why?" Svetlana's voice rang out insistently. "Everywhere this Dark One has appeared, Others or people have died. He's a killer! Are you going to allow him to carry on killing?"

The judge remained imperturbable. "While he has been in Moscow the Dark One Vitaly Rogoza has not once violated a single stipulation of the Treaty, and he has not once exceeded the limits of permissible force to defend himself. He has nothing to answer to the Inquisition for. We have no grounds to intervene."

"When the grounds appear, it will be too late!" Gesar said harshly.

The Inquisitor merely shrugged.

"He's going to take revenge for Shagron," one of the Light Ones said quietly and coughed.

Two magicians—a Light One and a Dark One—were approaching the entrance to the Moscow University building, and as the distance between them melted away, everyone at the Tribunal felt more and more certain that only one of them would make it up into the turret.

But who would it be?

*   *   *

I don't know why, but I got out of the car about three hundred meters away from the entrance to the university building. I could see spots of color, rays of light, and three-dimensional figures flickering above the building; I could sense that a power I didn't understand was restraining ordinary higher magic, not allowing it to be used. And I sensed that up there at the very top, just where the sharp steeple of the Moscow skyscraper began, there was a light gray cloud gradually swelling, and it reminded me of a time bomb.

I looked around as I set off along the sidewalk. In theory I ought to have been hurrying, but I walked at a medium pace. That must have been the way I was supposed to do it.

Just don't ask who had decided that.

My mini-disk player was oozing out another melody. I didn't like it, so I found the skip button by touch and pressed it. What would it be this time?

My name is an effaced hieroglyph,
My clothes are patched by the wind . . .
What I carry in my tight-clenched hands,
No one asks, and I will not answer . . .

The band Picnic and their song "Hieroglyph." That would do—a leisurely melody for someone who is already late anyway and whose only option now is to focus his mind and acquire the all-embracing, imperturbable calm of the sages of the East.

I wondered if there were any Others among those sages? Or maybe the question should be put the other way around—were there any human beings among them?

It would be interesting to find out . . .

I managed to adjust the security guards' minds—clearly the simplest, everyday spells were permitted even during a session of the Tribunal.

I walked across to the elevators—the vestibule was strangely deserted. Maybe subconsciously the people had sensed the presence nearby of all the most powerful Others in Moscow and were avoiding coming to this place? I pressed the button and the doors of one of the elevators opened immediately. I got out, automatically looking around to see if anyone else was hurrying for the elevator . . .

And I saw Anton. He'd just walked past the security guards, who were still out of action.

I wondered how he'd managed to catch up with me. Had he requisitioned a motorbike as well?

I stood there, waiting. Anton looked at me, as if he were pondering some thought, and waited too.

After a little pause, I pressed the button. The doors of the elevator closed and I went up. But not all the way to the very top right away, only about two-thirds of the way up the building. It turned out that the only way I could go higher was on a different elevator that served the upper floors. And then the only way to get where I needed to go was to follow a wide marble stairway with old blotches of whitewash on it. The stairway led to a door that was open in the Twilight but, naturally, firmly closed and locked in the ordinary world.

Just before the stairway, Picnic's ritual performance came to an end and the player selected another song at random:

> I dream of dogs and of wild beasts,
> I dream that animals with eyes like lamps
> Bit into my wings high in the heavens,
> And I fell clumsily, like a fallen angel . . .

I'd only heard snatches of this song by Nautilus Pompilius before, but now it suddenly struck an echo in my very soul. As I walked up toward the locked door and dived into the Twilight, I sang along together with Butusov.

> I don't remember the fall, I only remember
> The impact as I struck the cold stones.

How could I have flown so high and then
Tumbled down so cruelly, like a fallen angel?
Straight back down into the place that we
Had left behind, hoping for a new life.
Straight back down into the place from where
We stared avidly up into the blue heavens.
Straight down . . .

Any Other could have heard me and Butusov, even though the only real sound was coming from the little button earphones and faded away completely only one step away from me.

We entered the chamber where the Tribunal was taking place together. Me and the fallen angel.

I tried to be just and kind,
And I wasn't frightened or surprised
By the people gathering down on the Earth
To watch an angel fall . . .

Gesar. Zabulon. The Inquisitor Maxim. The Dark Ones I'd been drinking coffee with and talking to for the last few days: Edgar, Yura, Kolya, Anna Tikhonovna . . . The Light Ones I'd been sparring and fighting with recently, bending the rules almost to the point of breaking them: Ilya, Garik, Tolik, the shape-shifter, Bear. Others I didn't know, both Dark and Light, including some who were obviously not connected with the Watches. Two in loose robes— Inquisitors, I supposed.

And a light enchantress with a face contorted in grief. People and Others have expressions like that when they've just lost loved ones.

And the wind swirls into their open mouths,
Filling them with white snow, or sweet manna,
Or simply feathers flying down after
The one who has fallen, like a fallen angel . . .

And then I was dragged irresistibly up the transparent stairway, to the top of the mysterious pyramid I had been climbing all this time; at almost the very same moment, the two Inquisitors in robes rescinded the prohibition on higher magic. Svetlana hit me with that cloud I had seen, which had been ready to burst and explode at any moment. A field of Power that made a multi-megaton explosion seem tiny and insignificant.

Time stopped

And I understood everything. Everything that had happened. Everything that was happening now and everything that was destined to happen in the immediate future. I understood, and swallowed hard to keep down the lump that had suddenly risen in my cramped throat.

I had become the most powerful magician on Earth. A magician beyond classification. A Caliph for an hour . . . no, only for an instant . . . The only one in this dilapidated round hall who had no future.

There are some Others who have no future . . .

A Mirror! I was nothing but a Mirror. The Mirror of the World. A weight cast into the dangling pan of the scales when the balance between the powers of Light and the powers of Darkness is disrupted.

The Light had acquired a new Great Enchantress, but the Darkness had not been given an equally strong adept. The Light had been granted a chance to settle accounts with the Darkness once and for all.

But there is no Light without Darkness. And so the Twilight had produced me. It had found a strange Other who had not yet inclined to one side or the other, an Other with a pristine, pure aura, and then colored that aura Dark. It had taken away my former memories and given me the ability to reflect and absorb others' Power. The more powerfully I was struck, the more powerful I had become, jumping up onto the next step. And when there was nowhere left to jump, that was the summit, and beyond that there was only eternity and the Twilight—the Mirror was no longer needed. Because the Mirror had itself become capable of disrupting the equilibrium.

The Twilight was waiting for me. Eternal Twilight. I didn't know what would happen to the body of Vitaly Rogoza, who until only recently had been an Other with no destiny. I didn't know what would happen to his memory and his personality—it all happens differently every time a Mirror comes. I only knew that the one who had become aware of himself in that frozen park in Nikolaev on his way to catch a train to Moscow would disappear forever, be transformed into an incorporeal, powerless shadow, a ghostly inhabitant of the Twilight.

Or simply into a part of the Twilight . . . the Twilight that is not as inert as we are all used to thinking . . .

I understood all this in the brief instant before I drew in all of Svetlana's Power. She imagined that she had lost Anton Gorodetsky. And she imagined it because of a freak coincidence, because I walked into the Tribunal hall with a mini-disk player exactly like Anton's, with a copy of his disk in the player and with Anton's favorite song in my ears and my soul. I also understood that the Inquisition knew the truth. But none of the Inquisitors would say a word to reassure the Others of Moscow, who believed I'd had a skirmish with Anton and Anton had been killed.

The Light Ones knew his favorite songs.

"Die!"

No, I won't die, Svetlana. Or rather, I will, but not right now. I am a Mirror. In trying to destroy me, you grow weaker, and I only grow stronger. I can already see what lies ahead of you—thirty or fifty years spent on slowly restoring all the Power you've squandered so insanely. You'll have to collect together what you've lost, crumb by crumb. For three, or maybe more, decades—long enough for the Darkness to prepare for another attempt to disrupt the equilibrium by whichever side it happens to be. You have long years ahead of you to find happiness with Anton, or not to find it.

But in any case, throughout those years you will be equals.

Maybe you have lost your powers, but I'm giving you a chance . . . a chance that I don't have.

The music stopped. The magical blow had been too much for the player—technology reacts badly in general to powerful magic—and it shattered into shards of plastic. My cap went flying toward the door, and my jacket split in several places at once.

I was barely able to keep my feet, but I managed it.

"A Mirror!" Gesar exclaimed, his voice filled with an entire gamut of indescribable feelings and intonations. "The third time, and the third time for the Dark Ones!"

"Well, we don't set up global social experiments, my dear colleague!" said Zabulon, the head of the Day Watch, making no effort to conceal his triumph. Today he was one of the victors. And the Light Ones had suffered a defeat.

But just how many times had this already happened—or the exact opposite?

Svetlana, drained and shattered, had been crushed by grief only a moment earlier, but now she cried out, unable to conceal her joy: "Anton!"

He was standing by the door. Anton Gorodetsky. Light magician. Alive and unharmed. He had followed me up.

"Thank you, Anton!" Zabulon said to him in a tone of immense satisfaction. "You carried out my assignment perfectly. I hope you're pleased with your reward?"

"Assignment?" Gesar exclaimed. "Anton?"

Zabulon laughed quietly as he stood up. The head of the Night Watch only gave his triumphant enemy a swift glance and then looked back at Anton.

But Anton walked up to Svetlana, who was so happy she couldn't understand a thing, put his arms around her, whispered, "Just a moment," and moved toward me.

For a few seconds we looked each other in the eye. Enemy to enemy. Other and non-Other. I don't even know how to put it so that it sounds right. There are always at least two truths, after all.

"Take this," said Anton.

And he handed me his disk player to replace the broken one.

"Thank you," I whispered. I took the remains of mine off my belt, took out my disk without speaking, and stuck it into the player he had given me, as if that were the most important thing of all now. And I thought: *Now the Inquisitor will get up and say that I can go.*

I was right, of course. Magicians of that level don't make mistakes, even if they are non-Others.

"In the name of the Treaty," Maxim declared as dryly and dispassionately as ever, "since it has been demonstrated beyond any doubt that Vitaly Rogoza is not an Other in the ordinary meaning of that word, the actions of the Night Watch relative to Vitaly Rogoza are not a matter for investigation by the Inquisition. Likewise, Vitaly Rogoza does not come under the terms of the Treaty. He is free to pursue his own destiny."

As if I'd ever really had one. Me and the other Mirrors who had come before me, and the young boy Egor, whose time had not yet come . . .

"The Inquisition has concluded its consideration of all the cases," said Maxim, glancing around at the magicians present. "Do the Watches have any comments or suggestions?"

I pressed "play" and walked away. In my tattered jacket I looked like a cross between a street bum and a weird scarecrow. But who cared?

The disk player I'd been given was working in random mode. And yet again it picked out just what was needed from the dozens of tracks. Kipelov and Mavrin. "Troubled Times." All I had to do now was sing along.

So I did.

Troubled times!
The specter of freedom on a horse.
Blood up to your knees,
Like in some crazy dream.
The people amuse themselves
Killing the Old Gods,
The people pray,

Waiting for Righteous Words!
A comet in the sky,
A sure sign of imminent disaster.
Fallen Warriors of the Light
Are burned on bonfires.
Warriors of the Darkness
Have encircled the world.
Thousands of birds
Tumble down like rain.

Troubled times for the one who no longer has the right to call himself Vitaly Rogoza. For the one who rose, only to fall. For the fallen angel . . . the dark angel. Troubled times for you and for the Others. The end of the millennium. The time when it's impossible to tell the Light from the Darkness, or the Darkness from the Light. A time of deaths and battles. Troubled times.

We don't know who we are—
Children of the red star,
Children of the black star,
Or of the fresh graves . . .
The dance of Death is simple and terrible,
But until the hour strikes,
The sins of all our lives
Are punished by these troubled times!

I don't know whose child I am either. I only know one thing: The troubled times usually punish those who have not committed any sins for the sins of others. Or if they have committed any sins, they're not the ones they're punished for. But I wasn't allowed any choice. I wasn't given any destiny.

We're still alive.
Some will be saved, some will not

On a wild impulse
They put the lights out in our fortress,
The flag torn down
Is the sign
Of surrender to our enemies,
But you will not take it,
It's a lie—
For now we're still alive!

I am alive for now. And I'm singing. I'm singing, even though I know that Kipelov and Mavrin's next song contains the following lines:

Don't ask—I won't take you with me.
Don't look—I don't know the meaning of life.
Don't wish to learn another's secret
That's all—I am only a spirit, I am vanishing!

I'm only a spirit. I'm only a Mirror. A Mirror that has reflected everything it was made to reflect. But I can't help asking and believing. I am leaving now, only to vanish, but I ask, I hope, I want to believe—take me with you! Take me!

I believe.

I hope.

I believe.

I. . .

ANOTHER POWER

PROLOGUE

YUKHA MUSTAJOKI FLAGGED DOWN THE CAR—HE WAS THE senior member of their little group now. Yari Kuusinen and Raivo Nikkilya squeezed into the backseat of the old Zhiguli without speaking as Yukha took the seat in front.

"Take us to She-re-me-tie-vo," he said, speaking with emphatic clarity. Strangely enough, Russian had been the language of Mustajoki's childhood, although he'd managed to forget most of it afterward. But then he'd always had a talent for languages, and now he lived near the Russian border and made regular drinking trips to St. Petersburg. The others preferred the ferry to Sweden—on the overnight trip you could get really drunk on hard liquor bought in the duty-free shop, sleep it off during the day (who needed Stockholm, anyway?), and then indulge your expensive pleasure again on the way back. But Mustajoki had stubbornly kept on traveling to St. Petersburg. "Drive quick-ly and care-ful-ly," he said.

The driver drove. Quickly and carefully. Taking foreigners to the airport was a sheer delight for him. An out-of-work engineer making a living as a freelance taxi driver didn't often land a plum job like this. Especially at a time like this, just before the New Year, when the year 2000 was coming up and everybody was out working away, trying to make sure there'd be food for the festive table and good presents for the family.

The three Others sitting silently in the car weren't listening to the driver's thoughts, although they could have, of course.

After they'd already passed the Ring Road, Yukha turned to his comrades and said, "Are we really leaving then, brothers?"

Yari and Raivo nodded sympathetically. It really was hard to believe that it was all over—all the interrogations by the Night Watch, the visits by somber members of the Inquisition staff, the vigorous efforts of the Day Watch's adroit female vampire advocate, who was as well known among human beings as she was among Others.

They'd broken free. Broken free, been released from this terrible, cold, inhospitable city of Moscow, although they couldn't go home just yet: They were on their way to Prague, to where the Inquisition's European office had just relocated. But they had been released. With their rights restricted, with the obligation to register when they arrived anywhere, but even so . . .

"Poor Ollikainen . . ." Raivo sighed. "He was so fond of Czech beer. He used to say Lapin Kulta was the best beer in the world. He'll never drink beer again . . ."

"We'll drink a mug of beer for him," Yari suggested.

"Three mugs," Yukha added. "He was the most worthy of the Regin Brothers."

"And what about us?" Yari asked after a moment's thought.

"We are worthy too," Yukha agreed. "We did our duty."

For some reason when he said this all three of them lowered their eyes.

The small sect of Dark Others that called itself the Regin Brothers had existed in Helsinki for almost five hundred years. They were among the small number of Others who had not officially accepted the Treaty, but since they never committed any serious violations of its provisions, the Watches turned a blind eye to this. The Light Ones even seemed to be quite glad that twenty or thirty Dark Ones occupied themselves with harmless rituals, chanting, and archaeological explorations. The Dark Ones had made a couple of attempts to involve the Regin Brothers in the work of the Day Watch, but then they just gave up on them.

Until only recently Yukha, Yari, Raivo, and their friend who had been killed, Pasi Ollikainen, had regarded their involvement in the sect as a kind of curious, even amusing game. Their grandfathers and great-grandfathers had spent their entire lives as members of the sect, and their children would be Regin Brothers too . . . Their adopted children, that is. An Other is rarely fortunate enough to have a child who is also born with the abilities of an Other. That's only the norm for the lower Dark Ones, the vampires and shape-shifters . . .

It wasn't at all easy for the magicians of the small Finnish sect. They had to scout around the world, searching for Other children they could adopt, educate, and introduce to the great cause of service to Fafnir. As a rule, these children were found in the more underdeveloped and exotic countries.

Raivo, for instance, came from Burkina Faso. The little boy with the bulging eyes, legs bandy from rickets, and a swollen, flabby stomach had been bought from his poor parents for fourteen dollars. He had been cured of his illness, educated, and taught Finnish. And now, no one looking at this handsome, well-built young black guy ever could have guessed how strange his destiny was.

Yari had been found in the slums of Macao. At the age of four, with the help of his magical abilities, he was already a remarkably successful thief, which was how he was discovered by his future adoptive parents. They hadn't even had to pay anything for him. Yari hadn't grown very tall, but the Regin Brothers had been delighted with his sharp, tenacious mind and natural talent for magic.

Then there was Yukha, from Russia. Or rather, from somewhere in the south of Ukraine. He had suffered from wanderlust since he was a child, and at the age of seven he had traveled right across the country by jumping freight trains and hitchhiking, then crossed the border on foot, and one day he'd knocked on the door of the small townhouse owned by the Mustajokis, devoted members of the sect. There was no way that could be explained except by magical predestination.

By a wicked irony of fate, only the deceased Ollikainen had been a genuine Finnish boy.

The driver had never had such a strange group of passengers before—a young white guy with Ukrainian facial features, a tall guy with skin as black as pitch, and a short Asiatic with slanting eyes. And all three of them were speaking Finnish, or maybe Swedish, absolutely fluently. But then, you saw all sorts of things nowadays . . .

The first thing the Brothers did at the airport was study the timetable, but even here Russia's muddleheaded cunning had a little snag in store for them: The flight to Prague turned out to have been postponed for the fourth time. True, there was another flight to Duisburg with a stopover in Prague. But the transit flight wasn't in the timetable, of course, while the plane to Madrid, also with a stopover in Prague, left at a very inconvenient time, and they had to redraw their plans right there at the ticket office. This reduced a burly young guy in a track suit, wearing a gold chain as thick as a finger and clutching a cell phone in his massive hairy hand, to a state of inexplicable fury. He was on the point of pushing little Yari out of the way, but Raivo concocted a hasty spell of respect, and after that the line that had gathered behind them stopped complaining about the leisurely manner in which the Finns were consulting.

"We'll take the Duisburg plane," Yukha decided at last. "It's more convenient. And we won't have to wait so long. They'll postpone the Prague flight another three times at least, won't they?"

Of course they would. The reality lines were woven into a tight knot, and the ill-fated flight wouldn't leave until late that evening.

The almost forgotten sensation of freedom was as intoxicating as their favorite Lapin Kulta beer. While Yukha was talking to the pretty girl at the ticket desk (who was already hassled out of her mind), Yari and Raivo enjoyed themselves staring around the large hall, looking at the passengers walking by, the sales assistants in the brightly lit aquariums of their little shops, the international airline offices that are always there in any major airport . . .

It was Yari who spotted the Other.

"Look!"

There was a Light magician standing at a counter near the exit to the boarding gates, drinking coffee from a small, dark green cup. And there was a half-empty travel bag lying beside his tall stool.

Yari and Raivo studied the Light One's aura for a while—he was perfectly composed and completely in control of his emotions. He must have noticed them, but he didn't give any sign.

"When are they ever going to leave us in peace?" Raivo sighed.

"Do you think he's following us?"

"Of course," Raivo said with conviction. "We have to present ourselves at a session of the Tribunal. And the Moscow Night Watch has to be certain that the witnesses they released have left for Prague. You'll see, he'll follow us all the way to the boarding ramp."

"But there's almost five hours left until our flight."

"The Other's in no hurry. He's working."

Yukha joined them with the tickets. There was a faint breath of magic coming from him—of course there hadn't been any tickets left for today's flight, so he'd had some taken from the special reserve by influencing the girl at the desk and the airport manager.

"Here, take them . . ." he began, but suddenly broke off. He looked closely at the other Brothers and asked, "What's wrong?"

"A spy. Over there at the counter, drinking coffee."

Yukha looked and saw the Light Other.

And just at that moment a murky red stripe cut across the even azure tone of the spy's aura.

"Something's upset him," Yari said

"Another One!" said Raivo. "Over there, by the way out!"

There was a dark-haired, stocky man aged thirty-something standing right beside the glass doors, wiping his forehead with his handkerchief with one hand, and holding a cell phone to his ear with the other. He wasn't saying anything, either, but obviously listening to lengthy instructions from someone. There was a small black brief-case standing beside him.

This Other was a Dark magician.

"And they're following us too," muttered Raivo.

"Why would anyone be interested in us?" Yukha asked doubt-fully. "Any number of Others could have business at Moscow's international airport!"

"Remain vigilant, brother!" Yari reminded him. "Fafnir is sad-dened and alarmed by carelessness."

Yukha thought gloomily that after the hopeless failure of the operation to deliver the Talon to Moscow, the resurrected Fafnir ought to incinerate all four of them. Or at least the three survivors. But, as usual, he didn't say anything out loud.

Meanwhile the Light One finished his coffee, cast a glance of dis-pleasure at the Dark One, and set off in the general direction of the restaurant. His aura had returned to its even azure color, with a barely visible hint of cherry-red where the stripe had been.

The Dark One was still talking on his cell phone. Or rather, lis-tening.

"They want to make sure we leave!" said the shrewd Raivo. "As if we weren't delighted to go—what have we got to do here?"

But Raivo was wrong.

The Light magician wandered around the airport for a while and then settled at the counter again, reading some book and sipping coffee. The Dark magician finished his conversation and walked across to the ticket desk, and the Brothers sensed a trace of magic. Quite strong magic, too—about fourth level.

"What's he doing there?" Raivo asked, getting worried. "Is he getting a ticket too? Eh? Yukha, he's not going to bother us, is he?"

"Why would he?" Yukha asked. "Look!"

The Dark magician walked away from the window in the counter with a ticket in his hand.

"They've canceled a ticket someone had already paid for," Raivo guessed. "Would you believe it? There'll be an uproar . . ."

And there was an uproar, when the passengers were registering for the flight four hours later, when they all found themselves in the same line, including the Light magician. One of the passengers was politely informed that his ticket had been sold to him by mistake, that the airline apologized to him and offered him a seat in business class on the next flight . . .

The Dark magician watched the outraged passenger's complaints as if nothing unusual was happening. He actually seemed to be smiling. But the Regin Brothers had no reason to smile   the Dark magician and the Light magician were flying on the same plane as them.

"They've decided to see us all the way to Prague," Raivo eventually announced. "They're taking this business seriously."

Yukha shook his head. "No, brother. No. Something's not right here. You'll see—they'll come up and want to talk to us . . ."

CHAPTER 1

GESAR HAD SUMMONED ANTON IN THE EVENING, WHEN THE analysts and the technical staff had already gone home, and the field operatives who happened to be on duty that night had only just begun arriving at headquarters. The corridors on the second floor smelled of freshly brewed coffee, hot cinnamon buns, and mild, fragrant tobacco—that year a fashion for smoking pipes had swept through almost the entire Night Watch staff. Even the women hadn't escaped it.

It was about a year already since Anton had worked in the IT department; Tolik had replaced him as boss of the computers and the girls who operated them. A second-level magician—Anton had been classed as second level at the beginning of the year—was too important a figure to be spending his time stuck in a chair, tapping away at a keyboard and debugging programs.

"Like some coffee?" Semyon asked. Anton nodded, and just at that moment the phone rang. Silence fell instantly in the little room where the four field operatives—Anton, Semyon, Garik, and Bear—were sitting. They could all sense a call from the boss.

And who it was for.

Anton's colleagues watched closely as he picked up the receiver.

"Come in to see me as soon as you're free," Gesar ordered him without saying hello. "Finish your coffee and then come in."

"Very well," Anton replied in a steady voice. "As you wish, Boris Ignatievich."

He thought for a moment and then lit his pipe. If Gesar hadn't warned him time was short, it meant there was no great hurry.

"You in line for a dressing-down?" Garik inquired. Anton just shrugged. He could be in line for anything, from a charge of betraying the cause of the Night Watch to a promotion, from being told to stay in the office and not stick his nose outside to being ordered to storm the Dark Ones' headquarters. When a magician of the highest level got some idea into his head, it was pointless trying to guess his plans. Especially if that magician was in the kind of bad mood that Gesar had been in for the last few months.

Basically they were all feeling pretty lousy. This year had been just one failure after another. It had all started in the summer, when the workaday, humdrum arrest of a witch practicing magic illegally had spilled over into conflict with the Dark Ones. Then the fine young magician Igor Teplov, who had drained his powers in that conflict, had been sent to the Artek children's camp to recover and run foul of a deliberate provocation by the Dark Ones. A witch called Alisa Donnikova had managed to enchant him and make him fall in love with her. She was Zabulon's girlfriend, the same Dark bitch who had interfered time and again in the Night Watch's most complicated intrigues. This time Alisa hadn't gone unpunished—Igor had killed her. But in the process he had exceeded the limits of force permissible in self-defense, and now his fate hung by a thread.

About a month later Vitaly Rogoza had turned up, and that had proved to be a real disaster. At first they'd taken him for an ordinary Dark One, then they'd begun to suspect the visiting Ukrainian was an emissary, sent to assist the Day Watch. But Rogoza had turned out to be a Mirror—that very rarest of phenomena, which has been recorded less than ten times in the entire history of the Watches. He was a direct creation of the Twilight, a monstrous fighting machine molded out of a quite unexceptional individual, who might not even have been an Other. If only they'd realized that straightaway . . . but they hadn't. And in the struggle with the Mirror, Tiger Cub had been killed, Svetlana had lost her powers, and several other magicians had suffered to a greater or lesser degree.

Things were very, very bad . . .

Anton had cursed himself over and over again for not realizing the need to conduct a detailed analysis of the circumstances in which the Mirror had appeared. After all, there were similar cases in the secret archives—the appearance of a magician who evaded classification, a rapid increase in his powers, a decisive skirmish—and then he disappeared. Everything fit. Right down to the final moment, when Vitaly Rogoza had melted into thin air, dematerialized, and vanished into the depths of the Twilight that had given birth to him.

But never mind Anton, never mind even Garik or Semyon. For them a Mirror was one of those numerous exotic occurrences they'd only heard about in lectures or read about in the archives. Why hadn't Gesar or Olga, with all their experience, realized the truth immediately? They'd run into Mirrors before, after all . . .

Things were bad. Nothing was going right. As if the Darkness had been infuriated by the Night Watch's recent successes and was striking blow after blow. And very successfully too, it had to be admitted.

Anton shook his head to refuse the second cup of coffee that Semyon offered him. He carefully cleaned out his pipe, casting an involuntary sideways glance at Bear.

He was cleaning out his pipe too. The little pipe with a long, thin stem that had belonged to Tiger Cub. The girl had only smoked it occasionally, mostly to keep her friends company. But now that Tiger Cub was gone, Bear smoked his own pipe and hers by turns. It was probably the only way he had expressed his feelings since Tiger Cub's death—the gentle way he handled that pipe . . . and perhaps that fixed stare when Vitaly Rogoza had begun to dematerialize. A gaze full of regret: Bear hadn't had a chance to get his hands on Rogoza, he hadn't been able to satisfy his thirst for vengeance . . .

Like Alisher, the Light One from Uzbekistan whose father had been killed a year earlier by Alisa.

Anton had his own accounts to settle with the Day Watch and its chief, too. But of course the accounts would never be paid. The Treaty shackled both Watches, the Inquisition made sure it was observed, and the only way around it was to cut right to the chase and challenge an enemy to a duel . . . which was what Igor had done, for instance. And what was the result? The witch was dead, but now the magician was facing dematerialization, waiting for the decision of the European office of the Tribunal. And it wasn't hard to guess what it would be . . .

Anton got up, nodded to his friends, and made for the boss's office on the third floor.

He was feeling really sick at heart, not looking forward at all to the approaching New Year festivities that people everywhere around the planet were anticipating so eagerly, as if the number 2000 could change anything. What did it all really matter? But when Anton reached the door of the office, he felt a faint stirring of interest.

The magical defenses there were very strong. The Night Watch building itself was protected against observation, and the employees' offices and conference halls had additional screening. But it seemed like today Gesar had put in a lot of extra effort to ensure confidentiality: The air in the corridor was still and stifling, saturated with energy. And this invisible wall extended into the Twilight, much farther down than the first two levels that were accessible to Anton.

He walked into the office and closed the door firmly behind him. He sensed a slight movement behind his back as the defensive field closed together after being torn for a moment.

"Sit down, Anton," said Gesar, and asked in a perfectly friendly voice, "Tea, coffee?"

"Thanks, Boris Ignatievich," Anton replied, calling Gesar by his human name, "but I've just had one."

"A mug of beer then?" Gesar asked unexpectedly.

Anton had to stop himself rubbing his eyes or even pinching his arm. Gesar had never shunned the joys of life. He could leap about with the young people at a discotheque, flirt a bit with the silly young girls, and even take off with one of them for the whole night. He enjoyed sitting in a restaurant over dishes of exotic food, driving the waiters backward and forward, and setting the cooks trembling with his knowledge of exotic culinary subtleties. He could even go out with his staff, acting like one of the boys and drinking beer with smoked bream, vodka with freshly salted pickles, and wine with fruit.

But there was one thing Gesar never did, and that was to hold parties at the workplace. The ten members of the analytical section who drank a bottle of cognac to celebrate the birthday of Yulia, the watch's youngest enchantress and a universal favorite, had been punished with genuinely brilliant originality. Not even an intercession by Olga, who had been involved in the misdemeanor along with the others, had helped. The punishment had been devised individually for each of them, and it had been the most hurtful possible. Yulia, for instance, had been made to stay away from the Watch offices for a week and instead attend an ordinary school with teenagers her own age, go to the ice-cream parlor with the girls in her class, and go to the movies and discotheques with the boys. Yulia had returned to the Watch, fuming with indignation, and for ages she'd kept repeating: "God, if you only knew how stupid they all are! I hate them."

For those three words "I hate them!" she received another day's penalty and a long lecture from Gesar on the subject of "Can a Light enchantress entertain negative feelings for people?"

So now Anton was standing there in front of Gesar, frozen over the chair he'd been about to sit down in. He'd forgotten what he was doing.

"Sit down, will you?" Gesar prompted him. "No point in standing. So will you have a beer?"

"It's not quite the weather for it," Anton replied, indicating the window with his eyes. Outside there were large, heavy flakes of snow swirling through the air. A genuine Christmas blizzard. "Not the right weather . . . and not the right place?"

He surprised himself by making the last phrase sound like a question.

Gesar thought for a moment. "Yes, we could go to some amusing little place," he said, with a note of real interest in his voice. "For instance, that little café in the South-West district, where all the dentists go. Can you imagine it? The favorite café of Moscow's tooth-pullers? And there's a little pizzeria at the Belorussian station, that's a real blast . . ."

"Boris Ignatievich," Anton asked, unable to resist, "where do you dig all these placcs up from? The mountain-skiers' restaurant, the lesbians' bar, the plumbers' snack bar, the philatelists' *pelmeni* joint . . ."

Gesar shrugged and spread his arms: "Anton, my dear fellow, let me remind you once again what we work with. We work with . . ."

"The Dark Ones," Gorodetsky blurted out, and sat down in the chair.

"No, my boy, you're wrong. We work with people. And people are not a herd of cloned sheep who chew their grass in synchronized motion and all fart at the same time. Every human being is an individual. That is our joy, because it makes the work of the Dark Ones harder. And it's also our misfortune, because it makes our work harder too. In order to understand these people, whose souls, after all, are what the endless battle between the Watches is fought over, we have to know them all. It's not just that I have to, you understand. We have to! And we have to understand every one of them—from the pimply-faced kid who chews Ecstasy tabs at the discotheque to the ancient professor who's the last in a dying line of blue-blooded aristocrats and spends all his time growing cacti . . . Oh, by the way, the bar where cactus-lovers get together has rather interesting cuisine and highly original décor. But you and I can't go anywhere right now. Did you sense the defenses?"

Anton nodded.

"Believe me, I had good reason to install them. And sound se-curity arrangements in a crowded place would be far more complicated. I don't think I can really afford to waste that much Power at the moment . . ." Gesar rubbed his hand across his face and sighed. He looked really tired, all right. "By the way . . . take this. A small present."

Anton accepted the small object from his boss's hands with a surprised expression. It was something like a globe: a ball that was made out of thin needles of bone . . . yes, it was bone . . . bent into arcs and stuck into two little disks of wood at the poles. The ball was empty . . . But no, it wasn't. It was full of Power. Power that was sleeping, constrained.

"What is it?" Anton asked, almost in a panic.

"Don't worry. It's not liquefied bliss."

"Er . . . what's liquefied bliss?"

Gesar sighed: "How should I know? It was a joke. A figure of speech. A turn of phrase. A metaphor. I'm not even sure that bliss exists, let alone whether it can be liquefied. What you're holding in your hands is something like a magical white noise generator. If you need to have an absolutely—let me emphasize that—absolutely secret conversation, one that nobody can listen to, no matter what means they use, simply break the ball in your hand. You'll probably cut your hand, that's just the unavoidable price. But then for the next twelve hours there'll be no way anyone can monitor or check what's happening in a sphere ten meters across, with you at the center, no matter what technical or magical means they use."

"Thanks," Anton said gloomily. "Somehow a present like this fails to inspire me."

"You'll thank me again for it yet. So, will you have a beer or not?"

"Yes. But why does it have to be beer?"

"To avoid too serious a violation of my own rules," Gesar said with a contented smile. "We're at work, after all."

He pressed a button on the intercom and said quietly: "Olya, bring us some beer."

Nothing in the world was going to surprise Anton now. But Gesar released the button and explained anyway.

"Galochka's a magnificent secretary. But she's a fourth-level en-chantress. And she could give information away to the enemy with-out even realizing it. So just for today I changed my secretary."

A minute later Olga came in with a tray on which there were two immense glass mugs full of light-colored beer, an impressive crystal jug holding about two liters of the same drink, and a plate with an assortment of cheeses.

"Hi there, Antoshka," Olga said in a very friendly tone of voice. "You like Budweiser, don't you?"

"What Light One doesn't like light Czech beer?" Anton asked, trying to joke. The joke fell flat, but his readiness even to attempt a pun was amazing. He hadn't felt like doing that for ages . . .

"How's Sveta doing?" Olga asked, still in the same tone.

Anton gritted his teeth. The weight that had fallen from his heart returned for a moment.

"Still the same . . ."

"Nothing?"

Anton nodded.

"I'll call around to see her this evening," Olga told him. "I think she's ready for visitors now. And I'll find some way to make her feel better . . . trust me."

It was true. Who better to console a Great Enchantress who had lost her magic powers for a long time than another Great Enchant-ress who had been deprived of her powers for many decades in pun-ishment for a misdemeanor?

"Yes, come round, Olga," said Anton. "Sveta will be very glad to see you."

Gesar cleared his throat gently.

"You've got plenty of time," Olga snapped. "Anton, you know . . . I wish you luck. I sincerely wish you luck."

"Luck with what?" Anton asked, puzzled.

Instead of answering, Olga leaned down over him and kissed him tenderly on the lips.

"Well now!" was all Gesar could find to say.

"Ever since Anton and I swapped bodies," Olga remarked casually, "you don't really have any right to be jealous of me with him. And especially over such a tiny thing. Right, boys! Behave yourselves, don't drink too much, and if there are any problems—call me."

"Any problems?" Gesar echoed with a frown. But Olga was already on her way out. The Great Magician watched her go, and when the door closed, he sighed and said, "Living with a Great Enchantress is a real ordeal. Even for me. How do you manage it, Anton?"

"Svetlana didn't have time to become a genuinely Great Enchantress," Anton remarked. He picked up one of the mugs and took a mouthful of beer. It was excellent. Just the way real beer ought to be.

"But you're glad of that, surely?" Gesar inquired.

"No." Anton took a piece of strong-flavored goat's milk cheese. "I'm not."

"Why not?" Gesar asked with gentle curiosity. "Now you have several decades of happy life as equals ahead of you. Ideally fifty whole years."

"Gesar, what happiness can there be if the woman I love feels like a worthless cripple?" Anton asked sharply. "And if it's my fault, at least partly."

"Partly?"

Anton nodded. "Yes, exactly. Partly."

Gesar paused. Then he asked the question Anton had been expecting three weeks earlier but had already stopped expecting.

"Tell me, what happened between you and Zabulon."

"He came to my apartment again. Like the first time."

"And he entered with the help of your vampire friend again?" Gesar inquired.

"No, after the other time I closed my home to him. I simply don't understand how Zabulon could have got through."

Gesar nodded and took a drink of beer.

"Then Zabulon suggested I should commit . . . an act of betrayal. He said that Vitaly Rogoza was a Mirror-Magician created by the Twilight in response to the increasing strength of the Night Watch.

That his main goal was to kill Svetlana or deprive her of her powers. And if I was late for the session of the Inquisition, then Rogoza would strip Svetlana of her Power and dematerialize."

"And you agreed?"

Anton thought before he formulated his answer. He'd run through this conversation with Gesar plenty of times in his head. But he'd never found the right words . . .

"Gesar, the only other alternative would have been continuing confrontation. Obviously, either Svetlana would have been killed, or . . ."

"Or?" Gesar was clearly interested.

"Or many Others would have been . . . less exalted members of the Watch. To weaken us to the same extent overall."

Gesar nodded. "You figured it out for yourself?"

"No, not entirely. I rummaged in the archives and found a few similar cases, one of which ended with the annihilation of the entire Kiev division of Night Watch, apart from its leader, Alexander von Kissel. That time, the Mirror's target was apparently von Kissel, but he managed to protect himself. The result was that ordinary operatives and magicians died."

"But why didn't you contact me?" Gesar asked. "Why didn't you warn me about Zabulon's visit?"

"How could I know what he was expecting to happen? Maybe just that—for me to go dashing to you for advice. Zabulon was clearly trying to trick me, but I couldn't figure out what the trap was. It could have been a mistake to contact you, or to keep quiet. So I chose a third way. I tried to prevent the Mirror getting to Svetlana. Using a very primitive method—I rammed his car."

"Bravo," said Gesar in a strange, squeaky voice. "Well done, Anton. It didn't work, but it was a good try. But why didn't you tell anyone who Rogoza was?"

"Why didn't you tell anyone, Boris Ignatievich?" Anton asked, raising his head. "Or are you trying to tell me it wasn't you who led the investigation into the events in Kiev in October 1906? Or is one lousy century too much for your memory to retain? The entire situation was a perfect parallel. A certain Vladimir Sobolev came to Kiev from Poltava and registered with the Night Watch. He was later found at the scene of the murder of a young streetwalker, where there were clear signs of vampirism, then he was caught near the spot where a witches' coven was dispersed . . ."

"What did I summon you for?" Gesar asked in a very loud, indignant voice. "To question you about the dubious circumstances of your relations with Dark Ones or to hear you accusing me?"

"You summoned me, Boris Ignatievich, to have a drink of beer. And to ask me to do something for you."

Gesar started breathing heavily. Then he shook his head. "No, I'm not going to ask. I still have the right to order you."

"Go ahead," Anton said, pleased. "I won't argue, I'll carry out my orders. Right down the line. Only that's not what you want, is it? An obedient agent without any initiative?"

Gesar shrugged. "All right. You win. I want to ask you to do something for me, Anton . . ."

"First answer me . . . about the Mirror."

"Then listen. Mirrors have appeared nine times—if we take just the documented and proven instances. Only two of them have been on our side. The last three appearances of a Mirror have been on the side of the Dark Ones, each time at a place where the forces of Light had a significant advantage and plans were being made for . . . for a large-scale operation of some kind. It's impossible to fight a Mirror. He beats off any magical attack by rising to the level of his enemy and defends himself against ordinary attacks by using magical means. All you can do is choose who to sacrifice—a dozen of the rank-and-file magicians or one of the Great Ones."

"And you decided to let him have Tiger Cub and Svetlana."

"I didn't decide a thing! In the first place, until Tiger Cub was killed I wasn't even sure that what we were facing really was a Mirror!" Gesar smashed his fist down on the desk, spilling the beer. "And nobody was supposed to die. It was all supposed to end with Rogoza being captured—which would have meant he wasn't a

Mirror at all, just an ordinary visiting emissary—or with us retreating. I didn't expect Tiger Cub to blow her top like that!"

"She was a very impulsive girl."

"No, Anton. You're wrong. She was an energetic and impulsive Other, but she had excellent control. And this outburst of hers . . ." Gesar paused. "It seems that I underestimated the strength of her feelings for Andrei Tiunnikov . . ."

"They'd been seeing each other a lot just recently," Anton admitted. "He even went to her place out in the country, and Tiger Cub was very fond of her privacy. And when Andrei . . . well, just why did he go into Rogoza's room?"

"To show off to Tiger Cub . . ." Gesar sighed. "Ah, you little boys and girls, still green, boasting to each other, showing off your magic, your battle scars, talismans, and amulets . . . why is there so much human stupidity in all of you?"

"Because we are people. People who are Others, but still people. And we don't become genuine Others right away."

Gesar nodded. "You're right again, Anton. You have to live a complete human life, eighty years or a hundred, lose your family and all your loved ones who are human, see how ridiculous the politicians are, building their empires to last a thousand years, and the philosophers, creating their eternal truths for one or two generations . . . that's when you become an Other. But while you live your first, human life, you're still a human being. Even if you can enter the Twilight, cast spells, and read the reality lines . . . You're still a human being, Anton. And so is Svetlana. And Tiger Cub and Andrei were human beings. And your human side is where the Darkness catches you out. Your weaknesses, your emotions."

"Is love really a weakness?"

"If you have love in you, it's a strength. But if you are in love, it's a weakness."

"We can't do it any other way yet."

"Yes, you can, Anton. It's hard for you, but you can . . ." Gesar looked into his eyes. "Well, are you still angry with me?"

"No. I believe you tried . . . your best."

"Yes, I tried. And I pulled it off—that's the amazing thing."

"Tiger Cub and Andrei dead, Svetlana powerless—and you say you pulled it off?" Anton exclaimed indignantly.

"Yes. Because all the other options were far worse. And surprising as it may seem, what's happened doesn't simply play into the hands of Zabulon and his mangy curs." Gesar smiled. A cold, ironic smile. A very disturbing, suggestive smile.

"That still won't do Svetlana any good . . ." Anton began. Then he stopped, because Gesar shook his head.

"It's not finished yet, Anton. In fact, it's only just begun."

The chief of the Night Watch poured them each a second mug of beer, took a sip, and leaned back in his armchair.

"Boris Ignatievich . . ."

"Anton, I understand everything. You're tired. I'm tired too, we're all tired, we're full of bitterness, pain, anguish. But we're at war, and this war's a very long way from over yet. If you want to withdraw from it—then go. Live as an ordinary Light One. But while you're in the Watch . . . you are in the Watch, Anton?"

"Yes!"

"Well, that's excellent. Do you like the beer?"

"Yes," Anton muttered.

"Well, that's excellent too. Because you're flying to the homeland of this divine beverage. To Prague."

"When?" Anton asked stupidly.

"Tomorrow morning. Or rather, afternoon. The morning flight will be postponed until six in the evening and you'll take another flight with a stopover in Prague."

"Why?"

"You know that the European office of the Inquisition has moved from Berne to Prague?"

"Yes, of course. Because of Fafnir's Talon, the artifact that those idiots stole . . ."

"Precisely. Even without that, the Inquisition has a tradition of changing its location every fifty or a hundred years, and it was a very serious embarrassment for the Berne Watches. Anyway, they've settled in now and finally got around to considering our case."

"So that's why I got this present . . . Igor?"

"Yes. He's already there. We've lodged an official complaint, claiming that the Dark Ones organized a deliberate provocation and Alisa Donnikova enchanted Igor, which was the reason for his nervous breakdown . . . and that unfortunate incident in which a boy drowned. The Dark Ones, of course, are claiming that Igor enchanted Alisa in an attempt to recruit her to our side . . ."

Andrei snorted at the absurdity of the accusation—recruiting a witch! As if a Dark One could ever stop being Dark. Frighten her, force her to collaborate, bribe her or blackmail her—all that was possible. But to recruit a witch . . .

"Well then, the Tribunal will decide who was to blame and what degree of responsibility Igor bears. The lad challenged Alisa to an officially registered duel, so the Watch has nothing to answer for. But if the Inquisition accuses him of exceeding the limits of force required for self-defense or deliberate provocation—there's only one outcome for him. Into the Twilight. He's only half-alive as it is . . . and he doesn't even seem to want to fight. But we need Igor, Anton. You have no idea just how badly we need him!"

"Boris Ignatievich, what really happened down there?"

"Really? I don't know. We didn't arrange any provocations, you can trust me on that. I sent Igor on vacation because the lad had drained himself completely. Do you know how good working in a young Pioneer Camp is for restoring your powers? Smiling children's faces, happy laughter, cheerful voices . . ." Gesar's voice warmed so much that Anton was almost expecting the serious boss of the Night Watch to lick his lips and start purring at any moment. But Gesar broke off and then continued: "Either our accusation is just, and then there's a chance of saving Igor. Or everything that happened was just a tragic coincidence . . . in that case, there's nothing the Inquisition can accuse us of, but Igor won't survive the whole business. He's punishing himself for the death of that boy . . . and Alisa."

"What does Alisa matter?"

"He really did fall in love with her . . . yet another half-baked Other." Gesar watched as the expression on Anton's face changed and nodded. "Yes, he fell in love, no doubt about it. So, you're going to Prague. As our representative at the Tribunal. Defender and prosecutor in the same person. I'll give you all the necessary documentation in a moment."

"Ah . . . but . . ." Anton was confused. "I don't have any experience."

"Nobody has. But you'll acquire it. My heart tells me that as things develop there are going to be more and more of these . . . legal conflicts. Instead of honest battle and open combat. And don't you look so worried—I'll probably come to Prague when the session starts. Possibly even with Olga and Svetlana."

"Why bring Svetlana?"

"Maybe we'll be able to prove that Svetlana lost her powers because of a provocation by the Dark Ones and receive permission to restore her."

"How?"

"The same way we did with Igor. The problem isn't that Svetlana can't restore her powers rapidly, in just a few months. She can. The problem is that I can obtain permission for healing a second- or third-level magician, but restoring the powers of a Great Enchantress is an extreme case. To do that, we need direct permission from the Inquisition. And not the Moscow branch—it has to be the European office at least." Gesar raised his mug and smiled. "Prosit, Anton. Let's drink to your success."

"Boris Ignatievich, even now you're still not telling me everything!" Anton almost shouted.

"No, I'm not. Although I've already told you more than I ought to. But if you really want to lie awake all night with insomnia . . ." Gesar thought carefully. "Then add up together everything that's happened over the last year: the Chalk of Destiny, the death of Alisa Donnikova, the appearance of the Mirror, those ludicrous buffoons the Regin Brothers, and Fafnir's Talon . . . and the hysteria everywhere over the end of the second millennium."

"But there isn't a single thread connecting all these things," Anton blurted out.

"Then sleep well," Gesar said with a smile.

Late December is a time of frivolity and bustling activity. A time of frantic preparation for the holidays, a time for presents and drinking champagne with colleagues, even during the working day. A time of brilliant illuminations in the streets, a time for New Year tree bazaars. With the approach of Christmas and the New Year, even the eternal confrontation between the Others dies down, and Light Ones and Dark Ones suddenly slip into a short-lived dreamy state and sometimes even feel like forgiving their rivals their old offenses. The less serious and deeply felt ones, that is.

Edgar, the Dark magician, was late for a daily operational briefing for the first time since he had moved to the Russian capital from Estonia. The reason was trivial, but any self-respecting magician would have been ashamed to admit it.

Edgar had been feeding the ducks at the pond on Chistoprudny Boulevard. He'd surrendered to the memories that had suddenly come flooding back and completely forgotten about the time. He'd got lost in his dreams, like a teenage kid after a glass of beer. And when he finally surfaced, he realized the briefing had already begun.

If age teaches you anything, then one of its lessons is certainly not to hurry if you're already late, so Edgar didn't rush off to flag down a car or make a headlong dash for the metro. He calmly finished crumbling the bun he'd bought for the mallards darting about nimbly at the edge of the unfrozen patch of water or scrambling across the ice, and only then set off toward the Chistye Prudy metro station, with the Christmas snow crunching cheerfully under his shoes.

Twenty minutes later Edgar entered the Day Watch office without hurrying and with his gravitas still intact. The elderly vampire couple on watch were decorating the New Year tree. They greeted Edgar just the way they were supposed to—meekly and respectfully.

"The chief's been asking for you," the vampire husband told him. "He said to go see him as soon as you turn up."

"Thank you, Filippich," said Edgar. "Is the boss in his office?"

"He is now."

"Aha. Happy holidays to you!"

"And to you, Edgar."

Edgar rode up to the top floors and sent Zabulon the sign of Hojd through the Twilight.

"Come in," Zabulon replied.

The chief of the Day Watch required the strict observance of hierarchical discipline from his subordinates, but at the same time he somehow managed to respect the freedom of even the shabbiest werewolf among the security guards and to trust the magicians at the top of the Watch. He didn't question Edgar directly about why he'd missed the daily briefing session. If he'd missed it, there must have been a good reason.

But there hadn't been any good reason, and so Edgar thought he'd better simply tell Zabulon the way it was and leave it at that, especially since there hadn't been any serious operations planned for today. If a tricky situation had come up, they would have reached out to him through the Twilight or they could have simply given him a call on his cell, so Edgar wasn't feeling particularly guilty.

"Good evening, Chief."

"Good evening, Edgar. How do you like this weather?"

"Snow and no wind. I like it. I'm sorry I missed the planning meeting, chief. There wasn't anything urgent, was there?"

"No. But there will be now."

Zabulon was dressed as usual in his favorite gray suit and gray shirt. Edgar thought he'd never seen the chief dressed any other way. Always a suit and a gray shirt when he was in the ordinary world. And without any clothes at all in his Twilight form.

"Would you believe it, chief, I was daydreaming. Walking on the boulevard at Chistye Prudy, remembering Samara and 1912."

Zabulon gave a faint smile and sang quietly: "The photo studio . . . Samara wrapped in mist again, it's 1912 . . ."

The chief of the Day Watch had a clear, resonant baritone voice. Even though the Dark magicians had known each other for many years, it was the first time Edgar had ever heard Zabulon sing.

"Were you feeding the ducks?" Zabulon asked.

"Yes."

Zabulon sighed as he indulged his memories briefly. Very briefly. Literally for half a minute. "Okay, Edgar. Tomorrow you fly to Prague."

"For the Tribunal?"

"Yes. It's going to hear several cases, including Alisa's murder and the Regin Brothers' case."

"But weren't they going to release them tomorrow?" Edgar asked in surprise. "Or have the Light Ones changed their mind?"

"No, they haven't. They've handed the case over to the European office of the Tribunal. And I think Gesar will try to lay the responsibility for what they did at our door. As if we'd planned it. Or incited them."

"But they don't have any evidence! Not a shred!"

"Well, that's why I'm sending you to Prague. You can take a look, see what's what. And don't take it easy on anyone. We've taken enough, we've given way to them over the last two years—it's time we held our heads up higher."

"It was the circumstances. That's what we gave way to," said Edgar. The prospect of spending Christmas and seeing in the year 2000 in the ancient Gothic city of Prague had really fired his enthusiasm. Edgar loved the solemn city—it was the embodiment of the European spirit, a city where Dark Ones felt free and at ease.

"By the way. You'll probably be flying on the same plane as those Regin Brothers. Take a moment to drop them a hint that the Moscow Day Watch has no intention of abandoning Dark Ones who have suffered on its territory. Tell them not to panic or lose heart."

"And are we really going to defend them?"

"Yes, we really are. You see, Edgar, I have a few plans that involve that absurd trio. For the time being I need this international alliance . . . So pay a bit of attention to them as well. The Light Ones will probably set a spy on their trail. Keep an eye on him too. Don't let him interfere. Don't get involved in any unnecessary conflict—just keep him at a distance, that's all."

"I understand, Chief."

"Take these," said Zabulon, opening the safe beside the desk and handing Edgar two amulets and a charged wand. "I don't expect you'll need to use the Mist. But just in case . . . And you know where to recharge the wand."

"At Kostnitsa? At that ossuary?" Edgar asked, reacting immediately.

Zabulon nodded.

"Darkness!" said Edgar, almost feeling envious of himself. "I haven't been there for seventy years!"

"And you can purge yourself at the same time," Zabulon advised him. "Do you know how?"

Edgar frowned. They might be friends, but after all, Zabulon was a magician beyond classification, and Edgar hadn't even reached the first level yet, although he obviously had the potential for it. Edgar still had to carry on using his ordinary human name, but on the other hand, his surname had been completely forgotten by now.

"I've mastered the technique. In general terms." It was obvious that Edgar didn't like having to say that.

"Then you can practice it," said Zabulon, closing the subject. "That's all—now go and get ready. If you have any business outstanding, hand it over to someone else. Shagron or Belashevich."

"I understand, Chief. I will."

"Good luck."

Edgar left the chief's office, then called into his own for a moment, composed a message for Shagron, and suspended it in the Twilight before he set out for home. On his way out he ran into Alita.

"Hi there, beautiful!"

"Hello, Edgar. How would you like to go to the skating rink?"

"I don't have time."

"Oh, come on," said the young witch. "It's almost New Year—what business could you have to deal with? The Light Ones are more concerned with the quality of the champagne that's being made than their usual mean tricks. Holidays are for having fun, not for working."

"That's debatable," Edgar said with a sigh. "But anyway, I don't have time. I'm going away."

"Where to?"

"To Prague."

"Ooh!" Alita said enviously. "For long?"

"I don't know. A week or so . . ."

"The New Year in Prague!" Alita sighed. "And not just any New Year—the year 2000 . . . Maybe I should go with you."

"Go if you like." Edgar didn't try to dissuade her. "But not with me. I'm not going to have fun . . ."

He felt a little envious too: If the witch went to Prague, she'd be able to relax with a clear conscience. But Edgar had been on too many of these work trips to entertain any groundless illusions that they wouldn't involve much work.

There was always plenty of work, and especially at holiday times, as bad luck would have it. And during the most important holidays (who would claim that a change in the first figure in the number of the year wasn't an important event?) there was always more work than even the gloomiest prognosis suggested.

On his way home Edgar quickly reviewed the probabilities and established that the morning flight to Prague would be delayed until the evening and he would have to take an afternoon flight with a stopover in Prague. Of course, there weren't any tickets in the ticket office, and he couldn't really count on the special reserve either. But that didn't bother Edgar too much—what could be simpler than the old trick with the double-booked ticket? And, of course, the "right" ticket would turn out to be the one bought by the Other. Even if he only bought it a minute before check-in.

Packing for a trip doesn't take an Other long. Why bother taking things with you when it's simpler to buy them on the way? His entire luggage consisted of the amulets, the wand, and a brief-case containing a solitary magazine and several wads of American currency. Of course, an Other can get everything that money can buy without spending a kopeck or a dime. But it's not worth wasting the Power. And not all interventions are the same. Manipulate a sales assistant's mind for a piece of cake, and the Night Watch would nail you for an unsanctioned intervention. That would be just like them.

And apart from that, Edgar would simply have felt sorry for the sales assistant. The cake wouldn't have bothered him, of course. What if he suddenly needed to steal a jeep from an automobile sales room? People were the Other's foundation. Their feed base and sub-stratum. They should be treated with consideration . . . And there was no need to worry about that kind of ideology sounding too much like the Light Ones'.

The Dark Ones could tell the difference between treating human beings with consideration and doting on them.

They could tell it very clearly.

Edgar used the night to catch up on his sleep, although it was harder than he expected to get to sleep at such an unusual time. Even as he was sinking into slumber, Edgar regretted that he hadn't gone to the skating rink with Alita.

In the morning Edgar discovered that someone had put a lot of work into improving his natural magical shell, strengthening it and weaving in stiff, tightly connected reinforcing threads. Zabulon, of course, who else? It couldn't be anyone else. *Hm . . .* thought Edgar. *Could this mission really turn out to be complicated and dangerous? Or is Zabulon simply playing it safe?*

Since clashes with the Light Ones had become more frequent, Zabulon had installed personal protection for a lot of the members of the Day Watch. Just where did he get all the energy to maintain so many shields?

There were probably only two Others in Moscow who knew the answer to that—Zabulon himself and his eternal opponent Gesar. And maybe the Inquisition. At least its top bosses.

Shagron offered to give Edgar a lift to the airport. It seemed like the newly repaired magician simply enjoyed driving his newly repaired BMW around Moscow when the city was in a holiday mood. The excuse he invented couldn't have been any simpler or more convincing: a briefing on current business. Not that there was much business for Edgar to brief him on. The hysterical response of a thirteen-year-old girl who had discovered that she could enter the Twilight and accidentally looked at herself in a mirror while she was there. Win her confidence, talk some sense into her, support her . . . an assignment for a beginner. And then there was the gerontophilic succubus who was the laughingstock of half of Biruliovo.

This wasn't even work. It was just a couple of trifling problems. Minor domestic turbulence.

Just as he was walking into the airport terminal, Edgar got a call from another magician high up in the Day Watch—the magician whom his colleagues knew as Yury, although he could obviously have used a Twilight name quite openly. Shagron had one for his special services to the Watch, and Yury was significantly more powerful and much older than Shagron.

"Hi, Edgar. On your way to Prague?"

"What of it?" Edgar asked, Odessa-style.

"Listen, and don't interrupt. I know a thing or two about the chief's plans. And why you're being sent there. It's not all as simple and clear-cut as it seems at first glance. There are several Light Ones leaving for Prague today and tomorrow, and I wouldn't be surprised if Gesar himself goes there in a few days. There are a few little signs that indicate the Light Ones are setting up a large-scale operation. Of course, Zabulon is planning an appropriate response. So you just be careful. Especially while you're traveling."

Yury stopped, as if he were expecting a reply from Edgar, but Edgar didn't say anything—he remembered he'd been told not to interrupt. He just reached into the Twilight, attempting to locate Zabulon—but he couldn't find the slightest trace of the chief. He couldn't tell where he was, what secret crannies he was lurking in, or what deep levels of the Twilight he was roaming through. The most powerful magicians had their own paths and their own motives, incomprehensible to those around them.

"You remember the chief sent Alisa Donnikova on vacation?" Yury went on. "Remember what happened to her. Of course, you want to know why I'm telling you all this. I'll tell you right now. Because I'm a Dark One. And also because I've worked with you for quite a while already. Take it any way you like, but I'd prefer to see you as a live, healthy Other, and not just another shadow in the Twilight. See you, Edgar."

Edgar stood there for a while, thoughtfully squeezing the cell phone in his hand. Then he put it back on his belt, picked up his briefcase, and set off for the ticket desks.

Darkness! the magician thought to himself. *What was that? A warning of some kind? And obviously behind Zabulon's back. And he brought up that business with Alisa. . .*

Zabulon had simply sacrificed the witch Alisa. Coldly and without any unnecessary pity. Like a pawn in a game of chess. In the games played between the Watches it was absurd to develop any feelings for the faceless figures on the board . . . but Others know how to feel and love as well. Edgar felt genuinely sorry for Alisa, but he wouldn't have lifted a finger to save her, not even if he had known everything in advance. Every game has its own inflexible rules, set once and for all. And nobody who has joined in a game can ever withdraw from it, or go against the rules. The witch Alisa had made her exit, and the witch Alita had made her entry. The law of conservation in action. In fact, Alita promised to be more likeable . . .

Working on autopilot, Edgar brainwashed the girl at the desk, still absorbed in his own thoughts. She gave him a little blue booklet with his ticket and canceled the ticket of some other unfortunate passenger. Unfortunately, he would just have to take a later flight, because in the world of people and Others, it was the latter who set the rules. *Why did Yury feel the need to warn me?* Edgar wondered as he stood at a bar counter with a glass of beer that was very expensive, but not very good. *Surely not out of altruism? Nobody breaks the rules of the game that way.*

He recalled in passing that when Zabulon left Moscow, he hadn't left Yury or Nikolai as his deputy in charge, although they were the Day Watch's most powerful Dark magicians after the chief. He had appointed Edgar, who was substantially less powerful than either of them. Yury had already been acknowledged as a magician beyond classification in the nineteenth century, and Nikolai just recently, after the war. Edgar still hadn't even reached first level, and if he was honest, he hadn't even mastered the second level completely. Sure, Edgar was a powerful magician. Sure, he was more powerful than most of the Others in Moscow, Dark or Light. But he still couldn't match Yury and Nikolai.

Just why had Zabulon done that? Was Yury trying to take a bit of petty revenge? Out of simple envy? Trying to scare him or even (you could never tell!) simply having a joke at his upstart colleague's expense?

The way Edgar had been brought in from Estonia had been hasty and illogical too. There he was, living a quiet life up in the small Baltic country, running its small, drowsy Day Watch, and then suddenly—slam bang! The urgent summons to Moscow, the mad scramble to get his successor in Tallinn up to scratch—who was a classical "hot-headed Estonian boy," barely even fourth level . . . Edgar ought to give him a call, by the way. And then what had happened in Moscow? Edgar had been thrown straight into the crucible of a hectic two-week operation, and then, not long after that, he'd taken part in a wild cavalry raid to rescue from the Light Ones a witch who'd been practicing without a license. And that was all. After that, there'd been more than three months of routine work until the middle of November, when he'd suddenly been appointed acting chief of the Day Watch while Zabulon was away, and then there'd been the Mirror's visit and the Tribunal at Moscow University.

If he thought about it, it was quite possible that the old Day Watch magicians could try to teach this newcomer from the Baltic a lesson because he was making a career for himself too fast, but they could hardly believe he was actually conspiring to take over from the chief. Zabulon didn't leave Moscow very often. And when Zabulon was there, Edgar was no more than just another operational agent. A powerful one, of course, an elite operative, but he only had the same rights as the others.

By the time his glass was empty, Edgar had decided to stop guessing at the reasons behind it all. His best bet was to try to figure out a line of conduct that took account of . . . of everything. Even the very wildest possibilities.

All right. What was it that had finished off Alisa? She hadn't gathered enough Power in time. She hadn't recognized the Light Other, even though he was so close to her. She hadn't refused a duel that she was certain to lose. And most important of all—she'd given way to her emotions. She'd tried to appeal to a Light One's feelings.

Well, then, Edgar wasn't short of Power, and Zabulon had even given him some of his own. His two amulets were a real treasure house of Power, especially the one charged with the Transylvanian Mist. If Edgar used that one, every Other in Europe would sense the monstrous discharge of energy. Plus the battle wand—a highly specialized weapon, but it was fast and reliable. Shahab's Lash was nobody's idea of a joke!

That meant Edgar had to keep as close an eye as possible on the Light Ones. Oh yes, about the Light Ones . . . Just at that moment there were three of them in Sheremetievo. First, there was his old friend from previous operations, Anton Gorodetsky, whom the lower-level Dark Ones had nicknamed "Zabulon's favorite." In that business with the Mirror he'd done just what Zabulon wanted for some reason, and helped the Dark Ones . . . Or had he just made everyone think he helped the Dark Ones? Probably that was it—otherwise how could he have stayed on in the Night Watch?

Second, there was a middle-aged female healer who had no connection with the Night Watch, thoughtfully sniffing perfumes in the duty-free shop. She probably just happened to be traveling that day by coincidence.

Third, there was a militiaman who was an Other on duty at the check-in, as there was supposed to be in any airport.

Apart from Edgar himself, there were four Dark Ones in the international terminal of Sheremetievo-2. First, his charges, the trio of Regin Brothers, who kept staring guardedly by turns at Edgar and Anton, who had installed himself in the bar at the far end of the hall. Plus a weak magician over by the gambling machines who was paying no attention to anything; he seemed to be trying to earn a bit of extra cash by getting the mechanism to pay out the maximum winnings. His kind was perfectly described by the phrase "cheap trash."

The basic situation couldn't have been clearer.

Check-in and passport control went quickly; no visas were required for the Czech Republic. In fact, just in case, Edgar was carrying Estonian and Argentinian passports, both perfectly legal— Argentina was a wonderful country that traded its own citizenship quite freely.

Edgar spent the rest of the time until boarding in one of the bars. Naturally, not the one where Zabulon's favorite, the Light magician Gorodetsky, had installed himself. Edgar's glance and his had met just once—*I know you're here and you know I'm here, and both of us know that the other knows his opponent . . . and we're on similar missions. To defend our own at the trial and rout our enemies . . .*

To Gorodetsky's credit, he'd made his position perfectly clear: *When the trial starts, that's when we'll get to grips. Meanwhile, let's just enjoy the flight and not get in each other's way.*

Strange, how easily they understood each other. Maybe it was just a hangover from those ancient times before the Others were divided into Dark Ones and Light Ones, when they simply stood up together against fate and the vicissitudes of life. Back then, of course, any healer was closer to a vampire than he was to any simple, luckless human being in the faceless mass of other people like him. The Twilight can bring you together.

But the Twilight could separate you too. In fact, the Twilight was pretty good at it—nowadays you simply couldn't find more irreconcilable enemies anywhere on earth than Dark Ones and Light Ones. The puny conflict between the USA and the Islamic world was nothing in comparison . . . Even the old Cold War between the USA and the USSR that was now a part of history hadn't come close to the war of the Watches. They were just childish games for foolish human beings.

Edgar drank coffee that was extremely black, but not very good, thinking about everything at once and nothing in particular. For instance, why all these airport bars that were so expensive and didn't seem to be skimping on the ingredients of their food and drink managed to brew lousy coffee, pour bad beer, and make absolutely inedible sandwiches. Plenty of the problems of human life could be attributed to the struggle between the Watches, but this certainly wasn't one of them.

His charges—the entire ill-assorted trio of them—were peering at him disapprovingly from the waiting hall. Of course, the Regin Brothers regarded him as just another cop. Let them. They were boneheads. Brainless, heedless boneheads. And since that was what they were, they could be used to serve the cause of Darkness. Zabulon had been quite right to decide to make use of them. That business with Fafnir's Talon had certainly put the Light Ones off their stride during Rogoza the Mirror's visit. Without even knowing it, the Regin Brothers had taken one of the blows intended for the Day Watch and allowed the Mirror, who had already grown strong, to top himself right up with Power. That was really what had made certain that Zabulon and his cohorts would win out in the latest clash with the Light Ones.

And serve them right.

Edgar watched without the slightest sympathy as the courteous customs officers led away a furious gent in a prim, formal suit and expensive raincoat. It was his place that Edgar would be occupying on the flight to Prague.

When they were already on their way, Edgar waited until one of the Regin Brothers left his seat and then sat down next to the one who seemed to be the most sensible—the white one.

"Greetings, brother," Edgar said warmly.

The Finn looked at him with big round eyes. A cautious look.

"We are Dark Ones," Edgar went on quietly. "We don't abandon our own. I've been sent to protect you, if necessary. And we'll be able to defend you at the Tribunal—trust me. So hold your heads high, servants of the Darkness. Our hour will come very soon now."

Having said that, Edgar got up and went back to his place without looking back even once.

There. Now let them rack their brains over that.

How dramatic he had been! He'd really had to work hard to keep a solemn, stony face and avoid cracking a smile. But the expression in the Finn's big, round eyes had been the opposite of a smile—he'd been really frightened and worried.

"I really shouldn't have," Edgar muttered to himself. "They're like children . . . And I mock them."

Edgar sighed regretfully and opened his magazine. It was a nice short flight to Prague, not like flying to Yuzhno-Sakhalinsk, for instance. You were there before you knew it, without any other stops on the way or that hellish nightmare of having to sleep in your seat. But then, if you really thought about it, the most convenient form of transport was a Dark portal. Only setting up a portal from Moscow to Prague would be an unjustifiable extravagance. So he had to fly, like ordinary human beings.

But not quite like ordinary human beings . . . at least Others didn't have any problems with tickets.

CHAPTER 2

ANTON LOVED PRAGUE. IN FACT, HE SIMPLY COULDN'T UNDER-
stand how it was possible not to love the place. There were some
cities that confused you and suffocated you from the very first
moment, and there were some whose charm slowly and impercepti-
bly fascinated you. Moscow, unfortunately, did not belong in either
category. But Prague was like an old, wise enchantress who knew
how to pretend to be young, but did not see any need for it, since she
remained beautiful at any age.

And if you really thought about it, Prague ought to have become
the abode of Dark Ones. A city saturated to overflowing with Gothic
buildings, a city full of plague pillars—monuments to the medieval
pestilence of the Black Death—a city that had a ghetto during the
Second World War, a city that witnessed the opposition of the two
superpowers during the Cold War . . . where could all those emana-
tions of Darkness, the nutritional substratum of the Dark Ones, have
gone to? How had they been scattered, where to, and why had they
been converted into memory, but not into malice?

It was a mystery . . .

Anton didn't know any members of the Prague Night Watch in
person. They had occasionally exchanged information by courier or
email when something in the archives needed clarification. And at
Christmas and the New Year it was traditional to send greetings to
all the Night Watches . . . but nobody made any distinction between

the Prague Night Watch (active staff—130 Others, operational reserve—76) and the Night Watch of some small American town (active staff—1 Other, operational reserve—0).

Anton had been to Prague twice on vacation. Simply wandering aimlessly around the city from one beer bar to the next, buying cheap little souvenirs on the Charles Bridge, traveling out to Karlovy Vary to swim in the pool filled with hot mineral water and try the hot wafers in the café.

But now he was flying to Prague on business. Really serious business . . .

Anton stretched out in his chair, as far as the space in the Boeing 737's economy class would allow—the comfort level wasn't much different from an old Soviet Tupolev—and examined the backs of the Regin Brothers' heads. They looked tense—the Dark Ones' auras were full of fear and impatience. They knew Anton was there and they were dreaming of getting as far away from him as possible, as soon as possible . . .

If it wasn't for that incident at Sheremetievo airport, Anton might even have felt sorry for the luckless magicians. But once Anton had gone into combat with an enemy, he was an enemy forever.

As if he could read Anton's thoughts—although, of course, that was beyond his power—one of the Regin Brothers, the tall, strong black guy, turned around, glanced warily at Anton, and hastily averted his gaze. Raivo—Anton remembered his name. From somewhere in Senegal . . . no, from Burkina Faso, that was it. Picked up by one of the Regin Brothers' families and raised in the spirit of devotion to the great Fafnir . . .

Just how had the Regin Brothers come up with all this nonsense?

Once, long, long ago, something had happened, something that often happened among the Others. A Dark magician and a Light magician fought to the death. The Light magician was called Sigurd . . . Siegfried, if you pronounced it in the German manner. The Dark magician was killed . . . and he died in his Twilight form

of a dragon. He was called Fafnir. Later Sigurd was killed as well . . .
Anton wondered if Gesar had known him?

After that, things took a rather unusual turn. The Dark magician's disciples didn't scatter, as often happened, and they didn't
fight among themselves, as happened even more often. Instead they
decided to resurrect their master. They banded together to form a
sect known as the Regin Brothers and withdrew almost completely
from the usual struggle between Light and Darkness . . . which
suited the Light Ones very well, of course. The brothers lovingly
preserved the Talon torn from the Twilight body of the Dark magician. Later the Talon was confiscated by the Inquisition—just before
the Second World War the Light Ones had lodged a successful protest against such an extremely powerful artifact remaining in the
hands of Dark Ones. The Regin Brothers hadn't really argued about
it, but they handed over the Talon with the words, "Fafnir's time
has not yet come . . ." And then suddenly the European office of the
Inquisition had been attacked! There had been a battle in which
almost all the magicians in the small sect had been killed, together
with a substantial number of the Inquisition's bodyguards, who had
grown idle and lazy. Then the remnants of the sect had made their
absurd appearance in Moscow.

It was a well-known fact that human beings didn't have a mo-
nopoly on idiots . . .

But then . . . were they really idiots?

Anton remembered what an intense charge of Power the Talon
had given off. In part it was the Power accumulated in the Talon as
a result of the Regin Brothers' efforts over many years. In part it was
the Power of the Dark magician himself.

Others didn't die in the same way as ordinary people. They receded into the Twilight, losing their physical form and with it their
ability to return to the world of human beings. But there was something left behind—Anton had seen vague shadows and a quivering
mist that sometimes appeared in the Twilight, marking out the path

taken by dead Others. Once he had even met a dead Other . . . It wasn't one of his most pleasant memories. But there was something left, even there . . .

Was it possible to bring a dead Other back to life?

The answer was probably somewhere. In the labyrinth of the archives, classified as top secret, sealed by the Night and Day Watches, with access banned by the Inquisition. The Higher Magicians were bound to have wondered about where Others went when they died, the path that they themselves would eventually follow . . .

But Anton wasn't supposed to know the answer.

He looked through the window at the clouds stretching out below, at the weak glimmering of thousands of auras merged together that indicated cities. The plane was already flying over some part of Poland.

Just supposing it was possible to bring Fafnir back to life . . .

So what? Maybe he had been a powerful magician, maybe even a Higher Magician, a magician beyond classification . . . his resurrection wouldn't change anything in the global balance of power, especially since he would be estranged from human life. He wouldn't understand modern reality . . . and if he was stupid enough to set off around Europe in his Twilight form, he'd be torn to pieces by rockets, shot with lasers from satellites. They'd use tactical nuclear weapons . . . while the Japanese howled woefully that Godzilla had come back to life and been killed again . . .

What was it the Dark Ones wanted? Disorder, panic, people screaming about the Apocalypse?

Anton squirmed in his chair. He took the plastic cup and the small, two-hundred-gram bottle of dry Hungarian wine from the smiling stewardess. It was all right for Edgar . . . Like any Dark One, he was flying business class, so he had a crystal glass and superior wine . . .

There was something to that last idea. Fafnir . . . the Apocalypse . . . At least it made some sense of Gesar's remark about mass hysteria over the year 2000. But why would the Dark Ones want to stage the end of the world? And what about all the other things? The witch Alisa . . . the Chalk of Destiny . . .

Anton regretted that he didn't have his laptop. It would have been interesting to lay the situation out on the screen, shuffle the variants around and see what fitted with what. There was a standard program called Mazarini for analyzing intrigues, and it would have helped him understand a few things.

The Chalk of Destiny . . .

He took a gulp of wine, and it turned out to be surprisingly pleasant. Then he frowned. Gesar and Zabulon. They were really the two determining factors in the entire business. They were far more mysterious and complicated than ancient artifacts like the Chalk of Destiny and Fafnir's Talon, or Others like the Mirror and Alisa. They probably understood everything that was going on . . . and they were trying to outwit each other. As usual.

Gesar.

Zabulon.

The starting point for the analysis probably ought to be the Chalk of Destiny. When Svetlana, the new Great Enchantress, had appeared and joined the Night Watch, Gesar had tried to carry through yet another intervention on a global scale. Svetlana had been provided with the Chalk of Destiny—an ancient and extremely powerful artifact that could be used to rewrite the Book of Destiny and change human life. At first glance it had appeared that Svetlana was supposed to rewrite the destiny of the boy Egor, an Other with an indeterminate aura, inclined equally to the Darkness and the Light, and make him into either a future prophet or a future leader. But, with some assistance from Anton, Svetlana had failed to do this. All she had done was to bring Egor's destiny into equilibrium by removing all the influences exerted on him by the Watches in their struggle against each other.

But of course, there had been more than one level to Gesar's plan, and at the second level another Great Enchantress, his longtime girlfriend Olga, recently rehabilitated after being punished by the leadership of the Light Ones, had recovered her magical abilities and used the other half of the Chalk of Destiny to rewrite someone else's destiny—while all the Dark Ones of Moscow were watching Svetlana.

That was the truth that Anton knew. The second level of truth.

But maybe there was a third one?

Okay, he'd have to put that on hold for the time being. What had come next? Alisa Donnikova, a capable witch and member of the Day Watch, although she wasn't one of the elite. Following a fight between Dark Ones and Light Ones that had obviously been engineered by Zabulon, she completely lost her magical powers. Then she'd been sent on vacation to the Artek Young Pioneers' camp to recuperate . . . and Gesar had sent Igor, who had suffered a similar trauma, to the same place. A passionate love had sprung up between them—a terrible, deadly love between a Light magician and a Dark witch. And the outcome was that Alisa was dead, killed by Igor, and Igor himself was on the verge of dematerialization, weighed down by his violation of the Treaty and the burden of his own guilt. Then there was the boy who had accidentally drowned because of him . . .

This wasn't one of Gesar's intrigues. Its ruthless and cynical style bore the signature of the Day Watch. Zabulon had sacrificed his girlfriend . . . but what had he sacrificed her for? To get Igor out of the way? That seemed strange. It had been almost a straight swap. Alisa Donnikova had been a powerful witch.

So it was one intrigue in response to another . . .

Then there was the appearance of the Mirror. Gesar was certain it had been impossible to predict, so it must have been a coincidence. But no doubt Gesar and Zabulon had both immediately decided to exploit it . . . each for his own ends.

Anton suppressed the desire to swear out loud. There just wasn't enough data for an analysis. Nothing but conjectures, blanks, assumptions . . .

And not much was certain about the Regin Brothers either. They'd been lured to Moscow by Zabulon. Had he wanted to spread panic among the members of the Night Watch? Or feed the Mirror with Power? The only thing that could have lured the Dark magicians into their insane attack on the Inquisition was a promise to resurrect Fafnir. Naturally, the old magicians, who had seen Fafnir when he was alive, had agreed—it was just about their last chance of victory. Naturally, the young magicians had followed . . . all those young Finns of African and Asian origin who had been collected one at a time—they were too isolated in their own little world. They thought of what was happening as a game, not an outrageous crime.

But what had Zabulon been after?

No. Anton didn't understand a thing. He shook his head and accepted his inability to figure out what was going on. Well then . . . he'd just have to do the job he'd been given to do. Try to save Igor.

Try to make the charges against the Day Watch stick.

The plane was already making its approach for landing . . .

The latest issue of *National Geographic* didn't help Edgar relax. He just couldn't get into the article about the Italian custom of throwing old things out of the window at New Year and other amusing European New Year rituals. The only thing Edgar took away from the leading paragraphs was a firm determination not to go strolling around any narrow old streets in Italy at New Year.

The smooth hum of the turbine engines set his thoughts vibrating in sympathy. And despite himself, Edgar began thinking once again about his mission and the current situation of constant conflict between the Light and the Darkness in the persons of the Others.

All right, he thought. Let's take it from the beginning.

In recent times the Day Watch had significantly strengthened its position and struck several substantial blows against the Light Ones, inflicting losses that could not be made good on the spot. It would take time—not even years, but decades. Zabulon's natural move should be to build on success right now, without waiting for the Light Ones to gather strength again. To dash to victory while the enemy was still stunned.

What could weaken the Light Ones and strengthen the Dark Ones right now? After the Night Watch had lost a very powerful and highly promising enchantress? An attempt to take someone else out of the game?

Edgar pondered for a moment and regretted he hadn't brought his laptop with him. He could have weighed up the possible variants, run through all the White magicians with any real skills and tried to identify their weak sides . . . There was even a special program for that, called Richelieu—the Day Watch wasn't short of qualified programmers.

He would have to rely on his own natural computer—powerful but imperfect.

Who? Gesar was obviously not a candidate; he had already crossed that line beyond which an Other becomes almost invulnerable to his colleagues.

Objectively speaking, number two in the Night Watch hierarchy ought to be Svetlana Nazarova, but she would be out of the game for a long time, so Edgar had to award that honor either to the tricky Olga, an old specialist in combat operations, who had only just come back from being out of the game herself, or to Ilya, a first-level magician. In fact, Edgar suspected that was not the limit of Ilya's abilities. Eventually, he could quite easily develop his powers and become a Great Magician, but metamorphoses like that required time and colossal effort, primarily from the magician himself, and Ilya was still too young to abandon many of the simple, almost human, pleasures of life.

Who then? Olga or Ilya? Which of them should they go for now?

Like Stirlitz, the Russian spy at Nazi HQ in the cult film of the '70s, Edgar pulled down his little table and calmly sketched two symbolic portraits on napkins—a shapely female silhouette and a narrow face in spectacles. Olga or Ilya?

Olga. Intelligent, experienced, perceptive, worldly-wise, and cynical. Edgar didn't know her exact age, but it was reasonable to suspect that she was at least twice as old as he was. Edgar didn't know her true Power—he'd never had a chance to test it to make sure. And to be quite honest, he didn't really want to try . . . To deprive her of her powers again would certainly be incredibly difficult—if you've just been released from jail, you value your freedom very highly. Olga wouldn't just think twice, she'd think a thousand times before taking another risk and ending up in front of a Tribunal. Apart from that, she was Gesar's longtime love, and the boss of the Night Watch would certainly take great pains to protect her. In Zabulon's place Edgar would be wary of offending Olga, for an enraged Gesar was a far more dangerous enemy than the ordinary Gesar.

Edgar scratched his nose thoughtfully with the end of his felt-tip pen and drew a cross through the female portrait on the napkin.

Ilya. A very powerful magician with the face of a refined intellectual, who wore spectacles for some reason, although he could easily have corrected his own sight. At the moment he wasn't in Moscow, or even in Europe. He was somewhere in Ceylon. As a matter of fact, for the last five years or so Light Ones from the Moscow Night Watch had been making trips to Ceylon with suspicious frequency. Edgar wondered what they got up to there.

He made a mental note of that—he ought to pass the information on to the analytical section, let them rack their brains over it . . . Although most likely they were already monitoring this anomaly. But what if they weren't? Edgar would do better to play it safe, even if he did make himself look stupid, than to feel sorry later, if no one had paid any attention to the Ceylon business . . .

Ye-es. But if Zabulon was plotting something against Ilya, he would hardly be likely to choose Prague to carry out his plans at any time in the near future, unless he could lure him there somehow.

Edgar pushed the napkin away without crossing the portrait out and pulled a clean one toward him. The last one. He divided it into four sectors with two lines at right angles and set about drawing a portrait in each sector. The first three were sketched in sparing strokes but were remarkably vivid, in the comic-strip style of Bidstrup or Chizhikov.

In Edgar the world had probably lost a fine caricaturist.

Ilya, Semyon . . . Igor, the defendant at the Tribunal. Should he count him or not? Probably he should, especially since he was now the most vulnerable of all.

Edgar thought for a moment and then drew Anton Gorodetsky in the fourth sector—the only one who was still using his surname. But even so, he had already reached second level, which made him Edgar's equal, although less experienced.

Which one? Of course it was simplest of all to topple Igor. He already had one foot down among the shadows of the Twilight.

And then there was Gorodetsky—he was flying to Prague too. But these were only the simplest variants. How many were there altogether?

The mere thought of the number of theoretically possible variants set Edgar's teeth on edge. Ah, if only he had his laptop and the windows of Richelieu, with its heuristic module . . .

Stop, Edgar said to himself. Stop. How depressingly one-sided you are, Dark One!

The thought that had occurred to him was simple and surprising. Taking one of their enemies out of the game wasn't the only way to make the Dark Ones stronger. Why not the opposite approach— introducing a powerful Dark One into the battle?

But who was there to swell the all too thin ranks of the Day Watch? Vitaly Rogoza, whose appearance had filled Edgar with childish delight, had turned out to be no more than a Mirror. And after he'd done everything the Twilight had created him to do, he'd disappeared forever. Look for some promising young recruits? They were looking and they did find a few . . . But you couldn't mold any of them into a genuinely powerful Other overnight, and the Dark Ones hadn't come across any natural talents like Svetlana Nazarova for a long time now.

Even so, thought Edgar, I'm on the right road. I'm flying to Prague, the capital of European necromancy, and in time for Christmas before the arrival of the year 2000, at a time when countless prophets and soothsayers are frightening the world with all sorts of horrors, up to and including the end of the world itself . . .

Yes! That was it! Maybe Zabulon was planning to resurrect one of the disembodied magicians of the past? Prague, at a time like this! Darkness upon Darkness! As always, Zabulon had skillfully and unobtrusively hidden what was lying in open view.

Edgar breathed out heavily, crumpled up the napkin with the drawings and stuffed it in his pocket.

And so, in the city of necromancers, at a time of incredible energetic instability, Zabulon could easily try to pluck someone out of nonexistence . . . But who?

Think, Edgar . . . The answer should be lying on the surface too.

All right then, let's look at what we have. Prague, the Tribunal, the case of the duel between Teplov and Donnikova, Gorodetsky and Edgar seconded to the trial . . . Alita might come as well. Who else? Ah, yes the Regin Brothers too . . .

Stop. That was it!

The Regin Brothers! The servants of Fafnir! "I'll find a use for them, Edgar," Zabulon had said. "I have a few plans that involve them."

Fafnir!

Trying to maintain an appearance of calm, Edgar folded away his little table and settled more comfortably into his seat.

Fafnir. There was someone who would be very, very useful indeed to the Dark Ones. The mighty Fafnir, the Great Magician, the Dragon of the Twilight.

The faint echo of his Power, absorbed by the Mirror Rogoza, had allowed him to drain an enchantress like Svetlana with ease. *And if Zabulon really is going to attempt to resurrect Fafnir, he couldn't have chosen a better place and time during the last hundred years, or the hundred years to come,* Edgar thought as his eyes wandered idly across the paneling of the Boeing. *That's for certain, he couldn't have. . .*

The stewardess glanced at him, and Edgar fastened his seat belt. The plane was making its approach for landing.

Hello, Prague . . .

Edgar's ears felt like they'd been stuffed with cotton wool, but that didn't stop him from thinking. So it was a resurrection. That was something the Dark Ones hadn't tried for at least fifty years—not since Stalin's time. There hadn't been any opportunity to try it, because the level of energy turbulence hadn't been high enough since 1933 and 1947.

Why hadn't Zabulon told Edgar anything about it? Was it too soon? But then what was he to make of Yury's cautious warning? And then, what had this to do with what had happened at the Artek camp that summer? Because it had to be connected somehow—it had to be. A pawn had been sacrificed, and now maybe a more weighty piece's turn had come. A knight or a bishop—which of those would Edgar be? The two rooks, of course, were Yury and Nikolai, the queen was Zabulon himself, and the king, defenseless but crucial—that was the cause of the Darkness.

So one of the rooks had hinted to Edgar that there was a chance the Crimean Gambit might be used again—this time with a rook. Somehow Edgar didn't feel like being a knight. Let that vicious old hag Anna Tikhonovna play the horse—that would be just about right for her . . .

The plane shuddered as the wheels touched down on the runway. Once, twice—and flight was transformed into a rapidly decelerating dash over the concrete.

Surely Zabulon hadn't set up another exchange of pieces while he furtively pushed forward a few pawns (the Regin Brothers) in the hope that another black queen would appear on the board or, at the very least, a bishop?

It was insulting to be a throwaway piece.

And what if it's a test at the same time? Edgar wondered. *An endurance trial? Alisa let herself be gobbled up—Zabulon doesn't need pieces like that in his game. But if I can manage to survive, and without disrupting the chief's plans . . . Yes, that's the result we need!*

But how could it be achieved?

The other half of the exchange was Anton Gorodetsky, Zabulon's favorite. There was no doubt about that. The chief of the Day Watch couldn't carry on using him forever, and he understood that very well. It wasn't even really true that he could use him . . . Zabulon was always ready to put a good face on a poor result and make it look as if he'd tricked the Light magician . . .

The passengers stood up and began moving toward the exit and the goffered bridge that was so unfamiliar to the inhabitants of the former USSR. Edgar took his raincoat out and put it on, left his magazine in the pocket on the seat in front, picked up his briefcase, and followed the others.

The feeling of being in Europe and not Russia was instantaneous and strangely comprehensive. It was hard to grasp exactly what triggered it—the expressions on people's faces, their clothes, the cleanliness of the airport, the way it was laid out? Thousands of minor details. The announcements in Czech and English without a Ryazan accent. The far greater number of smiles. The fact that there weren't any of those gypsies or private taxi drivers that he detested on the square in front of the terminal building.

And there was a line of attractive yellow Opels at the taxi stand.

His taxi driver gabbled away equally freely in Russian and English and, of course, in his native Czech: Where to? A hotel. The Hilton, I suppose. Oh! Russians don't often go straight to the Hilton. And the ones who do, look different, wearing lots of gold, bigwigs with bodyguards, riding in expensive limousines . . . I'm not Russian, I'm Estonian. Yes, that's not the same thing any longer . . . It wasn't the same thing before either. Ah, even a Czech was almost the same as a Russian before . . . That's debatable. Yes, maybe it is.

The driver's chatter was distracting and Edgar decided to take a break from all his thinking. He wouldn't get any real work done on the day he arrived, in any case. He could actually relax—with a mug or two of beer, naturally. Who in his right mind wouldn't sip a mug of genuine Czech beer, provided his stomach was in good shape (or even if it wasn't)?

Only a dead man.

Just like in any Hilton, a free room could be found without any real problem, even when Prague was crowded with tourists just before Christmas. But just like in any country that had not yet cast off the shackles of its recent socialism, it cost crazy money for a non-Other. Edgar was an Other, and so he paid up right away without even a frown, although they were obviously expecting one from him. He was Russian, after all, and he didn't look like a nouveau riche bandit . . . A hundred years earlier Edgar wouldn't have been able to resist sticking his Argentinian passport under the administrator's nose. But he was a whole hundred years more mature now, and he made do with his Russian passport.

The person at the registration desk—the one that not everybody went to—was a Dark One. A very rare type, too—a Beskud. He glanced at Edgar, licked his thin lips, and opened his slit pupils wide. And then, at last, he smiled—his teeth were small and sharp, all the same triangular shape.

"Greetings! Here for the Tribunal?"

"Uh-huh."

"Here you go . . ."

He threw a small bundle of blue fire at Edgar—it was his temporary registration. The fire passed easily through Edgar's clothes and landed on Edgar's chest in the form of an oval seal that glowed in the Twilight.

"Thanks."

"You give them a roasting at the Tribunal," the Beskud told him. "A real roasting. It's our time now . . ."

"I'll try," Edgar promised with a sigh.

He went up to his room, just to get a wash and leave his briefcase there.

And now, Edgar thought enthusiastically as he rode down in the elevator, *I'm off to the Black Eagle! And I'm going to order the* peceno veprevo koleno.

This dish, roast leg of pork, was so popular he'd even come across a description of it in a fantasy magazine he'd read once.

As he waited for his order, Edgar took sips of his second mug of beer (he'd drunk the first one Russian-style, straight down, evoking a nod of approval from the waiter), and tried to focus on his thoughts. But something was preventing him. Or someone.

Edgar looked up and saw Anton Gorodetsky, who was standing near the table and staring steadily at him.

Edgar shuddered, thinking he must have been followed. But there was a puzzled expression in Gorodetsky's eyes too, and Edgar breathed a sigh of relief. A coincidence, nothing more than a coincidence.

And what's more, there weren't any places left. Except at Edgar's table.

Acting on a sudden impulse, Edgar nodded to the Light One and said, "Sit down. I'm taking a break. You should do the same—to hell with all this work!"

Anton hesitated and Edgar thought he was going to leave, but then he decided to stay. He walked up and sat down facing Edgar, giving him a sullen look, as if he found it hard to believe it when his old enemy claimed all he wanted to do was relax for a while. What was that saying the Light Ones had? Anyone you've done combat with once is an enemy forever.

Nonsense. Fanaticism. Edgar preferred a more flexible approach— if today it was advantageous to conclude an alliance with someone you hurled Shahab's Lash at yesterday, why not conclude an alliance? But then, after Shahab's Lash there wasn't usually anybody left to conclude an alliance with . . . Ashes didn't make a very good ally.

"And not a word about the Watches?" Anton asked ironically.

"Not a word," Edgar confirmed. "Just two fellow countrymen in Prague just before Christmas. I've ordered the *peceno veprevo koleno*. I recommend it."

"Thanks, I know it," said Anton, still without a shadow of a smile, and turned to the waiter who had come over to them.

No, these Europeans had no idea what a real frost was, what a real winter was . . . As Anton came out of the Malostranska metro station, he wondered if he ought to button up the collar of his jacket, but he didn't bother. Snowy weather, but there was no bite to it. Two degrees below zero at the most.

He set off along the street, strolling at a leisurely pace across the ancient cobblestones. Sometimes he gave in to curiosity and dropped into the souvenir shops—amusing wooden toys, curiously shaped ceramics, photographs with views of Prague, T-shirts with amusing inscriptions. He ought to buy something, after all. Just to make his mark, so to speak. Maybe that T-shirt with the funny face on it and the words "Born to Be Wild."

There were almost three hours left until he was due to meet the Inquisition's representative. He didn't even need to take a taxi or ride the metro—he could eat a leisurely lunch and stroll to the appointed place on foot. A rendezvous under the clock tower—what could be more romantic? What if the Inquisition's representative turned out to be a female, maybe even attractive, and a Light One? Then romance would really be in the air.

Anton laughed at his own thoughts. He didn't feel the slightest desire to play the field or start an affair. And anyway, the concepts of "Light" and "Dark" didn't apply to the Inquisition. They stood outside and apart from the two great powers.

Maybe the concept of gender did apply? But then, as far as Anton knew, when Maxim, the Light magician from Moscow they'd nicknamed the Maverick, became an Inquisitor, he had divorced his wife. Apparently they simply lost interest in all that petty human stupidity—love, sex, jealousy . . .

The Black Eagle was one of Anton's favorite restaurants in Prague. Maybe that was simply because he'd been there a few times on his first trip to the city. It doesn't take much to make a Russian happy, after all. Good service that isn't intrusive, good food, incredible beer, low prices. That last point was pretty important. It was only the Dark Ones who could afford to throw their money around. Even Rogoza, that creation of the Twilight, had appeared in Moscow carrying heaps of cash. It was possible to earn money honestly, but to earn a lot of money—you could never do that without compromising your conscience a little. And when it came to that, the Night Watch was definitely at a disadvantage compared to the Day Watch.

The street Anton was walking along divided into two, like a river, leaving a number of old, low buildings forming a long, narrow island along its center—most of them were restaurants and souvenir shops. The Black Eagle was the first in the row.

As he walked into the small courtyard, Anton saw a Light Other.

No, he wasn't a member of any Watch. Just an Other who preferred an almost ordinary, almost human life to the front line of the magical war. A tall, handsome, middle-aged man with a good figure, wearing the uniform of an officer in the US Air Force. He was on his way out of the restaurant, obviously feeling quite contented with the way he'd spent his time, with his girlfriend—a pretty Czech girl— and with himself.

He didn't spot Anton right away—he was too absorbed in conversation. But when he did spot him, he gave a broad, beaming smile.

There was nothing else for it—Anton raised his shadow from the snow-covered cobblestones and stepped into the Twilight. Silence fell, all the sounds were muffled in cotton wool. The world slowed down and lost its colors. People's auras shimmered into life, like rainbows—most of them calm and peaceful, not overloaded with unnecessary thoughts. The way it ought to be in a tourist spot.

"Greetings, watchman!" the American hailed him happily. Here in the Twilight there were no problems with language.

"Hello, Light One," Anton replied. "Glad to see you."

"The Prague Watch?" the American queried. He'd read the watchman's aura, but not made out the details. But then, he was a pretty weak magician. Somewhere around sixth level, and with a strong attachment to natural magic. There wouldn't have been anything for him to do in the Watch anyway, except maybe sit somewhere out of the way and keep an eye on witches and shape-shifters whose powers were as weak as his own.

"Moscow."

"Oh, the Moscow Watch!" There was a clear note of respect in the American's voice now. "A powerful Watch. Allow me to shake your hand."

They shook hands. The American airman seemed to regard the encounter as one more element of a pleasant evening.

"Captain Christian Vanover Jr. Sixth-level magician. Do you need my assistance, watchman?" The formal proposal was made with all due seriousness.

"Thank you, Light One, but I don't require any assistance," Anton replied no less politely.

"On vacation?" Christian asked.

"No. A business trip. But there's no assistance required."

The American nodded. "This is my Christmas vacation. My unit's stationed in Kosovo, so I decided to visit Prague."

"Good choice," said Anton with a nod. "A beautiful city."

He didn't want to continue the conversation, but the American was full of bonhomie. "A wonderful city. I'm glad we managed to save it in the Second World War."

"Yes, we saved it . . ." said Anton, nodding again.

"Did you fight back then, watchman?"

Anton realized Christian must be a really weak magician. Not to see his real age, at least approximately . . .

"No."

"I was too young too," the American sighed. "I dreamed of joining the army, but I was only fifteen. A pity, I could have got here fifty years earlier . . ."

Anton only just stopped himself from saying that Christian

wouldn't have had the chance, because the American forces never entered Prague. But he immediately felt ashamed of his own thoughts.

"Well, good luck," said the American, finally deciding to move on. "Some day I'll fly into Moscow to see you, watchman!"

"Only not the way you flew into Kosovo." This time Anton was too slow to stop himself, but Captain Christian Vanover Jr. didn't take offense. On the contrary, he smiled his broad smile and said, "No, I don't think it will come to that, do you? May the Light be with you, watchman!"

Anton followed the American out of the Twilight. Christian's girl hadn't noticed a thing. He took her by the arm and winked at Anton.

"And may the force be with you . . ." Anton muttered in Russian.

That was a stroke of bad luck . . . His good mood had completely melted away, like a lump of ice on a hot skillet.

He could tell himself a thousand times over that no arguments and disputes between states had anything to do with the concerns of the Light and the Darkness. He could accept that in a war this airman-magician was far more likely not to aim his bombs at civilians. But even so . . .

Just how could he manage to go out on bombing raids and drop his explosives on people's heads, and still remain a Light One? Because he was a Light One, no doubt about that! But he almost certainly had human lives on his conscience. How did he manage not to fall back into the Twilight? What incredible faith he must have in his own righteousness, to be able to combine active military service and the cause of the Light.

Anton entered the Black Eagle in a gloomy and depressed mood.

He immediately spotted Christian Vanover's fellow airmen. About ten of them, all ordinary human beings. They were sitting at a long table, eating goulash and drinking Sprite. They really were drinking Sprite.

In a Czech beer bar! On vacation!

And not because they were teetotalers. There were empty beer bottles on the table, American Budweiser, which Anton would only have considered drinking if he was dying of thirst in a desert.

Anton walked past the Americans. There were no more free tables—another stroke of bad luck . . . But there was someone over there sitting on his own, maybe he could join him . . . The person at the table looked up—and started. And Anton did pretty much the same.

It was Edgar.

CHAPTER 3

ONE THING THE DARK ONES CERTAINLY HAD WAS A LUST FOR life. Anton had never had any doubt about that. He only had to look at the way Edgar was dealing with that tasty-looking leg of pork that no dietician would ever have approved, larding it generously with mustard—the kind the Russians liked, of course, sweetish, but still with a sharp bite—and horseradish too, and swilling it down with plenty of beer.

Anton had always found that astonishing. He had always been on perfectly friendly terms with his vampire neighbors, and even they sometimes looked more full of the joy of life than the Light magicians. The Higher Magicians, that was—those whose powers were at Anton's level still hadn't finished "playing at people."

The unpleasant thing about it was that their love of life usually didn't extend beyond themselves.

Anton lifted his heavy mug of Budweiser and muttered, "Prosit."

It was a good thing the Czechs didn't have the custom of clinking glasses. Anton wouldn't have liked to clink glasses with a Dark One.

"Prosit," Edgar replied. He drained half of his mug in two swallows, savoring the beer, and wiped the foam off his upper lip. "That's good."

"It is," Anton agreed, although he was still feeling tense. No, of course there was nothing reprehensible about them drinking beer together like this. The rules of the Night Watch didn't prohibit contact with Dark Ones; on the contrary—if a member of the Watch was confident that he was safe, it was welcomed. You never knew what you might find out. You might even be able to influence a Dark One. Not turn him to the Light, of course . . . but at least stop him from pulling his next lousy trick. Anton surprised himself by saying, "It's nice to find at least one thing we can agree on."

"Yes," said Edgar, trying to speak amicably and politely, so that the Light One wouldn't blow his top over some imaginary insult or get suspicious for no reason. "Czech beer in Moscow and Czech beer in Prague are two different things."

Gorodetsky nodded. "Yes. Especially when you compare it with bottled beer. Czech beer in bottles is the corpse of real beer in a glass coffin."

Edgar smiled in agreement with the comparison and remarked, "Somehow the rest of Eastern Europe seems to have lost the talent for brewing beer."

"Even Estonia?" Anton asked.

Edgar shrugged. These Light Ones could never let slip a chance for a jibe . . . "Our beer's good. But it's not exceptional. Pretty much like in Russia."

Anton frowned, as if he'd just remembered the taste of the beer back home. But he said something quite different: "I was in Hungary this summer. I drank Hungarian beer, Dreher . . . almost the only kind they have."

"And?"

"I'd have been better off drinking sour Baltika."

Edgar laughed. Even when he strained his memory a bit, he couldn't remember a single type of Hungarian beer. But then, if Anton thought so poorly of it, it was better not to remember. Anton was a good judge of beer, an excellent judge, in fact. The Light Ones were fond of the pleasures of the flesh—you had to give them that.

"And these . . . valiant warriors . . . drinking their slops from back home," said Anton, nodding toward the Americans. "Peacemakers . . . Goering's aces . . ."

Both Edgar and Anton had finished their *peceno veprevo koleno* long ago. They'd both drunk enough beer to set their eyes aglow and their voices were growing louder and more relaxed.

"Why Goering?" Edgar asked in surprise. "They're not krauts, they're Americans."

Anton explained patiently, as if he were talking to a child. "Aces of the US Air Force doesn't sound right. Do you know any short, snappy term for the US Air Force?"

"No, I don't."

"All right, then. They can be Clinton's aces. At least the Germans knew they were fighting airmen like themselves, but this crowd has dropped bombs on villages where the only defense is a Second World War antiaircraft gun . . . And they get medals for it, too. But you just try asking them if there's anything in their lives they regard as sacred. They still think they were the ones who liberated Prague."

"Sacred?" Edgar echoed with a laugh. "Why would they need anything sacred? They're soldiers."

"You know, Other, it seems to me that even soldiers should still be human beings first and foremost. And human beings need something sacred to cherish in their souls."

"First you need to have a soul. The sacred bit comes later. Oh! Now we can ask one of them."

One of the American airmen, a guy with rosy cheeks in a uniform glittering with braid and various kinds of trimmings, was trying to squeeze past their table. A fresh strawberries and cream complexion, the pride of Texas or Oklahoma. He was probably on his way back from the restroom.

"Excuse me, officer! Do you mind if I ask you a question?" Edgar said to him in good English. "Is there anything in your life that you regard as sacred? Anything at all?"

The American stopped as if he'd stumbled over something. His instinct told him that a soldier of the very finest nation in the world had to rise to the challenge and give a worthy reply. He thought, his face reflecting the painful workings of his mind until suddenly it lit up. Inspiration. A smile of pride spread across his face.

"Anything sacred? Of course there is! The Chicago Bulls . . ."

"It's like a game of chess, you get it?" Edgar explained. "The bosses are just moving their helpless pieces—that's you and me—around the board."

The waiter's face grew longer and longer the more beer Anton and Edgar drank. The number of those big glass mugs he'd brought to this table would have been enough to get the entire American air squadron drunk, and the Chicago Bulls as well. But the two Russians just carried on sitting there, even though it was obvious they were finding it harder and harder to control their tongues.

"Take you and me, for instance," Edgar went on. "You're going to be the defender in this trial. I'm going to be the prosecutor. But we still don't carry any real weight. We're just figures on the board. If it suits them, they'll throw us into the thick of it. If it suits them, they'll set us aside for better times. If they want to, they'll exchange us. After all, what is this trial, really? It's a song and dance over a trivial exchange of pieces. Your Igor's been swapped for our Alisa. And that's all. They just set them on each other, like two spiders in a jar, and took them off the board. In the name of higher goals that are beyond us."

"No, you're wrong," Anton said sternly, wagging his finger at Edgar. "Gesar had no idea that Igor would run into Alisa. It was one of Zabulon's intrigues."

"And how can you be so sure of that?" Edgar asked derisively. "Are you so strong you can read Gesar's soul like an open book? As far as I know, the head of the Light Ones isn't too fond of letting his subordinates in on his fundamental plans either. It's the high politics of the higher powers!" he said very loudly and insistently.

Anton really wanted to object. But unfortunately he didn't have any convincing arguments.

"Or take that latest clash in Moscow University. Zabulon used you—I'm sorry, you probably don't like to hear me say that, but now that we've started . . . Anyway, Zabulon used you. Zabulon! Your sworn enemy."

"He didn't use me." Anton hesitated, but then went on anyway. "He tried to use me. And I tried to use the situation to our advantage. You understand—after all, this is war."

"Okay, so you tried to use the situation too," Edgar agreed dismissively. "Let's assume that . . . But Gesar did nothing—nothing!—to protect you. Why should he try to keep his pawns safe? It's wasteful and pointless."

"You treat your pawns even worse," Anton remarked morosely. "You don't even regard the lower Others—the vampires and shapeshifters—as equals. They're just cannon fodder."

"But they are cannon fodder, Anton. They're less valuable than us magicians. And anyway, it's pointless for you and me to talk about things and try to understand. We're puppets. Nothing but puppets. And we don't have a chance to become puppet masters, because for that you need the abilities of a Gesar or a Zabulon, and that kind of ability doesn't come along very often. And anyway, the places at the chessboards are already taken. None of the players will give his place away to a mere piece—not even to a queen or a king."

Anton drained his large mug sullenly and put it back down on the glass stand with the restaurant's logo.

He was no longer the same young magician who had gone out into the field for the first time to track down a poaching vampire. He had changed, even in the short time that had passed. Since that first mission he'd had plenty of opportunities to observe just how much Darkness there was in the Light. He was actually rather impressed by the gloomy position adopted by the Dark magician Edgar—they were only grains caught between the mill wheels as the big players settled accounts with each other, so the best thing to do was drink your beer and keep quiet. And once again Anton thought that sometimes the Dark Ones, with their apparent simplicity, were more human than the Light Ones, with their struggle for exalted ideals.

"But even so, you're wrong, Edgar," he said eventually. "There's one fundamental difference about us. We live for others. We serve, we don't rule."

"That's what all the human leaders have said," Edgar replied, obligingly falling into the trap. "The Party is the servant of the people, remember?"

"But there's one thing that distinguishes us from human leaders," said Anton, looking Edgar in the eye. "Dematerialization. You understand? A Light One cannot choose the path of evil. If he realizes that he has increased the amount of evil in the world, he withdraws into the Twilight. Disappears. And it's happened plenty of times, whenever a Light One has made a mistake or given way even slightly to the influence of the Darkness."

Edgar giggled quietly. "Anton . . . you've answered your own point. 'If he realizes . . .' What if he doesn't realize? Do you remember the case of that maniac healer? Twelve years ago, I think it was . . ."

Anton remembered. He hadn't been initiated at the time, but he'd discussed and analyzed the unprecedented case with every member of the Watch, with every Light One.

A Light healer with a powerful gift of foresight. He lived outside Moscow and wasn't an active member of the Night Watch, but he was listed in the reserve. He worked as a doctor, and used Light magic in his practice. His patients adored him—after all, he could literally work miracles . . . But he also killed young women who were his patients. Not by using magic—he simply killed them. Sometimes he killed them using acupuncture—he had a perfect knowledge of the body's energy points . . .

The Night Watch discovered what he was doing almost by accident. One of the analysts started wondering about the sharp rise in deaths among young women in a small town just outside Moscow. One especially alarming factor was that most of the victims were pregnant. They also noticed a remarkably high number of miscarriages, abortions, and stillbirths. They suspected the Dark Ones, they suspected vampires and werewolves, Satanists, witches . . . They checked absolutely everyone.

Then Gesar himself got involved in the case, and the murderer was caught. The murderer who was a Light magician . . .

The charming and imposing healer simply saw the future too clearly. Sometimes, when he received a patient, he could see the future of her unborn child, who was almost certain to grow into a murderer, a maniac, or a criminal. Sometimes he saw that his patient would commit some monstrous crime or accidentally cause the deaths of large numbers of people, so he decided to fight back any way he could.

At his trial the healer had explained ardently that Light magical intervention wouldn't have been any use—in that case the Dark Ones would have been granted the right to an equal intervention in response, and the quantity of evil in the world wouldn't have been reduced. But all he had done was "pull up the weeds." And he had been prevented from sinking into the Twilight by the firm conviction that the amount of good he had brought into the world was far greater than the evil he had done.

Gesar had had to dematerialize him in person.

"He was a psychopath," Anton explained. "Just a psychopath. With the typical deranged way of thinking . . . You get cases like that, unfortunately."

"Like that sword-bearer of Joan of Arc's, the Marquis Gilles de Rais," Edgar prompted eagerly. "He was a Light One too, wasn't he? And then he started killing women and children in order to extract the elixir of youth from their bodies, conquer death, and make the whole of humanity happy."

"Edgar, nobody's insured against insanity. Not even Others. But if you take the most ordinary witch . . ." Anton began, fuming.

"I accept that," said Edgar, spreading his hands in a reconciliatory shrug. "But we're not talking about extreme cases here! Just about the fact that it's *possible*, and the defense mechanism you're so proud of, dematerialization—let's call it simply conscience—can fail. And now think—what if Gesar decides that if you die it will do immense good for the cause of the Light in the future? If the scales are balanced between Anton Gorodetsky on one side and millions of human lives on the other?"

"He wouldn't have to trick me," Anton said firmly. "There'd be no need. If such a situation arises, I'm prepared to sacrifice myself. Every one of us is."

"And what if he can't tell you anything about it?" Edgar laughed, delighted. "So the enemy won't find out, so you'll behave more naturally, so you won't suffer unnecessarily . . . after all, it's Gesar's responsibility to preserve your peace of mind as well."

He raised the next mug of beer with a satisfied expression and sucked in the foam noisily.

"You're a Dark One," said Anton. "All you see in everything is evil, treachery, trickery."

"All I do is not close my eyes to them," Edgar retorted. "And that's why I don't trust Zabulon. I distrust him almost as much as I do Gesar. I can even trust you more—you're just another unfortunate chess piece who happens by chance to be painted a different color from me. Does a white pawn hate a black one? No. Especially if the two pawns have their heads down together over a quiet beer or two."

"You know," Anton said in a slightly surprised voice, "I just don't understand how you can carry on living if you see the world like that. I'd just go and hang myself."

"So you don't have any counterarguments to offer?"

Anton took a gulp of beer too. The wonderful thing about this natural Czech beer was that even if you drank lots of it, it still didn't make your head or your body feel heavy . . . Or was that an illusion?

"Not a single one," Anton admitted. "Right now, this very moment, not a single one. But I'm sure you're wrong. It's just difficult to argue about the colors of a rainbow with a blind man. There's something missing in you . . . I don't know what exactly. But it's something very important, and without it you're more helpless than a blind man."

"Why am I?" Edgar protested, slightly offended. "It's you Light Ones who are helpless. Bound hand and foot by your own ethical dogmas. And those who have moved up onto the higher levels of development, like Gesar, control you."

"I'll try to answer that," said Anton. "But not right now. We'll be seeing each other again."

"Avoiding the question?" Edgar asked, laughing.

"No, it's just that we decided not to talk about work. Didn't we?"

Edgar didn't answer. The Light One really had got him there! Why had he bothered getting into such a useless argument? You can't paint a white dog black, as they said in the Day Watch.

"Yes," he agreed. "It's my fault, I admit it. Only . . ."

"Only it's very hard not to talk about the things that separate us," Anton said with a nod. "I understand. It's not your fault . . . it's destiny."

He rummaged in his pockets and took out a pack of cigarettes. Edgar couldn't help noticing that they were cheap ones, 21st Century, made in Russia. Well, well. A Dark magician of his level could afford all the pleasures of life. But Anton smoked Russian cigarettes . . . and maybe it was no accident that he'd ended up in this small, cozy restaurant that was so inexpensive?

"Where is it you're staying?" he asked.

"The Kafka Hotel," Anton answered. "Zizkov, on Cimburkova Street."

That fit, all right—it was a small, second-rate hotel. Edgar nodded as the Light One lit up. It looked awkward somehow, as if he hadn't been smoking long or didn't smoke very often.

"And you're in the Hilton, aren't you?" Anton suddenly said. "Or the Radisson SAS at the very worst?"

"Are you following me?" Edgar asked, suddenly on his guard again.

"No. It's just that all Dark Ones are so fond of famous names and expensive establishments. You're predictable too."

"So what?" Edgar said defiantly. "Are you a supporter of asceticism and the poor life?"

Anton looked around ironically at the restaurant, the pathetic remains of his leg of pork on the knife-scarred wooden board, his latest mug of beer—how many had there been? It didn't seem like he even needed to answer, but he did: "No, I'm not arguing that. But the number of rooms and staff that a hotel has isn't the most important thing. Nor is the price of the dishes on the menu. I could have stayed at the Hilton too, and gone to drink beer in the most expensive tavern in Prague. But what for? And you—why did you come to this place? Not exactly top flight, is it?"

"It's comfortable here," Edgar admitted. "And the food's good."

"See what I mean?"

In a sudden fit of drunken magnanimity, Edgar exclaimed, "That's it! I think I've got it! That's what the difference between us is. You try to limit your natural requirements. Maybe it's some kind of modesty . . . But we're more extravagant, yes . . . With power, money, financial and human resources . . ."

"People are not a resource!" Anton's eyes were suddenly piercing and angry. "Do you understand? They're not a resource!"

That was always the way. As soon as the areas of contact came up . . . Edgar sighed. The Light Ones were really deluded. How could they be so deluded?

"All right. Let's change the subject." He took another mouthful of beer and couldn't help remarking, "There was an American airman sitting in here . . . and he was a Light magician . . . an absolute oaf, by the way; he didn't even notice me. I'll bet you he regards people as a resource. Or maybe as a stupid, dull-witted inferior race that can be nurtured and punished. The same way we regard them."

"Our trouble is that we're a product of human society," Anton replied gloomily. "With all its shortcomings. And until they've lived many centuries, even Light Ones still carry around the stereotypes and myths of their own country: Russia, America, or Burkina Faso—it makes no difference. What the hell, why can't I get Burkina Faso out of my head?"

"One of those idiots, the Regin Brothers, is from Burkina Faso," Edgar suggested. "And it's a funny name."

"The Regin Brothers . . ." Anton said with a nod. "What cunning business are your people up to with them? It was someone in the Moscow Day Watch who called them to Moscow. Promised to help them activate Fafnir's Talon . . . What for?"

"I am not in possession of any such information, and that is an official statement of my position!" Edgar replied quickly. You couldn't afford to give these Light Ones the slightest hint of a formal violation to clutch at . . .

"Don't bother admitting it, there's no need!" Anton said with a dismissive wave of his hand. "I'm not a little child. But the last thing we need is the appearance of an insane Dark magician of immense Power."

"Us too," Edgar declared. "That would mean all-out war. No holds barred. In other words, the Apocalypse."

"Then that means the Regin Brothers were lied to," Anton said. "They were persuaded to attack the Berne office, steal the Talon, and fly to Moscow . . . but what for? To feed Power to the Mirror?"

He's quick-witted, Edgar noted to himself. But he shook his head as he formulated a superb denial: "That's nonsense! We only found out who Vitaly Rogoza was after the Talon had already been stolen and the four survivors from the battle were on their way to Moscow."

"That's right!" Anton suddenly exclaimed. "You're right, Dark One! The appearance of a Mirror cannot be foretold—it's a spontaneous creation of the Twilight. But the Inquisition's official communiqué states that the sect began preparing to storm the artifacts repository two weeks before the actual event. Rogoza didn't even exist then . . . or, rather, he did, but he was an ordinary individual who was later transformed by the Twilight . . ."

Edgar chewed on his lip. Now it looked as if he'd given the Light One an idea . . . passed on some information to him or simply pointed him in the right direction. Oh, that was bad . . . But then, why was it? He wouldn't mind being able to understand the situation better himself. It was a matter of vital importance to him too.

Edgar mused out loud: "Maybe someone wanted the Inquisition office moved out of Berne?"

"Or decided it ought to be moved to Prague . . ."

They gazed at each other thoughtfully—a Light magician and a Dark magician, both equally interested in understanding what was going on. The waiter was about to approach them, but he saw they hadn't finished their beer yet and went to serve the Americans.

"That's one possibility," Edgar agreed. "But we didn't need the actual operation with the Talon. Don't even think of blaming us for that kind of nonsense!"

"But maybe," Anton exclaimed, "you needed to ruin some other operation . . . one of our operations? And Fafnir's Talon was a very good way to do that?"

Edgar cursed himself for being so talkative. Only in the figurative sense, of course. No Dark magician would ever set an Inferno vortex spinning above his own head.

"Nonsense, what other operation . . ." he began. And then he suddenly realized that by starting to defend the Day Watch so abruptly, he had effectively confirmed Anton's guess.

"Thank you, Other," the Light One said with sincere feeling.

Still mentally lashing himself, Edgar stood up. It was true what they said: Before you sit down with a Light One, cut out your tongue and wire your mouth shut!

"It's time I was going," he said. "I really enjoyed . . . our little talk."

"Me too," Anton agreed. And he even held out his hand.

It would have been stupid to refuse to take the hand that was proffered, so Edgar shook it. Then he tossed a five-hundred-crown bill onto the table and hurried out.

Anton smiled as he watched him go. It was fun to give a Dark magician a fright, especially one of the Day Watch's top ten. The fat watchman obviously thought he'd given away some terrible secret . . . but he hadn't given anything away: The explanation Anton had suggested was stupid, and even if it happened by chance to be the right one, Anton still hadn't learned anything worth knowing . . .

He squinted at the waiter and gestured, as if he were writing on his palm with his finger. A minute later he was handed the check.

Including the usual tip, it came to one thousand and twenty crowns.

Oh, those Dark Ones . . .

It was only a trifle, but Edgar had still saved money. After all those gibes about the poor Night Watch and that invisible counting on fingers . . .

Anton paid, stood up (the beer had had an effect after all—his body felt relaxed in a way that was pleasant and alarming at the same time), and walked out of the Black Eagle, toward Staromestka Square, where he had an appointment with a representative of the Inquisition. He was only just in time.

There were always a lot of tourists here.

Especially at the beginning of every hour, when the old astronomical clock began to chime. The little double windows opened and little figures of the apostles appeared in them, moving out as if they were surveying the square, and then retreating into the depths of the mechanism again. The indefatigable Staromestka Square clock . . .

Anton stood among the tourists with his hands stuck in his pockets—his hands were feeling cold after all, and he'd never liked wearing gloves. All around him videocameras hummed quietly, camera shutters clicked, and the members of the multilingual crowd exchanged impressions on their visit to the latest obligatory attraction. He even thought he could hear their brains squeaking as they ticked off one more spot on the tourist map of Prague: *Watch the clock chime—done.*

Why was he walking along in this faceless crowd, as if he were also ticking off the points of a tourist program in his mind?

Mental inertia? Laziness? Or an incurable herd instinct? The Dark Ones probably never walked around in the common crowd . . .

"No, I don't understand you," someone in the crowd said in Russian, a couple of steps away from him. "I'm on vacation, do you hear? Can't you decide for yourself?"

Anton squinted quickly at his fellow countryman, but the sight wasn't a very pleasant one. His compatriot was sturdily built, with broad shoulders, and was draped in gold. He'd already learned how to wear expensive suits, but not how to knot a tie from Hermès. The tie was knotted, of course, but with a "collective farm" knot that was awful to look at. There was a crumpled scarf dangling from under the unbuttoned coat of maroon cashmere wool.

The New Russian caught his glance and frowned as he put away his cell phone. He turned to gaze at the clock again. Anton looked away.

The third generation, that was what the analysts said. You had to wait until the third generation. The grandson of this bandit who had got rich and somehow managed to stay alive would be a thoroughly decent man. You just had to wait. And unlike people, Others could afford to wait for generations. Their work went on for centuries . . . at least the work of the Light Ones did.

It was easy for the Dark Ones to make the changes they wanted to peoples' minds. The path of Darkness was always shorter than the path of Light. Shorter, easier, more fun.

"Anton Gorodetsky," someone said behind his back. Someone speaking a language that was obviously not his own, but which he knew perfectly.

And with that intonation that was quite impossible to confuse with anybody else. The aloof, slightly bored intonation of the Inquisitors.

Anton turned round, nodded, and held out his hand.

The Inquisitor looked like a Czech. A tall man of indeterminate age in a warm, gray raincoat, and a woolen beret with an amusing hat pin with a design of hunting horns, weapons, and a deer's head. Somehow it was very easy to imagine him in a twilit park in autumn, strolling over the thick carpet of brown leaves thoughtfully, sadly, slowly—looking like a spy engrossed in his thoughts.

"Witezslav," said the Inquisitor. "Witezslav Grubin, let's go."

They made their way out of the crowd easily—for some reason the people moved aside for the Inquisitor, even though he didn't make use of his powers as an Other. They set off along a narrow little street, gradually moving farther and farther away from the idle tourists.

"How was your flight, Anton?" Witezslav inquired. "Have you had a rest, some lunch?"

"Yes, thank you, everything's fine."

A show of politeness from an Inquisitor, even if it was strictly formal, was a pleasant surprise.

"Do you require any assistance from the office?"

Anton shook his head, quite certain that Witezslav would sense the movement, even though he was walking in front.

"That's good," the Inquisitor replied in the same indifferent voice, but quite sincerely. "There's so much work to do . . . The office coming to Prague is a great event for us. We feel very proud. But our department is very small and there's a lot of work to do."

"As I understand it, the Inquisition hasn't had to intervene very often in Prague?"

"That's right. The Watches here are law-abiding. They don't violate the Treaty very much."

That's right, thought Anton. The Inquisition's job had always been to resolve disagreements between the Watches, but crimes committed by individual Others were dealt with by the Watches. The atmosphere of a normal European country was hardly likely to have a pacifying effect on the Dark Ones. But within the framework of an organization they'd learned to respect the law.

Or at least to break it less obviously.

"The Tribunal session to consider the case of Igor Teplov, magician of the second level, will commence tomorrow evening," said Witezslav. Anton appreciated the fact that he had used Igor's full name and given his status as a magician, and also the statement that the session would "commence" and not "take place." That meant the

Inquisition hadn't reached any conclusions yet. And it was prepared for a long hearing. "Would you like to see him?"

"Yes, of course," Anton said with a nod. "I have some letters for him from the other guys, some presents . . ."

He stopped short—that phrase about the letters and the presents had sounded very dismal somehow. As if he really had brought a parcel for someone in prison. Or to the hospital bed of someone who was seriously ill . . .

"I've got a car," said the Inquisitor. "We can stop at your hotel for the parcel and then go to see the detainee."

"Igor . . . is he somewhere in the Inquisition?"

"No, why would he be?" said Witezslav, answering a question with a question. He stopped beside a Skoda Felicia parked at the curb. "We might have kept a Dark One who was detained under observation. But your colleague is in an ordinary hotel. He signed a pledge not to leave the city."

Anton nodded, admitting it had been a stupid question. It was true, what was the point of putting a Light magician in a cell?

"Excuse me, Witezslav . . ." he said. "I know it has nothing to do with the work you do now, but I was wondering . . . just wondering, without any ulterior motive . . . I could probably try to probe you, but it's not appropriate somehow . . ."

"Who I used to be?" asked Witezslav.

"Yes."

The Inquisitor took out a key and pressed the button on the tag to switch off the car alarm. He opened the door.

"I'm a vampire. Or rather, I was a vampire."

"A Higher Vampire?" Anton asked for some reason.

"Yes."

Anton got into the front seat and fastened his seat belt. The vampire Witezslav started the engine, but waited before driving off, giving it a chance to warm up.

"I'm sorry, it really was an idiotic question," Anton admitted.

"Of course it was. Absolutely idiotic." The Inquisitor obviously didn't suffer from an excess of tact. "As far as I'm aware, Anton, you are still extremely young . . ."

He drove the car out into the street, carefully and smoothly. Of course, he didn't ask what hotel Anton was staying in—he didn't need to. He said, "You probably have certain illusions concerning the nature of the Inquisition and what kind of Others work in it. So allow me to explain a few things to you. The Inquisition is not a third force, as many ordinary members of the Watches believe. And we don't become some special kind of Others who aren't connected to the Darkness or the Light . . . We are simply Inquisitors. Selected from those Dark and Light Others who for various reasons have come to realize the absolute necessity of the Treaty and the truce between the Watches. Yes, we do possess certain information that you in the Watches don't have . . . apart, perhaps, from the very greatest magicians. And believe me, Anton Gorodetsky, when I tell you there is nothing comforting in what we know. We are obliged to stand on guard over the Treaty. Do you understand?"

"I'm trying to understand," said Anton.

"I'm a vampire," Witezslav repeated. "An absolutely genuine Higher Vampire who has often killed young girls . . . that's the most correct energetic . . ."

"Please don't lecture me on the physiology of vampires," said Anton. "I find it unpleasant, believe me."

Witezslav nodded, keeping his eyes fixed firmly on the road. Anton suddenly realized that the car was still new—it was well taken care of. The Inquisitor was clearly proud of it . . .

"Well then, I don't possess a soul, and I'm not even alive in the sense that Light Ones use that word," said Witezslav. "I regard the cause of the Light as a naïve, dangerous, and frequently criminal doctrine. And on the other hand, I sympathize with the cause of the Darkness. But . . ."

He paused for a moment, as if he were defining a complex pattern of thought. "But I have a very clear picture of the alternative to the present situation. And that's why I'm a member of the Inquisition. That's why I punish those who have violated the Treaty. Note that, Anton. Not those who are wrong—after all, there are always at least two sides to the truth. The Light has sometimes acquired great Power, and there have been times when the Darkness has triumphed. All the Inquisition does is stand guard over the Treaty."

"I understand," said Anton. "Naturally. But I've always wondered if a situation could arise in which the Inquisition would support one side or the other, not based on the letter of the Treaty, but on the truth . . ."

"There are always at least two sides to the truth," the Inquisitor repeated. "A situation . . ."

He thought about it.

"I've never come across a Light Inquisitor who would support his own Watch," Anton added. "But is the situation really the same with a Dark Inquisitor? Say what you will, but you have your own powers, your own esoteric knowledge. And I'm not talking about confiscated artifacts in the archives."

"Anything is possible," the vampire said unexpectedly. "Yes . . . I could see it. If open war broke out between the Darkness and the Light, not just a clash between the Watches, but real war between the Darkness and the Light. If every Other stood on his own side of the front, then what need would there be for the Inquisition? Then we would simply be Others . . ." He nodded and added, "Only by that time the Inquisition would probably have been destroyed in the attempt to prevent such a situation arising. There aren't that many of us. And what a few surviving Others who once wore the Inquisitor's robes might decide to do wouldn't change a thing."

"I understand what makes the Night Watch observe the Treaty," said Anton. "We're afraid for people. And I know what motivates the Day Watch—fear for themselves. But what makes you Inquisitors go against your own essential nature?"

Witezslav turned his head and said quietly, "The only thing that restrains you is *fear*, Anton Gorodetsky. For yourself, or for people—that's not important. But we are restrained by *horror*. And that is why we observe the Treaty. You have no need to be concerned about the outcome of the trial—there won't be any fixes. If your colleague has not violated the Treaty, he will leave Prague alive and well."

By the evening Edgar had recovered a bit from his annoyance. Maybe he'd been helped by a good dinner in an expensive restaurant with a bottle of vintage Czech wine (well, it wasn't French, or even Spanish, but it certainly wasn't bad). Or maybe the atmosphere of Prague at Christmas had a soothing effect. Naturally, Edgar didn't believe in God—not many of the Others, especially Dark Ones, suffered from superstitions like that. But he found the festival of Christmas really very enjoyable, and he always tried to celebrate it accordingly.

Maybe it was the influence of memories of his childhood? When he was a simple country boy called Edgar who helped his father on the farm, went to church, and looked forward to every holiday with his heart singing. Or maybe he remembered the 1920s and '30s, when he was already an Other, but not actively involved in the Watch, when he lived in Tallinn, had a good practice as an attorney, a wonderful wife and four little boys . . . His parents had died long ago, and he had buried his wife. One of his two surviving sons lived in Canada and the other in Pärnu, but he hadn't seen them for forty years. It would have been hard for the old men to believe that this youthful, sturdy man was their father, who had been born in the late nineteenth century.

Yes, it must be the memories, Edgar thought as he lit up his cigar. There had been a lot of good things in ordinary human life, after all. Maybe he should play at being human again? Get married, have a family . . . take thirty years' leave from the Watch . . .

He laughed hollowly. That was all nonsense. You couldn't step into the same river twice. He'd lived as a man, lived as an ordinary Other, and now his place was in the Day Watch. It was all right for Anton, with his unspent passion and fresh, vital emotions, but all that fretting and fussing wouldn't suit Edgar any longer.

Edgar caught the eye of the young woman sitting, bored and alone, at the next table. He smiled, and touched her mind with the gentlest of touches.

Not a prostitute, just a young girl out looking for adventure. That was good. He didn't like professionals. There was nothing they could surprise him with anyway.

He called the waiter over and ordered a bottle of champagne.

CHAPTER 4

THE INQUISITION HAD NOT BEEN MEAN WITH THE DETAINEES.
The hotel was a perfectly decent one and, while Igor was not in a
deluxe accommodation, he had a suite with two good rooms.

Anton hesitated for a second before he walked toward Igor.

How he had changed . . .

Igor had always been an operational agent. He'd joined the Watch
during the years after the war—there had been a lot of work to do
then. On the one hand there was an upsurge of Light emotions, and
on the other hand, during the difficult war years all sorts of petty
riffraff had multiplied. And with the general atheistic mood in the
country, it wasn't easy for anybody to accept that he or she was an
Other. But it had been easy for Igor to accept his true nature; he had
been glad to. He didn't really see much difference between parachuting in behind the fascist lines to blow up bridges and catching
vampires and werewolves on the streets of Moscow. His Power was
an honest third level, with little chance of advancing to anything
higher, but even the third level is fairly substantial, if it's reinforced
with experience, courage, and good reactions.

Igor had all of those in abundance. Perhaps he was just a little bit
short on experience, but then he had worked in the Watch at a time
when you could easily count one year as three. Perhaps he wasn't as
well-read or erudite as Ilya or Garik, and he hadn't taken part in
as many impressive operations as Semyon, but there weren't many

who could match him out in the field. And there was one other
thing that Anton had always liked—Igor had stayed young. Not just
physically—that was no problem for a magician of his level—but in
his soul. Who was it who would gladly accompany fifteen-year-old
Yulia from the analytical department to some place in Tushino for
the launch of the album "A Hundred Fifty Billion Steps" by the
fashionable band Tequila Jazz? Who was it who was happy to spend
time coping with a teenager riddled with complexes who'd just realized he was an Other? Who would enthusiastically devote five years
to extreme parachuting simply in order to verify the theory about
the high numbers of Others involved in extreme sports? Who was
always first to volunteer to take a colleague's watch or take on the
most boring assignment (there was no lack of volunteers for the dangerous ones)? Maybe it was a mistake, but for some time already
Anton had felt that it was safer to have your back covered by a partner who was reliable and cheerful, rather than powerful and worldly-
wise. A powerful and wise partner could always be distracted by a
more important job than covering someone else's back . . .

But the Other standing in front of Anton now didn't look either
powerful or cheerful. Igor had lost a lot of weight. There was a
strange, dull, hopeless yearning in his eyes. And he didn't seem to
know what to do with his hands . . . sometimes he put them behind
his back, sometimes he clasped them together.

"Anton," he said after a long silence. Without a smile, with only
the faintest trace of gladness. "Hello, Anton."

On a sudden impulse, Anton stepped forward and put his arms
around Igor. He whispered: "Hello . . . Now what are you doing in
such a state . . ."

Witezslav, who was standing by the door, said quietly, "I shan't
issue any official warnings about associating with detainees . . . since
you're Light Ones. Shall I wait for you, Gorodetsky?"

"No, thank you," said Anton, stepping back from Igor, but leaving one hand on his shoulder. "I'll make my own way back."

"Igor Teplov, the session of the Tribunal to consider your case will convene tomorrow evening, at seven o'clock local time. A car will come for you at six thirty; be ready."

"I've been ready for a long time," Igor said quietly. "Don't worry."

"All the best," the vampire said politely as he went out.

The two Light Ones were left alone together.

"Do I look damned awful?" Igor asked.

Anton didn't lie: "Worse than that. I've seen corpses that looked better. Anybody would think you were being kept on bread and water."

Igor shook his head seriously. "Oh no, I've been kept in good conditions."

There was a hint of irony in his words, as if he were talking about some animal sitting in a cage in a zoo.

"I've got a parcel here for you," Anton replied in the same tone of voice, clutching at that weak thread of life. "Is feeding the animals permitted?"

"Yes, it is," Igor said with a nod. "I just . . . I just can't eat, you know? I can't read books, I don't want to get drunk . . . or see anybody either. I switch on the television and watch it until three o'clock in the morning. When I get up I switch it on again. You know, I've already mastered the Czech language. It's very easy to understand."

"That's terrible," said Anton with a nod. "All right. As you can understand, when I left I was given confidential instructions—to give you back the will to live."

Igor actually smiled at that. "I understand. That's to be expected . . . well, get the things out."

Anton put a thick pile of letters on the table. There was just one name on each envelope—the name of the person who had written the letter.

"These are from all our gang. Olga said you had to read her letter first. But Yulia and Lena said the same thing. So you choose for yourself . . ."

Igor looked at the letters thoughtfully and nodded. "I'll throw a dice. All right, get out the rest. I don't mean the letters."

Anton smiled as he took a bottle wrapped in paper out of a plastic bag.

"Smirnoff No. 21," said Igor. "Right?"

"Right."

"I knew it. Carry on."

Anton carried on, smiling in embarrassment as he took out a small loaf of Borodinsky black bread, a stick of salami, salted cucumbers in a polythene vacuum pack, several purple Yalta onions, and a piece of pork fat.

"Why, you devils," said Igor, shaking his head. "Everything the way I like it. Semyon advised you, did he?"

"Yes."

"The customs officers must have thought you were insane."

"I made them look the other way. I'm on official business—so I have the right."

"I see. Okay, I'll just get everything ready. And you tell me what's been going on back there. I've been kept informed . . . but it's better coming from you. About Andrei, about Tiger Cub . . . about that whole damn mess."

While Igor was making the snacks, rinsing the glasses and drying them carefully, and opening the bottle, Anton told him in brief about the recent events in Moscow.

Igor poured vodka into four glasses without speaking. He covered two with slices of bread, set one in front of Anton, and took the last one himself.

"For the guys," he said. "May the Light show them compassion. For Tiger Cub . . . for Andriukha."

They drank without clinking glasses, and Anton looked at Igor curiously. Igor began coughing and looked at his glass, perplexed.

"Anton . . . wait . . . this vodka's fake!"

"Of course!" Anton confirmed happily. "Absolutely genuine fake vodka—pure alcohol diluted with tap water. I chose it specially. You wouldn't believe how hard it is nowadays to buy fake vodka in the shops!"

"But why?" Igor exclaimed.

"What do you mean, why? Why did I bring you Borodinsky bread? I could have bought a loaf of fresh, tasty black bread in any shop in Prague! And the salami too, and the pork fat. The onions would have been the only problem . . ."

"So this is a greeting from the motherland, is it?" said Igor, still wincing.

"Precisely."

"Oh no . . . I want to greet my last morning without a headache," Igor said seriously. He frowned and passed his hand above the bottle and the two full glasses. The liquid glimmered a lemon-yellow color for a moment. Igor explained in a slightly guilty voice: "I'm allowed to use lower magic."

"Then pour another glass."

"Are you in some kind of a hurry?" Igor asked, squinting at Anton as he poured the transformed vodka.

"No, where would I be going?" Anton replied. "I'd rather sit here with you and have a chat. Do you know why I changed the bottle?"

"So you're the perpetrator?"

"Yes, it was me. Semyon brought the real thing. But I wanted to remind you that a beautiful bottle doesn't always contain good stuff."

Igor sighed and his face went dark: "Gorodetsky . . . don't moralize with me. I was in the Watch before you were even born. I understand everything. But it's my own fault, and I'll take my punishment."

"No, you don't understand a thing," Anton shouted angrily. "You adopt this grand pose of yours: 'It's my fault, I'll take what's coming to me,'" he said, mimicking Igor. "But what are we supposed to do? Especially now, without Tiger Cub and Andrei? You know that Gesar's decided to give the girls who do the programming intensive training?"

"Oh, come on, Anton! There aren't any irreplaceable Others. The Moscow Watch has hundreds of magicians and enchantresses in its reserve!"

"Yes, of course. And if we whistle, they'll come running. Leave their families, drop their jobs and their usual concerns. They'll take up arms, of course they will. If the active members of the Watch have disgraced themselves and given up . . ."

Igor sighed and began speaking abruptly and energetically, almost like the old operational agent: "Anton, I understand all this. You're a bright guy, and you're doing the right thing now by making me angry. You're trying to inspire me with the will to live. You're trying to persuade me to fight . . . But understand one thing—I really don't want to fight! I really think I am guilty. I really have decided to . . . withdraw. Into nothingness, into the Twilight."

"Why, Igor? I understand that anyone's death is always a tragedy, especially if it's your fault, but you couldn't have foreseen . . ."

Igor looked up at him with eyes full of pain and shook his head. "No, Antoshka. It's you who doesn't understand a single thing. Do you think I'm punishing myself because that kid drowned? No."

Anton picked up his glass and drained it in a single gulp.

"I feel sorry for the boy," Igor went on. "Very sorry. But I've seen all sorts of things in my time . . . there have been times before when people died. And it was my fault. Children, women, old men. Have you ever, for instance, had to decide who to run to first, who to save—an uninitiated Other or an ordinary person? I have. Have you ever had to draw all the Power from a crowd—drain it completely? Knowing there's a ninety percent probability two people in the crowd won't be able to bear it and they'll kill themselves? I have."

"I've had to do a few things too, Igor."

"Yes, I understand. That hurricane . . . Then why are you talking such nonsense? Can't you believe it's not all about that unfortunate kid? That I fell in love with a Dark One?"

"I can't," said Anton. "I just can't! Gesar said that too, but . . ."

"You'd better believe Gesar," Igor said with a bitter smile. "I love her, Anton. I still love her, even now. And I'll go on loving her— that's the real tragedy."

He picked up his glass.

"Thanks at least for not setting a glass out for her on the table . . ." Anton could feel the fury beginning to seethe inside him. "Thanks . . ."

He broke off and followed Igor's glance to the glass-fronted cupboard, where there was a glass half-filled with vodka and covered with a stale piece of bread standing among the other glasses.

"You've lost your mind," Anton muttered. "Completely lost your mind! Remember, Igor—she's a witch!"

"She was a witch," Igor agreed with a faint, sad smile.

"She provoked you . . . okay, she didn't enchant you, but she still made you fall in love with her."

"No. She fell in love herself. And she didn't have the slightest idea who I was."

"Okay. Let's accept that, you ought to know. But even so, it was provocation. By Zabulon, who knew everything that was happening . . ."

Igor nodded. "Yes, very probably. I've thought about that a lot, Anton. That fight in Butovo was obviously prepared well in advance by the Dark Ones. At the very highest level, just Zabulon and another one or two Dark Ones. Lemesheva probably knew. Edgar and the witches didn't."

He didn't even think it worth mentioning the vampires and shape-shifters.

"Well, if you agree . . ." Anton began.

"Wait. Yes, it was a deliberately planned operation. One of Zabulon's intrigues. And a successful one . . ." Igor lowered his head. "Only what difference does that make to the way I feel about Alisa?"

Anton felt like swearing angrily. So he did, and then he said, "Igor, you've looked at Alisa Donnikova's file. You must have looked at it!"

"Yes."

"So you must understand how much blood she has on her hands! How much evil she has done? I've clashed with her myself several times! She's been responsible for ruining our operations, she . . . she served Zabulon loyally . . ."

"You forgot to add that she was Zabulon's broad," Igor said in a dull, lifeless voice. "That the head of Moscow's Dark Ones enjoyed having sex with her in his Twilight form, that she took part in covens when there were human sacrifices and in group orgies. Why don't you say it? Say it, I know it all anyway. Gesar gave me the full file . . . he tried really hard. I know all that."

"And you still love her?" Anton asked incredulously.

Igor raised his head, and they looked into each other's eyes. Then Igor reached out and gently touched Anton's hand. "Don't be angry with me, brother Light One. Don't despise me. And if you can't understand, you'd better go. Take a walk around Prague . . ."

"I'm trying to understand," Anton whispered. "Honestly, I'm trying. Alisa Donnikova was a perfectly ordinary witch. No better and no worse than all the rest. A clever, beautiful, cruel witch. Who left evil and pain in her wake wherever she went. How can you love her?"

"She was different with me," Igor replied. "A nervous and unhappy girl who really wanted to love someone. Who had fallen in love for the first time. A girl who, unfortunately for us, the Dark Ones spotted before we did. And for her initiation they chose a moment when there was more Darkness in her soul than Light. That's not too difficult to do with teenage girls—you know yourself. And after that it was all very simple. The Twilight drained all the goodness out of her. The Twilight turned her into what she became."

"It's not Alisa herself that you love," said Anton, failing to notice that he was speaking about Donnikova in the present tense. "What you love is her idealized . . . no, her alternative image! The Alisa that never existed!"

"She certainly doesn't exist now. But you're still wrong, Anton. I love her the way she became when she lost her powers as an Other. When she was freed for just a moment from that sticky gray cobweb. Tell me, have you never had to forgive somebody?"

"Yes, I have," Anton replied after a pause. "But not for something like that."

"You've been lucky, Antoshka."

Igor poured more vodka.

"Then tell me this . . ." Anton wasn't trying to spare Igor's feelings, but he still found it hard to get the words out. "Why did you kill her?"

"Because she was a witch," Igor said very calmly. "Because she caused evil and pain. Because 'a member of the Night Watch always protects people against Dark Ones everywhere, in any country, regardless of his personal attitude to the situation.' Have you never wondered about why the Regulations include that specific phrase? About our personal attitude to the situation? It ought to read 'personal attitude to the Dark Ones,' but that sounds rather pitiful. So they used a eum . . . euph . . ."

"Euphemism," Anton prompted him.

"A euphemism." Igor laughed. "Exactly. Remember when we caught the girl vampire on the roof? You were about to fire at her point-blank, but then your vampire neighbor turned up. And you lowered your gun."

"I was wrong," Anton said with a shrug. "She had to be tried. That was why I stopped."

"No, Anton. You would have shot her. And any other vampire who came running to help the criminal. But you were facing a vampire who was your friend, or at least one that you knew. And you stopped. But imagine if the choice had been between shooting and letting the criminal escape."

"I would have shot her," Anton said abruptly. "And Kostya too. There wouldn't have been any choice. I'd have felt very bad about it, I agree, but I . . ."

"And what if it hadn't just been someone you knew well, but the woman you loved? A human woman or an Other enchantress from either side?"

"I would have shot . . ." Anton whispered. "I would have shot anyway."

"And then what?"

"I wouldn't have allowed such a situation to arise. I just wouldn't have allowed it!"

"Of course. The very idea of loving never enters our heads if we see the aura of Darkness. It's the same for the Dark Ones if they see the aura of Light. But we were caught by surprise, Anton. We'd lost all our powers. And we didn't have a choice . . ."

"Tell me, Igor . . ." Anton paused and took a breath. The vodka hadn't done the trick, and even though the conversation was certainly intimate, it wasn't bringing any relief. "Tell me, why didn't you just throw Alisa out of the camp? Why didn't you ask Gesar for help and advice? That way you would have protected people and at the same time . . ."

"She wouldn't have gone," Igor said sharply. "After all, she had legitimate reason to be there at Artek. You know what's the most terrible thing about this whole business, Anton? Zabulon extracted the right for her to restore herself from Gesar in exchange for the same right for a third-level magician! Me, that is! Do you see how everything was all tied up together?"

"But are you sure she wouldn't have gone away?" Anton asked.

Igor lifted up his glass without speaking. For the first time that evening they clinked glasses, but no toast was proposed. "No, Anton, I'm not sure. That's the terrible thing, I'm not sure. I told her . . . I ordered her to clear out. But that was the very first moment, when we'd only just realized who was who. When my brain still hadn't kicked in, I was running on pure adrenaline . . ."

"If she loved you," said Anton, "she would have gone. You just needed to find the right words . . ."

"Probably. But who can say for certain now?"

"Igor, I'm really sorry," Anton whispered. "I don't feel sorry for the witch Alisa, of course . . . don't even ask me. I can't shed even a single tear for her. But I feel terribly sorry for you. And I really want you to stay with us. To get through this and not let it destroy you."

"I've got nothing left to live for, Anton," said Igor with a guilty shrug. "You understand, nothing! You know, I probably fell in love

for the first time in my life too. I had a wife once. I became an Other
in 1945 . . . I came back from the front, a young captain with a chest
full of medals, and not a single scratch on me . . . and I'd been lucky
in general. It was only later I realized it was my latent abilities as an
Other that had kept me safe. And then I learned the truth about the
Watches . . . It was a new war, you understand? And an absolutely
just one, it couldn't have been more just. I didn't really know how
to do anything except fight, and now I realized I'd found myself a
job for life. For a very long life. And that I wouldn't have to face
any of those human afflictions and annoying illnesses, those lines
for food . . . you can't even imagine what perfectly ordinary hunger
is like, Anton, what genuinely *black* bread tastes like, or genuinely
bad vodka . . . what it feels like the first time you laugh in the fat,
well-fed face of a special agent from SMERSH and yawn lazily in
response to his question: "Why did you spend two months on enemy
territory if the bridge was blown up on the third day after you para-
chuted in?"

Igor was beginning to get carried away now. He was speaking
quickly and furiously . . . not at all the way the young magician from
the Night Watch usually spoke . . .

"I came back and I looked at my Vilena, my little Lenochka-
Vilenochka, so young and beautiful. She used to write me letters
every day, honestly, and what letters they were! I saw how glad she
was that I'd come back—I wasn't hurt, I wasn't crippled, and I was
a hero as well. Very few women were so fortunate then. But she
was very afraid that her envious bitches of neighbors would tell me
about all the men she'd had during those four years, that my officer's warrant wasn't the only reason she'd been getting by quite
comfortably . . . even now you don't understand half of what I'm
saying, do you? But I suddenly saw it. All of it at once. The longer
I looked at her, the more I saw. All the details. And not only all her
men—from lousy speculators to others like me, soldiers who hopped
over the hospital fence and went absent without leave . . . And the
way she whispered to one colonel, 'He's probably been rotting in

the ground for ages . . .'—I heard that too . . . And by the way, that colonel turned out to be a real man. He got up off the bed, slapped her across the face, got dressed, and walked out."

Igor poured himself some vodka and drank it quickly, without waiting for Anton, then filled the glasses again. He said, "That's when I became what I am. When I left my home, with my medals jangling and Vilena roaring, 'It's all lies what they told you, the bitches, I was faithful to you!' I walked along the street, with something burning away in my soul. It was May, Anton. May 1945. Immediately after Germany capitulated, Gesar pulled me back from the front and told me: "From now on your front line is here, Captain Teplov." And back then people were . . . they were different, Anton. Their faces were all shining! There were plenty of foul Dark creatures around, I won't deny it, but there was a lot of Light as well. And as I walked along the street the little kids darted round me, looking at my chest full of medals, arguing about which one was for what. Men shook my hand and invited me to take a drink with them. Girls came running up to me . . . and kissed me. Kissed me like their own boyfriends, who hadn't come back yet, or had already been killed. Like their own fathers, like their own brothers. Sometimes they cried, kissed me, and went on their way. Do you understand me? No, how could you . . . You worry about our country too, you think how bad everything is right now, what a lousy hole we're all in . . . You suffer because the Light Ones won't all get together to help Russia. Only you don't know what it's like to be in a real hole, Anton. But we do!"

Igor drained his glass again. Anton raised his glass without speaking and nodded in support of the toast that had not been spoken aloud.

"That was when I became what I am," Igor repeated. "A magician. A field agent. Eternally young. Who loves everybody . . . and nobody. I'd already made up my mind that I would never fall in love. Never. Girlfriends were one thing, love was something quite different. I couldn't love a human being, because human beings were weak. I couldn't love an Other, because any Other was either an enemy or a comrade-in-arms. That was the principle I adopted for my life, Antoshka. And I stuck to it as closely as I could. It seemed like I was still the same young man who came back from the front, who still had plenty of time to think about falling in love. It's one thing to take a whirl with a girl on the dance floor . . ." he said, and laughed quietly, "or leap about in cool threads under the ultraviolet light at the discotheque . . . what difference does it make if it's jazz, rock, or trash, what length the skirt is and what the stockings are made of . . . It's all good. It's the way things ought to be. Have you seen that American cartoon, about Peter Pan? Well, I became like him. Only not a stupid little boy, but a stupid young man. And I felt just fine for a long time. Supposedly I've outlived the time granted to a man, and it would be a sin to complain—I haven't had any helpless old age or other problems. So don't you torment yourself unnecessarily, Anton."

Anton sat there with his head in his hands, not speaking. It was as if he'd opened a door and seen something behind it . . . not something taboo, and not something shameful either . . . Just something that had absolutely nothing to do with him. And he realized that behind every door, if—may the Light forbid!—he was able to open it, he would see something equally alien and . . . personal.

"I've reached the end of my road, Anton," Igor said almost tenderly. "Don't be so sad. I understand that you came here hoping to shake me up, to get all this nonsense out of my head, to carry out your instructions. Only it won't work. Like a fool, I really did fall in love with a Dark One. I killed her. And it turns out I killed myself too."

Anton didn't say anything. It was all pointless. He was overwhelmed by someone else's anguish, someone else's grief. Instead of simply bringing a parcel to a sick friend, here he was sitting with him at his own wake . . .

"Anton, don't go away today," Igor said. "I won't sleep anyway . . . soon I'll catch up on my sleep forever. To be honest, I've got another three bottles of vodka in the refrigerator. And there's a restaurant five floors down."

"Then we'll fall asleep at the table."

"We'll be okay, we're Others. We can take it. I want to talk. To cry on someone's shoulder. I've started feeling afraid of the dark. Can you believe that?"

"Yes."

Igor nodded. "Thanks. I've got my guitar here, we can sing something. Or I'll sing. You know, singing for yourself is just the same as . . . well, you understand. And apart from that . . ."

Anton looked at Igor—his voice had suddenly become more focused. Stronger.

"I'm a watchman, after all. I haven't forgotten that, you can be quite sure. And it seems to me that in all this mess, I'm no more than a pawn . . . no, probably not a pawn . . . A rook who has taken one of the other side's pieces and occupied a square in the line of fire. Only unlike the other pieces, I can think. I hope you haven't forgotten how to do that, either. I don't care about myself anymore, Anton. But I do care who wins this game. Let's think together."

"Where do we begin?" Anton asked, feeling amazed at himself. Surely he hadn't accepted what Igor had said and agreed to think of him as a piece who had already been removed from the board . . . or who at least was already doomed as the invisible player reached out his hand for him . . .

"With Svetlana. With the Chalk of Destiny," said Igor, watching carefully to see how Anton's face changed. He laughed smugly. "Well, have I guessed right? You've been having the same thoughts?"

"And so has Gesar . . ." Anton whispered.

"Gesar's a clever one," Igor agreed. "But we're no fools, are we? Anyway, why don't we try thinking with our heads and not our hands for once?"

"Okay, let's try," Anton said with a nod. "Only . . ."

He fumbled in his pocket for the amulet that Gesar had given him. He crushed the little ball in his hand and felt the bone needles prick his skin. There was never any gain without pain . . . He said:

"Now for twelve hours no one will be able to see us or hear us."

"Are you sure?" Igor asked. "Won't the absence of information alert the Inquisition?"

"There won't be any absence," said Anton. "As far as I understand it, if they have any observational devices here, or if they've cast any tracking spells—they'll provide false information. It's a quality scam."

"Gesar's a clever one," Igor repeated with a smile.

Edgar sat by the window, smoking and slowly sipping a glass of flat champagne. It still tasted good.

His girlfriend was sleeping peacefully in the next room, satisfied and happy. She had turned out to be a fine girl. A German student with some Scandinavian blood, reasonably passionate and reasonably cheerful. But a bit too fanciful in sex for Edgar's taste. Unlike most of his colleagues, Edgar was very conservative in such matters. He didn't take part in orgies, he didn't have underage girlfriends, and out of all the possibilities he preferred the classic missionary position.

But there was no denying that in that position he had achieved perfection.

Edgar stretched sweetly and carefully opened the window. He stood up and breathed in the cold, frosty air. The new day had begun and perhaps the Tribunal would give its verdict that very evening. Then he'd be able to relax and enjoy the festive season, without worrying about all these intrigues.

But who was behind this intrigue, after all . . . the Day Watch or the Night Watch?

And most important of all—what role had been assigned to him?

Could Yury's hint really be right, was he supposed to be sacrificed, just like Alisa?

"Here, look . . ." Igor spread out a large sheet of paper on the table and took a pack of felt-tip pens out of his pocket. "I've already drawn a few diagrams . . . and some things fit together. This is Svetlana."

Anton looked thoughtfully at the circle drawn with a thick yellow line and said, "It doesn't look much like her."

Igor laughed. "All right . . . very witty. But look at the way things shape up. We and the Dark Ones had a balance, a precarious one, but still a balance . . . Here are the magicians with first- to third-level powers on our side . . . here are their equivalents on the Dark Side . . . Both the ones in active service and the others who can easily be mobilized."

The paper was quickly covered with small circles. Then Igor divided the sheet in two with a sweeping gesture. At the top of one side he wrote "Gesar," and at the top of the other, "Zabulon." He explained: "They're not really in the game. They're the players, but we're interested in the pieces. Look at how things changed with Svetlana's appearance."

"It depends what piece we decide she is," Anton said cautiously. "Right now she's a first-level enchantress . . . or rather, she was."

"And what does that mean? Just look how many magicians there are at about the same level as her."

"She's a pawn," said Anton, feeling surprised at his own words. "Svetlana's no more than a pawn for years and years to come! While she nurtures her Power, learns to control her abilities, acquires experience . . . She's more powerful than me . . . or she was. But I'd have been able to handle her if I'd been on the other side."

"Precisely, Anton," said Igor, deftly pouring himself a glass from the second bottle of vodka—the first was already standing empty under the table. "Precisely! Svetlana made the Night Watch significantly more powerful. And in the future she could easily reach the same level as Gesar. But that's a matter of decades, or even hundreds of years."

"Then why all this activity by the Dark Ones? They almost violated the Treaty, simply in order to get Svetlana out of the game."

"Think," said Igor, glancing into Anton's eyes. "Let's take the chess analogy all the way . . ."

"A pawn that reaches the far side of the board . . ."

". . . becomes any other piece."

Anton shrugged. "Igor, that's obvious anyway. We're all pawns, but some of us have a chance to become queens. Svetlana has. You don't, I don't, Semyon doesn't . . . but it's a long way to the far edge of the board, and the Dark Ones don't need to be in such a hurry to eliminate Svetlana."

"The Chalk of Destiny," said Igor.

"What about it? Gesar wanted to use Egor, the boy without any destiny, to make him into . . ."

"Into what?"

Anton shrugged. "A prophet, a philosopher, a poet, a magician . . . I don't know. Someone who would lead humanity toward the Light. Or perhaps a Mirror? Another Mirror, like Vitaly Rogoza, only he would be on our side?"

"But Svetlana didn't want to interfere," Igor said with a nod. "The boy Egor was left with just his own destiny."

"But then . . ." Anton began, and stopped short. He didn't know if he had the right to tell Igor the truth he had discovered, even under the protection of the amulet.

"But then Olga rewrote someone's destiny with the other half of the Chalk," Igor said with a laugh. "That's an open secret already. The important thing is that the operation was successful anyway. Svetlana didn't do it, but Olga did. And incidentally Gesar managed to have Olga rehabilitated."

"Incidentally?" Anton queried, shaking his head. "Okay, let's say incidentally . . . But that's the second layer of the truth. I'm sure there's a third layer too."

"The third layer is the person whose destiny Olga rewrote. As soon as Zabulon heard she'd been rehabilitated, he realized he'd been duped. Taken in by a simple diversionary maneuver. And the Dark Ones started looking. They checked poor Egor a dozen times—in case the Book of Destiny had been rewritten twice for him . . ."

"And how do you know that?"

"I was keeping an eye on the boy. Gesar told me to—it was obvious the Dark Ones would start looking for a trick."

"And?"

"No, there were no tricks with Egor. It wasn't his destiny that was rewritten."

"Then whose was it?"

Igor looked into Anton's eyes without saying anything. As if he didn't have the right to say it himself.

"Svetlana's?" Anton exclaimed in sudden realization. And he suddenly thought that in his place any Dark One would have squealed, "Mine?"

"It looks like it. A brilliant and elegant move. There was such an ocean of Power raging around her that it was impossible for anyone to notice what was being done with her Book of Destiny. And the Dark Ones can't check her Book of Destiny—that would be as good as a declaration of war."

"Gesar wants to accelerate Svetlana's transformation into a Great Enchantress?"

"Out of the question. That's a violation of the Treaty. Dig a bit deeper."

Anton looked at the circles on the paper. He took a felt-tip pen and drew a bright scarlet line upward from Svetlana, then another circle where it ended. An empty circle.

"Yes," said Igor. "Precisely. You know what time this is now, don't you?"

"The end of the millennium . . ."

"Two thousand years since the birth of Jesus Christ," Igor said with a laugh.

"Ieshua was a supreme Light magician," said Anton. "I don't even know if we can call him a magician . . . he was the Light itself . . . but . . . Gesar wants a second coming of the Messiah?"

"You said it, not me," Igor replied. "Let's drink . . . to the Light."

Anton drank a full glass in total bewilderment. He shook his head. "No, but this . . . Igor, this is playing with the pure powers. With the foundations of the universe! How could he take the risk?"

"Anton, I'm certain that's the way it was all planned. Judge for yourself—there's a boom in religious faiths everywhere, one way or another everybody's expecting either the end of the world or the Second Coming . . . but then, they're the same thing."

"Not everybody . . ." Anton protested. "Don't exaggerate."

"Not everybody, but enough people for the torrent of human expectations to start reshaping reality. And if you could just help things along a bit, if you could rewrite someone's destiny . . . Gesar went for broke. Gesar wants to add someone new to our ranks, an Other so powerful that none of the Dark Ones will be able to match him. Not Zabulon, not a certain modest California farmer, not the owner of a small hotel in Spain, and not a popular Japanese singer . . . no one."

"That might be true," Anton admitted. "But Svetlana's lost her Power now, and for a long time."

"And what of it? Does that prevent her from having a child?"

"Stop," said Anton, waving his hands in warning. "Now we're getting ahead of ourselves! We can believe any hypothesis, but first let's look at the other events. The Mirror, for instance."

"The Mirror . . ." Igor frowned. "A Mirror is created by the Twilight. Zabulon couldn't make use of him directly . . . but he certainly could bring those stupid sect members to Moscow with that artifact of theirs and feed Rogoza with Power. And the reason for doing that is obvious—to destroy Svetlana."

"Rogoza didn't destroy her. He only drained her, but then that's . . ."

"One of us didn't play the game the way Zabulon had planned it," Igor replied. "Someone didn't make the move that would have led to the Mirror totally destroying Svetlana . . . as an individual. Maybe what saved her was the fact that Tiger Cub and Andrei had already died? A Mirror isn't exactly a Dark Other, and he isn't directly involved in the confrontation between the two Watches. You see, maybe he was expecting another blow of some kind? From you, for instance. From Gesar. But the blow never came . . . and he didn't strike back with all his strength."

"Then explain to me, Igor—why did Zabulon set you and Alisa up?"

"That was an accident," Igor muttered. "I told you, Alisa . . ."

"Okay, so *she* didn't know. But Zabulon knew, believe me! And he sent her to her death—he swapped one piece for another. Why?"

"I wish I knew," said Igor with a shrug.

CHAPTER 5

RAIVO BEGAN WALKING AROUND THE HOTEL ROOM, GESTICU-
lating with untypical fervor.

"I still think there's trouble ahead! We have no right to count on
assistance from the Day Watch of Moscow, of Prague, or Helsinki—
from any of them."

"But that Dark One promised to help us . . ." Yari objected.

Raivo frowned and waved his hands through the air picturesquely.
"He promised. Yes, of course he did. And who was it who promised
our brothers that Fafnir would be resurrected?"

"It seems to me," Yukha said in a quiet voice, "that it would have
been far more rational to serve the great cause of Fafnir's resurrection than actually try to resurrect the ancient magician . . ."

There was a moment's silence.

"Yukha . . ." Yari said reproachfully. "You . . . you can't just say
that . . ."

"Why can't I? The times when magicians used to play without
any rules are long gone. Do you want a global cataclysm?"

"But our . . ."

"Our decrepit leaders were out of their minds. And that's why they
were duped by somebody's promises. That's why they were killed in
Berne . . . And we won't get any help—Raivo's right about that.
Those who have departed can't be brought back. Pasi believed too—
and where's Pasi now? Dematerialized in the Twilight by Gesar."

The telephone on the table rang. Clearly reluctant to stop talking, Yukha picked up the receiver. "Yes."

The next moment he leapt in the air, dropping his glass of Czech beer. He shouted: "You? You . . . where are you calling from? What?"

He listened for a minute, with the expression on his face growing ever more joyful and confused. The expression of a man given good news after he has already braced himself to hear bad news and even managed to infect everyone else with his own pessimism. Finally Yukha put the phone down and whispered:

"Brothers . . ."

Anton couldn't decide if they'd been right or wrong to open the second bottle of vodka. On the one hand, it seemed like they were getting close to the essential truth of what was going on . . . but on the other, it was getting harder and harder to discuss the problem. For instance, Igor had become extremely skeptical, and he just couldn't understand what Anton was trying to demonstrate to him.

"Igor, in such a complicated setup, if even one episode doesn't fit in right, the whole thing collapses. There had to be a reason. Maybe you represented some kind of obstacle to Zabulon's plans?"

"Me?" Igor gave a bitter laugh. "Don't be silly. I'm an ordinary field operative. Third level . . . second level at a stretch . . . with no special abilities and no prospects. I couldn't have stood up against the Mirror. I don't know, Anton."

"But you have an idea about something," Anton muttered. He poured some vodka, paused for a second, and asked, "Igor, was there something between you and Svetlana?"

"No," Igor answered sharply. "No, and don't even think about it. There wasn't anything, there isn't, and there won't be. And if you're thinking I was supposed to be the father of the future Messiah . . ." He burst out laughing.

"It was just an idea . . ." Anton muttered, feeling like a total idiot.

"Anton, think about it . . . that's your jealousy speaking, not your head, I'm sorry! The ordinary human process of reproduction has nothing to do with all this. If Svetlana's Book of Destiny has been rewritten, if she has to be the mother of the new Messiah—that's a process that involves subtle matter, the energetics of the Light and the Darkness, the fundamental substance of the universe. What difference does it make who . . ."—he faltered for a moment and went on—". . . happens to be the biological father? It even depends on Svetlana only to a certain extent. No, that's nonsense. The only person Zabulon has to be afraid of is Svetlana."

"Then I don't see the point in eliminating you . . ."

"Neither do I. But there probably is one . . ."

They drank in silence, without clinking glasses. And then they both began staring at the sheet of paper.

"Let's start with the basics," said Anton, noticing that he was slurring his words a little. "So, a year and a half ago Gesar and Olga rewrote Svetlana's destiny? And now she's supposed to give birth to a Messiah?"

"Yes, that's the way it looks."

"And Zabulon tried to use the appearance of the Mirror to destroy her, but he failed . . ."

"Yes, that's it . . ."

"Okay, let's leave your part in all this aside for the moment . . . What could Zabulon's next move be? Now, when Svetlana has no magic powers at all and is defenseless?"

"She's not defenseless," said Igor, wagging his finger at Anton. "Why do you say that? I'm sure she's been given the finest possible protection. And in any case, to attack her is a violation of the Treaty. The Dark Ones are fond of their own skins, no one wants to face dematerialization . . ."

"What could his response be? Only one . . ."

"The appearance of an Antichrist, the only one capable of standing against the Messiah."

"And humanity is expecting the appearance of the Antichrist with no less eagerness," Anton exclaimed, "thanks to mass culture."

"Have you got a Bible?" Igor asked unexpectedly.

"With me? No, of course not . . ."

"Just a moment . . ." said Igor. He walked quickly, if not entirely steadily, into the other room and came back with a small, thick book. He gave Anton a rather embarrassed look and said, "Of course, I'm an atheist. But the Bible . . . you understand. Now . . ."

"Igor," said Anton, putting his hand on the book, "it won't help us. Why don't we try thinking logically?"

"All right," Igor agreed readily, setting the Holy Writ aside with some relief.

"Zabulon wants to live too. He doesn't want an Apocalypse . . . I hope. He needs a figure equal in Power to a Messiah of the Light."

"Fafnir . . ." Igor said thoughtfully. "Fafnir?"

"A powerful Dark magician . . ." Anton agreed. "But he's not the Antichrist."

"Six six six!" said Igor, squirming in his chair. "Come on, let's count what the letters in the name Fafnir add up to!"

"I don't remember how the name Fafnir is written in the original. But if we write it in Russian, then . . ." Anton thought for a moment ". . . then it's eighty-eight! Nothing like six hundred sixty-six."

"But eighty-eight is a strange kind of number too," said Igor, looking at Anton with blazing eyes. "Just think about it. Not eighty-seven. Not eighty-nine. Exactly eighty-eight. It's suspicious!"

"It is . . ." Anton agreed. The number really had begun to seem suspicious to him for some reason. "And it probably is possible to resurrect Fafnir, to bring him back from the Twilight . . . But . . ."

"Not just to resurrect him," said Igor. "This whole business depends on people, right? On their expectations, on their readiness to believe! And if Fafnir's return to life can be staged in the appropriate way, the insane magician can be made into an insane anti-Messiah."

"But how?"

"With those four horsemen of the Apocalypse . . . the emergence of the beast from the sea . . ."

Igor's eyes suddenly glazed over. "Anton, Fafnir was supposedly buried at sea! What if Alisa and that boy, Makar, dying in the sea was some kind of sacrifice . . . what a release of Dark Power . . ."

Anton shook his head and wiped his sweaty forehead. "Igor, maybe we've had too much to drink? Yes, I agree that Gesar's intending to use . . . could use Svetlana as the mother of a new Messiah . . . a reincarnation of Christ to some extent . . . or just a magician of unprecedented Power . . . It looks very much that way. And to counter that, Zabulon might try to come up with a figure of equal Power, but tying all this up with Armageddon, the Bible, and religion— that's pushing things too far!"

"What about the year 2000?" Anton almost shouted. "You understand? Magicians might intend to do one thing, but human dreams and fears shape reality in their own way. So the figures who appear will possess all the required qualities. Let's go!"

"Where?"

"To get some vodka. In the restaurant."

Anton sighed and glanced at the bottle. Yes, it really was empty.

"Why don't we just call and order some?"

"Oh no, I feel like a walk."

Anton stood up and put the amulet in his pocket. He nodded. "Okay, let's go . . ."

There was no one at the elevators, but they had to wait for a long time. Igor leaned against the wall and declaimed. "Look, this is how Zabulon can do it . . . Fafnir's Talon is taken out of the vault . . ."

"How?"

"What does it matter how? If they've stolen it once, they'll manage it somehow. Then they carry out the magical operation, plus staging all the mythological notions about the Apocalypse. All those locusts . . . the star Wormwood . . . the four horses . . ."

"I can just see Zabulon leading four horses by the reins . . ."

"He doesn't need any horses!" Igor said with a frown. "You know as well as I do what the magic of appearances can do. For instance, let's take four people, or better still—four Dark Others. One from Asia—he can be the red horse, one black-skinned—he can be the black horse, the third a European—he can be the white horse, and one, let's say, Scandinavian—the pale horse . . . We put them on wooden toy horses . . ."

The door of the elevator opened and Anton froze.

Staring out at the Light Ones in fright from the mirror-lined box were the Regin Brothers. The adopted children of the sect: the African, the Chinese, and the Ukrainian. Of course, where else would they be but in this hotel? They'd come for the Inquisition Tribunal too . . . Anton thought in a slow, leisurely way that the fourth fighter commando had been a Scandinavian.

It was a good thing he wasn't around any longer . . .

Igor seemed to have had the same thought. He muttered, "Three of them . . ."

In the deathly silence the doors of the elevator began to close. But Yukha Mustajoki suddenly stepped forward and stuck his foot between them, just where the sensor was. The doors reluctantly parted again.

"I'd like to thank the Night Watch of Moscow," he said unexpectedly. He was obviously agitated, but trying to maintain his dignity. "It was very humane."

"What was?" asked Anton.

"To spare Pasi Ollikainen. We . . . we appreciate the fact that he's still alive."

"Where is he?" exclaimed Anton.

"Downstairs . . . in the bar . . ." said Yukha, gaping in surprise at the two Light magicians.

"Four horses . . ." Igor said in a hollow voice. "Four horses. Four horses!"

Mustajoki staggered back rapidly and exchanged puzzled glances with his comrades.

The Light magicians were left alone.

"It all fits," said Igor, turning to Anton. "You see? Everything!"

"Hang on . . ."

Anton concentrated, remembering the movements. He raised his right hand, made a pass in front of Igor's face, then pulled his hand sharply downward and back up again, curving his fingers and cupping his hand.

"Damn you . . ." Igor groaned in a choking voice and went dashing for his suite. Anton followed him slowly. He looked at Igor's hunched-over back through the open door of the toilet and reached out to him through the Twilight. Igor began groaning.

The sobering-up spell isn't very complicated, but it's not very pleasant for the person it's cast on.

Two minutes later Igor came out of the bathroom. With his hair wet, his eyes sunk into his head and looking as pale as death.

"A pale horse . . ." Anton muttered. "Okay . . . Now you do it to me."

Igor eagerly made the passes, and then Anton leaned down over the toilet bowl. A few minutes later, after he'd washed his face and drunk some nasty-tasting water from the tap (the thirst had hit him immediately), he walked back into the room. Igor was already clearing away the remains of their drinking session. He looked at Anton and said mockingly, "A black horse . . ."

Anton went over to the refrigerator, took out several bottles of mineral water, pulled the top off one, and collapsed into a chair.

Igor took a second bottle from him. They drank water for a while in blissful silence. Then Igor admitted guiltily, "Yes . . . we got plastered."

"Toy horses!" said Anton. He smashed his fist down on the table and swore. "No, it's shameful, the nonsense we thought up."

"It all seemed very logical somehow," Igor said in an embarrassed voice. "Those damned Brothers . . . so the fourth one's alive too."

"He must be," Anton said with a shrug. "All I knew was that Gesar went after him in the Twilight and caught up with him . . ."

"Well, of course . . . why would he want to kill a suspect? He handed him over to the Inquisition. Probably right there in the Twilight. Anton, maybe we were right after all?"

"Are you still a bit tipsy?" Anton asked.

"No, I'm totally sober now . . . damn, I can't even get drunk properly! Yes, it's all nonsense. Zabulon wouldn't try to drag some ancient magician back out of the Twilight. What good would that do him? And as for staging the end of the world, creating an Antichrist . . ."

"And anyway, Fafnir wouldn't do for the job," Anton said. "He's not up to it. Wouldn't even come close."

"So all that stuff we came up with is nonsense?"

Anton looked at the sheet of paper, with its grease spots from salami and wet rings from their glasses. When had they managed to mess it up? He thought they'd been very careful.

"I'm afraid the bit about Svetlana isn't nonsense. But as for all the rest . . . Why did we get so excited over the number eighty-eight? What's so mystical about that?"

"It's kind of smooth and rounded, it reads the same in both directions . . ." Igor waved his hand through the air and burst into laughter. "Yes, you're right. It's drunken nonsense."

Anton picked up a felt-tip pen that had fallen on the floor and crossed out the circle with "Regin Brothers" written inside it. He said:

"They're not in the game. It looks like they completed their mission by charging the Mirror with Power. This is what we should be interested in, Igor . . ."

Igor looked at the circle with his own name in it. He sighed.

"I'd be glad to believe in my own special mission. To think I'd done something to really upset Zabulon and the Day Watch. But . . ." He spread his hands helplessly.

"Igor, you're the key," said Anton. "Do you understand? If we can understand why Zabulon is trying to get rid of you in order to fight Svetlana, then we'll win. If we can't, then the game's his."

"There's Gesar too. And from what I hear, he's coming this morning."

"We'd better try to manage without him," said Anton, sensing the note of irritation in his own voice. "His decisions are too . . . too global."

*   *   *

Edgar poured himself some more flat champagne, took a swallow, grimaced, and thought wryly: *Only aristocrats and degenerates drink champagne in the morning. And you, my dear fellow, don't look much like an aristocrat . . .*

The old watchman's habit of thinking all the time, in any situation, had not abandoned Edgar even during his nocturnal amusements. Last night Edgar had carried on thinking about what the leaders of the Moscow Watches were planning for this Christmas . . . but that hadn't prevented him from enjoying what he was doing.

Right, then, Edgar thought. *What have we got . . . We need to sort everything out neatly. Right down to the final detail.*

What could Zabulon squeeze out of the present situation? Edgar needed to construct a mental model of his chief.

A Tribunal that had drawn in forces from both Watches. Not the most important ones, but by no means the lowest either. Two magicians, both from the top ten. Edgar and Anton. There would be observers too. There was no doubt about that. And there was no doubt that during the actual session of the Tribunal neither side would make any moves—they would be haggling to extract some advantage for themselves from the indifferent and unbiased Inquisition.

But was it indifferent? Edgar had no doubts about its being unbiased. He'd lived a long time as an Other, and never, not even once had he had even the shadow of a doubt concerning the actions of the Inquisition. The servants of the Treaty had always been cool and decisive. Someone had once said that the Inquisition didn't judge who was in the right and who was in the wrong, but who had violated the Treaty. That was the essential worldview of any Inquisitor. Edgar had matured enough to understand that, but he still didn't understand what it was that made the Inquisition act that way and not any other.

He wondered if the Higher Magicians understood it. Gesar and Zabulon.

So, the Tribunal. The Light magician Igor Teplov could either be acquitted (which was not desirable) or found guilty. In the first case, the Night Watch would keep a third-level magician who was temporarily unfit for combat, but still powerful and, more important, highly experienced. Edgar had come up against Teplov before that battle in South Butovo, although only in passing, immediately after the war in the memorable operation Ashes of Belozersk. Back then the Moscow and Tallinn watches had operated in the most surprising places, such as the Vologda region. They didn't have enough men . . . Or rather, Others. The Dark Ones and the Light Ones were both short of numbers.

The other option was that the Night Watch would lose the magician forever. The question was: So what? Igor Teplov was not who he seemed to be. Or rather, there was something about him that was only obvious to top-flight magicians. All in all, it looked very much as if Zabulon was stubbornly and consistently aiming at two goals in the enemy's camp: Igor Teplov and Svetlana Nazarova. And in doing that he had been quite willing to sacrifice his own love, Alisa. Edgar still hadn't made out any logical connection between the battle in Butovo, the duel at the Artek camp, and the rather confused events that had accompanied the Dark Mirror's visit. But for him it was enough to sense very clearly that there was one. There was definitely a single thread running through all these battles and intrigues, connecting them all together, and it led straight back into Zabulon's hand.

All right, any attempt to eliminate a future Great Enchantress was quite justified and understandable. But why had Zabulon started scheming against the magician Igor? Why him especially? And why right now, and not earlier, when he was weaker and more careless?

There was only one answer that fit: Igor had only become dangerous after Svetlana had joined the ranks of the Night Watch.

All right. Let's move on.

The resurrection of Fafnir. You couldn't imagine a better time and place than the ones chosen: on the eve of the year 2000, in the center of European necromancy. How was this connected with the Tribunal and the Teplov–Donnikova case?

That was the problem.

Edgar sipped gloomily at his champagne, thinking that he was very short of time—he only had until the evening. So he took the only possible decision: to pay a visit to the local Day Watch office right away and request all available information about the duel between Siegfried and Fafnir, and also study the relevant section of the *Necronomicon*.

Edgar was a powerful enough magician to know about the mechanism for the resurrection of a great Dark One and understand which of the necessary conditions could be met at present and which couldn't.

The German girl was still sleeping serenely: Edgar took pity on her and didn't wake her up. He washed, shaved, and got dressed, gently touched her sleeping mind, and went out into the morning snow of Prague.

The Day Watch office was located on Vyshegrad, right beside the Valtava River, in the three-story brick building of a private house with a water pump that clearly still worked even though it was so old. The handle of the pump was like a twisted, pointing finger. Following tradition, Edgar got out of his taxi some distance away to give his colleagues a chance to spot him and decide what to do, if anything.

His colleagues were on the ball—they spotted Edgar about three hundred meters from the door. He felt a Light touch on his aura and opened himself up—exactly enough for the magician who was scanning him to realize that a Dark One was approaching, a Dark magician, a second-level Dark magician, coming on business. Just like that, increasing the dose of information each time.

Of course, Prague was a European capital, but it wasn't Moscow. The Beskud on duty—the only guard, as it happened—gave Edgar a toothy smile.

Another Beskud, Edgar thought, surprised. *Are they more common in Prague then? This is already the second one . . .*

There were only six Beskuds registered on the territory of the former USSR: two in Turkmenia and one each in the Crimea, Belorussia, Yakutia, and Kamchatka. Edgar knew that for certain, because fifteen years earlier he had a case outside Estonia in which all six of them had testified as witnesses.

The Beskud's Twilight image was almost classical.

"Greetings, colleague!"

"Good morning."

Of course, in the Twilight there were no language barriers.

"What brings you to our bastion? Business? Or simply a courtesy visit?"

"Business. Where's your archive here?"

"The second floor down, and then you'll see for yourself."

The second floor down, thought Edgar. *So they have a multilevel basement* . . . "Thank you. So can I go on down?"

"Of course. A Dark One is free to go wherever he wants, isn't that so?"

Edgar sighed. That was right, but not entirely . . .

"The elevator's over that way," the Beskud told him.

"Thank you," Edgar said again, and set off in the direction indicated.

A very, very old elevator took him down to two floors below street level. And that wasn't the deepest level: There were another five hidden under the ground. The Prague Watch was certainly firmly established!

The vestibule in front of the elevator was absolutely tiny: four meters by four. There was a door on the left and one on the right; the plaque on one said "Library," and the plaque on the other said "Computer Room."

Let's start with the library, thought Edgar. *In Fafnir's and Al-Hazred's time there weren't any computers . . . at least not in the modern meaning of the word.*

Edgar stepped toward the door on his left. It was closed, but not locked.

It was a classical library: a large hall with about ten tables and long rows of shelves with books. One glance at their spines was enough to understand that these venerable tomes remembered more than many of the Others . . .

Edgar stopped, and just at that moment an incredibly thin Other emerged from behind the shelves. A vampire. And a Higher Vampire—Edgar realized that immediately.

The ordinary vampires that were quite common in Moscow were the junior members of the team. The cannon fodder that Anton Gorodetsky had mentioned. They had hardly any magic, and even a degenerate Dark magician was still more powerful than they were. But Higher Vampires were a quite different matter, although for some reason there weren't any in Moscow, or anywhere in Eastern Europe—with the exception of the Czech Republic and Romania.

"Good morning. Can I be of any assistance?"

"Good morning. I'm interested in material on one of the magicians of the past."

"Who exactly?" the vampire inquired.

"Fafnir. The Dragon of the Twilight."

"Oho!" the vampire said respectfully. "He was a really mighty magician. One of the most powerful Dark Ones in the entire history of mankind. What exactly are you interested in?"

"The circumstances of his death. The reasons for his duel with Siegfried, the prehistory, the details . . . In short, I want to make a comprehensive study of this outstanding individual. But unfortunately, I only have a few hours in which to do it. And in addition I'd like to model the operation of bringing him back from the Twilight . . ."

The vampire smiled sadly. "Unfortunately, that's something that is effectively impossible. It would require interventions of such power and intensity that the right to make them could not be earned even by putting all—let me emphasize that—all the Dark Ones of the world into hibernation for a hundred years."

"Nonetheless," said Edgar, with a sweeping gesture of his hand. "I'd like to solve this problem, if only on paper."

"Then you should take a look at Al-Hazred's *Necronomicon*," the vampire advised him. "It describes all the necessary interventions for the rematerialization of essential beings with some precision. Are you a theoretical necromancer?"

Edgar smiled more broadly than before.

"Oh no! I've never really dealt with necromancy at all. But I've developed an interest . . ."

"Then you did right to come to Prague. People here know their necromancy, and there are any number of specialists . . . But unfortunately they are all theoreticians, and of course you understand why."

Edgar really did understand why. Because since the Treaty had been signed the Inquisition had only sanctioned rematerialization twice, and both times only temporarily. The Tribunal needed to question witnesses, and sometimes there really was an opportunity to bring a dematerialized Other back from the Twilight. Such opportunities had been exploited twice, but after questioning, the witnesses had gone back to the Twilight.

Edgar couldn't believe that a magician of Fafnir's level hadn't set up some loophole in advance to allow for his own rematerialization. He must have done it once he reached a certain level—as a matter of fact, Edgar was hoping to reach that level himself some day. He hoped with equal justification never to allow himself to be dematerialized, but life was such a strange business. It was always throwing up surprises, especially in conditions of continuous war.

"Go on through," said the vampire, indicating the tables. "I'll bring the books in a moment. I believe it's not the human experience of the time that interests you, but the chronicles of the Others. Is that so?"

"Of course, dear colleague. Of course."

"I'll just be a second."

The vampire really did come back very quickly. He had obviously been working as the custodian of the library for more than a decade and knew his books very well.

"There," he said, laying two large volumes on the table. The first was a huge, large-format book in an old binding of dull brown leather—the *Necronomicon* in Gerhardt Kuchelstein's translation; the second was a bit more modest—not so big, with a florid title that covered half a page: *A Life and Exposition of the Glorious Doings and Also the Prophecies and Numerous Unparalleled Discoveries of the Great Dark Magician Well-Known Among Others Under the Name of Fafnir, or the Dragon of the Twilight* by Johann Jetzer, Urmongomod. It looked like an original.

The title of Jetzer the Urmongomod's book was probably much more archaic in style, but Edgar didn't know Old High German, so he had to read the book through the Twilight. When you do that specific stylistic features are smoothed out and the text is leveled down, becoming much easier to understand.

Edgar ran his eye diagonally across *The Doings of Fafnir*: As was only to be expected, the contents of the thick volume interpreted events rather differently from the two Eddas and the *Song of the Nibelungen*. First, it was clear that Sigurd (a.k.a. Siegfried, a.k.a. Sivrit) and Regin and Khreidmar and Fafnir himself were all Others. Naturally, Khreidmar wasn't Fafnir's biological father and Regin wasn't his real brother. By means of long and carefully calculated plotting, Sigurd managed to make the Dark magicians quarrel and destroyed them all, some through the agency of Others, and some with his own hands. Sigurd's goal, of course, was not treasure at all, not useless pieces of metal and glittering stones. Sigurd and the others were searching for the heritage of the dwarf Andvari, but the Urmongomod's work did not explain what that was. It could have been some ancient and powerful artifacts or simply knowledge (in the form of books, for instance). Anyway, eventually Sigurd had killed everyone and taken possession of the heritage of Andvari, but what happened after that, Edgar didn't have any time to find out. Fafnir had been Sigurd's penultimate victim, before Regin. It seemed that Fafnir had taken certain secrets with him to the Twilight after all, but that didn't really bother the magicians of those times, who weren't bound by any Treaties or codes of law, and acted without any concerns about the Inquisition, since it hadn't existed then.

The main thing that Edgar had learned was that Fafnir possessed certain forgotten knowledge in the area of higher battle magic (which didn't appear to have helped him much in his duel with the crafty Sigurd), and he had taken this knowledge with him into the Twilight. So Zabulon could easily try to get hold of that knowledge.

Having arrived at this basically rather obvious idea, Edgar turned to the Necronomicon.

The first thing he discovered was that rematerialization was not at all the resurrection of an Other who had been dematerialized. It all turned out to be much simpler and more banal.

It was more like castling in chess. Someone withdrew into the Twilight, and in his place someone emerged from the Twilight. The higher the level of Power of the individual rematerialized, the more powerful the person dematerialized had to be. But the levels didn't have to be identical—a certain amount of leeway was allowed. If what the Urmongomod wrote about Fafnir was true, it meant the Dragon of the Twilight could be exchanged for a second- or third-level Dark magician, but only if the overall available energy input was adequate. And such a required input could easily be provided by acting out the Apocalypse—with the turbulent emotions of thousands of people generating such a squall that Fafnir would probably emerge reborn from the Twilight full of Power, a mighty Dark magician thirsting for vengeance and freedom. The freedom he had lost so long ago.

What would he do, this Great Magician from the past who had never even heard of the Treaty of the Inquisition? How was Zabulon planning to handle him? And was he planning at all? The Dragon of the Twilight in the skies over Europe at Christmas—what could possibly be more insane and terrifying?

Let's assume that if Fafnir runs wild and goes off burning cities and causing all sorts of devastation, if he simply goes for stupid brute force, then even people will be able to pacify him. With rockets. That Light flying ace who loved the Chicago Bulls will zap him with some devastating explosive device from his Phantom or his Harrier . . . they wouldn't kill him, but they'll pacify him. But what good will that do Europe? What does Europe want with nuclear mushrooms and her cozy little towns burned to cinders by Fafnir's flames?

But most likely Fafnir wouldn't simply run berserk; he would use his experience and cunning, and then watch out, Europe. Then there would be far more devastation and far more victims.

But why did Zabulon want all this?

Edgar couldn't understand.

What else was required for the resurrection of the Dragon of the Twilight? A second- or third-level magician in the right place . . . But what place was that?

Edgar spent about ten minutes calculating the answer from the stars and the shifting foci of energy. It was a problem of average difficulty: Fafnir had been cast down into the Twilight in the north of Europe . . . So, the most convenient place to rematerialize him on the cusp of the years 1999 and 2000 was . . . He had it.

Edgar wasn't very surprised by the result. The Czech Republic. Prague.

Edgar was immediately struck by a dark sense of foreboding. A Dark magician of the required level in the right place . . . In Prague . . .

That was him! Edgar the Estonian!

Edgar wiped away the cold sweat that had sprung out on his forehead and went back to his reading.

Not every magician would suit for Zabulon's purposes. For instance, the object of the castling move had to have been born in a specific place. It was rather unclear . . . What place exactly? When he figured it out it was Scandinavia, northern Germany, or the Baltic region.

The Baltic.

The chief of the Moscow Day Watch had suddenly summoned an Estonian to work in the Russian capital . . . And Edgar hadn't been able to see any obvious need for it . . .

Who else was there who had been born in Scandinavia, northern Germany, or the Baltic region and was in Prague just then?

No one. Only Edgar.

That was what Yury had warned him about before he flew to Prague. This had to be it. What else could it be?

All right. Easy now, easy. Just don't start getting nervous. Forewarned is forearmed. What else does the Necronomicon *have to tell us?*

Right, another four Dark Ones were required to form the Circle of Resurrection. Well, that was clear enough. The Circle was a kind of portal supported by the Power of the four Dark Ones, who were referred to very elegantly as their horses of Darkness.

And the horsemen were red, black, white, and pale. The precise scenario of the Apocalypse. Point for point.

And there were even magicians in Prague who would suit, although there were only three of them now—the Regin Brothers, who happened to be red-haired (the Asiatic), black (the African), white (the Slav), and pale (the Scandinavian that Gesar had killed).

Zabulon himself had said that this group had a place in his plans. Now Edgar could reasonably foresee what exactly those plans were. And Zabulon wasn't likely to be stopped by the absence of the fourth horseman.

Edgar studied the section of the *Necronomicon* to the end and discovered another two details that were small but, in the general context, important. Because Fafnir was a dragon, the canonical form of his resurrection should be to emerge from the sea—only that wasn't absolutely essential. What was essential was to make a sacrifice to the sea. In advance. Anywhere at all—it could be in China, or in the Falkland Islands.

Or even in the Crimea.

The person sacrificed was supposed to be "a youth or a maiden." No longer a child, but not yet an adult.

Artek, Edgar thought immediately. *The boy who drowned because of the duel.*

And then again, if Zabulon had set his sights on Edgar as the second figure in his castling move, then during the final twenty-four hours—no matter where Zabulon might be—he had to find an image of Edgar. A portrait or photograph. More likely a portrait. And keep this image with him. Until the moment when the move was made.

That was all—the library had no more help to offer Edgar. He hastily thanked the vampire librarian and hurried across to a computer.

Of course, he could have simply phoned Moscow. But a phone call was easy to trace, and Edgar didn't want to show his hand too soon. And he was absolutely certain that Alita was chatting on one of the IRC channels right at that moment.

The young IT manager—either a weak magician or a wizard—was glad to show him how to get onto the Internet. Edgar thanked him, and the young guy instantly stuck his nose into his own notebook computer, with its screen full of machine code. He was programming the old-fashioned way, without any of those newfangled Delphi Windows.

Edgar launched miRC and connected in the usual way to the Getborg DALnet server, with the funny cow in its logo (of course, the cow was drawn in pseudo-graphics—with letters and numbers). He identified himself, but he didn't log into any of the channels. He selected "Query" from the menu and put in the name he was interested in: Alita.

A new window opened.

What Edgar was most afraid of was a curt phrase appearing in the status window, saying: "No such name or channel."

But the Darkness was merciful—the reply came almost instantaneously. And from the right address—alita@ncport.ru.

"Edgar, hi! Are you in Prague?"

"Yes. Alita, I have an urgent question . . . it's rather strange.
And not for everyone's ears. Will you help me?"

"Do you need to ask, Edgar? Of course."

"Have you been in the chief's office during the last few
  days?"

In general, the likelihood of any witch being summoned by Zabulon himself was pretty low, but he had to start somewhere . . .

"Yes, I have, why?"

Well, well, Edgar thought to himself. *I guessed right!*
He typed in:

"You didn't happen to notice if he had a photograph or portrait
  of me in his office, did you? On the desk, for instance . . ."

"How did you guess?"

And Alita sent him a generous scattering of smiley faces to sym-
bolize her good mood.

"After you left the chief commissioned two drawings. Your
  portrait and a picture of a dragon. They're both standing
  in frames on his desk. I went to the arts and crafts salon
  on Tverskaya Street to get the frames. The chief gave me a
  bottle of Veuve Clicquot as a reward!"

Edgar closed his eyes. That was it. The final touch for the planned
switch of pieces. *Your death sentence, Edgar the Estonian. Now what are
you going to do?*
  "Thanks, Alita," he typed in with wooden fingers. "Got to run,
I'm snowed under with work . . ."

"Cheers, Edgar. Kiss!"

Edgar didn't even want to look at the smiley faces. He closed the window on the screen and got up from the table

The young programmer glanced at him from behind his notebook. "Is that it?" he asked without any real surprise.

"Yes," Edgar replied. "Thanks."

He reached the exit without thinking about anything—his head felt strangely dull and empty.

He'd been specially selected, like a cow for the Christmas kebabs. A reasonably powerful magician from the Baltic. He'd been lured in and treated well. Allowed to run things for a little while—in the Moscow Watch, not some dull backwater. But all the time he'd been nothing more than a sacrificial cow, who would be slaughtered when the right moment came. Used, just like a thing. Swapped, like a mindless chess piece.

After all, the game went on forever—it was only the presence of the pieces on the checkered board that was temporary.

But so what? If the time had come for one more black queen to join the game, did that mean it was pointless for the rook hastily drafted in from the periphery to dig in and clutch hard at the slippery surface of the board?

Oh no! thought Edgar. *I may not be a queen, but I'm certainly not a pawn. And I don't want to leave the board that easily. I'm going to kick up a fuss. And if I can manage it, I'll save half of Europe some serious problems.*

If all else failed, there was the Inquisition. Something told Edgar that the gray-robed officials were unlikely to be pleased by the idea of a visit from the Dragon of the Twilight.

Festive Prague seemed to have disappeared, faded, and receded into the distance. Edgar caught a taxi and rode to the hotel he needed without once looking out the window. He paid the driver automatically and walked into the vestibule, giving the doorman a look that probably made him wish he could disappear through the granite slabs of the floor.

Edgar strode toward the elevators so rapidly that his unbuttoned raincoat almost fluttered behind him. He walked toward the suite that he knew from his intuition as an Other.

Then he suddenly stopped as if he'd run into something and swallowed convulsively.

The Finns had just come out of the bar. The Regin Brothers. All four of them. Four, not three—the Chinese, the African, and the Slav had been joined by a genuine Finn, the one everybody had thought was dead.

But there he was, alive and well.

But of course—why would Gesar have wanted to kill a witness?

No doubt the artist is overwhelmed by a whole range of inexpressible feelings when he puts in place the final piece of glass in a mosaic. But what are you supposed to do when the glass pieces of the mosaic form the sparse words of your own death sentence?

"Brother!" one of the Finns said triumphantly to Edgar. "We want to thank you and the Day Watch of Moscow for your support. Why don't you join us? We're celebrating the survival of our brother Pasi—everybody thought he was dead."

The genuine Finn gave an embarrassed smile, his entire appearance showing how touched he was by his comrades' concern.

"Congratulations . . ." Edgar said in a hollow voice, although there wasn't really anything to congratulate them on—all four of them would be certain to die at Fafnir's resurrection.

"Brother Dark One . . ." Seeing Edgar's hesitation, the magician stopped pressing him. "Do you happen to know . . . the Light One who is also a defendant . . . why did he call us four horses?"

His colleagues all began nodding indignantly.

"Are we entitled to regard it as an unjustified insult?" the leader of the Regin Brothers asked hopefully.

"No," Edgar replied. "It's worse than an insult—it's the truth."

And he sprinted for the elevator.

CHAPTER 6

BY MIDDAY ANTON HAD GIVEN UP.

He and Igor hadn't drunk any more vodka, despite its remarkable ability to stimulate the imagination. Coffee already made him feel sick. And he didn't feel like drinking any of the wonderful Czech beer either.

Igor was standing by the window with a glass of Dannon drinking yogurt in his hand. He shook his head at Anton's latest suggestion. "No, come on. What sort of dragonslayer would I make? And I thought we'd abandoned the Fafnir scenario?"

"But what if it's right after all?"

"It makes no difference. It's a battle of magic, not a duel with a fire-breathing dragon . . ." Igor chuckled and added cynically. "And anyway, in a fight between Fafnir the Dragon and a pair of modern battle helicopters, I'd put my money on the choppers. There's no point in any more guessing, Anton. We won't come up with anything."

"But even so, Igor, you're the key."

"But what can we do about it? Nobody ever tells keys which doors they're going to open. Anton, I'm a perfectly ordinary Other. Only Zabulon knows what makes me so important. And Gesar probably knows too. He'll come upstairs and join us in a moment, then we can ask him."

Anton looked through the Twilight and said enviously: "Seriously? Is he already close? I can't sense him . . ."

"I can't sense him either: I just saw them through the window, walking into the hotel."

There was a gentle tap at the door. Just a token gesture of politeness, no more than that, and a moment later the visitors entered through the Twilight. Gesar, his silent shadow Alisher, and Svetlana. Svetlana was led through the Twilight by the magicians, and she only saw Anton when all three of them emerged from the Twilight into the human world. She smiled and gave a slightly guilty shrug, as if to say: "Just look what I'm like now." Once again Anton was overcome by a miserable feeling of guilt and tenderness, mixed with shame and anger at himself. Even though he'd had no other option but to let the Mirror take away all of Svetlana's Power . . . And the most important thing was that as a result, Svetlana was still alive . . . But he couldn't rid himself of the cursed feeling that the game had been lost.

Could Igor really have similar feelings when he remembered Alisa? Similar, but far more bitter? In that case Anton could only be surprised and delighted that he was still alive.

"Good afternoon, lads . . ." Gesar said in a soft voice.

He was wearing a modest, inexpensive suit and plain tie, looking like a run-of-the-mill businessman who bought his clothes from Marks and Spencer and always sent his employees modest presents for Christmas. In this case, of course, Gesar regarded himself as the very best present . . .

"Hello, Boris Ignatievich," said Anton. He couldn't bring himself to call this afternoon good. "Hello, Alisher."

He and Sveta simply exchanged glances again and he took her by the hand and led her across to a chair, as if she were an invalid . . . It was awful.

"Good afternoon, boss," Igor said calmly. "I'm glad to see you. Hello, Sveta. Hi, Alisher."

Gesar's bodyguard (that is, of course, if it was really possible to regard a third-level magician as a bodyguard for a Great Magician)—or, perhaps more accurately, his orderly, the son of a *devona* and a human woman—Alisher nodded to the magicians without speaking and moved into the corner of the room, where he froze with his arms crossed on his chest and partially withdrew into the Twilight. Anton sensed that Alisher's ability to observe in the Twilight had been heightened artificially, clearly by the boss. And he also noticed that the young magician was trying not to look at Igor. That was another crazy tangle—Alisher's father had been killed by Alisa Donnikova. And even though he hadn't been a human being or an Other . . . it was hard to formulate the precise status of a *devona*, a faithful helper of the Great Magicians. The *devona* himself did not perform any great feats of heroism, that was not his job. He merely served the heroes, removed minor obstacles from their path. And he strengthened family ties, facilitating the birth of great heroes . . .

Anton caught his breath.

As a rule, werewolves' children inherited the ability to transform, while magicians' children only became Others very rarely. But how did it work with *devonas*?

Who was Alisher: simply a magician or a *devona* like his father, who had been Gesar's assistant in Central Asia for many centuries? And what did the boss need the young Uzbeki magician for? Was it only for sentimental reasons that Gesar had taken him into the Moscow Watch and made him his retainer?

"Anton!"

He looked at Svetlana and only then realized that he was squeezing her hand too hard. "Sorry . . ."

Gesar was standing in front of Igor, looking into his eyes. He looked for a long time without saying anything. Then he sighed and walked away to a chair, hunched over and looking limp. He sat down and lowered his face into his hands.

"Boris Ignatievich," said Igor, "forgive me."

"No!" Gesar barked, with his hands still over his face, "I won't forgive you! So what if you fell in love with a witch? I won't condemn you for that—that's destiny. But you've given up on yourself—don't expect any forgiveness for that!"

Igor was clearly uncomfortable. As Anton looked at him, he suddenly realized he'd accomplished his mission after all. Not by simple, head-on tactics—it would have been stupid to expect to trick an experienced magician and restore his will to live with a simple drinking session and conversations about his friends. It would have been even more stupid to hope to convince him that the woman he loved was simply a repulsive, greedy bitch.

But their long nocturnal conversation, their attempts to understand what was happening and make sense of the latest stage in the war between the Watches had had an effect. Igor had been distracted from his misery and suffering. He had felt he was part of a team again.

Could that have been what Gesar was counting on? In that case, all of his behavior, including the present scene, had been carefully calculated!

But after all, the boss was right, Igor's mind was simply clouded.

"Gesar, there are things that even you have no right to ask!" Igor suddenly said. He said it abruptly, with a reawakened fury. With life in his voice.

"Yes, of course, Captain Igor Teplov." Gesar's voice was as cold as ice. "I have no right. But who had the right to ask you to swim down the Dnieper under fire in November '42? And who had the right . . ."

"That's different."

"Why is it?" Gesar stood up, walked over to Igor, and stopped still in front of him again, a head shorter than Igor, small and wiry, not looking at all heroic. "Do I have to explain to you, Teplov, what a war requires? It's not bodies that a war devours, but souls! And you knew that in the glorious city of Berlin, when you used your knife on that poor snot-nosed kid from the Hitler Jugend to make him give his friends away—you knew that."

Igor started as if he'd been slapped across the face.

"Conscience . . . love . . . honor . . ." Gesar said thoughtfully. "No one has the right to make anyone go against their conscience. No one has the right to make anyone betray love. No one has the right to persuade anyone to betray their honor. No one. You're right. But we do it! Of our own accord. When one pan of the scales holds our love, conscience, and honor, and the other holds a million loving, decent, honorable people. We're no angels, that's not for us. And I understand your pain, believe me! But you take a look at Alisher! And try to understand his pain! Ask Anton what he thinks about the one you love. Ask Svetlana."

"I can't condemn Igor," Svetlana said quietly. "I'm sorry, boss. Forgive me, Alisher. Maybe I'm just a fool . . . unworthy to work in the Watch. But I can understand all of you."

She said this in a very low voice, without any emphasis, but Gesar stopped talking and moved away from Igor. He spread his hands and asked, "Do you think I don't understand?"

The silence in the room was thick and heavy.

"Gesar, when it was my duty, I carried out my orders," Igor suddenly said. "Honestly, right down the line. Regardless of . . . what I thought or felt. But my duty's done now. I've reached the end of the line."

"No. That's where you're wrong, Igor." Gesar started walking round the room and took a cigar out of his pocket. He looked at it and frowned, put it back and took out a pack of democratic Pall Malls. He crumpled that and gestured in annoyance. "The Watch needs you. We all need you. I need you."

"Svetlana needs me . . ." Igor remarked casually.

"Svetlana, Alisher, Ilya, Semyon, Bear—all of us!" Gesar said very quickly. "Of course!"

Igor smiled, as if reconciling himself to the fact that he couldn't finish what he wanted to say. And then he suddenly asked in a businesslike, serious voice, "For long?"

"Twenty years at most," Gesar said quite calmly, as if he'd been expecting this question.

"Gesar, do you hope that will be long enough for me to stop loving Alisa?"

"That too," Gesar admitted. "But the Watch needs you right now. In the years immediately ahead."

"What do you want me to do, Gesar?"

"Don't get in our way, Igor. We're going to try to get you out of this. And we will get you out of it, believe me, if you just don't get in our way . . . or even better, if you help us just a little bit."

Igor thought about it. Then he said, "I won't accuse Alisa Donnikova of enchanting me. It's not true."

"But you can express the suspicion that your meeting was set up by the Moscow Day Watch?"

"Yes, I can," Igor said with a nod. "That's probably the way it was."

"That's enough," said Gesar with a shrug. "I don't ask anything else of you." And he really did look satisfied with that.

Anton cleared his throat and waited for Gesar to look at him. Then he said, "Boris Ignatievich, I'd like to ask you to do something for me. Can you explain what role Igor plays in our latest plot?"

"Just Igor?"

"Yes. What you need Svetlana for, and the *devona* Alisher, is clear enough already."

The young Uzbeki magician standing stock-still in the corner started.

"The new generation's coming along well . . ." Gesar said in a tired voice. "Shrewd. But stupid at the same time . . ." He hesitated and looked around at everyone there. Then he shook his head, and Anton sensed the Power spreading around them and flooding the room. The elastic wall was pressing something back, squeezing it out . . . "I can't tell you," Gesar admitted unexpectedly. "I can't tell you for one simple reason . . ."

"We'd refuse to cooperate?" Anton asked sharply.

Gesar shook his head. "No. On the contrary. I swear on the Light that what is going on will cause no harm to any of you. Neither to your magical or your human being . . . In fact, you would cooperate with genuine, sincere zeal. But . . ."

He was weighing every word now.

"What is taking place now really is the final operation of the Moscow Night Watch. Unfortunately, it is also the final operation of the Day Watch. Too much depends on the actions taken by everyone sitting here, as well as on the actions taken by our enemies. We are making our moves and our enemies are making theirs. They could be wrong, unsuccessful, mistaken. But the victory will go to those who make the final correct move."

"The victors are never judged," Anton agreed. "And the pieces on a chessboard are not given the right to move independently."

"Zabulon will easily read any move that any of you make!" Gesar barked. "And don't imagine, Anton, that when you rammed the Mirror's car it was a move that hadn't been foreseen! Yes, it was a successful move, the lesser of two evils. But even that was anticipated. By Zabulon . . . and by me." He paused for breath and went on more calmly: "Folks . . . to me you are not just pieces on a chessboard. Believe me. You're more than just tools."

"But one of us," said Svetlana with a smile acknowledging that she was the only woman in the room, "is the lathe for producing a tool?"

Anton didn't ask how she had realized. Maybe she'd been drawing up diagrams too—without letting even him know? Or maybe she'd already sensed something when she still had her powers?

Gesar paused, lowering his head. He seemed to be thinking hard . . . And then Anton realized that the strength of the protective cocoon around them had increased to a quite incredible level. Where was the limit to the Power of the Great Magicians? Was there even a limit to it at all?

"All right," Gesar said with a nod. "Svetlana, you're right . . . but only partly . . . ah, Light and Darkness!"

He lowered himself into an armchair, took out the cigarettes again, and lit one. He took two drags and started speaking: "Svetlana, you are a Great Enchantress. They're only born every few centuries. Potentially, you're more powerful than Olga . . . probably . . . But your value to the Light Ones—and I don't mean just our Watch, but Light Ones in general—is that you can become the mother of the Messiah."

"After Olga rewrote my Book of Destiny," Svetlana said.

"No. Not after that. It's not possible to rewrite the destiny of an Other as easily as the destiny of a human being. It was predetermined from the very beginning. We only corrected a few details. Minor ones. That don't affect you or the future . . . the prospective child."

"What details?" The anger could suddenly be heard in Svetlana's voice, the anger she'd restrained for so long. Now it was Anton who wanted to shout out as her fingers dug into the palm of his hand.

"Only the date." Gesar had no intention of giving way to pressure from Svetlana. "Nothing but the date. Two thousand years after the birth of Christ is the peak of human belief in the coming of the Messiah."

"Thank you very much," said Svetlana in a voice trembling with fury. "So you decided when I would have him and who his father would be?"

"In the first place, why 'him'?" Gesar asked.

Anton had been on the point of putting in a few words, mostly to clarify what Svetlana had said about the father, but he choked on this swift rejoinder. Svetlana's hand went limp too.

"For some the father and mother decide, for some it's the drunken obstetrician, for others it's an extra glass of vodka," Gesar said in a melancholy voice. There was no need for him to say "in the second place." "Svetlana, my child! It's dangerous to play with such forces, with such predetermination. Even I'm not trying to do that. It is predetermined that you can give birth to a daughter who will become the greatest figure in the war between the Light and the Darkness. Her word will change the entire world. Her word will make sinners repent. At a glance from her the greatest magicians of Darkness will go down on their knees."

"It's only a probability . . ." Svetlana whispered.

"Of course. There is no fate—which is both unfortunate and fortunate. But you must believe that an old, weary magician is doing everything he can to make it a reality."

"I should have stayed a human being . . ." Svetlana whispered. "I should have . . ."

"Have you looked at any icons recently?" Gesar asked. "Look into Mary's eyes and think why they're always so sad."

The room was very quiet.

"I've already told you more than I have any right to." Gesar spread his arms in a guilty shrug, and for the first time ever it seemed to Anton that he wasn't acting at all. "But I have told you, I've put one foot over the line of what is permissible. It's up to you to decide. To think who is a figure on a chessboard, and who is a rational individual, capable of seeing past imaginary offenses."

"Imaginary?" Svetlana asked bitterly.

"When they explained that you had to wash your hands after playing in the sandpit or made you tie the ribbon on your braid in a bow—that was interference in your destiny too," said Gesar. "And I think it was justified."

"You're not my father, Boris Ignatievich!" said Svetlana.

"No, of course not. But to me, you're all my children . . ." Gesar sighed. "I'll wait for you in the hall . . . that is, Alisher and I will wait. Join us if you want to."

He went out, and the *devona* followed him like a shadow.

Igor was the first to say anything. "What hurts most is that he's right about some things."

"If you'd been told that you have to give birth to a Messiah, then I'd talk to you about what's right or wrong," Svetlana replied abruptly.

"That would be rather, well . . . difficult for me," Igor admitted in an embarrassed voice.

Anton was the first to smile. He looked at Svetlana and said, "Listen . . . I remember how indignant you were about the injustice of destiny—that generally speaking, Others only have children who are ordinary people . . ."

"That was just an abstract indignation . . ." said Svetlana, throwing her hands up in the air. "Boys, I think someone's already been smoking in here . . ."

Igor handed her a cigarette without speaking.

"Why do everything like that, behind our backs," Svetlana complained as she lit her cigarette. "And what sort of mother would I make . . . for a Messiah? And a female one at that!"

"Well, Messiah is just the appropriate term, that's all," said Igor. "Relax."

"I'm no virgin!" Svetlana declared gloomily. "And in general . . . I don't think of myself as a paragon of virtue . . ."

"Don't draw irrelevant parallels."

Strangely enough, Igor seemed to have calmed down. For real. He was sharp and focused.

"Anton, why don't you say something!" Svetlana burst out. "Doesn't all this concern you at all?"

"I very much hope that it concerns me directly," replied Anton. "And I think we ought to go out now and join Gesar. It's tough on him sitting out there and waiting."

"He already knows everything . . . in advance . . ." Svetlana said, and turned away.

"No. He doesn't. If we're really not pawns, he doesn't know."

There was the soft sound of guitar strings. Igor was leaning against the wall, holding the instrument. He began singing so softly that Svetlana and Anton both had to stop talking.

The devils ask me to serve,
But I serve no one.
Even myself, even you,
Even the one who has power.
If he is still alive,
I do not serve even him.
I have stolen just enough fire
Not to need to steal any more . . .

Igor held the guitar out and gently lowered it into an armchair. People put their instrument down like that when they're sure they'll be back soon.

"Shall we go then?"

*   *   *

Edgar was the first Dark One to enter the Tribunal's meeting hall. That was the procedure. He entered through one door at the same time as Anton came in through the door opposite. They bowed their heads to each other in a polite greeting. Edgar did not feel any particular resentment for the Light One and he expected the feeling to be mutual to some extent

Yes, compared to the small, neglected room in Moscow University, this hall certainly made an impression. This was Europe, after all.

Stone vaulting—heavy and oppressive, but at the same time giving a sense of security and calm. A simple metal chandelier, but with about two hundred candles, and Edgar could have sworn the candles had been burning for more than one century already. They said the Berne department of the Inquisition was located in an ultramodern building, but the Prague department was in a truly ancient one.

Edgar liked the old style better.

The round hall was divided into two parts: One was faced with light marble, the other with dark. There was something at once naïve and exalted in this simple visual representation of the two Powers. The little desks for the prosecutors stood at the center, beside a circular metal grille covering a dark hole in the floor.

A wedge of gray marble reached almost to the very center of the hall. That was the Inquisitors' area, and they, of course, were already in their seats. Seven of them. In principle the Inquisition was not regarded as a power equal to the two Watches, but Edgar knew that those seven included two Great Ones—one Dark and one Light. If it wished, the European office could probably fight Gesar and Zabulon on equal terms.

That was good to know.

Anton was followed in by three Light Ones from Moscow. Gesar . . . well, of course, where would they be without Gesar!

Svetlana . . . that was natural too. And that Uzbeki, Gesar's secretary
or personal assistant.

The Dark Ones were already walking along the corridor behind
Edgar. Zabulon . . . Sensing the approach of his chief, Edgar involuntarily looked round—and received a friendly nod from the head
of Moscow's Dark Ones. *Well, well . . . smile, you Judas . . . you're even
worse than Judas: He betrayed his teacher, but you're betraying your disciple!*

But then another two Dark Ones followed Zabulon into the hall.
Edgar had been prepared to see Anna Lemesheva, but not Yury, who
winked mockingly at him. The same Yury who had given Edgar the
timely warning about Zabulon's underhanded schemes—he hadn't
been prepared for that!

Edgar forced himself to turn away from his colleagues and look
straight ahead.

Igor was brought in last. Two rank-and-file Inquisitors walked in
beside him and accompanied him to the circular grille, three meters
across, in the center of the hall.

There was no special magic in that circle, or at least Edgar
couldn't sense any. And the mechanism that had once been used to
invert the grille and plunge the accused into a deep well shaft looked
as if it had rusted up long ago and was no longer used. But even so it
didn't look as if standing on that circle was pleasant.

However, Igor paid no attention to that and stood in the center of
the circle with his arms crossed on his chest.

"In the name of the Treaty . . ."

One Inquisitor came forward from the group. The only one who
was not wearing gray robes. Witezslav, the Higher Vampire.

"We are Others. We serve different Powers . . ."

Edgar mechanically repeated the words of the Treaty, trying to
work out what Witezslav would start with. And how he could extri-
cate himself from this mess now.

"Today the European Tribunal of the Inquisition has to consider
a claim brought by the Night Watch of the city of Moscow, Russia,
against the Day Watch of the city of Moscow, Russia," the vampire

announced after the reading of the Treaty. "A counterclaim by the Day Watch of Moscow against the Night Watch of Moscow forms part of the proceedings. Its subject is the duel between the Light magician Igor Teplov, and the Dark witch Alisa Donnikova . . ."

There were no surprises so far . . . Edgar felt himself clutching the dark, cool wooden top of his desk and made an effort of will to calm himself down. After all, he was an experienced lawyer. And how were legal proceedings between people any different from legal proceeding between Others?

Except, of course for the nature of the sentence . . .

"However, the sequence of proceedings will be changed somewhat," said Witezslav. "The Tribunal is also obliged to resolve another two matters connected with the main claim. The first concerns a sect of Dark Ones who call themselves the Regin Brothers, who are guilty of attacking the Inquisition's vault and stealing the artifact known as Fafnir's Talon, smuggling it into Russia, and resisting the Night Watch of Moscow. Bring in the accused."

Another two young Inquisitors led in the four Finns. Faint smiles appeared on the faces of all the Others present—after all, it was impossible to imagine a more ludicrous-looking quartet.

"There is probably no need to recite the circumstances of the incident," said the vampire. "Everyone present is familiar with the materials collected by the Inquisition on this case. The Inquisition's job is to pronounce judgment. Just, impartial, and strict."

It was clear from the expressions on the faces of the four accused that they were not anticipating leniency.

"The punishment for a crime as grave as attacking employees of the Inquisition and stealing a highly dangerous artifact from the vault is unconditional—dematerialization," the vampire declared. He paused and then added something that made the Finns lift up their heads: "But . . . But the accused did not participate directly in the incident in Berne. As the materials of the case make clear, the leaders of the sect, who unfortunately were killed while being detained, made the four young magicians act as couriers. Therefore, the Inquisition qualifies their actions only as smuggling and resisting the Night Watch of Moscow. There are also extenuating circumstances: profound and sincere remorse, assistance rendered to the investigation after detention, the youth of the accused, and the absence of any previous offenses. If the Night Watch of Moscow can adduce any further extenuating circumstances and will withdraw the personal accusations against the Dark magicians, the Inquisition has the right to mitigate its sentence."

Gesar stood up to speak for the Light Ones. He spread his hands in a broad gesture. "The Night Watch of Moscow has no . . . personal charges to bring against the accused. In addition, we believe that the leadership of the sect of the Regin Brothers was provoked into committing its crime by a certain . . . a certain unidentified Dark magician."

"That has not been proved," said Witezslav.

"Only the identity of the provocateur has not been established," Gesar said with a smile. "The fact of his existence is in no doubt."

Witezslav nodded and turned to face his six colleagues. For a few moments the Inquisitors shared their thoughts with each other without speaking. Then Witezslav looked back to the four motionless Finns. "In the name of the Treaty, bearing in mind the clement attitude of the Night Watch, the absence of any grave consequences, and the other extenuating circumstances, the Inquisition offers you the right to choose your punishment. The first option—you are condemned to death by hanging, but your civil rights will not be affected . . ."

The large young black man sighed heavily and the Chinese and the Finn grabbed his elbows and held him up.

"The second possible punishment is that from this day until the end of your lives you will be forbidden to use magic. You will have the right to live ordinary human lives, without using magical means to prolong or improve the quality of those lives."

The Finns looked at the Inquisitor, stunned. Zabulon giggled shrilly, but immediately assumed a serious expression.

"The second . . . the second!" Yukha Mustajoki said in a choking voice. The others nodded.

"Does anyone present have any objections?" Witezslav asked.

Gesar got to his feet again. "As a small gesture of goodwill . . . we consider it possible to permit the accused to use magic . . . minor magic . . . with inanimate objects." It seemed as if Gesar had to struggle to pronounce every word, that he was forcing himself to show mercy. "Say, to find some . . . small item . . . that's been lost . . . a key or a coin . . . To drive the flies out of a room . . . according to the regulations, flies are regarded as inanimate, are they not? To clean the carburetor in a car . . ."

The vampire's face expressed faint surprise.

He doesn't understand, Edgar thought.

"The Inquisition has no objections . . ." the vampire said eventually. "Apply the seals to the accused!"

Two Inquisitors raised their right hands, and fine threads of glimmering energy streamed through the air toward the accused. The seals were applied permanently, leaving the condemned prisoners capable of only the very weakest forms of magic. Probably the Inquisitors really hadn't understood that Gesar's unexpected kindness had only made the punishment worse. It was one thing to be completely deprived of all magic and gradually come to terms with life as a human being. It was quite different to feel every day that you were a helpless cripple who had to manage with a pale shadow of your former abilities.

But then, the Finns hadn't thought about that yet. They were led out of the hall, absolutely crazy with happiness. Yukha kept trying to break away and shake everybody's hand, but the vigilant guards forced him to walk out simply by nudging and shoving him.

Edgar shook his head. He actually felt quite glad that the Dark Brothers had been saved. But what a price to pay . . . He would probably have preferred a quick death.

"The next matter for this hearing to consider has not been announced in advance," said Witezslav. "The Inquisition requests the

leader of the Night Watch of Moscow, known under the name of
Gesar, to step into the circle of the accused . . ."

Zabulon smiled in triumph.

"And also the leader of the Day Watch of Moscow, known under
the name of Zabulon."

Edgar was delighted by Zabulon's slightly perplexed expression.
But just how genuine was it?

"The Inquisition's first question is for the Great Magician Gesar."
Witezslav was speaking politely now, but very firmly. "Gesar, have
you carried out interventions in the Book of Destiny of the Great
Enchantress Svetlana Nazarova, here present, with the intention of
compelling the said Great Enchantress to become the mother of a
Light Messiah?"

The hall fell silent.

"Rephrase your question, Witezslav," Gesar said in a soft voice.
"Or I shall take offense."

The vampire bared his teeth in a smile. "Answer the substance of
the point, Great Magician Gesar."

"Very well," said Gesar with a nod. "I was not expecting these accusations, but . . . I will explain for the Tribunal."

You were expecting them, thought Edgar. *You were expecting everything, you cunning old schemer . . .*

"An intervention of that kind is impossible in principle. Even for
me," Gesar declared modestly.

Witezslav seemed confused by that.

"But, Great Magician Gesar, Svetlana Nazarova's Book of Destiny . . ."

". . . shows that she will become the mother of the greatest of all
Light enchantresses, in poetical terms a Light Messiah." Gesar smiled
happily. "This is a great joy for the Night Watch of Moscow . . .
and, indeed, for all Light Ones! But the respected Inquisition must
understand that such things cannot be *written into* a Book of Destiny.
Absolutely not. There is no way. Not even by using a certain artifact
familiar to you which belongs by right to the Night Watch."

"But interventions were made in Svetlana Nazarova's Book of Destiny?" the vampire continued to insist.

"Yes," Gesar said, and nodded. "As everybody, or almost everybody, knows, it is possible to make a new entry in a Book of Destiny, but it has a direct effect on the balance between Light and Darkness. It is fairly simple to introduce trifling changes in the destiny of an ordinary human being. It is rather more difficult to make even insignificant changes in the destiny of an Other. And the more powerful that Other is, and the more serious the change, the greater the disturbance suffered by the Light and the Darkness. Respected members of the Tribunal, can you calculate the consequences that would ensue from introducing into a Great Enchantress's Book of Destiny an entry that would make her the mother of a Messiah?"

No one replied.

"Any one of us . . . all the Others taken together, would be dematerialized if they attempted that kind of meddling. We'd be reduced to dust! The world would collapse! And you accuse me of committing such acts."

"Light magician Gesar, what changes were entered into Svetlana Nazarova's Book of Destiny?"

Gesar shrugged. "Nothing but trifling details. I am obliged to be concerned for my colleagues' well-being, am I not? A trip to some Italian resort or other . . . a course of lessons in a driving school . . . and something else . . . I can present a detailed list, if you wish. There's nothing serious. Just the small pleasures of human life."

Witezslav thought for a moment and asked, "Where were the new entries made? *Before* or *after* the entry about the birth of the greatest of all Light Enchantresses?"

"I think, *before* . . ." Gesar said with a smile.

"And in that way, you adjusted the time of the event." Witezslav was not asking—he was thinking out loud. "You maximized the probability that Svetlana's future daughter would be a Messiah of the Light . . ."

"Possibly," Gesar agreed. "But what of that? All I did was to improve the daily life of one of my colleagues."

"And could you not have used other methods to improve Svetlana Nazarova's living conditions? Free vacations, bonuses, friendly advice?"

Gesar looked genuinely offended now. "I made use of what came to hand. The Inquisition has a right to be surprised if I hammer in nails with a microscope . . . But there's no way you can charge me with that."

The Inquisitors exchanged glances. This time the silent consultation lasted for almost a minute. Edgar felt a trickle of cold sweat running down his back. It would really cause a ruckus if the Inquisition charged Gesar. The dematerialization of a Great Magician was not such a simple proposition as dealing with the four Finns . . .

"Not cognizable," Witezslav said eventually. "Great Magician Gesar, having heard your explanations, the Inquisition accepts that you have not violated the letter of the Treaty . . ."

"The letter or the spirit." Gesar corrected him sharply.

"The letter or the spirit," the vampire agreed in a voice that betrayed his frustration. "However, your actions are still considered to be dubious and dangerous."

"No more so than the attempt by the Day Watch of Moscow to eliminate Svetlana Nazarova shortly before her initiation," Gesar snapped. "Do you have any more questions for me?"

"No," said Witezslav. "You may return to your seat."

Throughout the questioning, Zabulon had stood modestly on the very edge of the circular grille . . . He didn't seem upset that no charges had been brought against Gesar. And that made Edgar feel uneasy.

"Dark magician Zabulon, the Inquisition has some questions for you," said Witezslav. "Was the attack by the sect of the Regin Brothers provoked by you?"

"No one is obliged to testify against himself . . ." Zabulon said in a dull voice.

"Is that a confession?" the vampire asked in a lively tone.

"No, it is a reminder of the law. You have no right to ask such a question. Therefore I shall not answer it."

"Very well. Your objection is accepted. Great Magician Zabulon, have you been planning, in order to oppose the future Messiah of the Light, to resurrect the Great Magician Fafnir, who was consigned to the Twilight and dematerialized more than a thousand years ago?"

Zabulon began blinking rapidly and exclaimed in a voice full of amazement, "Where did you get a nonsensical idea like that?"

"Did you act to prevent the initiation of Svetlana Nazarova and carry out other actions directed against her?"

"Yes, within the limits permitted by the Treaty," Zabulon replied briskly.

"And Fafnir?"

"What about Fafnir?" said Zabulon, answering a question with a question. He looked at Edgar and winked.

"Why did you send to Prague a certain member of the Day Watch, ideally suited for the rematerialization of Fafnir?"

"I have no idea what you're talking about!"

"Did you plan to exploit the following parallels: Fafnir as the Antichrist, the four members of the Regin Brothers sect as the four horsemen of the Apocalypse . . ."

Zabulon burst into laughter. He laughed and wheezed happily for a long time, the way someone might laugh if they had just pulled off a risky but very amusing hoax. Then he wiped away the tears that had sprung to his eyes and said in a calmer voice, "I am delighted by the sense of humor demonstrated by the members of the Inquisition. Fafnir was an insane psychopath. I actually knew him personally and there is nothing I would like less than to meet him again . . . in any case, he wouldn't suit as a Messiah of Darkness. That's beyond his level . . . Eliminating Svetlana, now . . ." Zabulon smiled. ". . . That's a possibility. But at such a price . . . oh, no, never. And as for those half-wit Finnish magicians . . . what did you say they were—the horsemen of the Apocalypse?"

Edgar felt like a total idiot. He looked imploringly at Witezslav. But the vampire hadn't given up yet.

"Why did you carry out the following actions: arranging the death of Alisa Donnikova, which can be interpreted as a ritual sacrifice for rematerialization, and ordering two portraits from a well-known Moscow artist—one of the Dark magician Edgar and one of the dragon Fafnir?"

Zabulon became more serious: "I would also like to understand the circumstances of Alisa's death better! As I understand, it is to be the subject of the next inquiry. Well, and as for the portraits . . ."

The head of Moscow's Day Watch reached inside his jacket and took out two small pictures in frames, about twenty by thirty centimeters. Edgar was horrified to recognize one as a portrait of himself. The other showed a dragon contorted by convulsions.

"This is a small Christmas present for one of my finest employees—please pardon an old man's sentimentality . . ."

And with that Zabulon took a step toward Edgar and held the portrait out to him. It was a good portrait—no two ways about it. But Edgar was only frightened even more by Zabulon's whisper: "Smart boy . . ."

Zabulon returned to the circle.

"And the second picture?" Witezslav asked.

"Pure sentimentality," Zabulon repeated. "Those Regin Brothers stirred up old feelings. I remembered Fafnir and . . . decided to have a portrait of him made as a keepsake . . ."

"You were not planning to bring him back to life?" Witezslav asked again. This time Zabulon answered very seriously and apparently with absolute sincerity. "Not for a moment. There are less disruptive ways to achieve my goal."

The Inquisitors exchanged glances.

"Great Magician Zabulon," said Witezslav. "The Inquisition has no charges to bring against you: You may return to your seat. However, we remind you that taken all together your actions appear extremely ambiguous and dangerous . . ."

"I understand, I understand," Zabulon muttered as he walked out of the circle. "Soon it will be impossible to pick your nose without permission . . ."

Edgar looked at Gesar, expecting the old intriguer to be angry.

But no. Gesar wasn't angry. He even seemed to have taken a genuine interest in what Zabulon had said. That is, he had been quite convinced that the head of the Dark Ones would wriggle out of everything, but he was interested in all the details.

They'd known all of this beforehand!

Edgar struggled desperately to gather his scattered thoughts. That meant Svetlana really was going to be the mother of a Messiah of the Light . . . and a female one—that was a surprise! Zabulon was fighting against it, but . . . but not by creating an Antichrist in the flesh . . . that had only been a diversionary maneuver, one in which Edgar had behaved like a naïve child.

But then what was the most important thing?

"The Inquisition now moves on to the consideration of the most important matter of the day, which is of exceptional importance for the Light and the Darkness," said Witezslav, as if he were answering the question that Edgar hadn't asked. "The case of Igor Teplov, a third-level magician of the Moscow Night Watch. Is everyone familiar with the materials of the case?"

Nobody said anything. Everybody had been familiar with the materials for a long time . . .

"I offer the prosecuting counsel, Anton Gorodetsky, the floor."

The Light One was standing opposite Edgar. He raised his head and nodded curtly to Witezslav.

"I shall be brief. In essence, our charges are simple—we accuse the respected magician Zabulon, here present, of deliberately sending Alisa Donnikova to the Artek camp, knowing that Igor Teplov would be there, restoring his powers. Zabulon had probably read the reality lines and realized that for Igor and Alisa those conditions would immediately lead to . . . to love between them. A tragic and hopeless love, since the young people served different powers. A love

that would end in a duel which would lead to the death of either
Igor or Alisa, while the surviving opponent would be condemned
by the Inquisition. We accuse Zabulon of the deliberate and cynical
elimination . . . attempted elimination . . . of the Moscow Night
Watch agent Igor Teplov. We therefore request the Inquisition to
withdraw the charge brought against Igor Teplov of violating the
Treaty and murdering Alisa Donnikova."

"Is that all?" Witezslav asked after a pause.

"No. We also request the court to consider the matter of the death
of a young boy who was not an Other, as a result of the duel. Insofar
as the duel was arranged by Zabulon . . ."

"Objection," Zabulon exclaimed in a squeaky voice.

"Objection sustained," the vampire ruled.

"Since we believe the duel to have been arranged by Zabulon, he
is also guilty of the boy's death, for which Igor Teplov cannot be
blamed. That is all."

Witezslav turned his head to look at Zabulon. "Can you reply to
the essence of the matter?"

"There will be no answer—I have already explained the reason,"
Zabulon replied coolly.

"I offer the floor to the counsel for the defense."

Edgar sighed and began. "My colleague's speculations are all highly
diverting. We are witnessing an attempt to shield a criminal . . ."

"Objection!" Anton put in quickly.

"To shield the accused," said Edgar, correcting himself. "Igor
Teplov is guilty of the murder of the young witch Alisa Donnikova.
And the worst thing about it is that he loved her with all his heart.
And worse again, in the grip of his maniacal passion, Igor Teplov
incidentally caused the death of the boy Makar Kanevsky. He killed
a child. A human child, who also had a right to live. And there is
more. As a result of his extensive gathering of Power from children
on vacation at Artek, seven of them suffered from nightmares for
three months. Two cases of persistent incontinence were recorded.
Nine-year-old Yurik Semetsky, a resident of Moscow, died of asphyx-

iation a month after returning from Artek, when he drowned in his bath. We do not know as yet if this was a result of the actions of Igor Teplov . . . the Light magician Igor Teplov."

He looked at the accused. Igor's face was stony. Impervious. Expressionless.

"The Light Ones can put forward their groundless accusations as long as they wish," said Edgar. "Without any proof, without even any cogent explanation as to why the Day Watch of Moscow would sacrifice a young and promising member of its staff who had already received several commendations from the head of the Watch, in order to eliminate a third-level Light magician who possesses no real talent . . . That is a matter for their consciences. We only request the Inquisition to consider the situation impartially and punish the guilty party for violation of the Treaty."

Edgar took a breath and added the final, decisive phrase: "We have heard a lot said about how Light magicians who commit some ethically unjustifiable act dematerialize themselves voluntarily. They withdraw into the Twilight under the burden of their shame . . . We have all heard a lot about this. But I, for instance, have never actually seen it. No doubt Igor Teplov regards the murder of a girl who was in love with him, and likewise the death and suffering of innocent human children, as ethically irreproachable actions."

He stopped speaking.

The Inquisitors exchanged glances. Then Witezslav asked, "Do the parties to the case have any proof that their assertions are correct?"

Gesar said nothing, but Zabulon asked in surprise, "Pardon me, but what proof can I offer that I'm not a camel? Let those who have uttered such nonsense attempt to prove it."

"The Inquisition has heard the opinions of the two sides," said the vampire. "Accused, do you have anything to add?"

Igor Teplov nodded. "Yes. I admit that my actions were not entirely justified . . . and I profoundly regret their consequences. I . . . I had . . ." He broke off, then started talking more quickly. "I had very strong feelings for Alisa Donnikova. But when I learned she was a Dark witch, it affected the balance of my mind. I do not ask for clemency. I have already condemned myself. But . . ."

He turned sharply toward Zabulon.

"You are the murderer! You sent Alisa to her death. And that is why I have to stay alive . . . I have to, so that you will not profit from your villainy."

Zabulon merely shrugged and gave a heavy sigh.

"Do you have any proof?" the vampire asked.

Igor shook his head.

"The Tribunal is aware of the significance of this case," said Witezslav. "Although neither side has adduced any evidence, the Inquisition considers it important to determine who is the real guilty party. Therefore . . ."

Edgar suddenly saw Zabulon's expression change: His face froze halfway through a sad smile.

"Therefore the Inquisition will continue to question witnesses. Alisa Donnikova will be temporarily rematerialized."

"Objection!" said Zabulon, rising to his feet. "This case is not important enough to disturb the peace of the departed!"

"Objection overruled. The Inquisition requests Anna Lemesheva, who has come here on the Inquisition's instructions, to advance to the center of the hall. Her body will be used for the temporary rematerialization of Alisa Donnikova."

Lemesheva began to squeal. But a moment later two young Inquisitors were already leading her, twitching feebly, out into the center of the hall.

"The expenditure of energy in this process will be borne by the Night Watch of Moscow and it will not be refunded no matter what the outcome of the trial," Witezslav continued. "Great Magician Gesar, do you possess the required reserves of Power?"

"Yes," said Gesar, getting to his feet, "I do."

Edgar felt he was completely losing the thread of events. What was so important about this Igor Teplov that Zabulon would sacrifice his lover for him and Gesar would expend such a colossal amount of Power?

"Proceed with the rematerialization," said Witezslav. "Any attempt to hinder it is punishable by immediate death."

Several of the Inquisitors moved forward slightly, and Gesar sighed and stepped toward Lemesheva. She squealed again, and then fell silent, staring at the Light magician with glazed eyes.

And then Edgar had to squeeze his own eyes shut.

There was such a colossal amount of energy raging in the center of the hall that he simply couldn't look. He sensed the Inquisitors erecting magical barriers around Gesar and Lemesheva, one after another. He sensed the barriers crumbling under the pressure of unimaginable Power. And he felt the Twilight shudder as it was torn open through all the layers that Edgar knew and those he had never even suspected existed. If this was temporary rematerialization, then what must a permanent rematerialization be like?

The storm died away. Gesar slowly stepped backward.

There were three figures left in the center of the hall—the Inquisitor Witezslav, the Light magician Igor Teplov, and the Dark witch Alisa Donnikova.

Alisa was trembling, coughing, and clutching at her throat.

Edgar shuddered. He didn't know what happened to Others there . . . in the Twilight. And he didn't really want to know, to be quite honest. But Alisa had just recovered consciousness at the moment when her human life had come to an end. She had come back to life with a searing pain in her lungs, still choking on seawater, struggling desperately with the pressure that Teplov had brought down on her.

"Alisa Donnikova," the vampire began. Even his voice trembled— temporary rematerialization was an infrequent procedure, very infrequent . . . "You have been temporarily rematerialized and are now in the premises of the European Tribunal of the Inquisition in Prague. Do you understand me?"

Alisa Donnikova straightened up, already controlling her wheezing. She was looking at Igor Teplov. And nobody else.

"Do you understand me?" Witezslav repeated.

"Why . . . in Prague?" Alisa asked. She was taking rapid, deep breaths, as if she simply couldn't get enough air—even the damp air in this dungeon.

"That is not important, Alisa Donnikova. You have been summoned to our world as a witness. A great deal depends on what you say."

"Can . . . can I stay here? Again? Forever?" Alisa asked.

But she was only looking at Igor.

"No," the Inquisitor replied honestly. "Will you answer my questions voluntarily?"

Alisa tossed her head to and fro, with a strange, desperate pride. "Yes, I will, Inquisitor. Ask."

But she was only looking at Igor.

"The questions concern your duel with the Light magician Igor Teplov, here present. Was the challenge to the duel made in accordance with all the rules?"

"Yes."

"Tell me, Alisa, do you accuse Igor Teplov of your death?"

Alisa smiled. She gestured with her hand—without turning around, but unerringly indicating Zabulon. "No."

She was only looking at Igor.

"Do you have any charges to bring against your . . . opponent?"

She only shook her head.

"Alisa Donnikova, can you accuse anybody who is present here of provoking the sad events that led to your death?"

"Zabulon," Alisa said in an absolutely indifferent voice. "It was his operation."

"You cowardly fool!" Zabulon shouted. "They won't rematerialize you anyway! What are you doing, witch?"

It was only then that Alisa Donnikova turned toward Zabulon. Under her gaze the leader of the Dark Ones fell silent.

"Zabulon, have you forgotten what you said to me when I appealed to you as I was drowning?"

"Stupid, vengeful little fool," Zabulon said in a calmer voice.

Alisa shook her head. She looked at Igor again and said in a strange, mocking tone of voice, "What has vengeance got to do with it . . . Love is also a great power, Zabulon."

"The Inquisition has no further questions," Witezslav said quickly. "Gentlemen . . . I think to continue with this scene . . . would be unworthy of Others. The charge against Igor Teplov of violating the Treaty is dismissed. Alisa Donnikova can . . . can go back now."

Edgar seemed to be watching in a dream as Gesar got to his feet. The triumphant, victorious Gesar, with Zabulon hunched over on his bench . . . the defeated Zabulon.

It was only when the faces of the Great Magicians suddenly trembled in surprise and confusion that he looked back at the center of the hall.

Alisa Donnikova was disappearing. Her body was changing, sinking into the Twilight as a pale, insubstantial shadow. Lemesheva was crawling on all fours toward Zabulon's feet.

But Igor Teplov was also disappearing.

Withdrawing into the Twilight.

Edgar hadn't lied. This really was the first time he had ever seen a Light magician dematerialize. Voluntarily. Without any fighting or screaming or streams of Power.

Just for one moment Igor Teplov, already transformed into an almost insubstantial shadow, turned to glance at his comrades. With a glance that looked guilty. But apart from that, he only looked at Alisa.

Then he disappeared.

The Twilight closed up. The air in the hall was icy, there was white, bristling hoarfrost clinging to the walls like a shroud of mourning. The triumphant smile was slowly returning to Zabulon's face. Gesar was looking at the empty circular grille with a weary, sad expression.

"Well?" Zabulon shouted. "Well? You see? Now where's your mentor? Where is he, the only one who was capable of *educating* the Messiah of the Light?"

He laughed and patted Lemesheva's head—she was standing on her knees in front of him. Then he turned to the Inquisition and said, "Yes, it was a Day Watch operation. Within the limits of the Treaty. The exchange of two equal pieces—Alisa Donnikova for Igor Teplov. Do you have any more charges to bring against us?"

"The Inquisition has no charges to bring against you . . ." the vampire said slowly. He rubbed his face with his hand. "In view of all the circumstances . . . The Inquisition will consider the question of the early restoration of Svetlana Nazarova's Power. But that . . . will be later. Everyone . . . everyone may leave the hall."

Svetlana was the first to get up from her seat. She walked up to Zabulon and stood for a second, looking into his face. Edgar suddenly realized with a sinking heart that the enchantress was going to hit the magician.

But all she did was say something to him, then turn away and walk out abruptly.

Edgar's legs felt stiff and awkward as he left his desk. He almost bumped into Gesar, who was musing sadly, engrossed in his own thoughts. Anton immediately came up to Gesar, pushing Edgar aside. He exclaimed, "So what does this mean . . . Svetlana's daughter can be an Other, but not grow up to be the Messiah of the Light?"

Gesar nodded.

"Why?" Anton asked with a stupid air. "Surely Svetlana herself . . ."

"Being a Great Enchantress and raising a Great Enchantress are two quite different things," Gesar said wearily. "Alas. I . . . so far I can't see anyone else to match Igor. I . . . I didn't know how much he loved that witch! I would have looked for some other way."

"Whose daughter will it be?" Anton suddenly asked. "Svetlana's and . . ."

"Whose? If you stop standing there like a fool, gaping at an old idiot, and go after your wife—it will be yours!"

Anton gave a feeble nod and went dashing out of the hall. Edgar also wanted to ask Gesar a couple of questions, but he caught the Light One's glance and decided not to risk it. He turned away and stepped onto the narrow gray wedge of the Inquisition that jutted out between the black and white halves of the hall.

The Inquisitors were already pulling off their robes. One of them casually tossed his robe into Witezslav's arms, opened a portal, and disappeared. The others left the usual way, through the door.

The vampire looked at Edgar and asked, "Want to try it on?"

"I'm not sure the cut will suit me," Edgar replied in a quiet voice.

"Who knows? But it's worth a try. Or are you intending to go back to Moscow?"

Edgar carefully took the crumpled gray material out of the vampire's hands. He asked awkwardly, "I beg your pardon . . . but what was it that Svetlana said to Zabulon?"

"An Inquisitor has to have good hearing." A crooked grin appeared on the vampire's face. "Almost nothing at all. I'd call it a curse, but the Light Ones don't even know how to curse properly . . . She said: 'May no one ever love you.'"

Edgar nodded. He shrugged and said, "He doesn't need anyone to, anyway."

MOSCOW–NIKOLAEV–LAZURNOE
JUNE–OCTOBER 1999

Coming in May 2014 from Harper,
the newest book in the internationally
bestselling Night Watch series:

New Watch

This is a dubious text for the Cause of Light.

—THE NIGHT WATCH

This is a dubious text for the Cause of Darkness.

—THE DAY WATCH

PART ONE

DUBIOUS INTENT

PROLOGUE

SENIOR SERGEANT DMITZY PASTUKHOV WAS A GOOD *polizei*.

Of course, for the purpose of enlightening drunks who got a bit above themselves he sometimes employed measures not actually prescribed by the regulations—a few good smacks in the teeth or well-aimed kicks, for instance. But only in cases where the dipso concerned was getting a bit too pushy about his rights, or refusing to proceed to the drunk tank. And Dima wouldn't actually spurn a five-hundred note shaken out of some lunk from the Ukraine or Central Asia who didn't have a residence permit—after all, what with police pay being so low, the offenders might just as well pay him their fines directly. Nor did he raise any objections when he was poured a shot of cognac instead of a glass of water in eating joints on the territory under his purview.

After all, it was a demanding job. It was dangerous and difficult. And at first glance people hardly even seemed to notice it. There had to be some material incentives.

But, on the other hand, Dima had never beaten money out of prostitutes and pimps. On principle. Something in the way he'd been raised wouldn't let him do it. Dima didn't waste time dragging slightly tipsy citizens off to the sobering-up station while they still retained a glimmer of reason. And when he uncovered a real crime he launched himself into pursuit of the perpetrators like a shot. He always searched conscientiously for clues and submitted reports on instances of petty theft (that was, if the victims insisted on it, of course) and he made an effort to remember the faces of persons on the "wanted" list. He had several significant arrests under his belt, including a genuine murderer—a man who had first stabbed his wife's lover (which was forgivable) and then his wife (which was understandable) and then, still brandishing the knife, had gone after the neighbor who had informed him about his wife's infidelity. Outraged at such black ingratitude, the neighbor had locked himself in his apartment and called the police on 02. Arriving in response to the summons, Dima Pastukhov had first detained the murderer, who was pounding impotently on the iron door with his blood-smeared, puny little intellectual's fists, and then struggled for a long time with his own desire to drag the whistle-blowing neighbor out onto the stairs and rearrange his face.

So Dima regarded himself as a good policeman—which wasn't really all that far from the truth. Compared with the example set by some of his colleagues, he stood out, seeming every bit as diligent as the militiaman Svistulkin in that old Soviet children's favorite *Dunno in Sunshine City*.

The only blot on Dima's service record dated back to January 1998: still young and green then, he had been on patrol in the Exhibition of Economic Achievements district with Sergeant Kaminsky, who was by way of being the young militiaman's mentor. (They were still called "militiamen," or simply "cops," back then: the fashionable word "policeman" and the slightly offensive term *polizei* hadn't come into use yet.) Kaminsky was very proud to be playing this role, but his admonitions and advice all basically came down to where and how you could pick up a bit of easy money. On that particular evening, when Kaminsky spotted this half-cut young guy (he even had an open quarter-liter of vodka in his hand) dashing out of the metro station towards the pedestrian underpass, he whistled in delight and the two partners moved in to intercept their prey. All the indications were that this drunk was about to part with a fifty note, or maybe even a hundred.

And then everything went pear-shaped. It was some kind of black-magic voodoo. The tipsy suspect fixed the two partners with a surprisingly sober stare (that stare was sober all right, but there was something savage and chilling about it, like the look in the eyes of a stray dog that had lost all faith in people a very long time ago) and advised the militiamen to get drunk themselves.

And they did as he said. They walked over to the trading kiosks (Yeltsin's chaotic reign was already in its final years, but vodka was still sold openly in the street) and, giggling like lunatics, they each bought a bottle exactly like the one carried by the drunk who had given them such sound advice. Then they bought another two. And another two.

Three hours later Pastukhov and Kaminsky, feeling very witty and merry at this stage, were picked up by one of their own patrols—and that was what saved them. They caught it in the neck, all right, but they weren't flung out of the militia. After that Kaminsky gave up drinking altogether and swore blind that the drunk they'd met must have been a hypnotist or even some kind of psychic. Pastukhov himself didn't slander the man pointlessly or indulge in idle speculation. But he clung on very tightly to the memory of him . . . with the sole intention of making sure he never crossed his path again.

Perhaps it was the powerful memory of that shameful binge, or perhaps Pastukhov had simply developed some unusual abilities, but after a while he started noticing other people with strange eyes. To himself Pastukhov called these people "wolves" and "dogs."

The first group had the calm indifference of the predator in their gaze: not malicious, no, the wolf harries the sheep without malice— more likely, in fact, with love. Pastukhov simply steered clear of their kind, trying hard not to attract any attention in the process.

The second group, who were more like that first young drunk, had a dog-like look in their eyes. Sometimes guilty, sometimes patient and concerned, sometimes sad. There was just one thing that bothered Pastukhov: that wasn't the way dogs looked at their masters, at best it was the way they looked at their master's whelp. And so Pastukhov tried to steer clear of them too.

And for quite a long time he managed it.

If children are life's flowers, then this child was a blooming cactus.

He started yelling the moment the doors of the Sheremetyevo-D terminal slid open and he came in. His mother, red-faced with anger and shame (the shouting was obviously a repeat performance), was dragging him along by the hand, but the boy was leaning backwards, bracing himself with both feet, and howling:

"I won't! I won't! I won't fly! Mummy, don't! The plane's going to crash!"

His mother let go of his hand and the boy slumped to the floor and stayed sitting there: a fat, hysterical, tear-stained, unattractive child, dressed a little bit too lightly for the Moscow weather in June—there was obviously a flight to warmer climes in prospect.

A man sitting at a cafe table about twenty meters away from them got up, almost knocking over his unfinished mug of beer. He looked for a few moments at the boy and the mother, who was trying to din something into her son's head. Then he sat down and said in a quiet voice: "That's appalling. What a nightmare!"

"I think so, too," agreed the young woman sitting opposite him.

She put down her cup of coffee and gave the boy a hostile look. "I'd call it sordid."

"Well, I don't see anything sordid about it," the man said gently. "But it's certainly appalling . . . no doubt about that . . ."

"I personally—" the young woman began, but stopped when she saw the man wasn't listening.

He took out a phone. Dialed a number. Spoke in a quiet voice: "I need a level-one clearance. One or two. No, I'm not joking. Try to find one . . ."

He broke off the call, looked at the young woman, and nodded. "I'm sorry, an urgent call . . . What were you saying?"

"I personally am child-free," the young woman declared defiantly.

"Free of children? Are you infertile, then?"

The young woman shook her head. "A common misapprehension. We childfree women are opposed to children because they enslave us. We have to choose—between being a proud, free individual or a social appendage to the population's reproductive mechanism!"

"Ah," the man said, with a nod. "And I thought . . . you had health problems. I was going to recommend a good doctor . . . But you do accept sex, though?"

The young woman smiled. "Naturally! We're not asexual, are we? Sex and marriage—that's all very good and normal. It's just . . . tying yourself to those creatures that are always yelling and running around and—"

"And pooping," the man suggested. "They're always pooping as well, aren't they? And they can't even wipe their own backsides at first."

"Pooping!" the young woman agreed. "That's it precisely! Spending the best years of your life serving the needs of undeveloped human juveniles . . . I hope you're not going to lecture me on morals and try to persuade me to change my mind and have a huge brood of kiddies."

"No, I'm not. I believe you. I'm quite certain you'll remain childless to the end of your life."

The boy and his mother walked past: the child was slightly calmer now or, more likely, he had simply resigned himself to the fact that the flight was going to happen. The mother was speaking to her son in a low voice—they heard something about a warm sea, a good hotel and bullfights.

"Oh God!" the young woman exclaimed. "They're flying to Spain . . . It looks like we're on the same flight. Can you imagine it, listening to that little tub of lard's hysterical squealing for three hours?"

"Not three, I think," said the man. "One hour and ten or fifteen minutes . . ."

A slightly scornful expression appeared on the young woman's face. The man appeared perfectly capable and competent. But then how could he not know the most ordinary things . . . "The flight to Barcelona lasts three hours."

"Three hours and twenty minutes. But suppose—"

"So where are you flying to?" asked the young woman, rapidly losing interest in him.

"Nowhere. I was seeing off a friend. Then I sat down to drink a mug of beer."

The girl hesitated. "Tamara. My name's Tamara."

"I'm Anton."

"You probably don't have children, do you, Anton?" asked Tamara, still unwilling to abandon her favorite subject.

"Why do you think that? I have a daughter. Nadenka. The same age as that . . . tub of lard."

"So you didn't want to let your wife remain a free, healthy woman?" Tamara laughed. "What does she do?"

"My wife?"

"Well, not your daughter . . ."

"By training, she's a doctor. But in herself . . . she's an enchantress."

"That's just what I dislike so much about you men," Tamara declared, getting up, "that vulgar affectation. 'An enchantress'! And no doubt you're quite happy for her to slave away at the cooker, wash the nappies, get no sleep for nights on end . . ."

"I am, although no one washes nappies any more—disposables have been in fashion for a long time."

At that the young woman's face contorted as if she had been offered a handful of cockroaches to eat. She grabbed her handbag and walked over to the check-in desk without even saying goodbye.

The man shrugged. He picked up his phone and raised it to his ear—and it rang immediately.

"Gorodetsky . . . Completely? No, third-level won't do at all. A full charter flight to Barcelona. You can accept it as second-level . . . Can't you?"

He paused for a while, then said: "Then one seventh-level for me. No, that's wrong. The boy has a first- or second-level gift of clairvoyance. The Dark Ones will dig their heels in . . . A single fifth-level

intervention—a change in the fate of one human and one Other . . .
All right, put it down to me."

He stood up, leaving his unfinished mug of beer on the table, and
set off toward the check-in desk, where the fat boy was standing in
the queue beside his mother with a stony look on his face, shifting
nervously from one foot to the other.

The man walked straight past the checkpoint (for some reason no
one even tried to stop him) and approached the woman. He cleared
his throat politely. Caught her eye. Nodded.

"Olga Yurievna . . . You forgot to turn off the iron when you were
ironing Kesha's shorts this morning . . ."

A look of panic appeared on the woman's face.

"You can fly on the evening charter," the man continued. "But
right now you'd better go home."

The woman tugged at her son's hand and then went dashing
toward the way out. But the boy, whom she suddenly seemed to have
forgotten completely, gazed at the man wide-eyed.

"You want to ask who I am and why your mum believed me?" the
man asked.

The boy's eyes misted over as if he were looking inside himself, or at something far, far away on the outside—something in a
place where well-brought-up children weren't supposed to look (and
where badly brought-up adults shouldn't look either, unless they
really had to).

"You are Anton Gorodetsky, Higher White Magician," said the
boy. "You are Nadka's father. Because of you . . . all of us . . ."

"Well?" the man asked keenly "Well, well?"

"Kesha!" the woman howled, suddenly remembering her son. The
boy shuddered and the mist in his eyes dispersed. He said: "Only I
don't know what all that means . . . Thank you!"

"Because of me . . . all of you . . ." the man murmured pensively,
watching as the woman and her child rushed along the glass wall of
the terminal building towards the taxi rank. "Because of me . . . all

of you will live lives of luxury . . . All of you are doomed. All of you have been bankrupted . . . All of you are, will, have been—what?" He swung round and walked unhurriedly toward the exit. By the entrance to the "green corridor" he stopped and looked back at the queue that had formed at the check-in desk for Barcelona. It was a large, noisy queue. People going away for a holiday at the seaside. There were lots of women and children in it, lots of men, and even one child-free young woman.

"God help you," said the man. "I can't."

Dima Pastukhov had just taken out his lighter to give his partner Bisat Iskenderov a light even though Bisat had his own lighter – it was simply a routine they'd got into. If Dima took out a ciga-rette, Bisat reached for his lighter. When the Azerbaijani decided to smoke, Dima offered him a light. If Pastukhov had been inclined to intellectual reflection, he might have said this was their way of demonstrating their mutual respect for each other, despite their dif-ferences of opinion on many things—from problems of nationality to which car was classier: the Mercedes ML or the BMW X3.

But Dima wasn't inclined to reflections of this kind—he and Bisat both drove Fords, preferred German beer to Russian vodka or Azerbaijani cognac and had quite friendly feelings for each other. So Dima clicked on the button, summoning up the little tongue of flame, glanced briefly at the exit from the airport terminal building—and dropped the lighter just as his friend's cigarette was reaching for it.

There was a "dog" walking out through the doors of the depar-ture lounge. A middle-aged man who didn't look frightening at all—quite cultured, in fact. Pastukhov was used to seeing people like this, but this one wasn't simply a "dog," he was *the* "dog" . . . from the Exhibition of Economic Achievements district, from way back in the distant past. Only he didn't look drunk now, more as if he had a bit of a hangover.

Pastukhov turned away and started slowly groping for the lighter on the ground. The man with watchdog's eyes walked past without taking the slightest notice of him.

"A drop too much yesterday?" Bisat asked sympathetically.

"Who?" muttered Pastukhov. "Ah . . . no, it's just that the lighter's slippery . . ."

"Your hands are shaking and you've turned as white as a sheet," his partner remarked.

Pastukhov finally gave him a light, checked out of the corner of his eye that the man was walking away toward the car park, took out a cigarette and lit up himself—without waiting for Bisat's lighter.

"You're acting kind of funny . . ." said Bisat.

"Yes, I was drinking yesterday," Pastukhov muttered. He looked at the terminal building again.

This time there was a "wolf " coming out of it. With a self-confident, predatory gaze and determined stride. Pastukhov turned away.

"You should eat *khash* the morning after," Bisat admonished him. "But only the right *khash*—ours. That Armenian *khash* is poison!"

"Ah, come on, they're absolutely identical," Pastukhov replied in his usual manner.

Bisat spat disdainfully and shook his head.

"They may look the same. But in essence they're completely different!"

"They might be different in essence, but in reality they're absolutely identical!" Dima replied, watching the "wolf," who had walked past and was also going toward the car park.

Bisat took offense and stopped talking.

Pastukhov finished off his cigarette in a few quick drags and looked at the door of the terminal again.

His first thought was angry, even resentful: *Are they holding some kind of grand get-together in there today?*

And then the fear hit him.

The individual who had walked out of the doors when they slid open and was now standing there, gazing round thoughtfully, wasn't a "dog." But he wasn't a "wolf," either. He was someone else. A third kind.

A kind that ate wolves for breakfast and dogs for lunch. And left the tastiest parts for supper.

The classification that immediately occurred to Pastukhov was "tiger." He said: "I've got stomach cramps . . . I'm off to the can."

"Go on, I'll have a smoke," replied his partner, still offended.

To have asked Bisat to go to the toilet with him would have been strange. There wasn't any time to explain anything or invent anything. Pastukhov turned round and walked away quickly, leaving Iskenderov in the path of the "tiger." "He won't do anything to him . . . He'll just walk straight past, that's all . . ." Pastukhov reassured himself.

Pastukhov only looked round as he was already walking into the departure hall.

Just in time to see Bisat salute casually and stop the "tiger." Of course, his partner couldn't spot them—there wasn't any incident in his past like the one Pastukhov had experienced. But this time even he had sensed something—with that policeman's intuition that sometimes helped you pull an entirely unremarkable-looking man out of a crowd and discover that he had a rod stashed in a secret holster or a knife in his pocket.

Pastukhov suddenly realized that his stomach cramps were genuine now. And he sprinted into the airport's safe, noisy interior, full of people and suitcases.

Since he was a good *polizei*, he felt very ashamed. But he felt even more afraid.

ABOUT THE AUTHOR

Sergei Lukyanenko was born in Kazakhstan and educated as a psychiatrist. He began publishing science fiction in the 1980s and has published more than twenty-five books.

Andrew Bromfield (translator) is a founding editor of the Russian literature journal *Glas*. He is known for his acclaimed translations of Victor Pelevin and Boris Akunin, and his work has been short-listed for numerous translation prizes.

THE NIGHT WATCH SERIES BY
SERGEI LUKYANENKO

NIGHT WATCH
Book One in the Night Watch Series

Available in Paperback and eBook

Set in contemporary Moscow, the Night Watch series tells the story of the Others, an ancient race of magicians, shape-shifters, vampires, and other supernatural beings that live among us, and swear allegiance to either the powers of Darkness or the forces of Light.

DAY WATCH
**Book Two in the
Night Watch Series**

Available in Paperback and eBook

In *Day Watch*, we follow the Dark Others, including a young witch with the tragic misfortune of falling in love with a Light Other, a powerful warlock who struggles to understand his purpose in the war, and a top lieutenant who worries that Zabulon, the leader of the Day Watch, is planning to betray him.

TWILIGHT
WATCH
Book Three in the Night Watch Series

Available in Paperback and eBook

Twilight Watch returns to the perspective of Anton Gorodetsky, now married, with a daughter who has limitless potential as a Light Other, and an important destiny. When an ancient book of spells with the power to turn ordinary humans into Others falls into the wrong hands, Anton and the Night Watch must join forces with the Day Watch to find the culprit and prevent total war.

COMING SUMMER 2014
NEW WATCH
The newest chapter in the Night Watch series